Skulduggery Pleasant
A MIND FULL OF MURDER

DEREK LANDY

Skulduggery Pleasant
A MIND FULL OF MURDER

HARPERCOLLINS
CHILDREN'S BOOKS

First published in the United Kingdom by
HarperCollins *Children's Books* in 2024
HarperCollins *Children's Books* is a division of HarperCollins*Publishers* Ltd
1 London Bridge Street
London SE1 9GF

www.harpercollins.co.uk

HarperCollins*Publishers*
Macken House, 39/40 Mayor Street Upper
Dublin 1, D01 C9W8, Ireland

1

HB ISBN 978–0–00–858582–2
WATERSTONES SPECIAL EDITION ISBN 978–0–00–870023–2
ANZ TPB ISBN 978–0–00–858584–6
EXP TPB ISBN 978–0–00–858583–9

Derek Landy asserts the moral right to be
identified as the author of the work.

A CIP catalogue record for this title
is available from the British Library.

Typeset in Baskerville MT 11.5/15 pt by
Palimpsest Book Production Ltd, Falkirk, Stirlingshire

Printed and Bound in the UK using 100% Renewable Electricity
at CPI Group (UK) Ltd

This book is dedicated to Natalie.

There are many stories to remember you by, Natalieeb.
The time you turned the toaster on to its side to make
cheese on toast, for example, only for the bread to get
flung across the countertop and land, much to your
disappointment, cheese-side down on the floor.

Or the time you ripped your tights off in the middle
of a nightclub and screamed "I'm the Hulk!"

Or even the time you broke up with a boyfriend
because of his "weirdly large" eyelids.

You were odd. You were loud. You were argumentative
(though never to me). You were wonderful and special,
and the first time we met you proposed to me. I let you down
gently and a few years later ended up with your best friend,
but you never let your heartbreak show. I admired that.

I had included some of your funniest stories in this book,
actually, which I felt would be a sad but loving tribute
to your memory. But I had to cut them for space.

SIX YEARS LATER...

1

It started with phone calls.

A withheld number and a long, empty silence. Whenever Gavin tried to envisage the caller, he always saw him – or her, his imagination could never decide on the gender or appearance – just standing there, head down. Never sitting, never walking – just standing. He could almost feel it in the silence, that expectation, that potential for quick, sudden movement. As if the caller was conserving energy. As if the caller was getting ready to strike.

He didn't know why he'd been targeted or who was doing it. Undoubtedly, some kid somewhere, bored of video games or whatever, having dialled this number at random had decided that, yep, this is the person I'm going to torment. Kid singular. Not kids. This was not a fun prank played with friends. There was never any giggling or hushed voices on the line. Just the long, lonely silence.

So Gavin did what anyone would do – he stopped answering the phone to withheld numbers. An easy fix, he reckoned, as he went to work, as he played with his dog, as he fell asleep with his wife. He had enough to be doing with his time than answering some dull prankster's calls: the water, for instance. It was giving him trouble again. The local council were as helpful as they could be, but they reminded him that his house was, technically, outside their jurisdiction, and he could tell they were getting tired of his complaints.

Gavin did not like complaining. He had never once sent a plate back to a restaurant kitchen and couldn't imagine a time, ever, when he'd demand to speak to the manager of a store.

This didn't mean he was a pushover. He was the guy in the cinema who made his way over to whoever was causing a disturbance and asked them, politely but firmly, to stop talking or to put away their phone. When it came to enjoying movies, Gavin was quite prepared to kick up a fuss.

So, when his own phone rang, loud and obnoxious, in a packed cinema, right as the masked killer was stalking the final girl through the old house littered with the bodies of her dead friends, it was beyond mortifying.

He always put his phone on airplane mode the moment he settled into his seat. It was his ritual. He put the drink in the cup-holder, then the straw in the drink, then he tapped on airplane mode and, lastly, he cleaned his glasses, whether they needed it or not.

As every last person in the theatre turned to glare at him, he yanked the phone out of his shirt pocket and stabbed at the screen, but the thing just wouldn't shut up. He tried turning it off, but messed up and somehow made it louder. He hurried down the steps, tucking the phone under his armpit, then burst through the doors into the quiet, carpeted corridor.

His grip was so tight he wouldn't have been surprised if the phone cracked in his hand. He didn't recognise the number on the screen, just like he didn't recognise the ringtone. He didn't even use a ringtone – he hated the bloody things and always had his phone on vibrate. He swiped to answer and clamped the device to his ear.

"Yes?" he said, hating whoever was calling. When they didn't respond, his anger grew. "Yes? Hello?"

Still no response. They could undoubtedly hear the anger in his voice – but none of this was their fault. He was the one who'd screwed up. He took a deep breath and let it out and said, as calmly as he could, "Hello, Gavin Fahey speaking?"

The caller didn't reply, but didn't hang up, either.

"Can I help you?" Gavin asked.

Nothing. It was the prankster again. It had to be. Only this time they hadn't withheld their number – which meant that Gavin could now block it. He hung up and did exactly that, then put the phone on vibrate only and shoved it back in his pocket before re-entering the theatre.

He didn't head back to his seat, though. He didn't want to cause any more of a disturbance than he already had, and he really didn't want to suffer more glares from his fellow audience members. Besides, the film was almost over. He stood against the wall as the final girl shot the masked killer, as the killer flipped backwards over the banister and fell all the way to the floor.

The final girl took the stairs down, watching the killer the whole time. She knew her stuff, this girl. She knew that if she took her eyes off the bad guy for even a moment, he'd disappear. So down the stairs she came, gun gripped in trembling hands and a thin trickle of blood running from the perfect cut along her cheekbone.

Shoes crunching on broken glass, she approached the unmoving figure. Gavin reckoned she had, at most, two bullets left. She moved around, staying away from the killer's hands. Crouching, she reached for the mask, pulled it off to reveal the actor from that TV show.

Huh. Gavin could usually spot who the bad guy was in these things. This one had caught him by surprise. He liked that.

The killer's eyes snapped open and the final girl jerked back, pulling the trigger. But the gun, in fact, was empty, and the bad guy dived at her, and Gavin's phone rang again.

He spun, barged out, striding away from the doors even as they closed behind him. Another number he didn't recognise. He swiped to answer.

"Yeah?" he said, properly angry this time.

No response.

He didn't say anything, didn't curse at the prankster, didn't want to give them the satisfaction of knowing they'd got to him. He just hung up and blocked the number. He once again turned his phone to vibrate only. He'd figure out what had gone wrong in the morning. Tonight, he wasn't in the mood.

The shopping centre was quiet as Gavin strode to the car park. It was always a surreal experience, walking through a space designed to be packed with people that was suddenly empty. Shop windows were dark; doors were shuttered. Somewhere, someone was polishing the floors.

He paid for parking, then passed the stairs. Glass doors slid open and he walked out on to the fourth floor of the car park. His Lexus – twelve years old, silver, in great condition despite its dire need of a wash – sat waiting across all that empty concrete. His footsteps echoed as he walked. A scenario straight out of a horror movie, like the one whose final few minutes he was missing right now.

He was halfway to his car when the theme from *Halloween* blasted from his pocket and actually made him jump.

He pulled out the phone – he hadn't known it even *had* the *Halloween* ringtone – to end the call without answering, but his wife's name flashed at him. He took a breath and resumed walking as he answered.

"Hey," he said. "I'm just leaving now. There's something wrong with my phone so don't be surprised if it cuts out halfway through this call. What's up?"

Jessica didn't answer right away.

"Hello?" Gavin said. "Can you hear me? The signal might not be great – I'll call you back when I'm on the road, OK? Sweetie?"

"Sweetie," said a voice that was not his wife's.

Ice water flooded Gavin's veins and he stopped walking and blinked.

Something wrong with the line, a corruption of sound in some way, distorting her voice, that's all it was.

"Jessica?" he said.

"Jessica," the caller repeated, mocking him.

A new kind of fear took hold, unlike any Gavin had ever known, as the possibilities and the implications of those possibilities invaded his thoughts. Someone had his wife's phone. Someone was at the house right now with his wife's phone in their hand and his wife was – what? – hurt? Injured? Dead?

"Who is this?" he asked. "Where's Jessica?"

"Downstairs," said the caller.

Rushing air filled Gavin's ears and he nearly toppled. "Don't hurt her," he whispered.

The caller laughed softly.

"Don't you hurt my wife!" Gavin screamed into the phone. He ran for the car, unlocked it and jumped in. He started the engine and, as he peeled out, the car took the call and he was able to drop the phone on to the passenger seat.

"You'll never make it in time," said the caller.

Gavin ignored the taunt, taking the first ramp down. The undercarriage knocked against the ground and in any other situation he'd have winced at that, but damaging his car was the least of his worries right now. The ramp curled round and he went faster, roaring into the third floor of the car park, which was just as empty as the fourth. He swept on to the next ramp and the bumper shrieked against the wall and the tyre hit the low kerb and he cursed but kept going. As long as he didn't wreck the car, as long as he didn't sabotage his drive home, none of it mattered.

He sped out on to the second floor. Two more ramps to go, then out through the barrier. Steering with his left hand, he searched his pockets for the ticket. Where the hell had he put it?

"How long will it take you to get home?" the caller asked. "Fifteen minutes? Think you can do it in half the time if you go fast enough? This time of night, with the roads empty, you might be lucky. It still won't be fast enough to save your wife."

"Shut up," Gavin snapped. He found the ticket, put it

between his teeth, almost smashed into the ramp wall, but yanked on the wheel just in time.

"Hurry," the caller said. "Hurry."

Gavin reached for the phone, but it slid away from him. He reached again, snagged it, held it with his thumb hovering over the red X on the screen. To call the cops, he'd need to hang up. To hang up would mean the caller would no longer be delayed.

The car's undercarriage smacked painfully off the ground again as Gavin roared on to the first floor and swung round. He braked, jolting forward in his seat, and slammed the heel of his hand on to the horn. A Hyundai with L-plates, its reversing lights on, blocked his entry on to the final ramp. Gavin's window whirred down and he snatched the ticket from between his teeth.

"Move!" he screamed. "Get out of the way!"

The voice on the other end of the phone laughed.

The Hyundai backed up a little and then stopped, and the white lights went out as the driver shifted gears, and Gavin slammed the horn again. The car inched forward, the driver frantically turning the wheel, but it still wasn't going to manage the manoeuvre.

Gavin screamed another curse and put his car in Park and opened the door to jump out, but the Hyundai jerked back, then forward, and then straightened, and Gavin shut the door. The Hyundai started to crawl down the ramp, Gavin right behind it.

"It sounds like you're busy," the caller said. "I should let you go. I've got things to do."

Keep the caller talking. He had to keep the caller talking. "Who are you?" Gavin asked. "Why are you doing this?"

The Hyundai's learner driver was too nervous, too hesitant. They were only halfway down the curving ramp.

"You want to know who I am, Gavin?" the caller asked.

"Yes. Please, you have to tell me."

"You'll die not knowing," said the caller, and ended the call.

Ahead of him, the Hyundai stopped.

Gavin blasted the horn, but the Hyundai didn't budge. Then, astonishingly, the driver turned off the engine.

"Move!" Gavin screeched through his open window.

The driver sat there, nothing more than a dark shape.

Gavin opened his door and lunged out, and the Hyundai's door opened in response.

"Move your car!" Gavin shouted. "Please! This is an emergency! Please get back in and move your car!"

The driver got out. At first, Gavin thought he was wearing a hat, a woollen hat, maybe, but it wasn't a hat, woollen or otherwise. It was a mask, a black mask made from plastic or something, that covered his whole head, a mask with a blank, expressionless face, like a mannequin's. Only the eyes showed any humanity – or the eyes behind those narrow eyeholes, at any rate. They glittered in Gavin's headlights.

A thousand thoughts battered their way into Gavin's mind. This was the caller. But if the caller was here, then he wasn't about to go downstairs and kill Jessica. So Jessica was safe. But Gavin wasn't. Not even remotely.

All those movies Gavin loved, where the good guy is confronted by the masked killer, he'd always wondered how he would fare in the same situation. Would he be fast enough to escape? Would he be strong enough to fight? Would he be smart enough to win? And here he was, staring at his very own bad guy, and he didn't know what to do and his legs wouldn't work and he couldn't even shout or curse or threaten or scream.

But something bubbled inside him, a churning kind of energy, and he realised it was adrenaline and all of a sudden he was moving, turning to dive back into the safety of his car, but the driver was moving too, raising his hand, and he was holding something – a knife? Was that a knife? – and then Gavin was behind the wheel and the car folded in around him from all sides, crushing his legs, his ribs, his shoulders, his arms and his spine and his skull.

He stayed alive for a few seconds in the sudden silence and stillness that followed, but he couldn't see anything and all he could hear was the air escaping his ruined lungs, and footsteps, slow footsteps, getting fainter. And then he died.

2

Cadence Clearwater felt like she was under arrest. The interview room was small and grey. To her left was a two-way mirror, allowing observers to see in, but not letting her see out. To her right, a binding sigil was carved into the wall, restricting all magic. The chair she was sitting in was straight-backed and bolted to the floor. The table was small, also secured in place, with two stainless-steel loops for chains to be threaded through, should the suspect be in need of restraint.

There were no restraints on Cadence. She wasn't a suspect. She just felt like one.

Her foot tapped the ground incessantly. She realised that she was picking at her fingernails. There was dried blood there. There was dried blood on her clothes and splashed across her cheek. It wasn't her own.

The door opened and she went cold. She was expecting another detective, maybe someone she knew. She wasn't expecting *her*.

Valkyrie Cain walked in, carrying two cups of coffee. Cadence knew her face – everyone in the magical communities did. This was the face of the girl who'd saved the world and it was also the face of Darquesse, the being who had murdered thousands of mages on Devastation Day, who had then gone on to wreak havoc across countless dimensions before returning to save reality itself by restarting the universe.

Valkyrie looked younger in person. She was as tall as Cadence had heard – six foot – and she had the broad shoulders and strong legs that could be seen in the photographs and Network footage that every mage had watched. Her outfit didn't disappoint, either: jeans and scuffed boots and a long-sleeved top, army green, that stretched lightly over her muscles. She dressed like she was ready to chase down a bad guy or fight to the death, whichever came first. Her hair, dark with a middle-parting, had a gentle wave to it now, which softened her face. She looked a few years younger than Cadence's own twenty-four years, though she must have been thirty-one or thirty-two by now.

But when Valkyrie sat at the table Cadence changed her mind. Lines or wrinkles or crow's feet didn't give away Valkyrie's true age, but those dark eyes did. They'd seen too much, and they were haunted. Bright but haunted.

"Hi," Valkyrie said, her voice gentle as she held out one of the coffees.

Cadence took it. She'd never developed much of a taste for coffee, but if Valkyrie Cain offers you a coffee, you take the coffee.

"You know who I am?" Valkyrie asked. Cadence nodded. "Then you know I'm here to help. You've been through a traumatic experience and you want time to process what's happened, but you also know why we need to speak to you so soon, right?"

"It's important to get as many details as possible from a witness while they're still fresh in the memory," Cadence told her dutifully. "Before the memory itself starts to take short cuts."

"My partner will be joining us in a moment, and we'll begin. How are you doing, Cadence?"

Cadence smiled shakily. "Not well."

"I'd imagine not. How long have you been a detective for the Sanctuary?"

"Two months."

"Before that you were an operative for, what, ten months? And before *that* you were with the Roarhaven Police Department, right? For three years? Not everyone from the RPD gets to make the move over to the Sanctuary, and not everyone gets to move from operative to detective. And then to be assigned to a murder case within two months? That's impressive."

"I just... I needed to do something with my life. Something positive. Something that would help people."

"There are easier ways to help people than becoming a detective."

"I needed a change. I wasn't happy at the RPD and then, well, I broke up with my boyfriend and that kind of messed me up. I wasn't in a good place, you know? He... well, I found out he was seeing someone else and I suddenly felt like I had no worth any more, so..." She gave a thin laugh. "Sorry. This is completely irrelevant."

Valkyrie didn't look like she minded. "Go on."

"I just realised I had to either embrace failure or grab

on to my career with everything I had, so I grabbed. Getting assigned to this case might sound impressive, but I practically begged Detective Garde to let me tag along."

"Why this one in particular?"

"I thought I might be able to help. That I might be able to offer a different perspective."

"You didn't think Detective Garde would be able to handle it on his own?"

"No, God, no, nothing like that."

"I wouldn't blame you if you *did* think that – he is new to the Irish Sanctuary, after all. How much do you know about him?"

"Detective Garde doesn't really talk a whole lot about his past, but I know enough. He's one of the detectives trained by Cogent Badinage. I know they went after some pretty serious bad guys in their time, mostly in the American Sanctuary."

"Nothing worse than a corrupt Sanctuary operative. So why did you think your perspective could offer anything new?"

"Um, well... no offence to him, but he was born in the 1600s. I thought it might aid the investigation to have someone a little closer to the age of the victims."

"And Detective Garde agreed?"

"Eventually, yes. I suppose I can be determined."

Valkyrie shrugged. "Nothing wrong with determination."

Cadence's voice shook a little, but she controlled it. "How is he?"

"Still in surgery."

Cadence gave another nod. It was his blood she was splattered with.

Skulduggery Pleasant entered the interview room. Tall and narrow in a dark blue three-piece suit, crisp white shirt with a dark tie and matching hatband. His gloves were black. He sat in the chair beside Valkyrie and put his hat on the table. The light gleamed off the top of his skull. Shadows danced in his empty eye sockets. His jaw opened when he spoke and his voice was deliciously clear and smooth despite the fact that he had no lips and no tongue.

"The first victim," he said, "was Gavin Fahey. Mortal. Forty-three years old. Crushed eight days ago when someone turned his car into origami."

"Yes," said Cadence.

"The second victim was Sarah Boyle. Mortal. Thirty-six years old. Killed three days ago when her body was diced into four hundred and eighteen perfectly symmetrical cubes in the fifteen seconds she was out of her sister's line of sight."

"Yes."

"And the third victim," Skulduggery said, "was Avant Garde. Mage. Detective. Four hundred and two years old. Attacked and seriously injured four hours ago by an unknown assailant." He leaned forward. "From the beginning, Detective Clearwater."

Cadence put her coffee on the table, but then her hands had nothing to do so she picked it up again. "Detective Garde was assigned the Gavin Fahey murder. I read the report on the Sarah Boyle case and I brought it to him. I pointed out that they were both killed by an unknown discipline of magic so they might be connected. He, um, agreed to take me on as a partner, and we went to Sarah Boyle's house to look for something linking her to Gavin Fahey."

"And did you find anything?" Skulduggery asked.

"We didn't really get a chance." She took a sip of coffee. It tasted horrible. "I was in the kitchen. Detective Garde was in the living room. When we'd arrived, Sarah Boyle's sister was there with her parents, but Detective Garde spoke to them, you know, using their given names. He calmed them down immediately, told them we were cops, told them the best thing to do was to go home and deal with their grief, talk about their feelings, that sort of thing. He was like a... like a therapist, I suppose."

"How long were they gone before you were attacked?"

"Maybe five minutes. So, we were searching, and I heard the door open and I thought either they'd come back or another friend had turned up and I went out to intercept them."

"Who did you see?"

"A man wearing a black mask. I only caught a glimpse before he waved his hand and I hit the wall."

"So he's an Elemental?" Valkyrie asked.

"Maybe," said Cadence. "Though I didn't feel that blast of air, you know? I just felt something hit me and I went flying."

"What happened then?"

"Detective Garde ran out and the suspect turned to him and, like, waved his hand again. At that time, my view was blocked, and all I saw was a splash of blood and he fell. The suspect spoke to him and then came over to me."

Skulduggery tilted his head. "You heard the suspect speak?"

"Yes, sir. I think he said, 'You fail,' or something like that."

"Did you notice an accent? Could you identify the voice if you heard it again?"

"I'll never forget the voice, but there was no accent that I could make out. It sounded artificial, unnatural. I think the mask did something to it."

"What did the suspect do then?"

"He came over, looked down at me. I was winded. I couldn't get up."

"The doctors treated you for three broken ribs, didn't they?" Valkyrie asked. "How are you now?"

"I'm better," said Cadence. "There's not even any bruising. But I thought he was going to kill me. I actually thought he was going to kill me and I just lay there. I wouldn't have been able to do anything to stop it. I'd have just let it happen."

Valkyrie reached over, covered Cadence's right hand with both of hers. "You're safe," she said, "and you survived. That means that whatever you did, or whatever you didn't do, was the right thing."

Cadence swallowed, and used her other hand to wipe a tear away. "He looked down at me, the suspect, and he said, 'Do better.' Then he walked into the living room. When I got up, he was gone."

"Do you think he teleported away," Skulduggery asked, "or just climbed out the window?"

"I don't know, sir. After that, I called it in and performed first aid on my partner. I actually didn't really know where to start. His entire torso was..."

"We know," Valkyrie said gently.

Skulduggery sat back, folding his arms. He tapped his fingertips against his chin.

"Can I ask a question?" Cadence asked. "Why are you investigating this? Sorcerers killing mortals isn't exactly a rare occurrence, especially in the last few years, so why are the Arbiters getting involved?"

"The moment a Sanctuary operative gets killed or injured," Skulduggery said, "it's always best for a third party to head up the investigation."

"I suppose that makes sense. If I can—"

He held up his hand. "You're about to offer us your assistance in whatever capacity we might need, even though you're aware that your personal stake in this could very well lead to an unconscious bias that would derail our enquiries. So we have to politely decline your offer. Thank you for your help, Detective Clearwater. Your captain will be in shortly to debrief you."

"But I know this case. I can help you with—"

"We work better on our own," Valkyrie told her, not unkindly. "You've been through a lot and your partner is in a critical condition. You focus on yourself, OK?" They stood.

Cadence stared. "Do you even have the jurisdiction to do this?"

"We're Arbiters," Skulduggery said, putting his hat on. "We have jurisdiction over every Sanctuary investigation around the world. We answer to no one and we choose our own cases. We've chosen this case, Detective. We're taking over."

Valkyrie took her coffee and walked out and Skulduggery followed.

3

Gavin Fahey's wife, in an effort to process his death, had
obviously gone on an intense cleaning spree. The floors of
their house were freshly washed, the bookshelves polished,
the cushions plumped and perfectly arranged. Everything
was in its place. Even the fridge magnets were symmetrical.

She was now upstairs with the specially trained Sensitive
from the Sanctuary, deep in a trance that, as well as helping
her through her grief, would also serve to wipe the memories
of this little visit from her mind.

Valkyrie had found nothing of note anywhere else in the
house and was now conducting a very thorough, very
conscientious search of the living room, making sure to return
anything she moved back to its original position. The Faheys'
dog, a grinning golden retriever, kept her company the entire
time. The retriever was strong and healthy and young, and
reminded Valkyrie of Xena when she was a puppy. Except
Xena was a hell of a lot smarter than this dimwit.

She heard a car pull up outside, and a few moments later
Skulduggery walked in. As soon as the front door closed
behind him, the skin, hair and face he'd been wearing

flowed back to the sigils etched into his collarbones. Years ago, he'd needed to activate the façade with a tap of his fingers, but these days it was all done with a thought.

"You're late," Valkyrie said, perusing the shelves. As well as a number of hardbacks by Stephen King, Grady Hendrix, and Joe Hill, Gavin Fahey had a nice collection of movies on disc and albums on vinyl. Valkyrie dug that.

"Couldn't be helped, I'm afraid," Skulduggery responded. The retriever came over and sniffed him. For a walking skeleton, Skulduggery had a surprisingly calming effect on animals. "Have you found anything?"

"Nothing to link Fahey to Sarah Boyle. He worked in finance; she worked in publishing. She was younger and had an active social life whereas he seemed content with his wife and a few close friends. Neither victim was especially religious; neither had strong political views; neither had any extreme or extremist affiliations... They seemed pretty normal, all things considered."

Skulduggery moved through the room, tilting his head at various items.

"We might be dealing with two victims picked entirely at random," Valkyrie said.

"That may, indeed, be the case," Skulduggery responded. "But even then there could be a pattern. In the 1970s, there was a serial killer in New York who liked to choose his victims as they emerged from various subway exits across the city. At six minutes past six on whatever day, he would wait for the sixth person to walk by and then follow them home. He'd spend some time watching them, getting to know their habits and their routine, and then eventually he'd break in and kill them."

21

"What did they call him?" Valkyrie asked. "The Six-Six-Six Slasher? The Number of the Beast Butcher? Subway Jack? Something like that?"

"Nobody called him anything," Skulduggery said. "No one else ever linked the murders. I tracked him down because of a single stubbed-out cigarette I found outside a victim's window. He only detailed how he selected his targets afterwards in the interview room."

"Some bad guys do like to talk. Was he a mage?"

"Mortal. A strange little man of average intelligence with a grievance against the world."

"Then how come you got involved?"

He shrugged. "I've always liked a good mystery."

Valkyrie picked up her not-actually-leather jacket and put it on. "Well, I'm done here. You want to give the place the once-over, I'll be outside."

She left him to wander and stepped out into the wet June morning, tapping the number for the High Sanctuary Medical Department into her phone. She was immediately put through to Doctor Synecdoche.

"Hey, Reverie," she said. "Any word on Detective Garde?"

Reverie sounded tired. "He's stable," she said. "The wounds to his torso are extensive and there was major damage to some vital organs, all of which came very close to killing him."

"Is he going to be OK?"

"We'll do what we can, but for the moment we've induced a coma to give him some chance of healing."

"Any idea when he'll wake?"

"There's no way to be sure if he *will* wake, let alone give you a timetable. Sorry."

"What about the type of magic used in the attack?"

"We have no idea. His injuries are... unusual. That's all I can say right now. You'll be the first one I call if anything changes."

Valkyrie put the phone away as it started to rain. The clouds were grey and heavy from one side of the built-up, penned-in sky to the other – but screw it. At least there *was* a sky. At least there *was* rain to fall, and a Dublin city for it to fall on to. At least the world still spun, and the galaxy still whirled, and the universe still existed. She couldn't let a little bad weather ruin her mood when there was still a reality in which bad weather could form.

Skulduggery came out, the rain bending around him as his façade flowed up over his skull and over his body, covering the bones of his wrist that had been visible in the slight gap between his sleeve and his glove.

She raised an eyebrow. "That was quick. Did you check the whole house?"

"I did."

"Even upstairs?"

"Yes, although the Sensitive didn't like me walking in. She said it risked upsetting Mrs Fahey. I miss the days when we didn't have to call in Sensitives for things like this."

"Well, now we do."

"I just can't help but remember that among your many talents—"

She cut him off. "I'm not doing the psychic stuff any more."

"But it was very handy."

"It was also very dangerous, gave me splitting headaches, and left me vulnerable to possession."

"So handy, though."

"And the last time I was possessed, I tried to kill a whole bunch of people."

"So incredibly handy."

Valkyrie pointed at her hair, which was quickly getting wet, and he sighed and bent the rain around her, too.

"You just want me to use those abilities because you've come to the realisation that Sensitives don't like you," she said.

"They don't like anyone whose mind they can't read."

"So it's got nothing to do with you mocking them right to their faces?"

"I don't mock all of them. I never mocked Cassandra or Finbar. I don't mock Philomena. I just mock the pretentious ones, the ones who annoy me. God, they're so annoying. Everything about them annoys me. Especially their shoes."

"Getting back to the murder investigation: did you find anything in the house that links the victims?"

"I did not," he said as they walked over to the Bentley, "but if solving murders were easy, Valkyrie, everyone would be doing it."

Sarah Boyle's apartment was small but pretty. She'd lived alone, and the place had a pleasing sort of mess to it, with everything on the cusp of being put away. Valkyrie was the same, and she knew it'd have taken Sarah no time at all to tidy up if she had company coming. The only reason Grimwood House didn't resemble Sarah's apartment was the fact that Militsa liked to know where things were at all times, and insisted on imposing order on Valkyrie's carefully contained chaos.

A big-screen TV dominated the living room. Fairy lights trailed between framed black-and-white photographs on the wall. The sofa was a two-seater – orange – with a pair of chocolate-brown cushions. There was an acoustic guitar on a stand in the corner.

The kitchen had wine glasses on the draining board. The fridge needed to be cleaned out. The table was small, with three chairs. Two of them were neatly pushed in. The third had a pile of washing that Sarah would never get round to sorting through.

In the bedroom there was a wardrobe stuffed with clothes, a fabric shoe rack below the window, and a dresser littered with various brands of make-up. There was an old rumpled teddy bear on the bed, sitting up on the pillow.

At one end of the corridor that ran from the kitchen to the apartment door, a mirror had fallen from the cracked wall and smashed. That was where Cadence Clearwater had hit it. At the other end of the corridor, the floorboards and walls were splattered with dark dried blood. A single brown leather shoe lay on its side. That was where Avant Garde had almost died.

Skulduggery and Valkyrie searched. They found nothing to connect Sarah to Gavin Fahey, and nothing to indicate why Sarah had been targeted. When they were done, Skulduggery took a last, quick sweep of the apartment to see if anything jumped out at him. He had a knack for that – for spotting the noteworthy in the seemingly inconsequential.

While she waited, Valkyrie made a few calls, arranging for the clean-up crew to come by, pick up the evidence and get rid of the blood. Skulduggery came in and they looked at each other.

"Are we stumped?" Valkyrie asked. "Is that what we are?"

His head tilted. "Of course not. We simply don't have enough data to draw any conclusions. What we need is another victim."

"You realise that hoping for more dead mortals is kinda morbid, right?"

"Murder is a morbid business."

"That should be our motto."

"We can add it to the list."

Valkyrie's phone buzzed and she glanced at the screen. "Sarah's phone had been wiped but I'm looking at her records now. She was killed at eight thirteen on the evening of the fifth. She received a call from a blocked number one minute before that which lasted eleven seconds. Another blocked number called her earlier in the day, lasting nine seconds. Another the previous day, thirty-one seconds. The day before that, twenty-seven seconds. I'll ask the Sanctuary techs to bypass that block, but if it was the killer calling, they were probably using a shielded phone so we won't get a whole lot."

"But even that will tell us something," Skulduggery said. "It will tell us the killer likes to call their victims. Ask the techs to access Gavin Fahey's records, too."

"We should let her family pack up her stuff. You remember where everything is in case any of this becomes relevant, right?"

"I do."

"Then I reckon you should drive me to Roarhaven. I'm having lunch with my girlfriend."

4

Tier nodded to a blonde girl walking on the other side of the campus courtyard, a pretty girl who hugged her books to her chest and laughed with her friends.

"Know who that is?" he said. "That's Valkyrie Cain's sister."

Winter watched the blonde girl walk away. "You sure?"

"She's in my history and magical history classes," Tier said. "Everyone knows who she is, but no one ever says it out loud."

"What's she like?"

He shrugged. "Kind of stuck-up. She skates by on Cain's reputation and doesn't bother associating with anyone not up to her high standards. Like, *my sister saved the world, why are you even talking to me*, you know? We started in this place at the same time and she's never spoken more than three words to me."

Winter decided not to mention that, until five minutes ago, Tier had barely said more than a dozen words to *her*, so she didn't quite know what he was complaining about. Also, it was one of the worst-kept secrets in Corrival

Academy that Tier Galling was the son of Eliza Scorn, notorious ex-leader of the Church of the Faceless, so if there was anybody doing any skating on someone else's reputation...

But he was cute, and his dark hair kept falling over his eyes, and he had a mean line to his mouth that, for whatever reason, Winter sort of liked, so she didn't press the matter.

"What are you going to do over the summer?" she asked, and tried not to cringe once the words left her mouth.

If Tier wanted to roll his eyes at the blandest question she could possibly have asked, he restrained himself admirably. "Probably nothing," he said. "I'll be spending most of it on my own, back in England, and there's not a whole lot to do where I'm from."

"Yeah," said Winter. "Same."

He looked at her. "I thought you had loads of friends."

Winter laughed. "I have, like, one."

"Compared to me, that's loads."

"Fair enough," she said, smiling. "Then yeah, I've got loads of friends, but they don't live anywhere near me, so I'll be on my own."

The bell rang and Tier muttered something, then dropped from the wall they were sitting on. He held out his hands and Winter's heart actually fluttered as she took them and he helped her down, even though she was easily as tall as him. They were suddenly nose to nose, his hands still holding hers, her heart still fluttering.

"Walk with you to class?" he said.

"Sure."

They stopped holding hands, but they were walking so close to each other that their arms kept brushing, and each touch sent tingles through her. She was being so incredibly stupid right now, but she didn't care.

They passed Tenacity Yates heading the other way, and she nodded at Tier and he nodded back.

"You know her?" Tier asked when Tenacity was out of earshot.

"I mean, I've chatted to her, yeah," said Winter.

"You hear she saved the world just before Christmas?"

Winter glanced behind them. "Seriously?"

"There was a... Ah, Jesus, why can't I remember these things? There was a thing about a guy and he was trying to bring back some old sorcerer who'd died, like, during the war, I think. Anyway, Tenacity stopped him. Beat the hell out of the dude, from what I was told."

"Wow."

"Yeah," said Tier, and then frowned. "I've never understood that."

"What part?"

"The saving-the-world part. Like, Tenacity is actually a pretty cool person, and I'm glad she did it because I am actually *in* the world, and, as miserable a place as it can be, I do like some aspects of it – but I just don't get why so many students here get sucked into these stupid adventures."

"Ah," said Winter. "Yes, I've been noticing the same thing."

"It's not just me, right?"

"Not just you."

"And not only do they get sucked into stupid adventures, they *allow* themselves to be sucked into stupid adventures. They want to do it. They want to solve a mystery or stop a bad guy or save Roarhaven from this thing or the world from that thing."

"But isn't that what the Sanctuaries are for?" Winter asked.

"Thank you!" said Tier, actually grinning now. "That's their job. Someone wants to bring some freaky old sorcerer back from beyond the grave, you call Tanith Low and she gets her Cleavers to cut him up into little pieces, or the Sanctuary sends their detectives out, or Valkyrie Cain and Skulduggery Pleasant come swooping down out of the sky to save us all at the last minute. But why would you want to go off and do it yourself? I can barely get out of bed for class in the morning, and you want me to go save the world? Nuh-uh. Not happening."

"So if it was ever up to you..."

"Oh, we'd all be dead," Tier responded. "We'd be so dead you wouldn't believe how dead we'd be."

"*Tier, to save the world, all we need you to do is wake up fifteen minutes earlier than usual and push this button.*"

"Nah, couldn't be *bothered*," Tier said, and they both laughed.

The corridors were emptying fast and Winter realised where they were. "Wait," she said, "my class is in the opposite direction."

He blinked at her. "Then why are we walking this way?"

"I was following you."

"But I don't know what your next class is."

Mia Pizazz was suddenly there, linking her arm through Winter's, dragging her back the way she'd come. Winter had time for a quick wave before she had to devote her full attention to her friend.

"Oi, oi," said Mia, grinning, "what's all this, then?"

"He does *not* sound like that."

"I beg to differ, guv'nor," said Mia. "Behind that common-

or-garden English accent, 'e's as cockney as Dick Van Dyke, that lad. You mark my bleedin' words."

"I don't know who or what a Dick Van Dyke is."

"You've never seen *Mary Poppins*? *Chitty Chitty Bang Bang*? Dear God, Winter, what have you been doing with your life?"

"Not watching crappy old musicals on TV, that's what."

"I'll have you know that those *crappy old musicals* are a big part of my mother's culture."

"Your mother's Ethiopian."

"And she adores *Mary Poppins*, so I will thank you to not impugn the majesty of the 1960s musical."

"Impugn?"

"It means to call something into question."

"I know what it means. I just didn't think *you* knew what it means."

"Not just a pretty face, Winter." The corridors were totally empty now and they increased their walking speed. "So how did it happen, anyway? You and the Brood King of Broodville?"

"I was sitting on the wall, waiting for you, and he was sitting on the wall, reading a book, and I said something about reading and that started a whole conversation."

"What did you say about reading?"

"Like, about how good it was."

Mia stared at her. "You said reading was good?"

"Not in those exact words, but... yeah."

"And he still talked to you? Wow."

"Shut up. And reading *is* good."

"Reading is *very* good, yes. I think we can both agree. What book was it?"

31

Winter kept her mouth shut and Mia's grin widened.

"What book was it, Winter? What was he reading? What was the Brood King of Broodonia reading?"

"I thought it was Broodville."

"The kingdom expanded and had to be renamed. What was he reading?"

Winter took a deep breath. "*The Catcher in the Rye.*"

Mia howled with laughter.

"You're overreacting," Winter said, trying her very best to scowl. "And also, quiet down, for God's sake."

They hurried by the closed classroom doors on either side, and Mia managed to gain control of herself. "The broodiest boy in Broodtown with the flickiest hair and the dreamiest eyes, the tortured son of Eliza Scorn and Baron Vengeous, just happens to be sitting on the wall next to you, reading – what I'm imagining to be – a very *battered* copy of *The Catcher in the Rye.* Have I got that right?"

"It was quite dog-eared, yes. And what the hell happened to Broodonia?"

"There was a civil war and it all got divided into individual fiefdoms." Mia put her hand over her mouth. "Oh, Winter. Oh, he's perfect for you."

"Shut up. Also, his dad is not Baron Vengeous."

"Of course he is."

"How does that even work? He's fifteen, the same as us, and Vengeous has been dead for, like... nineteen years?"

"Baron Vengeous is totally his dad. Everyone knows it."

"Everyone does not know it."

"Where'd he put the book?"

"Baron Vengeous?"

"Tier," said Mia. "Where did Tier put the book? He wasn't carrying it just now, so..."

"He put it in his pocket."

"His back pocket?"

"It may have been his—"

"So the tall, gorgeous, angst-ridden existentialist, the son of Eliza Scorn and Baron Vengeous, walks through school with a battered, dog-eared copy of *The Catcher in the Rye* sticking out of his back pocket? How fast was your heart beating?"

"He's not an existentialist."

"Nobody that gorgeous could be anything *but* an existentialist. How fast was it beating?"

"Pretty fast."

"You're destined for each other."

"We just had our first conversation ten minutes ago."

"Yeah, after years of long, lingering looks across the classroom. This is what they write love songs about. I would totally listen to a Korean pop song about this. It would be a *banger*, do you hear me? An absolute *bop*. It'd be called something like 'Luv U, Girl', or 'In the Stars', or, like... 'Brood King and Ice Queen Go for Ice Cream and a Mood Ring'."

"That's definitely a song that should exist. And I'm the Ice Queen in this scenario, am I?"

"You're Winter Grieving," said Mia. "Of course you're the Ice Queen."

Mia led the way into the classroom without knocking. Mr Herringbone stood by the board, raising an eyebrow at them.

"Sorry we're late, sir," said Mia. "Winter had a toilet emergency."

The class cheered and Mr Herringbone had to hide his smile, and Winter glared at her grinning friend as they took their seats.

"And it's just you two, is it?" Mr Herringbone asked. "Brazen wasn't with you during this emergency?"

"Just me and Winter, sir," Mia answered.

Brazen's desk, on the other side of the room, sat empty.

5

"They're staring at you again," Militsa said, cutting into a tomato and then spearing it with her fork. When she popped it into her mouth, she took another look. "Yep. Definitely staring."

"Let them stare," Valkyrie said, focusing on her own food. "So long as they don't come over, it's cool."

Militsa glanced at her, amused. "They're going to come over. You know they are. They can't not come over. They're tourists, and you're part of the reason Roarhaven even has a tourist industry."

Valkyrie grunted out a laugh of derision at that, even though she knew Militsa was right. She just didn't like to admit it. Admitting it seemed... *tacky*.

And of course they came over. A family of sorcerers: the mother wearing a – frankly amazing – leopard-print top, the father in a freshly purchased Ireland rugby shirt, and the boy and girl with eyes so wide it's a wonder their heads had room for the rest of their features.

"Excuse me," said the mother. They were American. "You're not Valkyrie Cain by any chance, are you? It's just, we're visiting and we're all such big, such huge admirers of yours, and we saw you and I said to my husband, I said, you know who that is, don't you? And he hadn't seen you."

"I had my back to you," the father added by way of explanation.

The mother nodded. "He had his back to you. And I said, you know who that is? That's Valkyrie Cain. And the kids – these two are ours, little Kyle and little Amanda – it was the first time they'd looked up from their tablets and, well, you can see their faces. Kids, go on now and say hi to Miss Cain."

The boy went red and said nothing and the girl croaked out a "Hi".

Valkyrie smiled at them both, and shook their hands. "Hi there, Kyle. Hi there, Amanda."

"When I'm older," Amanda whispered, "I want to take Valkyrie as my name, too."

The mother laughed self-consciously. "She's been saying that practically since the day we told her about taken names, but we told her—"

"We told her there's only one Valkyrie Cain," said the father, chuckling.

"Only one Valkyrie Cain, we said. Miss Cain, we're sorry for interrupting your lunch, but we really had to come over and say... we had to just say thank you. Darquesse is... she's a part of you. She is you, in a way, and you're her, and we'd just... we pray to her every day to thank her for this world we live in and for bringing us all back. Ever since the Deletion, ever since the Great Reset, we have valued each and every moment we're given. Thank you for that, Miss Cain. Thank *you*."

"Thank you," said the husband, almost bowing.

Valkyrie smiled, didn't know what to say, so she said, "Cool."

The mother wiped a tear from her eye. "Could we trouble you for a photo?"

Militsa continued on with her lunch, doing her best to hide her grin, while Valkyrie posed for a series of pictures and then said goodbye to the family as they headed for the exit. She called Amanda back, and the little girl hurried over.

"When you're older," she told her, "you can *absolutely* take the name Valkyrie if that's what you want."

Amanda beamed, and then skipped out of the door.

Valkyrie turned back to her plate.

"You're such a softie," Militsa said.

"Shush. I'm busy being a role model and inspiration to little girls everywhere."

"You'll make a great mum someday," Militsa said, and Valkyrie choked on her food while Militsa laughed. The day was saved by a message coming through on Valkyrie's phone.

"Gotta go," she said.

"Tell Skulduggery I said hi."

Valkyrie kissed her and left the café. The sky had cleared since the morning and so she tied her hair back and tapped the black metal skull on her belt. The necronaut suit flowed over her clothes and she took off, trailing white energy as she left the ground behind her.

She flew over Corrival Academy. Usually teeming with students, the summer months meant the campus was quieter, with a lot less drama and a drastically reduced number of life-threatening injuries. They still happened – even the adult sorcerers, like Militsa, managed to get themselves into all sorts of trouble while conducting their research and experiments – but once the adventures of a certain number of intrepid students were removed from the equation things tended to get a lot safer.

Valkyrie skimmed over the streets, keeping her speed down. She should really have been wearing the white, stylised skull mask that she could pull down from her hood. The last time a speck of grit had got in her eye she'd crash-landed on Decapitation Row in front of dozens of people who were too busy taking pictures of her to bother helping her up. But she loved the feeling of the rushing wind against her face, so she left the mask in the hood and she left the hood where it was.

She approached the twin structures that towered over the city: the Dark Cathedral – where they worshipped Darquesse and sang hymns to Valkyrie – and the High Sanctuary, which the Grand Mage and his Council of Elders shared with the mayor of Roarhaven. She veered towards the High Sanctuary, landing at the top of the steps so suddenly that a man shrieked and dropped the files he'd been carrying.

"Sorry," she said to him, the suit flowing back into the black skull as she passed through the doors. She crossed the foyer, took the elevator up and stepped out. Skulduggery was waiting for her. He tapped his pocket watch before putting it away. "You're late."

"Now you know how it feels," Valkyrie replied, shaking her hair out of the ponytail as they started walking. "But at least you know *why* I'm late – I was having lunch with a hot chick. Why were you late this morning?"

"I had things."

"Things?"

"To do."

"Things to do. You had things to do. That's all you're going to say?"

"I would happily go into more detail, but it seems as though we're about to be interrupted."

Cerise came forward, her tablet held close to her chest.

"Arbiters," she said, "the Grand Mage is ready for you. If you'd like to follow me?"

She led the way to the Grand Mage's door, opened it, and allowed them to pass through.

Since taking his post, Ghastly had allowed the mayor to commandeer the huge office at the top of the High Sanctuary, and had moved into a slightly more modest space a few floors down. It was still a big office, lined with shelves on which rested important books and ancient artefacts, and it still had a magnificent view of the city, but it revelled less in its authority. There was a round oak table in the middle of the room and Ghastly's desk was off to one side – a desk on which Ghastly Bespoke had laid his sleeping head.

The top of Ghastly's head – like the rest of Ghastly's head – was ridged with perfectly symmetrical scars. His sleeves were rolled halfway up his thick forearms, and his shirt stretched across his shoulders and biceps. His waistcoat was grey and Valkyrie knew, even though the desk obscured his legs – that the rest of his outfit matched perfectly. Tailor by trade. Boxer by birth. Grand Mage by necessity.

Skulduggery slammed his fists on the desk and screamed.

Ghastly leaped to his feet, his left hand out to grab whoever was attacking him, his right fist pulled back and covered in fire.

He registered Skulduggery's presence and the flames went out as he covered his face with his hands. "You're a terrible person."

"I'm awfully sorry," Skulduggery said. "Did we disturb you?"

"I understand that you don't have to sleep, Skulduggery, but the rest of us need to grab our rest when we can, especially after late-night meetings with boring people."

Valkyrie perched on the edge of the round table. "When was the last time you went home?" she asked.

"I'm home all the time," Ghastly replied. "I have my apartment in this very building."

"I mean *home* home."

"I stopped by last week," said Ghastly. "Wait, is it still April?"

"It's June."

"Oh."

"I thought the situation had calmed down," Skulduggery said.

"The previous situation has calmed down," said Ghastly. "But now there are twelve new situations that need to be dealt with – including the one I asked you in today to discuss. I've been looking forward to this, actually. I derive so little enjoyment from the day-to-day business of running a Sanctuary that I take my pleasures where I can find them."

"This sounds interesting," Skulduggery said.

Ghastly grinned, pressed a button on his desk. "Cerise, could you send in Mr Quiddling, please?"

"Of course," came Cerise's reply, and a moment later a gentleman in a nice suit entered the office. The suit was expensive and well tailored, but it wasn't exquisite. It wasn't like the suits Ghastly made for Skulduggery.

40

"Detective Pleasant," Ghastly said, "Detective Cain, allow me to introduce Aldous Quiddling, representing the English Sanctuary."

Quiddling was a good-looking man, trim and smiling, with brown hair in a conservative cut. "Arbiters," he said, shaking their hands, "it's an honour to meet you both. But it's important to note that not only do I represent the Sanctuary in England, I am also acting as a representative of the Scottish and Welsh Sanctuaries, the French and Spanish Sanctuaries, the American Sanctuary, the—"

"Multiple Sanctuaries, then," Skulduggery said. "That's very good to know. It's always terrific news whenever multiple Sanctuaries send someone to talk to us. It bodes well."

Quiddling chuckled. "I understand your scepticism, Detective Pleasant, and I admit that it is not without cause. In the past, the international Sanctuaries have not made life easy for you – as you, indeed, have not made life easy for them."

"This is starting so well," Ghastly said, smiling broadly as he sat at the round table. He motioned to the other chairs. "Please, everyone."

Valkyrie sat beside Skulduggery and Quiddling took a seat on the opposite side.

"I'm not here with bad news," Quiddling assured them. "Quite the opposite, actually. I think you'll be rather thrilled with what I have to suggest."

"I doubt that very much," Ghastly said happily. "Please continue."

Quiddling fixed them with a professional smile. "Since re-establishing the Arbiter Corps ten years ago, you have done sterling work. You helped to keep Supreme Mage

Sorrows and Supreme Mage Creed in check, and, when they exceeded their mandates, you were instrumental in, ah, *foiling their plans*, as it were."

"As it were," Valkyrie agreed solemnly.

"You did this because of the unassailable authority of your position – because the Arbiters have always been an independent force for truth, justice and democracy."

Skulduggery didn't respond.

"Obviously," Quiddling continued, "circumstances have changed since you brought the Arbiter Corps back. The High Sanctuary is no more – it's merely the name of this splendid building. The Supreme Mage is no more – authority has been rightly returned to each individual Council of Elders. The transgressions – some would say crimes – of the Irish Sanctuary system have all been admitted to and corrected, and the international community certainly appreciates these positive, progressive steps forward."

"I think a round of applause is owed to Grand Mage Bespoke for all these wonderful changes," Skulduggery said, as he and Valkyrie both raised their hands to clap.

"Absolutely," Quiddling agreed, clapping enthusiastically as Skulduggery and Valkyrie dropped their hands.

Quiddling stopped his applause, and chuckled, though the reddening of his cheeks suggested he didn't find it all that funny.

"You'll have to forgive the Arbiters," Ghastly said. "They may be intelligent and ruthlessly efficient, but they're also alarmingly immature. I would agree with you, Mr Quiddling, and I would say that everyone at the Sanctuary here in Ireland is committed to making up for the mistakes of the past. When Darquesse gave us all another chance at life, we embraced the opportunity to correct old mistakes that have plagued the magical community for far too long. Take the African Sanctuaries for example."

Quiddling shifted awkwardly in his seat. "Quite."

"Why," Ghastly continued, "it was the international community itself that imposed the original restrictions, was it not? Three Sanctuaries, one Council of Elders, spread across the entire African continent as, what, punishment? A punishment imposed by people who had no authority to do anything of the kind?"

"With the benefit of hindsight," Quiddling said, "some of the Sanctuaries' actions hundreds of years ago were, indeed, regrettable."

"Not all the Sanctuaries, though," said Valkyrie. "Didn't the other two Cradles of Magic object to what everyone else was doing?"

"They did, indeed," Quiddling said. "Arbiters, Grand Mage, I am not claiming that the international community is blameless. We have certainly made our share of mistakes. We are well aware of the burdens that come with responsibility. That's why I'm here. The Arbiter Corps was once the main source of law and justice in the world. The Arbiters were many and found their strength in numbers. Now, the Arbiter Corps has only two officers."

Valkyrie shrugged. "We're doing OK."

"You are," said Quiddling, "but how long can this continue? How long before the next world-shattering threat comes over the horizon?"

"You want to expand the Arbiter Corps," said Skulduggery.

"Eventually, yes, we do," Quiddling replied. "But we don't want to force new members upon you. Apart from anything else, we don't have the right. Only the Arbiters can decide who else joins. You need to trust your fellow officers implicitly. So, going forward, we hope to work out a system with you that might, one day, see the Arbiter Corps become the force it once was."

Skulduggery and Valkyrie watched as Quiddling leaned forward.

"Arbiters, you are stretched thin. You need support. That's what we're offering: logistical support. How much time do you spend sorting out which cases to take, which investigations to prioritise, which threats to engage with first? How much time do you spend doing paperwork?"

Valkyrie's eyes widened and she looked at Skulduggery. "We're supposed to do paperwork?"

He patted her hand. "Don't let the bad man scare you, Valkyrie."

"We can also offer you the very latest in technological and magical advances. We've always sought to use technology to replicate magical disciplines. A thousand years ago, before there were cloaking spheres, invisibility was a popular discipline for assassins and suchlike. Can you even name one sorcerer alive today whose discipline is invisibility?"

"Gleeman Shakespeare," said Valkyrie.

"Who?"

"Mr Glee."

"Oh, yes. Well, apart from the notorious serial killer, I can't think of one, can you? That's entirely down to the invention of the various types of cloaking spheres. And the research and development hasn't stopped there." He took a square sticking plaster from his pocket, its surface

44

shimmering like a heat haze. "This is a cloaking skin. Instead of generating a sphere of invisibility around a space, it generates a field that follows the contours of the individual. It is, essentially, a layer of invisibility that covers you like a second skin."

Valkyrie reached for it. "Can I see that?"

Quiddling put it back in his pocket. "I'm afraid not. There are only two prototypes in existence and so I am unable to let this out of my possession. Huge apologies."

"Whatever," Valkyrie muttered.

Quiddling continued like he hadn't even noticed her scowl. "But that's not all. In the last ten years, we have seen huge advancements in shunting devices, meaning we can open doors between worlds without relying on Shunters, who are now free to use their powers purely to explore other dimensions. And now it's the Teleporters' turn."

Skulduggery tilted his head. "You have teleportation devices?"

Quiddling smiled. "Indeed we do, for we are duty-bound to focus on the more difficult disciplines. For a time, Fletcher Renn was the only Teleporter in the world. Thanks in large part to his instruction, there are now dozens, but even so their power is among the rarest in the world. Technology will ease them of this burden." He held up what looked like a metal butterfly, the size of a large coin. "This wonderful device is called a Gadda-Da – I have no idea why – and it has a twin. The twin is placed a few metres away. When the Gadda-Da is activated, it seeks to be reunited with its twin, and it does so by accessing the teleportation energies that it has been suffused with. Anyone holding it or touching it is, of course, brought along for the ride."

"I'm sure Teleporters would accuse your technology of taking their jobs," Skulduggery said.

"Progress can be ruthless, it's true – but, if anything, our teleportation devices highlight just how valuable a good, human Teleporter really is. Apart from the limited range of our device – limited for now, of course – a piece of tech is no match for the real thing. Someone who can think on their feet? Who can improvise? Who can solve problems creatively? Sorcerers will always be able to outperform whatever technologies we come up with."

"Mr Quiddling, I assume you're nearing your point."

"I am, Detective Pleasant. Yes, we can offer reinforcements and the latest gadgets, but where we think we would be most useful is in taking the burden of paperwork from your shoulders. We sort through the mess, we identify the priorities, we present you with the urgent cases and we support you in whatever way you need. If that means providing Cleavers, mages, research departments, if that means stepping out of your way entirely and just letting you do your job the way only you two can do it, then we're happy to help however we can."

Skulduggery looked at Ghastly. "And where do you stand on all this?"

Ghastly shrugged. "I got a call a few days ago and they outlined their intentions, asked for my support. I told them I'd have to remain neutral for personal reasons, but requested that I at least be in the room when they suggested it to you. I really didn't want to miss this."

Skulduggery returned his attention to Quiddling. "What you're proposing is setting up an oversight committee."

"No," Quiddling said immediately. "Not at all."

"The international community knows full well that the Arbiter Corps acts independently of the Sanctuary system."

"We're not seeking to change that."

"The Arbiter Corps must be free to investigate whomever and whatever we choose."

"Absolutely."

"This may, from time to time, necessitate investigations into matters that various Sanctuaries would prefer to keep quiet."

"All part of the—"

"We'll be investigating the Sanctuaries, Mr Quiddling. The Sanctuaries, therefore, cannot be part of any stage of that process."

Quiddling went quiet for a moment. "We're not trying to interfere..."

"That's exactly what you're trying to do."

"Detective Pleasant, surely you have to recognise the dangers of any organisation operating with impunity. *Quis custodiet ipsos custodes?*"

Valkyrie scowled. "Settle down, Socrates. We have a rule here: no Latin before five."

"Who watches the watchmen?" Skulduggery translated for her. "A question that could very well be asked of the Sanctuaries themselves. If we overstep our bounds, the rest of you can swoop down to stop us. But who is there to stop you once you cross that line, if we're no longer in a position to do so?" He stood. "It's a disingenuous offer, which might be insulting if you were capable of insulting us."

Valkyrie got to her feet beside him. "It makes me wonder what you've got coming over the horizon that you're going to want to cover up."

"Don't be ridiculous," Quiddling said, irritation flickering across his features for the first time.

"Well," Ghastly said, standing up, "this has been a lot of fun. Mr Quiddling, I could have told your superiors that this is exactly how this conversation would go, but I really felt that you had to experience it for yourself. I hope you've enjoyed it as much as I have. We have a Teleporter waiting to take you back home – a genuine, actual human one – so happy travels, and say hi to everyone in London for me. Skulduggery, Valkyrie, you may now leave my office. Apparently, I have actual work to do."

He went back to his desk and Valkyrie left with Skulduggery. Cerise was standing outside. When they walked by, she tapped once on her tablet, then gave them a smile. Valkyrie smiled back.

6

That familiar smell of chlorine, sharp but lovely, hit her the moment she pushed through the doors of the sports centre, as shrieks and laughs and yells and distant splashes echoed from one corner to the next.

Colleen was exhausted. She had been exhausted for eight days straight with no time off, shift after shift of helping patients, coping with doctors, filling out forms, and dealing with various requests, complaints, demands, and outbursts. She'd been doing this for nine years so she knew she could handle it, but it didn't get any easier.

Just twenty minutes ago, she'd had to make a concerted effort to leave the hospital when she was *supposed* to – and not hang around to clear something up or take care of something else – and come here, to the public swimming pool, to her safe place, so she could at least get the exercise her system so desperately needed.

In the changing rooms, she found a row that was mostly empty and dumped her bag on the bench. She put on her swimsuit and flip-flops and packed her nurse's uniform neatly in her bag with her shoes, her knuckles brushing against a phone that she hadn't even glanced at all day. The screen lit up. One voice message, one text, and fourteen missed calls: three from a blocked number, and eleven from Eimear Shevlin, whom Colleen hadn't spoken to in years. Frowning slightly, she picked up the phone and tapped. The text message said, simply, *Call me.*

She sat on the bench, considering the device. Eimear wasn't someone who'd keep calling unless there was an emergency, but Colleen was tired of emergencies. She was tired of beeps and alarms and rushing into rooms and hurrying along corridors. She just wanted to swim, then go home and sleep.

"I don't think you're allowed to use that in here," a middle-aged woman said from a bench further up.

Colleen looked at her, genuinely puzzled. "Sorry?"

The woman, who was tucking her hair into a swim cap, looked pointedly at Colleen's phone and then to the sign on the wall.

"Oh, yes," Colleen said as she put the phone back in her bag.

She leaned back and closed her eyes, rested her head against the wall. On any other day, she might have argued with the woman, told her to mind her own business. Colleen loved a good argument if the mood was on her. But this evening she didn't want to argue with anyone, didn't want to fight, didn't want to do anything but sit here and maybe go to sleep. That would have been nice.

She opened her eyes again. No. All she needed was to muster the energy to swim hard for maybe half an hour, just long enough to flood her system with all those lovely endorphins, to focus on cutting through the water like she was cutting through the hassles and the pressures and the responsibilities she took on whenever she dressed in that uniform.

But before all that she needed to sate her curiosity, just a little bit. After making sure there was no one else around, Colleen took her phone back out, tapped it, and held it to her ear.

"Colleen, it's Eimear. Eimear Shevlin. Please call me. I'm not sure... There's been an accident. Gavin was in a car crash and he – he didn't make it. And Sarah's gone, too. I'm not sure what happened to her, but first the cops said she died during a break-in at her apartment and now they're saying she died in an accident. They've changed their story. I think something's going on." A hesitation. "Colleen, have you been getting any strange calls? I've been getting strange calls and I think... I think there's someone after us. I think we're all—"

The message ended.

Colleen sat there, the sounds of the swimming pool fading. Gavin and Sarah. She blinked, realised her thumb was hovering over the CALL button.

She moved it away slowly. The fear in Eimear's voice was misplaced. It wasn't fear she was feeling, it was shock that was manifesting as paranoia. Eimear had an overactive imagination. They all knew that.

There was no threat. There was no one after them. Gavin had died and Sarah had died. It was tragic and heartbreaking and Colleen wanted to burst out crying, but accidents happened every single minute of every single day. Colleen knew that better than most. She was one of the people who got to see the results.

She put the phone in her bag and took it to her locker in the small alcove, dialled the combination and stuffed the bag inside. She closed the door and stood for a moment, resting her forehead against the cool metal. Every day, Colleen saw people at their extremes. She was there to see the joy, the laugh-out-loud relief, when tests came back negative, and she was there to see the devastation when an illness overcame the feeble attempts to stop it. She saw every kind of reaction, and every stage of grief. She would have thought that she'd have picked up some way of dealing with it herself, but that was a trick she'd yet to learn.

She needed to swim. She needed to let this news settle into her mind, to take whatever shape it was going to take, while her body was busy doing something else. Her flip-flops padded across the rubber mats lining the floor of the alcove. When she stepped out, the changing room fell so silent it was like she'd been slapped. The shrieks and splashes from the pool continued to bounce off the walls, but the chatter in here had cut off as if a mute button had been pressed.

There were some women slightly ahead of her. Colleen could see the elbow of one, the shoulder of another. She stepped forward. One was standing, one was sitting, but their heads were down, their eyes were closed and they were asleep.

"Excuse me?" Colleen said. "Hello?"

They didn't stir.

She went to the next row. A mother and her two daughters, dressed and ready to go, stood with their shoulders slumped.

Colleen hurried over to them, sniffing the air for gas, for something she didn't recognise. She shook the mother's arm.

The woman didn't wake. Colleen shook her again, harder this time. Still nothing.

They weren't in any obvious, immediate danger and they didn't seem close to toppling over, so Colleen left them and hurried for the exit, barging into the reception area where the man behind the desk snored gently in his chair.

"Hey," Colleen said. "Hey!"

He was a big guy, a lifeguard, and when she darted behind the desk she grabbed his shoulders and shook him violently. His head lolled, but his eyes didn't open. She slapped him, once. Slapped him harder.

"Wake up!" she shouted, right in his face.

She pushed him to one side, the wheels of his chair rolling easily. She grabbed the phone, dialling the emergency services. First, call for multiple ambulances, then call the cops. It didn't matter if this was an accident, some kind of gas leak, or an attack – her priority was ensuring the safety of as many people as possible.

The call hadn't even gone through when the phone went dead. Colleen stared at it, dropped it, looked around for the fire alarm.

The main doors into the sports centre were glass. A man walked across the car park, the evening sun reflecting off the black mask he wore.

It was like something out of a horror movie, and now Eimear's words came back to her: *I think there's someone after us.* The doors slid open and the man in the black mask came inside.

Colleen bolted.

Back to the changing room she ran, leaving her flip-flops to tumble in her wake.

A shadow moved on the floor ahead, but instead of diving into the row to grab this new ally, instead of babbling out an explanation, Colleen came to a sudden stop. She'd seen those horror movies, and this was the part where the killer, whom everyone thought was still lumbering along behind, somehow leaped out in front of the fleeing victim.

The shadow was still, waiting for her to pass.

Bare feet stepping silently, Colleen crab-walked to the other end of the row, squeezing by a sleeping elderly lady wrapped in a towel. The shadow moved but Colleen took two big steps to the partition. She stood with her shoulder jammed against its edge, trying to make herself thinner, still holding her breath.

She blocked out the sounds of splashing and laughter and focused on the killer's slow footsteps. He didn't know where she was, but now she didn't know where he was, either. Behind her terror, her mind struggled to figure out how he could have got from the reception area to the changing room. There were only two doors into this place: the door back to reception, and the doorway out to the pool area. Unless there were two killers, working together.

Colleen had seen those movies, too.

If there were two killers, or if there was only one who could somehow do the impossible, then it meant that sneaking from one hiding spot to the other was only going to delay the inevitable. She needed to get help. She needed to get to the pool area.

Colleen risked a peek into the row. It was clear, so she took two steps to the next partition.

The killer had either come to a stop and was listening for her, or he was moving so quietly that she couldn't hear him over the splashing. She peeked again, then snapped ramrod straight.

The killer was at the halfway point of the next row, his back to her.

She didn't know if that meant he was walking in that direction, away from her, or he had just turned to check behind him as he came in *this* direction. She didn't know if she should hurry back or hurry forward or just stay where she was. Her legs trembled, her knees actually knocking together. She wanted to pee and scream and run and curl up on the floor all at the same time.

She was breathing quickly through her open mouth. She tried to stop, but couldn't. She was going to hyperventilate if she didn't do something. If she didn't make a decision. When Colleen was a kid, playing hide-and-seek with her sister and brothers, she used to get so anxious when the seeker was near that she'd burst out of her hiding place because she couldn't handle the mounting tension. The irrational side of her brain wanted to do the same thing right now.

She took a big step forward, turning to the row as she did so, and gave a silent sob when she saw that it was empty. Her knees went and she hunkered, holding her fist to her mouth, her teeth biting into her knuckles. Keeping her hand there, she turned her head and counted. Just five more rows to the doorway, to the step down on to the rubber surface filled with sterilising water. From there she'd just need to round the corner and step up and she'd be surrounded by people. Safety was a short sprint away.

Colleen straightened, took a big, big breath, shook out her arms and legs, and bolted, and right as she passed the last row the black-masked killer lunged, shoving her into the wall.

Her head cracked against the tiles and the world exploded in a flash of white, but then she rebounded and scrambled against her attacker. She glimpsed a curved knife, and Colleen knew she had to keep that away if she had any chance of making it through this. She probably had concussion, but she wasn't dead yet. She was pretty far from being dead.

She got a bare foot to the tiles and pushed herself off. The killer toppled beneath her and the curved knife went skittering, coming to a stop against one of the rubber mats. The killer turned, searching for the weapon, and Colleen stumbled for the doorway, missed the step and fell into the sterilising water. She put a hand to the back of her head and it came back covered in blood. Definitely concussion.

Heaving herself up, she pressed her hand to the wall for balance and hurried round the corner, leaving a bloody trail on the white tiles. She tripped on the next step, probably breaking some toes but not feeling it, and arrived in the pool area on her knees. Dozens of people were in the water, maybe a dozen more standing along the edges. There were two lifeguards. A lot of alarmed faces.

People rushed towards her, helping her up, startled by the blood, the lifeguards hurrying over. Colleen pointed behind her as the killer followed her out.

He waved the knife and the people all went suddenly still, their chins dropping to their chests, their eyes closing.

Colleen ran for the emergency exit but she slipped and fell sideways and the water pulled her in. She twisted, broke through to the surface, her hair plastered over her eyes, her blood turning the water red. The other people in the pool floated serenely on their backs. The killer stood on the edge, looking down at her.

The emergency exit was at the other end of the pool. Colleen wondered if she could swim it faster than the killer could run it. She twisted again, her bladed hands slicing through the water, her feet kicking behind.

Halfway there, she risked a glance back. The killer hadn't moved. She remembered the two-killers possibility and suddenly stopped, checking ahead of her, making sure there wasn't a second black-masked figure waiting beside the exit. But no, it was clear. Just the one killer. She turned, treading water, looking back at him.

"What do you want?" she shouted. "Why are you doing this?"

He raised the knife. Now that she wasn't scrambling, she could see that it wasn't a knife. It was curved and pointed, but it wasn't made of steel; it was made of something that was slightly off-white.

The killer flicked his wrist, and Colleen burst into flames.

She screeched and writhed in the water, the water that was doing nothing to douse the fire. The pain overwhelmed her. She couldn't see, couldn't hear, couldn't breathe.

Then the pain faded, and everything else faded, too. The world was dark and quiet and Colleen was weightless.

She died in the dark, and the quiet.

7

Valkyrie parked, locked the car and walked over to the steps leading to the main doors of the sports centre. It was a nice morning, sunny and hot. Her linen trousers were loose, her trainers light, her T-shirt plain – a summer outfit – though all in black, of course. She had an image to maintain.

A staff member stood outside the entrance, smiling regretfully as she approached. She scanned the messages on her phone, found his name, and before he could apologise and inform her that the pool was closed for the day she said, "Alan Coleman, you've successfully turned me away."

Alan Coleman's eyes glazed over for just a moment and he nodded, more to himself than to her, and Valkyrie entered the building. Two mages she knew stood guard in reception and she nodded to them, but frowned at the presence of Cadence Clearwater.

"They won't let me through," Cadence said.

"Because you're not on the case," Valkyrie told her.

"Detective Cain, please. I'll do whatever you need me to do, even if it's just, like, securing the scene."

"We already have Sanctuary operatives doing that."

"Then I'll help with the witnesses. There were dozens of them, right? It's going to take another few hours to get through them all."

Valkyrie folded her arms. "Dealing with witnesses is a delicate procedure. These people were traumatised and that trauma needs to be dealt with. It can't just be swept away by telling them they didn't see what they saw."

"I know that."

"Do you have any training in that area? Are you a Sensitive? Or were you just planning on using their given names to insist nothing weird happened last night?"

Cadence didn't have an answer.

"I get that you want to be involved. I really do," Valkyrie continued. "Your partner is lying in a coma and you feel the need to see this through. But we have a killer targeting mortals, and this is going to sound cruel, but we don't have the time to hold your hand. We'll need to move fast when the situation calls for it and you just don't have the experience."

"But I've been on this case since the beginning," Cadence said. "Surely I can offer insights or observations or I'll be able to spot a pattern or—"

"If there's a pattern," Valkyrie interrupted, "we'll spot it. You want a bit of advice, which could serve you well in the future? The weird thing about patterns is that if you go looking for them, you'll find a coincidence and fool yourself into thinking it's more important than it is."

"My dad always said there's no such thing as coincidence."

"No disrespect to your father," Skulduggery said, standing in the doorway to the changing rooms, "but that's ridiculous. Of course there's such a thing as coincidence. The world is built on coincidence. Dismissing coincidence is dismissing the beautifully random nature of the universe."

"Detective Pleasant," said Cadence, turning to him, "can I please help in this investigation?"

"No," Skulduggery said.

"Leave this to us," Valkyrie told Cadence as she walked away. "You'll get your chance at a big case soon enough."

She and Skulduggery headed into the women's changing room, the door swinging shut behind them. There were a few sorcerers she recognised sweeping for clues. "I'll say this for her: she's eager."

"A case like this would make a young detective's name," Skulduggery replied. "She probably looks at what Avant Garde has accomplished since Ghastly hired him, going from one big case to the next in the space of a year, and decided that if there's anyone in the Sanctuary to emulate right now, it'd be him."

"What's he like?"

"I don't know Detective Garde at all – but I knew his mentor, Cogent Badinage, who only trained the absolute best. Every single one of his investigators was precise, ruthless, and determined."

"What happened to Badinage? Is he dead?"

"Cogent Badinage disappeared under mysterious circumstances in 1961."

Valkyrie raised an eyebrow. "Mysterious circumstances? That's all you're going to tell me?"

"I'm afraid so. Cogent was highly intelligent, impeccably dressed, and resolutely incorruptible, and he demanded the same from his squad. They specialised in bizarre cases no one else would touch and, when called upon, crimes committed by Sanctuary operatives and officials. His group was so secretive that none of his detectives even knew the identity of any of the others. From what I gather, Avant Garde might be the last one left alive."

"Huh. Interesting."

"You have something to say, Miss Cain?"

"If I didn't know any better, and if I hadn't just lectured Cadence on keeping things professional, I'd say this might be personal for you."

"I repeat, I do not know Avant Garde."

"But Cogent Badinage sounds like he was a friend of yours, and if Avant Garde is his last student..."

"That's a somewhat tenuous assumption to make."

"Yeah, maybe."

They passed a large smear of dried blood on the wall, indicative of a violent impact.

"Tell me about the victim's home," Skulduggery said, leading the way through to the pool area. A gesture, and the sterilising water parted for them, allowing Valkyrie to keep her trainers dry.

"A small house in Beaumont," she said, eyes on the bloody imprints leading round the corner. "She rented, with another nurse. Had been living there for three years. Messy, in a *nobody has time to tidy up* kind of way. Two busy women working long shifts. No pets, no boyfriends, no girlfriends."

They emerged into the pool area. More sorcerers here, and only eight blank-faced mortals left to deal with, all of them sitting against the wall. Sensitives sat opposite, holding their hands, speaking gently. Valkyrie didn't know what the mortals were being told, but it was probably that they had witnessed a terrible drowning, a tragedy that they would need professional counselling to work through.

"Shared living space," she continued. "Full of personality, but at the same time it doesn't tell us a whole lot about Colleen herself. Her bedroom has everything you'd expect from a woman in her mid-twenties, with a splash of teenager in there. It's like she transplanted her childhood bedroom into her new home when she moved in and had just never got round to updating it. Posters on the walls, little figures on the shelf – Beetlejuice, Pennywise – and boxes full of books and movies and music. Clothes everywhere. Medical textbooks on the desk."

Skulduggery waved his hand as they stepped from the edge into the pool, and they walked across the surface of the water. A buoy floated ahead of them. Colleen Griffin's body had already been taken away.

They reached the buoy and the water solidified round it, holding it in place.

"This is as far as she got," Skulduggery said.

"Cameras?" Valkyrie asked.

"The footage has been corrupted. It's been taken back to the Sanctuary to see if anything can be salvaged."

"You ever hear of someone burning alive underwater?"

"Unfortunately, yes," Skulduggery replied, "though there was nothing magical about it. There are versions of napalm, containing white phosphorus, that will continue to burn provided it has an oxidiser to react with. But that doesn't seem to be the case here. It looks like the victim burst into flames while she was already submerged. I don't know of any fire, not even fire conjured by magic, that could do that."

"Show me the note."

From his inside jacket pocket, Skulduggery took a piece of paper, wrapped in an evidence bag, and handed it over. Valkyrie scanned the tightly packed lines full of weird symbols, and groaned. "It's in code."

"I told you it was in code."

"Yeah, but I thought you meant, like, a riddle. Not a made-up alphabet." She frowned. "Is it a made-up alphabet or is it one of the magical languages?"

"It's a made-up alphabet."

"I hate those." She gave it back to him. "So I did my part, now you do yours. What's it say?"

"Your *part* was searching a house. That is not the same as deciphering a hitherto unknown code."

"Yeah, but you're the genius, as you're always reminding me. You found this stuck to her locker, what, two hours ago? If you haven't solved it by now, I'm going to be really disappointed in you."

He sighed, put his finger to the first line and started tracking it along as he translated.

"I am Ersatz. I am the killer, the slayer, the executioner of these mortals whose names are not worth the ink it would take to write them. I have killed them and I will kill more. Mortals are nothing but animals. They are vermin. They are insects. I am the tenth ancile, protecting our kind from the mortal plague, but you will try to stop me. You will try to obstruct me in my sacred mission, my divine calling, my solemn duty, my hallowed purpose. Skulduggery Pleasant and Valkyrie Cain, you are being tested."

Skulduggery returned the note to his pocket.

"Well," said Valkyrie, "our serial killer sounds delightful."

"We don't know yet that Ersatz is a serial killer," Skulduggery cautioned, leading the way back to the edge of the pool.

"They've left a taunting note, addressing it to the very people who are hunting them."

"Classic serial-killer behaviour, I would agree. Even the construction of the code is reminiscent of the first cipher that the Zodiac Killer sent in 1969, containing both homophonic substitutions and transposition. But it strikes me as a cheap copy, more of an homage than a naturally occurring method of communication."

They stepped back on to solid ground and the water surface relaxed behind them, rippling and splashing slightly.

"It seems contradictory, though," said Valkyrie. "Here we have a sorcerer paying homage to a mortal serial killer in a note in which he's otherwise acting superior to mortals in general, calling them animals, vermin, and insects. Then he names himself Ersatz, a word that means an imitation of the real thing. So does Ersatz reckon he's superior to mortals, or inferior?"

"Like you say – contradictory."

"What's that word he used? What's an ancile?"

"The ancilia were twelve sacred shields in ancient Rome."

"And what's the significance of the tenth one?"

"As far as I'm aware, there is none. Only one of the twelve was an actual sacred shield – the rest were exact copies made to fool thieves – so perhaps the tenth one was the original. I'd have to research that to confirm if the theory has any validity." He took out his phone, read a message, and tilted his head as he put it away.

"What's wrong?"

"The victim's phone was in her locker. I asked for it to be examined."

"And?"

"It's blank. The call history, voicemails, and contact details have all been wiped."

"Annoying, but so what? The killer wiped Sarah Boyle's phone, too, and probably would have wiped Gavin Fahey's if it hadn't been crushed to bits."

"But this phone was in her locker, in her bag, tucked away beneath her clothes."

"So the killer didn't have to physically *hold it* to wipe it – assuming he *was* the one who wiped it. All right, so did he have a gadget to do that, or did he use magic? Is he some sort of advanced Elemental *and* a Technomage? He's got two disciplines? Who do we know who's got multiple disciplines? We haven't heard from Crepuscular in a while."

"You think it might be my grandson?" Skulduggery said. "I doubt it. No. Whoever's doing this is killing these people for a reason. It's elaborate. Sadistic. Personal."

"Then just who are we dealing with here?"

"I don't know," said Skulduggery. "But I can't wait to find out."

8

Winter scrolled through her phone while she lay on the bench outside Mirror Hall, her legs stretched out, her ankles crossed. Classes had ended twenty minutes ago and everyone was off doing their extracurriculars or their homework or studying or just, in some cases, hanging out with their friends. Mia, she guessed, was doing the latter. Unlike Winter, Mia didn't have a problem making friends. People gravitated towards her. They found her charming and warm and nice to be around. Which was weird.

Winter could be charming and warm and nice to be around, but only for Mia or, once upon a time, Brazen. OK, and maybe Tier Galling, if things worked out. When it came to just about everyone else, she was pretty unfriendly.

Sometimes she worried about stuff like that, worried that her lack of a significant social group was more down to an inability to maintain one rather than disinterest in establishing one, but she had a wonderful way of ignoring thoughts she didn't like, so that's what she tended to do.

Familiar footsteps approached. Her own footsteps.

Winter's reflection stopped and stood there without moving until Winter tapped her screen off and sat up.

"Hey," Winter said.

Expression flooded the reflection's face like it had just switched itself on. "Hey," it said back.

Winter patted the bench and the reflection sat beside her. It didn't need to sit – it didn't get tired – but basic compassion was at the heart of Corrival's Rules of Reflections, ever since Principal Sorrows had started allowing reflections to be used as learning aids. Winter knew plenty of students who viewed their reflections with borderline contempt, but she figured this said more about how those students felt about themselves than how they felt about their reflections. If you could be nasty to something that wore your face and was filled with your memories, then there was something darker at play.

"Mia's late again," the reflection said.

Winter smiled. "She has too many friends."

"Or you have too few."

"I was just thinking something along those lines," Winter said, "so I don't need you saying it out loud, thank you very much."

The reflection nodded. "You said you'd call home this afternoon."

Winter soured. "Oh, yeah."

"You're not going to."

"Probably not. I'll be home for the whole summer. They can do without me until Friday."

"In England, they only get six weeks of summer holiday," the reflection said, telling her something she already knew.

"Good thing we're not in England," she replied. Then, "Do you mind if we don't speak?"

"Not at all," said the reflection, and sat very still, looking straight ahead.

Sometimes Winter was in the mood for idle chat, and doing the small-talk thing with the reflection was really good practice for talking to real people – but sometimes it just depressed her. The only times the reflection had anything of interest to say was if something of interest had happened to it since it had stepped out of the mirror. Otherwise, it just regurgitated stuff that was already in Winter's head. Sure, it was also unimaginably useful as a memory prompt, but mostly Winter just wanted to sit in silence.

Mia and her reflection came round the corner, chatting and laughing. Winter envied the ease her friend had with people – her own reflection included. It was something Winter could never quite manage.

"*Annyeong, naui eol-eum yeowang,*" Mia said. "Shall we?"

Winter and her reflection stood and they all walked towards Mirror Hall.

"When was the last time you saw Brazen?" Mia asked, mouth twisting in that adorably cute way of hers.

"Haven't a clue," responded Winter, glancing at her reflection.

"Sunday at three forty-four pm," it said. "She was sitting in the courtyard, texting."

"There you go. Why?"

Mia shrugged. "I'm just wondering where she is, that's all."

"I wouldn't waste your time. She doesn't care about us; we shouldn't care about her."

Mr Peccant was on duty outside Mirror Hall, marking student essays. "Names," he said as they approached his desk, even though they'd both been in his class for years.

"Mia Pizazz and Winter Grieving," said Mia.

Peccant made a note in the ledger by his elbow, and nodded. "Go on."

"Mr Peccant," said Mia, lingering, "could I ask you a question?"

"You could," said Peccant, "providing the question is about maths."

"It's actually about Mr Herringbone."

"Carry on into Mirror Hall, Miss Pizazz."

"I'm just wondering, sir, if Mr Herringbone is married?"

"I don't discuss fellow staff members with students, Miss Pizazz. I don't discuss anything with students that isn't maths."

"Mr Peccant, sir, you know that you're my absolute favourite teacher—"

"I am nobody's favourite teacher, Miss Pizazz – now carry on into Mirror Hall or your reflection privileges will be revoked until the end of term."

"You're tough but fair, sir."

"How wonderful for me," Peccant muttered, returning to his marking.

"I just want you to know that you are so embarrassing to be around," said Winter as they entered Mirror Hall. "Having a crush on the teacher is such a cliché."

"And having a crush on the school bad boy is any better?" Mia shot back with a grin as they reached the first two mirrors in a corridor lined with them. "You do know that I don't really have a crush on him, right? Reflecky, back me up here."

"She pretends to fancy Mr Herringbone because it leads to amusing situations and allows her to be what she regards as funny," Mia's reflection said.

Now it was Winter's turn to grin. "*What she regards as funny*. Even your own reflection is mocking you."

Their reflections stepped into the mirrors, their features and clothing gently flipping to the opposite side as they turned. Mia tapped the mirror and Winter did the same, closing her eyes as six hours' worth of alternate memories swarmed her mind like a shoal of fish before easing into the currents and eddies of her own.

"Don't get me wrong," Mia said as they walked back, "Herringbone is a fine-looking man, but I just don't have time for crushes, you know? I've got my exams to think about."

Winter nodded. "Because you care so much about exams."

"We've got two more years of this place, and when I graduate I swear to God I will make the world a better place. You just watch me."

"Hey," said Winter, "I believe it."

"As well you should. Have you decided what you're going to do with your life once we finish here?"

"Haven't a clue."

They passed the desk outside Mirror Hall and Mia waved, but Peccant didn't even look up to scowl.

"Your grumpy demeanour doesn't fool me for a second, Mr Peccant," Mia called.

"I'll put you in detention, Miss Pizazz."

Mia sighed happily. "He's adorable. He reminds me of my granddad, if my granddad was old and crotchety instead of looking like he's my big brother." She clapped her hands. "Right. Let's go find Brazen."

"I'm sorry? What?"

"Millicent and Violante haven't seen her in days. Her stuff is still by her bed, though, so she hasn't gone home."

"Mia, why do you care where she is?"

"Because she's our friend."

"She was our friend, and then she turned weird and nasty. I mean, when was the last time you actually spoke to her?"

"I speak to her all the time."

"And when was the last time she responded?"

"That's not important. She *was* our friend and if we don't look for her, who will?"

Winter sighed. "Have you checked with her folks?"

"Oh, yeah, because that'd be a good conversation. *Hey, we were just wondering if Brazen returned home to you guys without taking any of her stuff? I thought she was safe in school. Oh, she totally is! Nothing to worry about here!*"

"I'm confused. How many voices were you doing there?"

"The first was me, the second was both her parents, and the third was you."

"The third sounded nothing like me."

"You're just saying that because we never like our own voices played back to us."

Winter looked at her friend, torn between not caring and really not caring, and then sighed again. "Fine. Only because I know you're going to keep bugging me about this, let's go ask the one person who could know where she is."

"Ah," said Mia, "the stalker."

They returned to their dorm room and got changed out of their uniforms. Mia dressed in black leggings and an oversized pink hoody that went with her trainers. She was a blast of colour, that girl – a blast of positivity and brightness – unlike Winter, with her dark clothes designed to blend into the background. They left the school and took the tram to the bookshop on Effervescent Avenue. Mia searched the ground floor and Winter searched the first, all the way from Science Fiction to Horror, and they both arrived on the third floor at the same time. They found Brazen's stalker sitting in the coffee place in the corner.

Winter dropped into the seat opposite, startling Aphotic Atramentous out of the book he was reading.

"Whatcha got there?" Mia asked, giving him a smile as she slipped daintily into the remaining chair.

"Edgar Allan Poe," Aphotic said warily.

"You a fan?"

"He's my favourite writer."

"What's your favourite book?"

"This one."

Winter peered at the cover. "*The Selected Works of Edgar Allan Poe*. That's like saying your favourite Foo Fighters album is their *Greatest Hits*."

"I only like the Foo Fighters' early stuff," Aphotic said.

"Of course you do."

"I don't know them," admitted Mia. "They're an old band, right? Yeah, don't know them."

Winter frowned at her. "How are we even friends?"

Mia gave her a shrug, then looked at Aphotic. "Have you seen Brazen today?"

"Why?"

"Just tell us," said Winter impatiently. "We're looking for her."

He hadn't always been Aphotic. The first name he'd taken, the name he'd had when he'd started at Corrival aged twelve, was a perfectly fine name, even if Winter couldn't remember it right now. But he'd changed it in an attempt to give himself a darker edge, to turn himself into the kind of guy someone like Brazen Yarrow would go for. She liked the bad boys, did Brazen. The bad boys with the tortured souls. The last time Winter had spoken to her of such things, back when they were still friends, Brazen had been pining over Tier Galling.

"I don't know where she is," Aphotic said.

"You always know where she is," Winter responded.

"That's just because we hang out at the same places."

"No, it's because you hang out at all the places she hangs out. There's a difference."

Aphotic glowered. "I don't know where she is," he repeated.

"When was the last time you saw her?" Mia asked, all smiles, the good cop to Winter's irritable, easily annoyed cop.

"Sunday evening."

"In school?"

He shook his head. "I passed her on the street."

"What street?"

"Just outside the museum."

"That's a bit out of the way, isn't it?" Winter said. "What were you doing in that part of town?"

"Nothing."

"You weren't following her, then?"

Aphotic shifted in his chair like he was getting ready to leave.

"Hey," Mia said, frowning at Winter, "he was out walking. People are allowed to go out walking. Aphotic, you passed her. Was she with anyone?"

A resentful moment dragged by, and Aphotic grunted. "Yeah. She was with a few people."

"Did you recognise them?"

He shrugged.

Winter sat forward. "Aphotic, who was she with?"

"I didn't—"

"If I have to beat it out of you," Winter said, "I absolutely will."

Aphotic laughed. "You're not going to attack me in the middle of a bookshop."

Winter got up and leaned over him, gripping the arms of his chair so that he had to shrink back. "I don't like you," she said.

"You don't like Brazen, either."

"But for a few years I did, and, when we were friends, you asked her out four times and each time she said no. You've never been able to accept that she doesn't reciprocate your weird, twisted little feelings, have you?"

"They're not—"

"Brazen's missing," said Winter. "No one knows where she is. You're probably the last person to see her. You know what that makes you? The prime suspect in her disappearance."

"I only recognised one of them," he said weakly.

Winter straightened up, but didn't move back. "Who?"

"Remember that guy with the tattoos? He graduated last year?"

"Alter Veers?"

"Yeah, him."

Mia frowned. "What's Brazen doing hanging around with Alter Veers?"

Alter was cool enough, from what Winter had heard, but he'd been three years ahead of them, and their paths had never really crossed. Aphotic had an expression on his face like he had news he just had to share. Winter prodded him. "Spill."

"I don't know much," he said, "but, when Alter Veers left Corrival, he... This is just what I've heard, OK? But, when he left, he fell in with a crowd of, uh..."

"For God's sake, just tell us what—"

"Mortal-haters."

Winter shut her mouth and watched him.

"What kind of mortal-haters?" asked Mia. "Like, there are different degrees, you know? Are we talking just Isolationists or something... worse?"

"I heard Alter joined the Order of the Ancients."

The bookshop carried on around them, and the world carried on around it, but here, right here, time suddenly stood very, very still.

"So what are you saying?" Winter asked. "I mean, if that's true – if Alter Veers is a member of the Order of the Ancients – then what are you saying?"

"I'm not saying any—"

"Yes, you are," Winter interrupted. "You're saying that because Brazen is hanging out with Alter, Brazen is a... she's a... You're saying she's a terrorist, aren't you?"

Aphotic hesitated. "I'm saying she might be, yes."

Winter loomed over him again. "You know what you're going to do now? You're going to ask around and find out where we can talk to Alter Veers."

"Why would I—?"

"If we talk to Alter, we'll be able to talk to Brazen and maybe snap her out of whatever this is before the trouble really starts. You want to help Brazen, don't you?"

He swallowed. "Yes. But why do you?"

"I don't," said Winter, and jerked her thumb at Mia. "She does. And if my friend is dumb enough to want to help some toxic, nasty witch we once sat with at lunch, then I'm dumb enough to want to help her. Now get out there, Aphotic, and go find us some terrorists."

9

"Twelve more," Panthea said as Valkyrie's arms trembled. "Just twelve more and you're done."

Valkyrie barked out a laugh, but kept it short. The grips hurt her hands and her legs were too tired to stay curled behind her and so each breath she expelled needed to be in service of the movement.

"Come on!" Panthea shouted. "You can do this! You've already done this ten minutes ago!"

Valkyrie wanted to point out that ten minutes ago meant forty push-ups ago, and forty lateral raises ago, and thirty bicep curls ago, and thirty air-squats ago, but she didn't point out any of that because each breath she expelled needed to be in service of the movement.

Down she went, holding herself off the ground by the grips and the grips alone, and then back up. And then back down. And then back up.

Panthea counted out each dip, but Valkyrie stopped listening, stopped focusing on the idea of finishing. Her whole world was the triceps dip she was performing. And when it was done her whole world was the next one, and then the next one.

All of a sudden, Panthea cheered, and Valkyrie uncurled her shaking legs, found the steps, took her weight off her arms. Panthea gripped her on either side of the waist and kept her steady as she hopped to the floor.

"Nicely done," Panthea said, grinning.

"You've killed me," Valkyrie murmured, allowing herself to just stand there, arms flopping uselessly, sweat soaking through her shorts and top.

"Nonsense," said Panthea, slapping her on the back. "You can do that kind of workout in your sleep. On Thursday, we'll do legs, but then let's fit in a heavy session next Monday, what do you say?"

"That wasn't a heavy session just now?"

"You're funny. You're tiny and funny."

"I'm only tiny to you. I'm actually pretty big to just about everyone else."

Her trainer smiled at her, the way she'd smile at an adorable puppy. "Of course you are."

Valkyrie retrieved her empty water bottle and her towel and dragged herself to the showers. Once upon a time, she'd have chewed on a hanna leaf to get rid of the muscle ache before it really kicked in, but she didn't do that any more. Painkillers were now used only when absolutely necessary. She quite liked the ache. It was a reminder that she'd done something good, something healthy. Something positive.

She stood with her eyes closed and her head down while the hot water blasted her scalp. Valkyrie could have stayed like this all day, her thoughts light and floaty, but the real world was waiting. She reached out, turned the dial all the way round, and raised her face into a torrent of ice water that made her gasp. She withstood as much as she was able and then cut it off.

She cheekily asked an Elemental to dry her, then pulled on jeans and boots and a T-shirt and carried her gym bag out into the sunshine, where Skulduggery was leaning against the Bentley.

"We're going to Texas," he said.

Valkyrie held out her bag. "Tell me."

He took it, opened the car boot and dropped it in. "Ersatz's note. It annoyed me. Not the taunting part – killers have sent taunting notes before and it's been nothing but helpful. The annoying part was when he broke the rule of three."

"The rule of three. Yes. Excellent. Explain it to me like I'm an idiot."

He closed the boot. "People process information in a variety of ways – one of these ways is the rule of three. You'll see it utilised most often in novels and movies, but you'll also find yourself using it in your day-to-day life. If you want to give enough examples of a thing to establish a pattern, three examples will do so in a pleasing, satisfying, and memorable manner. Did you see what I just did? *Pleasing, satisfying, memorable.* I just used the rule of three."

Valkyrie watched him. "It feels like you're teaching me something, and you know that I hate being taught things."

"Ersatz understands this rule. He calls himself the *killer*, the *slayer*, and the *executioner*. He calls mortals *animals*, *vermin*, and *insects*. Then he calls what he's doing a *sacred mission*, a *divine calling*, a *solemn duty*, and a *hallowed purpose*. The third time, just when he's about to *complete* the rule of three, he *breaks* the rule of three."

"The scoundrel," Valkyrie. "He clearly must be stopped."

"He ends the note by telling us that we're being tested. When he attacked Avant Garde, he told him he'd failed. When he let Cadence Clearwater live, he told her to do better."

"So Garde and Cadence were being tested, too."

"Garde failed the test, and Cadence must have passed, or maybe her test isn't over. If we are being evaluated, it stands to reason that any interaction we might have with Ersatz is also a test."

"In which case," said Valkyrie, "we passed the first one, right? We cracked the code."

"I cracked the code."

"But I believed in you, so I can take half the credit. Continue without arguing, please."

"If Ersatz is testing us, then at the very least he knows what we've done and how good we are. He knows we're better than anyone else, so our test is going to be harder than anyone else's."

"OK. And?"

"The phrase that broke the rule of three – *hallowed purpose*. Ersatz put that in there for a reason – to draw our attention."

"At the risk of repeating myself: OK. And?"

"I did a little digging, searching for that particular phrase. There's a church in a small magical community in Texas – the Church of the Hallowed Purpose. I think we should go there and ask the good people of that town some questions – subtly, just to see if they're somehow connected to what's going on."

Valkyrie shrugged. "Sure. What's the town called?"

"It's a lovely little place, by all accounts. Quaint is the word that's most used to describe it."

"And what's it called?"

"What's what called?"

"The name of the small town, Skulduggery, the name of the magical community, the one you're trying to avoid saying. What is it called?"

"I'm not trying to avoid saying anything."

"What is it—?"

"The town's called Hellfire," Skulduggery said.

Valkyrie looked at him, and sighed. "Sounds delightful."

They drove to the High Sanctuary, parked beneath it and rode the tiles up to the foyer. Skulduggery went to ask one of Cerise's assistants to arrange for a Teleporter, and Valkyrie headed for the canteen. She sat with a plate of chicken and a coffee.

"Another balanced meal," Fletcher Renn said, sitting opposite.

She raised an eyebrow as she chewed. "You're our Teleporter?"

"You have that honour, yes. I've already been to the charming little town you're going to as part of my Magical Mystery Tour, so we can travel straight there when you're done eating."

"Your Magical Mystery Tour?"

"That's what I call it. I advise all the Teleporters in my class to travel to every magical community around the world. I tell them, I *guarantee* them, that they'll need to deposit those locations in the ol' memory bank."

"And how many of them take that advice?"

"That I know of? One."

Valkyrie almost spat out her coffee. "One student has taken your advice in, what, ten years?"

"It hasn't been ten years," he said, and then frowned. "Has it? Anyway, none of them want to actually do anything that they won't get tested on, no matter how essential it is. As far as I know, Never's the only one who actually did it. Not at all coincidentally, but who is the world's second-best Teleporter right now, the best being me?"

"That would be Never."

"Yes, it would."

"Have you spoken to them lately?" Valkyrie asked. "Ever since that thing with the mascots, they've been positively *friendly*."

"Lessons were learned, Valkyrie. Never is living proof that people can change. As a moulder of young minds, that's what I try to incorporate into my classes.

"Uh-huh," she said. "And how's that going for you?"

He shrugged. "Teaching is the greatest job ever during the summer. I find that's when the students are at their best."

"When they're not in school, you mean."

"Yes."

"And you've got no desire to head up the Sanctuary's Teleportation Department?"

He messed his hair one way, then messed it right back again. "Working for the Sanctuary is going to get me killed, so I try not to do it too much. Besides, agreeing to the occasional assignment makes them appreciate my rarefied skills, and allows them to treat me like the rock star I am."

She thought about mentioning the teleportation device

Quiddling had shown her, then decided against it, and instead said, "I'd say being a teacher in Corrival Academy isn't a whole lot safer than working for the Sanctuary."

Fletcher laughed. "Yeah, there's definite danger in going into work during termtime. In practically every class, there's a group of friends who have adventures – and they're not silly adventures, either. They're proper adventures. Even calling them adventures makes it sound silly, but that's what they are. They're the kind of adventures you used to drag me into – end-of-the-world, battling-the-forces-of-evil-type stuff."

Valkyrie smiled along with him, then frowned. "My sister's not involved in any of that, is she?"

Fletcher held up his hands. "Not that I know of. If she was, I'd tell you. I promise."

She nodded. "Good. Thank you. So you're managing to keep out of adventures for the most part, yeah?"

"For the most part. It still isn't easy being a teacher, though – not when you look like this."

"I'm sorry? When you look like what?"

"Like this," he said, gesturing to himself. "You must get it, too. I mean, we're gorgeous. I'm not saying that to brag, but you and me are two very, very good-looking people. And we're going to stay young for hundreds of years. I'm thirty-five years old and I look twenty-one. You're thirty-two and you look nineteen."

"I don't look nineteen."

"Valkyrie, we look amazing, so let's accept that and move on. But looking amazing and young and beautiful is not good for a teacher. I actually yearn – I *yearn* – to look middle-aged and grizzled. Then I might stand a chance of getting some respect from these kids. But they look at me standing at the front of the class, imparting wisdom, and half of them don't take me seriously, and the other half have crushes on me. *Of course* they have crushes on me. Not a line, not a wrinkle, not a hint of grey – combine that with this bone structure and this hair and it's a recipe for a roomful of lovestruck teenagers barely listening to what I have to say. And it doesn't help matters that I've obviously been working out."

Valkyrie blinked. "You have?"

Fletcher laughed. "What, you think this definition happened by accident?"

She peered closer. "You have definition?"

"It can't be any easier for you. You've got to project absolute authority when you're dealing with the killers and bad guys you encounter every single day. How do you cope? How do you project authority?"

"I... well, I mean, the first thing I do is I *have* authority."

"Yes?"

"And then I *project* it."

"Well, yes, it's just that I have authority, too, but I'm hampered by how good-looking I am."

"Oh, Fletcher."

"I know," he said miserably.

Skulduggery came over. "Are you ready?"

Valkyrie stood quickly. "Yes."

10

Fletcher took them to a handful of thirsty, brittle trees on the outskirts of Hellfire, Texas, and then teleported away. It was just gone nine in the morning there, and it was already hot. The ground was dry and the sky was drier.

The people here were sorcerers, but not everyone reacted well to a living skeleton roaming among them, so Skulduggery's façade flowed over his body beneath his black suit. This one had stubble on the jaw, and the eyes were shaded by the brim of his hat. They walked the town's main street, such as it was. Ramshackle homes sagged next to a ramshackle general store. There was a post office that doubled as a barber shop, and opposite that a bar. Dust-covered cars and pick-ups sat quietly. People frowned at them as they passed.

At the end of the street was a gas station and, beside it, a small wooden church, its doors open. They went inside. There were six pews on either side of the nave, and religious paintings hung on the walls. The altar consisted of a simple table and a cheap podium and, elevated behind it, a naked store mannequin, white and chipped and missing its arms. Its head was black, a calm expression carved into the plastic.

A man in black prayed on his knees before the mannequin. "I've been expecting you," he said without looking round.

Valkyrie hesitated. "Are you talking to us?"

"He said you would come."

"I think he's talking to us," she whispered to Skulduggery, loud enough for the man to hear.

He stood and turned. He was slender, of average height, with dark hair, receding slightly. He had a kind face and his clerical collar was as black as his shirt.

Skulduggery tilted his head. "When you say *he* said we would come, who exactly are you referring to?"

"Arava Kahann," said the priest.

"That's your god, is it?"

"Yes, he is."

"What kind of a god is he?" Valkyrie asked. "I don't know how to say this exactly, but, like... is he a good god? Is he a fan of peace and love? Or is he the other kind?"

"Arava Kahann is a wonderful god," the priest said.

"That doesn't really answer my question," Valkyrie responded, walking closer to one of the paintings. It was disturbingly violent, depicting a woman being pulled apart by crows. "See, this picture here doesn't fill me with confidence that Arava Kahann is a nice guy, which would lead me to suspect that maybe you, yourself, could be a... well." She side-eyed the priest. "Are you a devil-worshipper?"

The priest smiled. "To your mind, yes, I suppose he would be the Devil, and his kingdom would be Hell, for you and others like you. He is the Devil, but he is not Satan, or Lucifer. He goes by many names, but we know him as Arava Kahann, the Hidden God."

Valkyrie's own smile faded. "Yeah. I know him."

"You do," the priest said, nodding. "And he knows you. He saw you, three hundred years ago, through *La Porta dell'Inferno*."

Valkyrie rejoined Skulduggery in the centre of the nave. "Yep. That was me. So how's he doing? What's he been up to?"

"He's been watching you."

"Oh, good, that's not creepy."

"He sees the potential for greatness in you, Valkyrie Cain. If he can convert you, he believes the world can still turn against Darquesse. Humanity can still be saved."

"Saved from what?" Skulduggery asked.

"From a life of slavery," said the priest.

"You think Darquesse has enslaved them?"

"Arava Kahann trusted her," the priest said. "He believed her lies. When she told him of her plan to delete the events that led to the deaths of billions, to fix what had gone wrong, and then to restart the universe and make this reality a paradise without restriction, he helped her. He added his strength to hers. But she betrayed him. She stole his power and then cast him out, and she rebuilt the universe as a prison for the souls of the innocent. Arava Kahann wants to free those souls. He wants to free you."

"You realise," Valkyrie said, "that none of that is true, right?"

"I don't expect you to believe me. Not right away. You'll need proof. You'll need persuasion."

"You know us," Skulduggery said, "and we know your god, but what is *your* name?"

"My name is Fervor," said the priest with a smile. "Bilious Fervor."

"Utterly charming," Skulduggery said, taking out his gun.

"I hope you don't think this is too forward of me, Bilious, but it's obvious that you are, as Valkyrie would put it, a bad guy, yes? So I might just shoot you now to save us the trouble of shooting you later."

Valkyrie scowled. "You can't shoot him."

"Yes, I can," he said, pointing with the gun. "He's right there. It'll be easy."

"He hasn't done anything yet. You can't just shoot him if he hasn't done anything yet."

"So I'm only allowed to shoot him *after* he's attacked us?"

"Well, no, you don't have to wait until *after*. I'd rather you didn't shoot him at all, but if you shoot him the moment you think that we or someone else is in danger, then that's, I suppose, acceptable."

"My way would save us so much time, though."

"Skulduggery."

"Fine," Skulduggery said, "but I'm not putting my gun away."

"OK then," said Valkyrie, looking back at the priest. "I wouldn't make any sudden moves if I were you."

Fervor nodded. "Duly noted."

"Bilious, you seem to me like a practical, reasonable fellow, praying as you were to a clothes-store mannequin, so why'd you do it? Why'd you kill those people?"

"I haven't killed anyone," Fervor said. "Not recently, anyway."

"Not even a few little mortals? I mean, they barely count as people, right?"

"Mortals and sorcerers are equal in the eyes of the Hidden God. Half of the good citizens of Hellfire are mortals. We live together in peace and harmony."

"Huh. So you're *not* Ersatz? You're not the serial killer we're looking for?"

"I'm afraid not."

"We'll probably just take you in for a quick scan, though, just because we don't believe you."

"I doubt your Sensitives will be able to breach my defences," Fervor said, "but if that's something you feel you ought to do, then so be it."

"Thank you for being so understanding. Would you like us to find someone to take care of your mannequin while you're gone?"

"That's very nice of you to offer, but the good people of Hellfire will see to my church."

"Fair enough," said Valkyrie. "Is that an accurate representation of him, by the way? Arava Kahann?"

"Honestly, I do not know," Fervor said. "He has yet to appear to anyone but his most deserving of acolytes. This is my feeble attempt to embody his essence in a way that makes sense to my limited eyes."

Valkyrie nodded. "Yeah, OK, I get that. Hey, since we're chatting about random stuff like two old pals who haven't seen each other in a dog's age, you wouldn't happen to know where we could find our pesky little serial killer, would you?"

"I would, actually."

"And would you be willing to tell us?"

"I can show you, if you'd like."

Skulduggery tilted his head. "By all means."

But, instead of leading them to a second location, Fervor just smiled.

Valkyrie tilted her head, the same as Skulduggery, and they turned.

A figure stood in the open doorway. The black mask he wore was identical to the mannequin's expressionless face. Skulduggery thumbed back the pistol's hammer while Valkyrie turned sideways, one hand pointing to Ersatz, the other raised towards Fervor.

"You're under arrest," Skulduggery said, and Ersatz flicked his wrist away from his coat slightly and Valkyrie saw now that he was holding something and Skulduggery vanished.

Magic charged through her system and white energy crackled around her hands. "Bring him back," she ordered. "Wherever you sent him, whatever you did, bring him back or I'll fry you where you stand."

Ersatz just looked at her.

The phone in her pocket buzzed three times. Skulduggery was trying to call, which meant he was still alive and somewhere with mobile-phone reception. That was good. What wasn't quite so wonderful was her positioning – directly between Ersatz and Fervor. She suddenly felt very vulnerable. Skin rippling with gooseflesh, every instinct screamed at her to tap the black skull on her belt, to cover herself with the necronaut suit. But that would mean dropping a hand, even if it was only for a moment.

She realised that the object in Ersatz's hand, which she had assumed to be a curved knife, was actually a bone – what looked like a human rib. From the way Ersatz was holding it, and now that she'd seen what it could do, Valkyrie knew that a human rib wasn't *all* it was.

"Real sorcerers," she said, "don't use wands."

11

Ersatz moved, swiping the air with the wand, and Valkyrie released a stream of lightning that faded before it even reached its target. She tried to generate more, tried to call upon that energy to crackle around her, but it was gone.

It wasn't just bound. It wasn't just restricted. It was gone.

Something hit her from behind, flinging her to the floorboards. She went to tuck and roll, but didn't manage it and sprawled painfully instead. Fervor stalked after her.

Valkyrie got to her feet. *Screw it.* She'd had to fight without magic before; she could do it again.

She darted to meet him, but her punch was awkward and anyway he slipped outside it, returned fire with a hook to the ribs. Valkyrie grunted and he hit her again, just above the temple, and the world spun as she staggered. He came forward, weaving like a boxer. She feigned being more hurt than she was – a small part of her alarmed at how much she *was* hurt – and then grabbed him, going to stomp on his foot and follow with a headbutt. But nothing was working right and she fumbled the grab and when he hit her, flush on the chin, he rocked her so hard it was as if she'd never been punched before. Her legs went and she sat heavily on the floor.

And all the while Ersatz stood there, watching.

"If I were you," said Fervor, "I'd stay down."

Valkyrie had to laugh at that through the sudden headache that was smashing the inside of her skull, and got up.

She lunged, but Fervor saw her coming and drove his fist into her belly. Valkyrie wheezed, doubled over, and fell to her knees. The priest grabbed two handfuls of her hair and started dragging her to the doors.

She couldn't help it. She screamed.

Kicking wildly, she clawed at his hands, then did her very best to grab his wrists in order to take the pressure off her hair as Ersatz stepped aside and Fervor pulled her out of the church. She cursed and wailed and struggled and Fervor just kept going, her hip and her back, where her T-shirt rode up, scraping along the ground.

He dumped her in the middle of the street and Valkyrie rolled into a protective ball, hands clasped to her head, waiting for the pain to subside. He walked around her, the picture of calm.

Glaring, Valkyrie tapped the black skull on her belt but, like she expected, it didn't activate the suit. They had an audience now – townspeople were gathering.

"My name is Valkyrie Cain," she said loudly as she got up. "I am an Arbiter. I came here to investigate a series of murders. I need one of you to call the Sanctuary. This man is assaulting me."

Not one of them moved.

"The people of Hellfire are good people," Fervor told her. "They don't like to see this sort of thing, but they know it's for the greater good. They know that your death will have purpose."

"I thought you wanted to convert me."

Fervor smiled. "I'll convert you if I can. I'll kill you if I must."

"My life is in danger," she said, speaking even louder now. "Are you going to let him murder me right here, this morning, in front of you? Are you going to let him do that?"

When no one responded, Fervor shrugged. "If it is the will of Arava Kahann."

Valkyrie shook her head. "I don't think you know how much trouble you're in right now, Bilious. Can we not just talk about this?"

He went to respond and she jabbed, caught him square, felt his nose crunch beneath her knuckles. She followed the jab with a right cross as her left hand grabbed his upper arm, and before he could recover she smacked an elbow into his face, staying with him and smacking him again as he stumbled. She tripped him and he went down, and she went to break his arm, but she fumbled the hold and he was free, and rising, and swarming her with punches that sent her crashing to the ground.

She groaned and turned over, blood dripping from her nose and lips. Something was wrong with her, with how she was fighting. She wasn't going to beat him unarmed, she knew that. She wiped the stinging tears from her eyes, and realised there was a hardware store beside her.

Hardware stores had hammers.

"Give up, Valkyrie Cain," Fervor said, wiping the blood from his own nose.

Groaning again, this time with the effort of heaving

herself to her feet, Valkyrie ran for the store. There was an old man in the door and she barged her way past, knocking him back a few steps.

"You should pray to him," the old man said as she searched through the shelves. "He'll forgive you if you pray to him."

She found the hammers, grabbing one in each hand and turning as Fervor entered the store.

"It's OK," the priest said, patting the old man's shoulder, "I'll take it from here."

The old man nodded and stepped back.

"You're not going to win," said Fervor.

Valkyrie grinned with bloodied teeth. "You haven't heard? Winning is what I do."

"But you're not you, are you? Not really. You're not the woman you were. I mean no offence, but when you walked in my church a few minutes ago, you were a lot more... imposing."

She flung the hammer in her left hand and he jerked to the side to avoid it and she leaped, swinging the hammer in her right. But he caught her hand, hit her, then kicked her full in the chest. Valkyrie flew back and hit the ground so hard it would have knocked the air out of her lungs if there had been any left. She curled up, making stupid noises as she tried to breathe. When she opened her eyes, she fixed her bleary gaze on the tattoo on her wrist, a Chinese symbol, even though she didn't have a Chinese symbol tattooed on her wrist.

As she fought for control of her lungs, she splayed her hands. Her nails were longer. Her knuckles were smooth and soft.

Fervor saw her examining herself and he nodded kindly. "Do you know what I think Ersatz has done, with that magnificent wand? I think you've been swapped."

94

Her hair was longer, she realised. Her jeans were looser around the thighs, but tighter around the waist. She got up, moving awkwardly, sucking in tiny slivers of air as her stomach muscles fought to relax. There was a selection of mirrors behind her and she backed up to them.

"I think there's a version of you out there," Fervor continued, "in the endless number of alternate worlds, that has no magic. A version, perhaps, that has chosen a different path in life. And her form has been plucked from that world and you wear it now. Maybe she wears your form. Wouldn't that be something to see?"

Valkyrie got to the mirrors, glanced at her reflection and then looked again, transfixed. Behind the blood, it was still her face, but it was different. She had the beginnings of laugh lines round her nose and mouth, and faint crow's feet at the corners of her eyes. She took a step back. She was still wearing the clothes she'd arrived in, but her shoulders were narrower. Her arms skinny. She looked her age. She looked thirty-one years old.

"This must be a stark reminder of your own mortality," Fervor said. "Mages, mortals, we're all living to a deadline, are we not? Every moment we spend on this Earth is a moment lost. Arava Kahann offers us a way out. He offers an eternity of moments to those who follow him."

Her body, which was not her body, ached. It was unused to this kind of pain. It didn't know how to deal with it. She didn't have the strength or the speed she was used to. She had the knowledge of the fighting skills, but she didn't have the muscle memory to make use of it. She took one of the mirrors down off the wall.

Brute force it was, then.

She yelled as she hurled the mirror. It was big and heavy and Fervor laughed and jumped back to avoid it as it smashed at his feet. She ran at him, plucking a plastic-wrapped toilet seat from a cardboard bin and swinging at his head. He got an arm up to fend it off and she let it clatter and charged into him, driving him back into a display stand. He sprawled across the floor and she tripped and fell on top of him, but scrambled up and ran on, towards the door. Her new plan was to get the hell out of town.

The old man was half turned away, but when she passed he swung a sledgehammer, low and one-handed, and it crunched into her left shin and Valkyrie screamed and flipped and tumbled out of the door. Tears of pain running down her face, mixing with the blood, she rolled off the pavement on to the street, banging her head against a pick-up's exhaust pipe. But she didn't care about that. She didn't even feel it. All she felt was her shattered shinbone.

The people of Hellfire gathered round, and Fervor came out, once again patting the old man on the shoulder.

"I'm sorry, Reverend," the old man said. "I saw her coming and I didn't know what to do."

"You did well, my friend," Fervor replied. "You've got nothing to worry about."

"Is she hurt?" the old man asked. "I ain't never hurt no one before. Do you think maybe her leg's broke?"

"Arava Kahann forgives you for acting in his name," said Fervor, and looked down at Valkyrie. "The Christian Bible proclaims that pride goeth before destruction, and haughtiness before a fall. I don't know if you were ever a Christian, Valkyrie. Maybe, as your name suggests, you were a follower of the Norse gods. Did you pray to Odin? Not that it matters.

We're watching all the old religions come to an end and new ones take their place. In your city of wickedness, do you not have a Dark Cathedral where the Faceless Ones have been replaced by Darquesse? She is the True God, apparently. Her way is the True Way. The people of Roarhaven chant and pray and sing to their True God, following along blindly. And then there are people like us, humble servants of the Hidden God, and we are here to spread his word and to speak his truth."

He hunkered down. "My point is, if this were a Christian world, I would be gloating over my triumph. I would remind you of your arrogance as you came into this town and point to where you are now, rolling around in the gutter, crying. Screaming. But this is no longer that world. None of us here take any joy from your pain. Your tears do not make us happy. We see you, we see a fellow human being in distress, and we want to help you up. Help you stand. Help you heal. But you must let us. You must surrender. That's the first step, Valkyrie. You must touch the bottom before you can rise back up."

Even if she wanted to throw out a retort or an insult, Valkyrie was incapable of it. All she could do was clutch her leg and bite her lip and taste her blood.

Fervor straightened. "Stay down, and you will be saved."

The body she wore was not used to this kind of punishment, but her mind had been through a lot worse, so Valkyrie grunted and turned over. She grabbed for the pick-up and hauled herself, painfully, to one foot. The other foot, the one attached to the broken leg, she kept off the ground.

"You think you're being brave," Fervor said.

She did her best to spit at him, but only ended up splattering her own chin.

The crowd parted. Ersatz approached.

"So is that what this is?" she said, her voice strained. "You're killing those people as a sacrifice to the Hidden God?"

"Ah, no, you misunderstand," said Fervor. "Ersatz isn't yet part of our church, or of our religion. But we are hopeful that the same circumstances that guided him to a covenant with Arava Kahann can also bring him to a deeper understanding of his own spiritual needs. Maybe one day we will indeed stand together beneath the shade cast by the Hidden God. Until that time, we will pray for his eternal soul – as we pray for yours."

Fervor punched, snapping Valkyrie's head back. She hopped, trying to maintain her balance, and then toppled.

Ersatz and Fervor stood side by side, looking down at her.

When the pain had subsided a little, Valkyrie clambered, once again, to her feet. Fervor sighed and stepped forward and threw another punch. Valkyrie covered up and lunged at him, but put her weight on her bad leg and crumpled. He drove his knee into her chest as she did so and she fell sideways.

Ersatz watched her and she felt like she was being evaluated on how long it took her to try again. Something clicked, and this time when the pain faded enough for her to stand, she sat up, instead.

"Screw you," she said. "I surrender."

"Arava Kahann is pleased," Fervor said, frowning slightly as Ersatz raised the wand. "Wait. She surrenders."

He reached out to grip Ersatz's wrist and Ersatz flicked

the wand towards him. Fervor crashed into the side of the pick-up and the townspeople shouted in alarm and moved back. Ersatz pointed the wand at Valkyrie again and she arched an eyebrow.

"This is a test, right?" she said. "You're about to tell me I've failed, and then you're going to kill me. Skulduggery gets tested on the puzzles he can solve, so what's my test? Is it how much punishment I can take? Or maybe you just get someone to beat the crap out of me and so long as I keep getting back up, I pass. Is that it?"

She laughed. "And why would I keep getting back up? You've taken away my magic; you've taken away my strength; you've taken away my ability to fight effectively. Now I can't even run. Why should I get back to my feet if I'm just going to get hurt? You think this is a test of my character? My indomitable will? That's ridiculous. Fighting when you know you're going to lose is macho nonsense. It's a hell of a lot smarter to conserve what's left of your strength for when you've got an actual chance. So you wanna kill me? You go ahead. Your test is stupid."

Ersatz grabbed her throat with his free hand, but Valkyrie didn't fight back. He hauled her up and she just glared at him. The people around them waited warily. His grip tightened and her head began to pound – and then he let go. She gasped for breath and the wand flicked and Ersatz vanished and Valkyrie's pain went away. Magic flooded her system. Her leg was her leg again, and unbroken. She looked at her hands: long fingers, short nails.

"Everyone go back to your homes," Fervor said as he was helped to his feet. "Go on with your day now. Go on."

The townspeople reluctantly dispersed and Valkyrie

stepped to the pick-up, checking out her reflection in the wing mirror. She was back to her old self, which was her young self. Didn't even have any blood on her face.

"Somewhere in some parallel universe," Fervor said beside her, "there's a version of you with a broken leg who's just started to scream."

"You might want to compare notes," Valkyrie said, swinging at him and breaking his jaw.

He dropped and she took out her phone, called Skulduggery.

"Are you OK?" he asked immediately.

"I'm good," she said. "I'll tell you about it later. Where are you?"

"Ireland," he said. "Kilkenny. I was teleported to a graveside. Ah, I'm about to have company, it seems. I'll call you back."

The call cut off, and she rang Fletcher.

"You're still alive!" he cried.

"Just about."

"Skulduggery called and I've been trying to teleport back to Hellfire, but—"

The line crackled and went dead, and a moment later Fletcher came running out of the church. She waved, and he teleported over.

"I couldn't get in," he said, putting his phone away. "There was a barrier I couldn't get through. I've never – that's never happened before. Are you OK? Who's this guy?"

"This is Reverend Bilious Fervor," Valkyrie said. "I'd like you to teleport him to a cell in the High Sanctuary, if you don't mind. He is most definitely under arrest."

12

While the Sensitives tried to break into Bilious Fervor's mind, Valkyrie waited for Skulduggery outside a grand old building that had been converted to apartments in one of Dublin's more salubrious suburbs. She stood in the small car park, protected from the street by a copse of healthy trees, and watched him approach, a fast-moving speck in the white clouds. When he was directly over the apartment building, he plummeted, his hands in his pockets. If anyone happened to glance up, they'd barely have time to make him out, let alone take a second look.

A heartbeat before he smashed into the ground, his plummet turned into a gentle descent and a façade flowed over his skull. "You're looking well for someone who's just had her leg broken," he said.

"That poor me," Valkyrie responded, then frowned. "That's not self-pitying, is it? If I say *poor me*, but I don't mean poor *me*? No, it can't be. That poor girl. She's just living a normal life and then suddenly she looks ten years younger, and the next thing she knows she's back to normal, but she's got blood all over her and her shinbone's smashed and she's in agony."

"You want to find her, don't you?" Skulduggery said. "Track her down, shunt over, send her flowers and chocolates?"

"Yeah, pretty much. I feel awful. She didn't have anything to do with it." They climbed the steps to the door. "And she looked so... she looked great, actually, but older. She looked her age, I mean. My age. Whatever. Fervor, when he was rambling, said something about how it must be a reminder of my own mortality. And it was. It really was." Valkyrie shrugged off her discomfort. "So why are we here?"

Skulduggery took his lock picks from his jacket and crouched, started on the door. "Ersatz teleported me to a grave on a private plot of land on a hill in Kilkenny. The only building in sight was a house across a meadow. The grave was that of a sorcerer, one Rumour Mills."

"Rumour Mills," Valkyrie repeated, smiling slightly. "I like it." On the panel next to the door were the buzzers for five apartments. The fifth apartment had *R. Mills* written in the slot beside it.

"She had an apartment here," Skulduggery said, "until she died last September, at the age of twenty-three. The house across the meadow belongs to her parents, Salter Such and Catherine Dennehy. Salter's a big man. Strong. Angry. A mage. Catherine is mortal. Nondescript. They're both still grieving."

The door clicked open and Skulduggery led the way inside. "When Salter noticed me standing by the grave, he came out to inform me of how much I wasn't welcome.

Catherine emerged a minute later to defuse the situation."
They started up the wide, sweeping staircase.

"How did Rumour die?"

"They weren't clear on that. Catherine may have divulged that information were she on her own, but not with her husband there. I've asked for any Sanctuary reports to be sent over to us."

"And did they say anything about Ersatz?"

"They didn't know who I was talking about."

They got to the next floor. There were three apartments up here, and they went to Rumour's. Skulduggery took out his lock picks again and then grunted. There was no lock to pick. Instead, there was a sensor above the door handle.

"I hate the future," he muttered.

Grinning, Valkyrie moved her hand close and sent a shock of energy into the sensor. It beeped and the door clicked.

Inside they were greeted by a framed poster for *A Nightmare on Elm Street*, the original, signed by the cast in silvers and blacks. There were other posters on the walls, mostly horrors and thrillers from the seventies and eighties, the kind of movies Tanith had introduced Valkyrie to.

The rest of the living room was pretty conventional. A large couch faced a large TV. The coffee table was low and wide and held two remotes, placed side by side, and an empty reed diffuser. There was a bookcase with actual books on it, and another packed with movies on disc. Skulduggery deactivated his façade as he went to the table below the *Elm Street* poster and sifted through the mail collected there. There was a smell to the place of stale, still air.

A short corridor led to the kitchen. It was neat. Even the coffee maker on the granite worktop had been cleaned.

"Her father didn't strike me as the type, but her mother had the right kind of nervous energy to come in and tidy." Skulduggery didn't have to say it: Rumour's mum had probably packed away any clue that might have given them answers.

Valkyrie moved into the bedroom while Skulduggery checked the rest of the apartment. The bed had a sheet over the duvet and pillows, protecting them from dust. She rummaged gently through the bedside table and drawers. Searching the homes of suspects was a thrill – a vital discovery was always a possibility – but searching the homes of the dead was draining. It emptied her heart, bit by bit. She was sifting through a life left behind, cataloguing and then dismissing the objects that had once been so important to someone, objects that had now been stripped of their meaning.

"Anything?" Skulduggery said from behind her.

Valkyrie shook her head. "Nothing connecting Rumour with Ersatz or the Hidden God, or with Gavin Fahey, Sarah Boyle, or Colleen Griffin."

"Keep in mind," Skulduggery said as she left the bedroom, "that we don't know yet that the murders actually *are* connected to the Hidden God."

"Oh, Fervor was quite clear in that regard. Ersatz made some sort of deal with Arava Kahann, but he isn't one of them – not yet, anyway." She sat on the arm of the couch. "Any idea what to make of the wand?"

"Not really," Skulduggery said. "There was a Necromancer who used a wand, but that was just to direct his power, like any other Necromancer object. This could be like that."

"I don't know," Valkyrie replied. "The way Fervor talked about it, it was like the wand had power of its own."

"Then, if we're lucky, the good Reverend can expand on that during interrogation, maybe while he's also telling us more about his god."

"What do we know about him?"

"Arava Kahann? Very little. There have been a few churches set up to worship him over the centuries, but they're all very... secretive is the polite way of putting it."

"What's the impolite way of putting it?"

"Paranoid, suspicious, and downright hostile. The first one of these churches to appear on the Sanctuary radar was in 1708, in Italy."

"Five years after the Gate to Hell was activated."

"And then promptly deactivated, thanks to you."

"Hey, I'm just a time-travelling adventurer havin' time-travelling adventures." She chewed her lip. "And now I'm wondering if these churches had always been there, or if they only popped into existence once I reset the timeline."

"Do not start down this track."

"But doesn't it mess with your head? Doesn't it bake your noodle?"

"My noodle is unbaked."

"Only because you can hold all these conflicting thoughts in your head at the same time. The rest of us aren't so lucky."

"Absorbing the memories of a malfunctioning reflection for so long has made you more prepared than most to grapple with two timelines simultaneously."

"But this is holding two *histories* in your head. In fact, it's more than that: it's two histories and a third history that was erased for everyone else except me and, possibly, a bad guy. It gives me the most massive headache."

"Which is why I advised you not to start down this track."

"Why is life so complicated? Is it because it hates me?"

"Presumably." Skulduggery's phone rang and he stepped away to answer.

Valkyrie refocused her thoughts on Rumour Mills as she went to the bookshelves and scanned the movie titles.

"This was a girl who liked her physical media," she said to Skulduggery once his call had ended.

"Sorcerers tend to. When you expect to live for hundreds of years, you gravitate towards permanence wherever you can. That was Rumour's mother on the phone – she's convinced her husband to talk, and invited us over tomorrow." A façade flowed over his head. "Come on, let's go have a word with Rumour's neighbours."

"Not with that face," Valkyrie said. "Sorry, but you look nineteen. Put on the grumpy one."

"I don't have a grumpy one," Skulduggery said, cycling through some of his more regularly-used façades until he got to the grumpy one.

"Perfect," said Valkyrie.

They left Rumour's apartment. There was no answer at Number Four, but the door to Number Three opened after they knocked and a young man in a shirt and tie and shorts stood there. Valkyrie tried to remember the name next to the buzzer outside, but Skulduggery spoke before she could manage it.

"Mr Driscoll," he said. "First name?"

"Uh, Vincent."

"Vincent, how are you? I am Detective Inspector Me; this is Detective Sergeant Her. We'd like to ask you a few questions, if you don't mind."

"Me?" said the young man.

"Yes, you."

"No, sorry, I meant... You both have very unusual names, is what I meant. And what are the chances of the two of you being partnered up together, eh? I'd say it's a million to one odds. Maybe. I don't know much about odds, though. What can I help you with?"

Valkyrie could feel Skulduggery's disappointment and it resonated with her own. Usually, their *Me* and *Her* routine went on for a lot longer.

"We just have a few questions about Rumour Mills, from Apartment Five," Skulduggery said, all the enthusiasm gone from his voice.

Driscoll nodded. "Of course. May I ask, uh, why?"

"I'm afraid not, Vincent. Did you know Miss Mills?"

"Yeah. I mean, yes. We talked. She was friendly and nice."

"What did you talk about?" Valkyrie asked.

"Like, movies mostly. What she was watching on TV and stuff. She liked horror movies and I like horror movies, so..."

"So you talked about horror movies."

"Yes. She was really nice."

"What do you know of how Miss Mills died?" Skulduggery asked.

Driscoll scratched the back of his head. "I don't know much. I was just – the landlord told me she'd passed away because of a long-term medical condition, but he didn't know what it was. I wanted to go to the funeral, but it must have been private because, like, I didn't see any notices for it." His voice went quiet. "I would have liked to have gone."

"Can you describe her for us?" asked Valkyrie. "What

she was like, how she interacted with people, that kind of thing?"

"Yeah, sure," he said, and smiled. "She was great with people. She really was. I don't go out much – I work from home. Most of my social interactions are over a video call. But she was nice to me. She was always nice to me, even when she was..."

"When she was what?"

"Upset," said Driscoll. "She cried a lot. I heard her sometimes. I'd knock on her door with a movie or something, to cheer her up? Sometimes she answered and her eyes were all red, but sometimes she just..."

"She wouldn't answer," said Valkyrie. "When she was like this, did she dress any differently?"

"I suppose, yeah. Like, tracksuit bottoms. Sloppy T-shirts. Hoodies. She didn't really leave the apartment when she was like that, but... yeah."

"And how long would this last?"

"I don't really... I didn't time her moods, or anything. Maybe a week. Two weeks at most."

"But you liked her?"

He nodded, smiling again. "She was cool. She was lovely. Always so kind and always so nice."

"Did she have many friends? A boyfriend or girlfriend?"

"Don't know about boyfriends or girlfriends, but she didn't really have a lot of people over. She used to. About six or seven years ago, she had a group of friends who'd come round every few weeks, stay for a few hours, laugh a lot, and then leave. But, like I said, that was years ago."

"Was Rumour acting differently in the few days leading

up to her death?" Skulduggery asked. "Did she seem jumpy? Anxious?"

"I didn't really notice anything, sorry."

"I see. How long have you lived here?"

"Eight years. Rumour already lived here when I moved in. It's really not the same without her."

"Thank you for your time, Vincent." Skulduggery's phone buzzed. He glanced at it, then put it away. "If we need to speak to you again, we know where to find you."

13

Aphotic texted, told them about an event taking place that evening, an event that Alter Veers was likely to attend. They arranged to meet, and Aphotic turned up dressed all in black, with some kind of a frock coat to complete the ensemble. In contrast, Mia was wearing blue jeans, a Hello Kitty T-shirt and pink trainers. And then there was Winter, stuck between them like their boring cousin who just wanted to spend the evening curled up watching TV. Which was pretty much exactly what she did want.

But there was an ex-friend that needed finding, and so they took the tram to Effervescent Avenue, and started walking.

"Are you sure this is the way?" Mia asked, checking the map on her phone. "It's not showing up here."

"That's because it's a secret underground bar," Aphotic said. "If the secret underground bar was easily viewable on your phone's app, then it wouldn't be very secret, now would it?"

Mia put her phone away. "Then how do you know where it is?"

Aphotic shrugged. "I found out."

"How?"

"By asking people who knew."

"And how do you know people who knew?"

"I know a lot of people," said Aphotic.

Mia said something witty and Aphotic responded, and they had a bit of a back and forth that Winter stayed out of. Aphotic wasn't as bad as she'd expected. In fact, he was actually sort of funny, in his own, self-serious way, and was turning out to be quite handy. Certainly, they wouldn't have found out about this Isolationist meeting if it wasn't for him.

Butterflies fluttered in Winter's belly, and not the good kind. There were plenty of mages in Roarhaven and elsewhere who resented the mortals for the things they'd done during the Deletion, and plenty of reasons to want to isolate the magical community from the mortal world – but the fact that Alter Veers would be at this meeting indicated that something darker was at play. For all they knew, they could have been about to step into a roomful of full-blown, mortal-murdering terrorists. The Order of the Ancients may not have racked up as many kills as groups like the Soldiers of Magic, but they were all travelling the same path.

When they got to the bar, it was almost ten and the sun was close to setting and the streetlights were on. They passed the main entrance and Aphotic led them round the corner, down some steps and in through a side door. A large man stood waiting, his arms crossed. Winter didn't know what she'd say if he asked for ID, but he just nodded and they walked by. Aphotic looked terrified.

They stayed away from the crowd of people who were standing around, talking. There was a stage set up with a microphone – the place looked like it doubled as a live music venue. Everyone here seemed pretty normal, all things considered. Winter didn't know what she'd been expecting. Nazis, maybe?

Two men walked onstage. The younger of the two was in tattered jeans and a T-shirt and looked like he worked behind the bar. The older was dressed in a suit, and looked like every mid-level businessman Winter had ever seen.

The guy in jeans tapped on the microphone. "Hey," he said. "Thank you all for coming. Quite a big turnout this evening. Welcome back to everyone who's been to one of these before, and a big hello if you're joining us for the first time. But you're not here to listen to me so I'll shut up and introduce our speaker for the night. Friends, please put your hands together for Icious Staid."

The man in the suit stepped forward, basking in the enthusiastic applause. When he spoke, he had a Scottish accent. "Thank you, thank you. It's always a genuine pleasure to visit Roarhaven. If you could have told me, as a young man, that there would one day be a grand city of magic, a city of sorcerers, I'd have been a lot happier, I'll tell you that much!"

For some reason, this made people laugh, and Staid chuckled, too. He continued saying nice things and Winter took the opportunity to scan the crowd. It was pretty much an even split between male and female, with an age range that seemed to go from early twenties to early sixties – though, of course, this being sorcerers, there was no actual telling what age anyone really was.

Winter and Mia and Aphotic were the youngest here, though, and there was no sign of Alter Veers or Brazen.

"I hear this a lot," Icious Staid was saying. "I'm a mortal-hater, apparently. I've been told that so much lately that those words, those two words, put together like that, have ceased to have meaning to me. It's just a nasty accusation that people throw out. It's an easy insult for those who disagree with me. What's tragic about the whole thing is that if I were able to sit down with these people, if they'd stop throwing insults for just five minutes, they'd find out that I'm not the Devil. They might find out that we have something in common!"

Murmurs of agreement rippled through the audience. The crowd parted slightly, just for a moment, and Winter glimpsed Tier Galling, his eyes fixed on the stage. Then he was gone.

"I don't hate mortals," Staid continued. "I'd hazard a guess that nobody here hates mortals. Of course we don't – we live beside them. We share this world with them. But there's a difference, isn't there, my friends? There's a difference between hating mortals and seeing them for what they truly are. *We see them.* Unlike our mortal-loving brethren, we have seen what they've done and we have not forgotten. I'm not even talking about what they did during the Deletion – I'm talking about what they've done throughout history!"

The audience gave a few shouts of support.

"I'm talking about the wars, my friends," said Staid. "The constant wars. We've had wars, don't get me wrong. We had a Three Hundred Year War. Oh, yes, we did. But we did not ravage the world while this war was being waged. Oh, no. It's mortals who do that. It's mortals who use poverty and oppression and racism as weapons, as cudgels, to beat the weak into submission. It is mortals who have developed

113

political systems – whether it be capitalist, communist, socialist, fascist, democratic, republican, whether it be a monarchy or an oligarchy, whether it be totalitarian or authoritarian, liberal or conservative... It's mortals who have developed radically different political systems that somehow – *somehow* – are all the same."

More cheers.

"The weak get weaker. The poor get poorer. The rich get richer. The strong get stronger. They bash their enemies over the heads until they've knocked the fight out of them. They attack those different from themselves until they've been beaten completely out of shape, until they look and sound and think just like everybody else. And those who refuse to conform? Those who can't fit in? They disappear. They're brushed aside. They fall between the cracks of the pavement and they drown in the dirt beneath."

Staid took a steadying breath. "That's what mortals do," he said. "They are a petty, spiteful species. They are a dangerous, hateful species. And they're in charge. They have the overwhelming numbers. We can't fight them even if we wanted to – and we don't, because we don't hate them. But we have seen what will happen if they ever find out about us. We've seen how the mortal governments, how the mortal *people*, will react to our existence. We've been blessed with a second chance, thanks to Darquesse. Since the Great Reset, all those old arguments about whether we should reveal magic to the world have been well and truly silenced. We know what they'd do, don't we, my friends?"

More murmurs of agreement.

"They'd hunt us down. They'd kill us. Our only chance to live and flourish, to allow our unique culture to grow and evolve, is to leave them behind. It's an awful thing to say, but we must abandon the mortals. We have no other choice. As an Elder on the Scottish Council, I am a lone voice of reason. My fellow Elder and my Grand Mage, in all her wisdom and benevolence, simply cannot fathom such a... such an ambitious move. Well, I am nothing if not ambitious." He chuckled. "And yet it's not a self-serving ambition that drives me. It is a self-*preserving* ambition. To preserve our way of life, our movement must grow. We must attract new members, like we have done tonight. We must preach not hatred but love. Not violence but peace. Our path is clear. We must simply be brave enough to walk it."

The bar erupted in cheers and applause and Winter saw three men talking to Tier, crowding around him. One of them had his hand on Tier's shoulder and was speaking directly into his ear.

The guy in the tattered jeans came back onstage as Icious Staid stepped away from the microphone, waving to his audience.

"Let's get out of here," Mia said quietly.

"This is the kind of stuff Brazen's been going to?" Mia asked as they walked back to busier streets. "Like, she goes to those meetings voluntarily?"

Winter glanced at Aphotic. "Did you know?"

"I knew she was hanging out with people like that," he replied, looking like his entire world was falling down around him. "I didn't know she felt the same."

"She didn't," Mia said. "She doesn't. She can't. Brazen doesn't hate mortals."

"We don't know what she hates," Winter reminded her. "Not any more."

"And that guy," Mia said, "the guy talking, he's an Elder? He's an actual Elder from an actual Sanctuary? How is he even allowed to go to places and say all that?"

All three of them turned to the sound of running footsteps. Tier slowed as he approached.

"Hey," he said, his eyes on Winter. "Didn't expect to see you at something like that."

"We're looking for our friend," said Mia before Winter could respond. "Brazen Yarrow. Have you seen her?"

"You're friends with Brazen? I didn't know that. But no, I haven't seen her in... I don't know. A few days."

"Do you go to many of these things?" Winter asked.

"I've been to a few, yeah. They're not illegal, if that's what you're worried about."

"The Order of the Ancients is an illegal terrorist organisation," said Aphotic.

Tier side-eyed him. "And do you know for a fact that anyone there is a member of the Order? No, you don't, because they're all just Isolationists, and there's nothing illegal about being an Isolationist. Nuru Yewahi and Contumacious Cross are Isolationists. Would you call them terrorists?"

Winter didn't know who Contumacious Cross was, but Mia had told her all about Nuru Yewahi, the sorcerer who'd turned down the position of Grand Mage in the Ethiopian Sanctuary three times so far. She was a good person, a peaceful person who, until the Deletion, had always believed mage and mortal were destined to co-exist side by side. She had since changed her mind.

"Who were those men you were arguing with?" Winter asked.

Tier's look of bored defiance slipped a little. "I wasn't arguing with them, I was just not agreeing. They're recruiters for... something. I never let them get far enough into their pitch to find out exactly what they're trying to recruit me into. They talk a good game, though. They get you to confess how much you really hate mortals without, like, making it obvious that that's what they're doing."

Mia frowned. "Did they recruit Brazen?"

"I don't know," said Tier. "They could have."

"And why haven't they recruited you?" Winter asked. "You keep going to the meetings, right? You do hate mortals, don't you?"

"Don't you?" Tier responded. "Because if you don't, you should. I was nine during the Deletion, but I remember it perfectly. I remember what they did. I remember how scared I was. So yeah, I hate mortals, but no, they've never managed to recruit me because they're full of crap. They've got this big demonstration planned for the Humdrums and they're hyping it up like it'll change anything, like it'll be important. It won't be important. The Order of the Ancients is a joke."

"I knew it was the Order of the Ancients!" said Aphotic.

"You didn't know anything," said Tier. "If I don't know for a fact that they're recruiting for the Order, then you *definitely* don't."

"I know Alter Veers is a member."

"Then you've heard the same stories that I've heard. Big deal."

"Have you spoken to Alter?" asked Winter.

"Yeah. He hangs around those guys and, fair enough,

I've seen Brazen hanging around, too. But that doesn't mean you should take them seriously. The Order of the Ancients want to be the Soldiers of Magic, but the Soldiers of Magic are actually hardcore terrorists who *do* kill people. If Brazen were mixed up with them, then you would have a right to be worried. But instead she's mixed up with the Order of the bloody Ancients. Have you seen who leads them?"

"Imperator Dominax," said Aphotic.

"Imperator Dominax," repeated Tier, failing to stop the smirk of disbelief from forming. "He's an embarrassment. With all the black leather and the spikes and everything?"

"They're organising a protest in the Humdrums?" Mia asked.

Tier nodded. "They're mortal-haters with delusions of being badass, so they want to make a scene, but they don't want to go too far out of their way. So they figure, hey, let's demonstrate at the Humdrums. Let's shout nasty things at the mortal refugees from the Leibniz Universe who happen to live right here in Roarhaven. It's mean-spirited *and* convenient."

"Brazen might be there," said Mia. "When is it planned for?"

"The demonstration? Haven't a clue. Sometime in the next week."

"Can you find out?"

He laughed. "You mean go back in there and ask them? No. I can't."

Mia glanced at Winter.

Winter sighed. "Will you go back in there and ask them?"

Tier laughed again. "I'm on my way to Corrival. In case you've all forgotten, we have an exam tomorrow."

"Yeah?" said Winter. "What is it?"

Tier hesitated. "I want to say gardening."

"Gardening is not a class we take. Tier, please could you go back to the bar and find out when and exactly where the demonstration at the Humdrums is due to take place?"

Tier crossed his arms and looked at her, his feet planted like he had no intention of ever moving. Then he sagged. "Fine," he said. "Whatever."

14

When Skulduggery had described Rumour's father as *a big man*, that didn't really do him justice.

Salter Such was as tall as Skulduggery, a slab of meat packed on to muscle, all contained by dirty jeans and scuffed work boots and a faded shirt. He looked to be in his fifties. His hair was grey and long and tangled and his brow was heavy. His eyes were intelligent, his nose had been broken in the past and he'd never bothered to reset it, and his mouth was a thin, straight line. He sat forward, elbows resting on the table, his sheer size making the chair look like a piece of doll's furniture.

The kitchen was nice. Modest. A horseshoe hung over the door. There were framed photographs of Rumour with her parents on one of the walls, next to an east-facing window that showed the tree across the meadow and, beside it, Rumour's headstone.

If Skulduggery had failed to adequately prepare Valkyrie for Rumour's father's appearance, then he hadn't even bothered to prepare her for Rumour's mother. *Nondescript*, he'd said. Catherine Dennehy was a mortal so if she looked like she was in her late forties, that meant she probably was. And she was stunning. A beautiful woman with a few grey hairs in that tousled blonde mane and light make-up, it was all Valkyrie could do not to stare.

Catherine gave Valkyrie a coffee and put her own down beside her husband. She sat next to him. He didn't acknowledge her. His eyes moved between Valkyrie, sitting in front of him, and Skulduggery, wandering round the kitchen.

"You have a lovely home," Valkyrie said.

"Thank you," said Catherine, smiling slightly.

No one said anything for the next few seconds.

Valkyrie took a sip that raised her eyebrows. "This is delicious."

"Isn't it?" said Catherine. "Rumour found that blend when she was in France last year."

"Not last year," Salter rumbled. "Year before last."

"The year before last, that's right," said Catherine. "They all seem to blur together, don't they? The years?" Her hands were shaking slightly, and she put her cup down on the saucer.

Skulduggery took two slim boxes from a shelf.

"They're just Mother's Day and Father's Day cards," said Catherine. "I always thought I was silly to keep them, but now I'm... now I'm glad."

"Do you mind if we look through them?" Skulduggery asked, placing the boxes in front of Valkyrie. "Any insight into who Rumour was as a person could be helpful. It would also be useful to look round her old bedroom, if it's still as she left it?"

"Of course," said Catherine.

While Skulduggery went back to his wandering, Valkyrie hesitated, then awkwardly opened the first box and took out roughly two dozen home-made Mother's Day cards. She wasn't sure what she could glean from them, other than that the early ones were adorable and full of love hearts and childish scrawls, and the later ones were no less adorable, but a lot more artistically satisfying. Someone – Catherine, presumably – had written Rumour's current age on the back of each card. The one she'd made when she was eight was particularly cute.

"As I said earlier, Valkyrie and I had an altercation in Texas, at the Church of the Hallowed Purpose," Skulduggery said. "We encountered a man in a black mask called Ersatz, a man who has killed two mortals that we know of and attacked two Sanctuary operatives. He teleported me to Rumour's grave."

"Do you think he's the one?" Salter asked. "The one who killed her? The one who killed our daughter?"

Valkyrie glanced at Skulduggery, then to the grieving parents. "Mr Such, quite honestly, sir, we haven't received the Sanctuary file yet. We don't even know how she died."

Salter kept his clenched fists on the table. "Somebody broke her neck. We found her in the park near here. The park she used to play in when she was a kid."

"And you called the Sanctuary?"

Salter nodded. "They sent someone. A detective. We didn't get any answers."

"We call," said Catherine. "Every week, we call for an update. There's never any news."

"We'll look into that," said Skulduggery, tilting his head at a collection of rusted antique butcher's knives and old painted plates displayed on top of the cabinets. He turned. "Can you tell us about your daughter? How was she before she died?"

"Rumour had been depressed," Catherine said. "The medication she was on, it wasn't working. She was allergic to some of it, and she had a bad reaction and... anyway. She had to stop. She was seeing a psychiatrist, but she wasn't happy with that, and then..." Catherine cleared her throat. "Obviously, I didn't grow up knowing about magic. I grew up here, in the area, and I had a very, I suppose, normal life. Then I found out there was magic in the world."

"It comes as quite a shock," Valkyrie said, offering a smile.

Catherine laughed. "Yes. Yes, it does. I didn't know what to think. My entire world was upended."

Valkyrie opened the second box, the one filled with cards for Father's Day. With the exception of two that were shop-bought, sent when Rumour was eleven and twelve, they showed the same progression from childish scrawls to a more adult artistry as the cards to Catherine. Rumour hadn't been a bad artist. The card she made when she was thirteen seemed determined to compensate for the lack of effort in the previous two years, emphasising how wonderful a father Salter was. Valkyrie stole a glance. The man sat there, a glowering monolith, and she could well believe it. In her experience, stoicism was a dam that held back the unfathomable depths of pure, swirling emotion.

"How did you find out?" Skulduggery asked.

"Sorry?" Catherine said.

"About magic."

"Oh. A guy I was seeing. I didn't know it when we started dating, but he was a sorcerer."

"That's not all," Salter said.

Catherine looked uncomfortable. "No. He was also a narcissist and, I think, some kind of sociopath. I may not have been the best judge of character back in those days."

"It obviously didn't work out between you," said Valkyrie.

"It really didn't. I broke up with him and he didn't take it well, but the one good thing about him was that, through him, I met Salter. They had been... not friends but acquaintances, I suppose. We became close and fell in love and got married. Salter's stayed away from magic, for the most part. He's never been interested in the Sanctuaries or their business or that whole community. I mean, look at him. He's just a normal man."

"And then Rumour came into your lives."

Catherine smiled genuinely for the first time. "Her given name was... Well, it doesn't matter what her given name was. She took the name Rumour when she was old enough. She was a godsend. She took after Salter so much – she didn't see why all the sorcerers had to live in just one city, or even a community. She liked magic, she loved it, she loved what she could do, but she didn't want it to define her.

"Her best friend was a local girl, a mortal – Simone Ruddy. Rumour told Simone about magic when they were kids because she needed someone to talk to about it all. As far as I know, Simone is the only mortal she ever told. Our daughter was a good girl. She was happy."

The smile faltered. "Then, five or six years ago, she began to fall into these... black holes, almost. She'd just get so down. We took her to a doctor – a mortal doctor – and she was put on medication, and when that didn't work out we turned to, um, your kind of doctor. A magical doctor."

"He was an acquaintance of an acquaintance," Salter said. "A psychiatrist. He said he could help."

Catherine hesitated. "He said he could not just treat depression but cure it completely."

"What was this psychiatrist's name?" Skulduggery asked, sitting down in the chair beside Valkyrie.

"Elysian," Salter said, his lip curling in disgust. "Cyrus Elysian. You've heard of him?"

Skulduggery nodded. "The Sensitive. He has quite a record of success."

"Which is why we went with him," said Catherine. "He told us he could enter a mind and restructure it, taking out the trauma, removing the... the bad parts. He said it'd maybe take a year and, to begin with, it was really working. Rumour was immediately brighter. She was more optimistic. She started thinking about the future again. But then she got worse. Much worse."

"He broke her mind," Salter said in that deep, rumbling baritone. "He went in and he broke it until it didn't work any more. And I'd sent her to him."

Catherine looked away, pinching the skin on the back of her hand until she could look up again. "Rumour called us. She was supposed to be in her apartment in Dublin, but she called to say she was coming home. That she was on her way. She spoke to Salter and then to me. She told me she loved me. She told me she was sorry for all the things she had put me through." Tears rolled down her cheeks. "She hadn't put me through anything. There's not one moment where I wasn't thankful to have her in our life – but she couldn't see that. She said she'd be home soon. She said she was making herself better. Then she hung up. The last thing she ever said to me was, 'I'm going to make you proud.' I was already proud of her. I was already so proud."

"I thought she might be close so I went out looking for her," Salter said. "I drove around all night. Didn't think to... to check the park."

Catherine's voice was quiet. "We don't know why she was there."

"The detective, from the Sanctuary, said that more than likely she was killed by a mortal," Salter said. "Said these things happen. That sometimes there's no accounting for it."

"I'm so sorry," Valkyrie said.

Skulduggery shifted a little in his seat. He didn't have to shift, Valkyrie had learned, but he'd found that small movements put people at ease. He had no eyes to blink or lips to twitch, had no access to the subtle movements that spoke to the unconscious minds of the people he interacted with, and so he compensated with the delicate, but deliberate, shifting of position. "Do you, yourselves, have any suspects?"

Catherine didn't say anything, but Salter practically growled. "I don't know if it was this Ersatz person who broke my little girl's neck, but Cyrus Elysian killed our daughter just as much as whoever attacked her that night. Whatever she was trying to do, however she was trying to fix herself, it's because of him. He got into her head and he..."

Catherine reached out for her husband, but he flinched, his face tight with fury. Catherine withdrew her hand.

"Have you spoken to the Sanctuary about Elysian?" Skulduggery asked.

"They say there's nothing they can do," Catherine said.

"We'll talk to him," said Valkyrie.

Salter sneered. "And do what? You work for the Sanctuary. You all protect each other."

"We're Arbiters. We work for no one. If Elysian did anything wrong, we'll find out."

"And when you find that he *did* do something wrong? When you find that he needs to be punished? What will you do?"

Valkyrie met Salter's eyes. "Then we'll punish him."

15

Valkyrie had looked up Rumour's friend, Simone Ruddy, on social media. On Tuesdays and Thursdays, Simone liked to start her day with a smoothie before the gym, so Valkyrie had figured out the coffee shop she frequented and, coffee in hand, sat opposite the girl with the incredible figure and the workout clothes. Around them, people talked. Above them, music played. Behind them, baristas worked.

"Good morning," Valkyrie said.

Simone glanced up from her phone. "Someone's sitting there," she said.

Valkyrie smiled. "No, they're not."

"There are plenty of other free tables to sit at."

"I don't want to sit at a free table. I want to sit at your table."

Simone lowered her phone and looked at Valkyrie, then narrowed her eyes, like she was trying to place her.

"Don't bother," Valkyrie said. "You don't know me. But I know you, and I'd like—"

Simone's eyes went wide and she pointed right at her. "Oh my God, you're God!"

"Ah, hell."

"You're God! You're that new God! Oh my God! Oh! Sorry! Did I just take your name in vain? Please don't smite me, please. I didn't mean to!"

Valkyrie leaned forward, fixing a smile on to her face, and spoke softly. "All right, Simone? You're going to have to calm down, you hear me? You're being way too loud for my liking."

"Just don't smite me!"

"I'm not going to smite you, Simone. Jesus! I don't even know *how* to smite someone! How did you know about...?" She gestured to her face.

"My friend told me."

"Rumour Mills."

Simone paled. "You *are* all-knowing."

"She told you about Darquesse?"

"Yes, Lord. She showed me pictures, too. Your hair's different. I like it."

"Thank you – but I'm not Darquesse. My name is Valkyrie."

"Valkyrie, Valkyrie," Simone muttered, then, "Valkyrie Cain!"

"That's right, yes. I'm not Darquesse, so you can calm down now, can't you? I'm completely normal."

"You're a sorcerer, though."

Valkyrie sighed. "Yes, OK, I'm a sorcerer, but apart from that I'm completely normal. I'm just here to talk."

"About what? Oh, no. Do I know too much? Are you here to silence me?"

"You don't know too much, Simone. I just want to talk to you about Rumour."

"That's all?"

"You know what I do, right? I'm a kind of magical cop? Me and my partner, we're looking into Rumour's death."

"Skulduggery Pleasant," Simone said, eyes widening. "Is he here? Can I meet him?"

"He's not here, sorry."

Then, like the information was just taking its time to reach her brain: "Wait, you want to know about Rumour?"

"You were her best friend, weren't you? That's what her parents told us."

"We were, yes, we were best friends since third class in school, when we were nine or ten, something like that."

"And when did she tell you about, you know... M–A–G–I–C?"

"On her sixteenth birthday."

"And how did you react?"

"Oh, I didn't believe her. Not even when she showed me, like, the fire thing and then the air thing for the first time. I thought it was a prank. She loved scary movies, and I hated them. And I thought this was, like... I don't know. I don't know what I thought. But it took a lot for her to convince me it was real. Why are you looking into her death? Oh my God, was she..." She lunged forward, to the edge of her seat, sudden tears in her eyes. "Was she murdered?"

Valkyrie froze. "Uh..."

"Oh my God. She was. I thought... Her parents told me it was an accident, but somebody murdered her? Who?"

"I'm afraid I can't talk about that."

"Do her parents know?"

"They're the ones who told us. They also told us about you. What do you think of them?"

"Her folks? They're nice," Simone said. She sat back, blinking. "Her mum's lovely, obviously, and her dad is, like, so scary." She smiled sadly. "I always thought he's what a concrete block would look like if it grew legs. But they've always been nice to me."

"Have you had much contact with them since Rumour died?"

She shook her head. "There's no reason to. I was at the funeral. There was just the three of us. I don't think her dad took it very well. I mean, Jesus, of course he didn't, but I think Catherine needed him to..." She hesitated, grasping for words.

"Open up?" Valkyrie suggested.

"Yeah," said Simone. "She needed him to open up and I think he was doing the opposite. It can't have been easy on them. Something like that, it'd put a strain on any marriage. How are they doing?"

Valkyrie didn't want to lie. "I don't know," she said. "They seem to be still together, though."

"Her dad blamed himself for pushing Rumour to go and see that psychic guy."

"Cyrus Elysian?"

Simone nodded. "He went into her mind, you know? He's got to be responsible for some of what happened to her. He's just got to be. Are you going to talk to him? You should definitely talk to him."

"We're already arranging an interview. We'll get to the truth of exactly what he did, don't worry. Simone, did Rumour have any strong beliefs that you know of? Political? Religious? Anything like that?"

"No. I mean, she supported LGBTIQA plus causes, if

that counts? And also animal rights. She loved animals. But she wasn't part of any organisation or group. She just, you know, supported them."

"Did she have any enemies?"

"No, none. If she had any, she'd have told me."

"What about girlfriends or boyfriends?"

Simone's face soured. "Her last boyfriend was magic, but not magical. Do you know what I'm saying? A sorcerer but a creep. They dated years ago and he broke her heart, and they got back together and I told her. I said he's gonna break your heart again, but Rumour... Rumour was an optimist. She told me this time it was different."

"But it wasn't different."

"He dumped her a month or two before she died."

"What's his name?"

Simone rolled her eyes. "Handsome Whitlock."

"Seriously?"

"Seriously, that's the name he took. Tells you everything you need to know about him."

"You obviously don't rate him."

"He was awful," Simone said. "I'm pretty sure he cheated on her, and he just... You should talk to him, too, and if you do, don't be nice to him."

"I won't, I promise." Valkyrie took out her phone, sent a message to Skulduggery, then put the phone away. "What was Rumour like, as a friend? This isn't for the investigation – this is just for me."

Simone looked at her and then, when her eyes became unfocused, Valkyrie knew she had stopped seeing her. "Rumour was great," she said. "She was so, so funny. Like, you know there's always one person that just makes you laugh, no matter what? That you just, you click with, and they get you, and everything they do is funny? That was Rumour."

Valkyrie found herself smiling. "She sounds great."

"Oh, she was the best. She really was."

"How are you doing since she passed away?"

Simone shrugged as tears ran down her face. "I'm doing OK," she said. "I miss her all the time. Like, every single day, multiple times a day, I think about her. I remember something she did or said or something reminds me of her. Even this song," she said, gesturing to the speakers as 'Karma Chameleon' played. "This was one of her favourites. I once sat in here for two hours and every single song reminded me of Rumour. I can't escape her and I don't want to. I'd hate to leave her behind. Oh, God, am I crying? I'm crying again, Jesus." Simone took a napkin and dabbed at her eyes. "I swear, I'm always crying these days. There must be something wrong with me."

"Or maybe you're still trying to cope with losing your best friend."

"Yeah," said Simone. "Who knows?" Through her tears, she laughed.

When Valkyrie left the coffee shop, Fletcher was waiting for her. He looked confused.

"Skulduggery sent me," he said. "But I don't understand his message. He's found a handsome guy and he wants me to take you to him, apparently. I've already teleported him over there."

"Over where?"

"Los Angeles," Fletcher said. "Why's he looking for handsome guys for you? Are you and Militsa breaking up?"

"Handsome is this guy's name. What time is it in LA?"

"About one am. Is he good-looking? Is he better-looking than me?"

"Fletcher, calm down. I'm sure he isn't half as gorgeous as you are. Can you take me? Please?"

He took her hand. "You'll tell me if he's better-looking, won't you?"

"Of course," she totally lied.

16

Skulduggery was waiting for Valkyrie in an expensive hotel lobby filled with glamorous people talking really, really loudly.

"He's waiting for us," Skulduggery said as they walked. "He sounds excited."

"Excited to be questioned? That's new. Who *is* this guy?"

"I looked him up, but I still have no idea."

"What does he do? For a living?"

"As far as I can tell, and this is purely based on my initial reading, it would seem that he is professionally good-looking."

They got into the elevator and a middle-aged couple of obvious wealth made to step in after them.

"I wouldn't advise it," Skulduggery said.

The man blinked at him. "I'm sorry? What?"

"Joining us in this elevator. I wouldn't advise it. We're in the middle of a private conversation. You should wait for the next one."

The man's face flushed red. "*We* should wait for...? Don't

be absurd. Do you have any idea who I am? Do you have any idea what I can—?"

Skulduggery's façade smiled. "A warning," he said. "If you are inside these doors once they close, I will reduce you to tears. My insults will shake the very foundation of who you think you are. They will strip you down and lay you bare. They will shatter your self-image. You won't be the same man leaving this elevator as you were entering. You will be free of all self-delusion. Your shortcomings will be exposed for the world to see and I will do all of this with an alacrity you will find most alarming."

The couple stared at him, and stepped backwards. The doors closed and Skulduggery pressed the button for the penthouse.

"Do we have an interview with Cyrus Elysian yet?" Valkyrie asked. "Simone's opinion of him isn't any higher than Rumour's folks."

"I spoke to Cerise," Skulduggery responded. "She said she'll have him for us to interview tomorrow morning."

"Good. I'm quite looking forward to making him squirm."

The elevator pinged. The doors opened. They got out.

The suite was decorated in a style Valkyrie didn't either recognise or, in fairness, appreciate. It was modern yet retro, the future as imagined by a science-fiction set-dresser in the 1960s. There was a long bar against the far wall and before the doors that led to the other rooms stood a large table, roughly the shape of an amoeba. There were three brightly coloured chairs-that-weren't-quite-chairs in a semicircle facing a floor-to-ceiling window looking east over the city. Strange light fixtures protruded from the walls like tapeworms.

Five people stood chatting by the amoeba table. The tallest of them, and the most muscular, saw Valkyrie and Skulduggery when they walked in and quickly ushered the others into another room. Then he came hurrying over, shaking first Valkyrie's hand and then Skulduggery's.

"It is so good to meet you," Handsome said. "Thank you for coming. It is an honour. It is an... I just want to say, on behalf of the whole world, thank you for saving us all those times."

Valkyrie was pretty sure he wasn't authorised to speak for the whole world, but she let it slide on account of how good-looking he was. His blue eyes sparkled, his white smile dazzled, his square jaw squared, and his perfect dark hair was perfectly dark and, indeed, hair.

Handsome Whitlock was a very handsome man.

"Come," he said, ushering them towards the unusually shaped chairs, "sit. Can I get you anything? Champagne?"

"Thank you, no," said Valkyrie. She sat in the lemon-yellow chair, surprised by how comfortable it was.

Skulduggery remained standing. "Handsome, is it?"

Handsome grinned bashfully. "I used to say *Handsome by name, Handsome by nature*, until someone pointed out how embarrassing that was. But yes, that's my name. My taken name. My given name is—"

"We don't need to know your given name," Skulduggery said, tilting his head at him.

"No, of course. Of course you don't. I don't know why I said that. I'm nervous, I guess. Well, more excited than nervous. Would you like something to eat?" He started walking to the door. "I can get my people to bring you something. The kitchen in this place does the best—"

"We're here to talk to you about Rumour Mills, Handsome. We're Arbiters and we need some questions answered. You are not our host and we are not your guests."

Handsome came quickly back, like an obedient puppy. "Uh-huh. No problem. I'm ready to answer whatever you've got to ask."

"Who are your friends?" Valkyrie asked, nodding to the room he'd been headed towards.

"They're my team. Don't worry, they won't bother us."

"What kind of team?"

Handsome spread his arms wide. "Team Handsome!" he said, laughing. "You know, PR people, assistants, advisors. Experts, really."

"Experts on what?" Skulduggery asked.

"Me," said Handsome. "And I'm only half joking!"

"I wasn't aware that was even half a joke."

Valkyrie rearranged herself on the chair. "What do you do, Handsome? As a job?"

For the first time, Handsome hesitated. "That's the problem," he said. "I don't know. I don't know what I want to do. And I know you're here to discuss Rumour and I'm down for that, I am, but I was hoping, while we're all in the same room, that I could pick your brains."

"About what?"

Handsome took a breath. "We all have something to offer the world, am I right? We all have something unique to bring to the table. Some of us are lucky enough to get certain... opportunities. I have a, I don't know if you know this, but I have a pretty big following."

Skulduggery's head tilted the other way. "You're the leader of a cult?"

"No!" Handsome said, then shrugged. "Well, kinda, yeah. I have a pretty big following on social media. A lot of the time, that means nothing, but occasionally large followings on social media equate to large followings IRL, too."

"In real life," Valkyrie translated for Skulduggery.

"I have an opportunity," said Handsome. "I have the backing to set up a serious media empire. I already have my socials, my video channel, my gaming channel, but I'm on the cusp of moving into the stratosphere. I'm talking major mainstream sponsorship deals. I'm talking sports, video games, book signings."

Valkyrie shifted in her seat. "You wrote a book?"

"It's being written as we speak. My life story. In my own words."

"So you're writing it?"

"My ghostwriter pulls from stuff I have said and stuff I would say, so it's essentially me, yes. We're looking at an October release to hit the Christmas market."

"This book," said Skulduggery, "how much detail will it go into?"

Handsome smiled. It really was a magnificent smile. "You're worried about the whole magic thing, aren't you? Don't worry, we only touch on that stuff. It's, like, the barest of hints."

"You can't hint about it."

"It's really subtle, my dude. I swear."

Skulduggery's voice went cold and flat. "I am not your dude."

Handsome's tan paled all of a sudden. "Right. Yeah. No, of course. I'll get someone to send it to the Sanctuary when it's done, you know? So they can check it and remove anything, like, too top secret."

Valkyrie doubted Handsome knew anything too top secret, but she let it slide on account of how good-looking he was.

"In fact, that's kind of what I wanted to talk to you about," he continued. "The magic stuff. I'm an Elemental, and that's how I was raised. Both my parents are mages and they taught me everything I needed to know. My mom works for the Sanctuary, but only part-time. She's in Legal, so there's a lot of negotiating between the magical matters and the mortal matters, but it's just a job for her. It's not like it's her calling. So I grew up, basically, with a foot in both worlds. And I never had this great need to do what you guys do, you know? Battle the forces of darkness, and stuff?"

"We'll struggle on without you," said Skulduggery.

"But that's the thing," Handsome said, turning to the window and looking out. "I'm wondering if I'm making the right choice. Do I focus on the social-media stuff, the sponsorship deals, the money and the influence... or do I abandon it all, and devote my talents to saving the world?"

He stood with his legs apart, his muscular arms down by his sides, and his head turned at a slight angle, like he was posing for a photograph that wasn't being taken.

"I think you should focus on social media," Valkyrie said.

"I agree," said Skulduggery.

Handsome wheeled, conflict etched on to his gorgeous face. "But isn't that just me being selfish? Isn't that just me thinking only of myself? I have more to give than just style guides and lifestyle choices and workout tips. I'm more than just... just this." He beat his well-defined pecs. "I can help people. I mean, I already help people through my channels. I communicate and educate. I lead and listen. I entertain and inspire."

He came over, sank into the seat beside Valkyrie.

"But then I look at you," he continued, "and you don't get the money and you don't get the fame or the adulation. Yeah, some people worship you as New God, but it's not like you'd be recognised walking down the street."

"It's not me they worship."

He snapped his fingers. "That's right! It's not even you! So you run headlong into danger every single day and nobody cares."

"I wouldn't say nobody—"

"And that's a different kind of fulfilment. Maybe that's the kind I need because I... there's an emptiness." He reached out, took her hand. "I'm not perfect, Valkyrie."

"Don't say that."

"It's true. I've been selfish in the past and I've had to be ruthless to get where I am today. Isn't it time I gave back?"

"I mean... maybe? Skulduggery, what do you think?"

"I don't care," Skulduggery said. "Handsome, how long did you date Rumour Mills?"

Handsome blinked a few times, like his thoughts were a train he had to shift on to another track. "I don't know. In total? Six months? I couldn't be sure."

"How did you meet?"

He looked away as he tried to remember, then smiled. "You know the Firehand, here in LA? It's a sorcerer nightclub. Or it might have been the Cauldron bar. Anyway, it must have been six, seven years ago, and I was there, having a good night, and Rumour comes up to me and throws a drink in my face. This girl, pretty as a picture, calling me every name under the sun in her funny little accent, and I just fell in love right there and then."

"Why did she throw her drink over you?" Valkyrie asked, adjusting herself on the chair.

"Apparently, I'd been rude to her friend. But then we got to talking and, well... That's how we met."

"You started going out soon after?"

He grinned. "Love at first sight."

"And you dated for how long?"

"About four months, initially. I remember because it's still the longest I've ever dated anyone. She was just special, you know?"

"And then you broke up?"

"Love runs its course."

"But you got back together again."

"Love finds a way."

"And then you dated for two months the second time round?"

"About that, yeah."

"Describe her," Skulduggery said.

"Uh, sure," Handsome responded. "About five foot seven, brown hair—"

"Describe her as a person."

"Oh, sorry. She was a five-foot-seven person, with brown hair—"

"What was she like?" Valkyrie said quickly, before Skulduggery could lunge. "Was she funny? Smart? Kind?"

"Oh, yeah," said Handsome. "She was all those things. The trifecta, you know? So kind and so funny. She was always making jokes that I didn't quite get, but that's because we had totally different senses of humour. We also had totally different kinds of intelligence, you know what I mean? She knew things out of books and she would talk about movies and history and politics. Whereas, my intelligence is more street-level. More real-world. I knew a lot more about moisturisers."

"Uh-huh," said Valkyrie. "What else can you tell us about her?"

Handsome sat back. "She cried a lot."

"Why?"

He shrugged.

"Did you ask?"

"Why she cried?" he said. "I mean, sure. But she'd just shake her head. A girl shakes her head, that means no. My dad taught me that. So I didn't ask again."

"We've spoken to a friend of hers, Simone Ruddy?"

"Yeah, I know Simone." He laughed. "She does not like me."

"Why's that?"

"People either love me or hate me," said Handsome. "It's been happening all my life. You just learn to deal with it, you know? Simone's one of those people who – you know what it is? She was protecting Rumour. That's what it was. She took one look at me and thought, *He's bad news. He's gonna hurt my friend.*"

"Did you?"

"Naw. I loved Rumour."

"You dumped her twice, though."

"Love runs its course."

"So you've said. Why did you break up?"

"Which time?"

"Either."

"I don't want to sound like a jerk, but it was the same reason both times. The crying was starting to get to me."

Valkyrie resisted the urge to punch his beautiful face. "Uh-huh."

"Did Rumour have any enemies?" Skulduggery asked. "Anyone she'd had a problem with, or anyone who'd had a problem with her?"

"Not that I know of," said Handsome.

"Did Rumour talk about her sessions with Cyrus Elysian?"

"We agreed that she should keep those conversations to herself. If we allowed any of it to spill over, it'd just... I was afraid it'd poison the well of our relationship. And I mean like a metaphorical well. Not an actual one. All I know is that she'd started going to him before we met up again and she was doing really good. So much better than when I'd seen her last. But then the crying started again and, like I said, it was getting to me, so I felt like the time had come to call it quits. I felt she needed to focus on her mental health."

"You're a terrible boyfriend," Valkyrie said.

Handsome laughed, then frowned. "Seriously?"

"She needed you to support her and you bailed."

"Love runs—"

"—its course, yeah. You said."

"Does that make me a terrible boyfriend?" he asked, apparently genuinely concerned. "Does it?"

Valkyrie worked a little to heave herself out of the ridiculous chair. "You tell us. How would you rate yourself?"

"Looks-wise?"

"As a boyfriend."

"I'm a good boyfriend. I bring positivity and fun to the table. I love with all my heart and, yeah, sometimes that flame burns brighter rather than longer, but that's how love is meant to be, isn't it?"

"And you've always been faithful?"

"Pretty much. I mean..." Handsome paused, then scratched his perfect chin. "OK, this does not paint me in a particularly good light, which is ironic, because I've been told that, on me, every light is a good light. That's why I pop on screen. I'm sure I have a bad angle, but honestly? If I do, the camera hasn't found it yet." He chuckled. "But yeah, sometimes my relations do overlap."

Valkyrie glared. "You cheat on your girlfriends."

"I'm a victim of my heart. But once I've realised that a previous relationship and a current relationship have overlapped, I end the previous relationship. I mean, that's just common decency, you know? I'm not a two-timer."

"And how do the women from the previous relationships generally react to this news?"

"They tend to be angry about it. I don't know if they blame the current girlfriend, but they *definitely* blame me. I get the majority of the anger." He shook his head, like it was hard to believe.

"They blame you because it's your fault," said Valkyrie.

"Well," Handsome said, "there are two sides to every story."

"But it *is* your fault, right?"

"There is fault on my part, yes. Some of the blame—"

"*All* of the blame."

"See, you're making it sound like it's *entirely* my fault."

"It *is* entirely your fault."

"How, though? I've just fallen in love with somebody new. How can I be blamed for that? Can either of you honestly tell me that you've never cheated on anyone?"

"I've never cheated on anyone," said Skulduggery.

"But you're a skeleton. I mean, no offence, but who are you gonna cheat on?" Handsome switched to Valkyrie. "But you – you're hot. Can you say you've never cheated?"

"I've cheated," said Valkyrie. "But at least I felt guilty about it."

"So would it make the cheating less bad if I felt guilty about it?"

She went to answer, then just glared. "We're asking the questions here."

"Yes," he said. "Yes, sorry."

The elevator pinged behind them and Fletcher stepped out. He faltered when he saw them, but summoned the courage to walk up.

"So," he said, puffing out his chest, "you're Handsome."

"Thank you," said Handsome.

"No," Fletcher said, frowning. "I mean, you are Handsome. That's your name."

"It is. And you are?"

"I'm handsome, too."

"We picked the same name?"

"What? No. My point is, I'm Fletcher. That's my name. I don't feel the need to go around telling people I'm handsome, because that's just – that's kinda sad."

Now it was Handsome's turn to frown. "But I have to tell people I'm Handsome. It's my name."

"Fletcher," said Skulduggery, stopping the conversation from going too far, "what are you doing here?"

"Sorry?" Fletcher replied. "Oh, yes. Murder. There's been another murder, back in Dublin. Sorry, I got distracted by... Anyway, the place is crawling with cops. Mortal cops. Guards, like. The Gardai. I figured you'd want me to take you straight there before they contaminate the crime scene."

17

Winter and Mia stood together in the Principal's Office –
arms by their sides, backs straight, no slouching, heads up
– like they were scared little kids who had just got in trouble
for the first time in their lives. That was most definitely not
the case, but even so, and despite her best efforts, Winter
still felt incredibly, ridiculously nervous.

The desk before them was large, the chair behind it empty.
Shelves lined every wall and on those shelves were the
scariest of books, the weightiest of grimoires, and the
obscurest of artefacts. Once upon a time, the principal of
Corrival Academy was reputed to have the most extensive
private collection of magical literature and objects in the
world. Winter didn't know if this was all that remained of
such a collection, or if it was only the tip of a very big,
very powerful iceberg.

The door behind them opened and then closed, and
China Sorrows came round the desk, aided by a glass cane
that churned with an unknown energy. Some students
believed the cane could fry an enemy to charred, blackened
remains – and China Sorrows had plenty of enemies – while

others believed it contained the soul of a man who had wronged her centuries ago. Winter didn't care too much about the cane – it was the woman who wielded it that commanded her attention.

She had seen photographs of China Sorrows in her prime and the woman had been an impossible, ethereal beauty. Now her black hair was bleached of colour, her slender frame bent and gnarled, her perfect skin lined and sagging. It wasn't youth that had fled from Principal Sorrows, but vitality. Her life force, her very *soul*, had been sapped as she struggled to contain a bomb blast that would have killed tens of thousands of mortals, leaving her a fragile shadow of the person she had once been.

Principal Sorrows sat, and rested her cane against the desk. She peered at them, her blue eyes clouded but inquisitive, like she knew you had a secret and she was coming after it.

"Miss Grieving," she said, "Miss Pizazz, thank you for coming to see me." They didn't exactly have a choice, but neither Winter nor Mia mentioned that. "How are the exams going, girls? You're not going to let the school down, are you?"

"No, miss," they both said, so perfectly in synch that they could have practised it.

"Good. Some students tend to think it's only the exams you sit in Sixth Year that are truly important, but I don't think they see the full picture, do you?"

"No, miss," they said again.

"The simple truth of the matter is that the exams you sit in Sixth Year don't matter, either."

Winter blinked. That was not what she'd been expecting.

Principal Sorrows eased back in her chair, a look of discomfort on her face quickly passing. "I've always loathed institutionalised education," she said. "How boring for the students, to learn what everyone else is learning. And how tedious for the teacher, to have to repeat themselves, year after year after year. I have no interest, girls, in churning out the same graduate again and again. What Corrival Academy seeks to do is foster the talents of the individuals we have here – individuals such as the two of you."

Winter didn't know how to respond, but Mia said, with great uncertainty, "Cool."

Principal Sorrows smiled, and there was an echo of the beauty she'd once been. "I'm sure it wouldn't surprise you that this school has produced more than its share of evil people."

"I'm sorry?" Winter said, frowning.

"Evil people," Principal Sorrows repeated. "I don't mean psychopaths and the like – although make no mistake, we have those in abundance. Some of your classmates are psychopaths. There is one budding serial killer among you that we're keeping our eye on. Can you guess who it is? No, don't answer. It's probably unprofessional of me to even ask. Oh, how I miss the days when I didn't have to mould young minds."

She sighed, then shook her head. "Magic corrupts. That's the inescapable truth. It always has and it always will. Human beings, most of us, are not meant to wield such power. Sorcerers have a command over reality itself. Should we be surprised that it results in psychopaths and megalomaniacs?"

Winter didn't respond, but Mia shook her head.

"But evil," Principal Sorrows continued, "is a few steps beyond, wouldn't you agree? Psychopaths are not inherently evil people, after all. I have known some wonderful psychopaths in my time. I myself *am* a psychopath, in my own way. Yes, for a long time I was on what could be considered the wrong side of the Three Hundred Year War, and I worshipped the Faceless Ones and I have murdered and manipulated and murdered again, but would you consider *me* evil?"

"Not at all," said Mia.

"Probably not," said Winter.

There was a ghost of a smile. "Truly evil people are quite rare in life, needing – as they must – a certain chain of events to make them the way they are. These events could be external or internal, and could take place long before they're even born. But they occur most frequently with those of a magical nature, where the combination of obscene power and long life and a dark, dark history often leads to behaviour that cannot be redeemed and individuals who are just too dangerous to attempt it."

"Principal Sorrows?" said Mia.

"Yes, Miss Pizazz?"

"Are you telling us this because you think one of us is evil?"

"No, my dear. I am telling you this so that you have some inkling as to the things that concern me. Magic is who we are, as sorcerers. But magic is also the greatest threat this world faces. The Sanctuaries have a function in our society: they act as our governments, as our leadership, and as our law enforcement. They are here to protect mortals from magic. To preserve the current way of life on this planet."

She tapped her fingernails on the desk. "But the Sanctuaries are not us, and we are not the Sanctuaries. Not every student who graduates from this Academy will work within the Sanctuary system. Corrival is not a factory. We do not produce Sanctuary agents, operatives, or detectives. Our students have a choice. They are in charge of their own destinies."

Winter and Mia waited.

"But while Corrival students are not obligated to work for, or with, the Sanctuaries, we are all in a symbiotic relationship with the mortals. We share this world with them. We need them, and we know it, and they need us, even though they have no idea."

"You want to know if we're Isolationists," said Winter.

"No. I do not want to know. It's not my place to ask, and if it were I wouldn't expect either of you to answer. Whether or not you believe we should be living apart from the mortals, our safety depends on the actions we take. I happen to believe that the actions undertaken by the so-called terrorist organisations are ill-conceived. You may disagree, but that is not what we are discussing."

"What are we discussing?" Winter asked.

"It has been brought to my attention that you two are orbiting some disreputable social circles."

Winter bristled. "Are you going to tell us not to talk to the people we're talking to?"

"I am not, Miss Grieving. But what I am going to ask is if you have spoken to Brazen Yarrow lately."

"We haven't."

"Her family is worried about her."

"So are we."

"They are concerned that she has been inducted into an illegal Isolationist organisation."

Winter nodded, but said nothing.

"Is there any light you can shed on this?" Principal Sorrows asked.

Winter glanced at Mia, noting the conflict on her face, and answered for them both. "No."

Principal Sorrows watched her. "You're sure?"

"Yes, miss."

"Because Brazen might be getting herself in a lot of trouble, and if that's the case, it would be up to her friends to say something. To tell people who could help her."

"We're not her friends, though."

A moment passed.

"Thank you, ladies," Principal Sorrows said, picking up a sheaf of papers. "You may return to class."

18

"Dermot Cairns," Skulduggery said, "you're feeling much calmer than you'd expect."

Dermot Cairns looked round at them, confused, grief-stricken. "Niamh," he said. "My wife. She's in there. She's still in there."

Skulduggery nodded, his façade showing sympathy. "We are terribly sorry for your loss," he said. "Dermot Cairns, you're deciding to be strong right now, in memory of your wife."

Dermot turned back, watching all the cops and the forensics specialists traipse in and out of his house. It was a warm and beautiful morning. Not the kind of morning that should be spent dealing with death. "They won't let me near her."

"They have to examine the scene," Valkyrie told him as gently as she could. A uniformed Guard walked over and she flashed her fake badge and he backed off, relieved that someone else was handling the husband.

"Dermot Cairns," Skulduggery said, "you trust us. You know we're here to help. Tell us what happened."

"I don't *know* what happened," Dermot said. Valkyrie doubted he was even aware of the tears rolling down his cheeks. "I took the bins out. I was gone for maybe two minutes. Niamh was talking to Halina, our neighbour, through the window. I could hear them laughing. When I walked back in, I found her. She was... It's not possible, what he did to her."

"What was done to her, Dermot?" Valkyrie asked.

"She was... she was in pieces."

Dermot's legs went, but Skulduggery caught him under the arms before he fell. He pulled him to the ambulance parked behind them and Valkyrie opened the rear doors so Dermot could sit on the edge. There were people standing at their gates all the way down the street, hugging each other, watching what was going on. Some of them were in their pyjamas.

"How did he do that?" Dermot asked. "I don't know how he did that. I need to see her."

"You've got to let them do their jobs," said Valkyrie. "You want us to catch whoever did this, don't you?"

"I know who did this. He's been calling her. He doesn't say anything, but he's been calling her for weeks. When it started, she joked. She said it was like in the movies, when the killer calls the girl alone in the house. But then she *was* alone in the house." His voice rose, hysteria creeping in.

"Dermot Cairns," Skulduggery said quickly, "you're calming down now. You're forcing yourself to think clearly and rationally."

Dermot covered his face with his hands and took a deep breath. "They think I did it. The police. They think I killed her."

"They did think that," said Skulduggery, "but they've spoken to your neighbour. They know now that you didn't."

"Is there anyone Niamh suspected of making those calls?" Valkyrie asked.

"No. She said it was coming from inside the house. She was joking. It's from the movies. She said it was from *Black Christmas* and... and something else. *When a Stranger Calls.*"

"Could we see her phone?" Skulduggery asked.

"I don't... Yes, you can, but I don't know where it is. I don't have it."

"When you find it, will you let us know? Thank you, Dermot. Did Niamh ever mention a Gavin Fahey, or a Sarah Boyle, or a Colleen Griffin?"

"I don't know. I'm not good with names. Maybe... maybe Colleen."

"What about a Rumour Mills?"

"Is that a person? I don't think she ever mentioned anyone like that."

"Thank you very much for your help," Skulduggery said, and looked him in the eyes. "Listen to me. The life that you knew is over. It's gone. All your hopes and dreams are different now. You'll never get over this, but you will adapt. You will learn to be happy again. Dermot Cairns, one day you will be OK."

Valkyrie turned away, unable to stand the pain in the poor man's eyes. She glimpsed a face in the small crowd that had gathered and she frowned, walked quickly over. She pointed at Cadence Clearwater and then pointed at the space beside her. Cadence dutifully came over and stood where she was instructed.

"What the hell are you doing here?"

"I just want to—"

"You want to help," said Valkyrie. "Yes, I know. Detective, you're not helping. What you're doing right now is interfering."

"My partner is lying in the Infirmary because I wasn't able to stop the man who attacked him!"

"Of course you weren't able to stop him," said Valkyrie. "No one would expect you to. But you think you're going to be able to solve this, to catch the killer, to save the day? That's not going to happen. Give it ten years – get the experience under your belt – and then you might have a chance. But, right now, all you're doing is distracting me."

"Detective Cain, please—"

"Go back to the Sanctuary," Valkyrie said angrily. "Carry out whatever duties have been assigned to you. Do not let me see you out here until all this is over."

She left Cadence there, strode back to where Skulduggery was waiting.

"You're scary when you're issuing orders," he said.

"I think I may have gone too far," Valkyrie replied. "Is she crying? I don't want to look. Is she crying?"

"It's hard to tell."

"Oh, God... I feel awful."

"You're keeping her safe and you're maintaining the integrity of the investigation. Feeling awful is a small price to pay."

They didn't have a car with them and it was too bright and sunny to fly without being seen, so they ducked under the cordon and went to find a taxi.

"This is depressing," Valkyrie said quietly.

"When we stop Ersatz, it will all be worth it."

She shook herself out of the dark mood that was threatening to descend. "I want to talk to Vincent Driscoll again."

"For any particular reason?"

"Rumour's the key. The more we know about her, the closer we'll be to figuring it out."

"Sound reasoning," Skulduggery said.

She looked at him. "That's where we were headed, anyway, wasn't it? Oh, God, I'm starting to think like you."

"That," he said, "can only be a good thing."

At Rumour's apartment building, they let themselves in. Skulduggery found the façade he'd been using last time and they knocked on Vincent Driscoll's door. Vincent answered, wearing baggy jeans and a vintage Megadeth T-shirt.

"Vincent," Valkyrie said, "we have a few more questions. Can we come in?"

"Sure," Driscoll said, "if you don't mind the mess."

He stood to one side and they entered. Movie posters covered the walls – old, tattered posters, stuck up without any thought to a coherent theme. Every surface and shelf that wasn't piled with books had some kind of statue or action figure from comics or cartoons or movies. More specifically, horror movies.

"Nice place," Valkyrie said.

Driscoll gave a short laugh. "Thanks, yeah. Nice place for a thirty-one-year-old adult, right? My mum says I stopped growing up when I was fourteen. I think she has a point." He tapped his T-shirt and made the devil horns sign. "Rock on."

Valkyrie smiled while Skulduggery looked around.

"Can I, uh, get you anything?" Driscoll asked. "I've got a couple of cans of Coke and, I think, some strawberries and cream in the fridge."

Valkyrie blinked at him. "How odd. Thank you, Vincent, but no. You're a horror-movie fan, I see."

"Yeah. Yes. Always have been. Always will be. Horror never dies."

"Indeed. And Rumour was a bit of a fan, too, wasn't she?"

Driscoll smiled sadly. "Yeah, she was. It was how we became friends. I mean, look at me, you know? No social life, nothing really to offer anyone and then, like, look at her. Lovely. Funny. Beautiful. We didn't really have much in common, so... I used to pass her on the stairs and we'd say a few words and she was always so nice and I figured, hey, this is another amazing girl who's going to barely know I exist. And then one day the power went out. It was only off for a few hours, but... Anyway, Rumour knocked on my door to ask if my power was gone, too, and she saw, well..."

"She saw the posters."

"Yes. I showed her around and... I don't show an awful lot of people around. And the people I do, they don't really get my whole thing. But Rumour... she got it." He laughed. "She really got it. We went over to her place and she showed me her books and her movie collection and we were comparing notes and talking about our favourites and it was... it was so cool. You should've seen the way her eyes lit up when she was talking about this stuff."

"Is it anything like the way your eyes light up when you're talking about her?" Valkyrie asked with a smile.

Driscoll blushed. "I suppose I had a crush on her."

"Did she know?"

"I'm not good with girls. I get all awkward and clumsy and I say stupid things... So she knew, yeah, but I never said anything."

"Did you love her, Vincent?" Skulduggery asked from across the room.

Driscoll seemed to shrink into himself, and he looked at the floor, and nodded.

Skulduggery wandered over. "That can't have been easy, to be in love with the girl across the hall – this lovely, funny, beautiful girl. Every time she left her apartment, you had to be wondering if this was the day she was going to meet someone else."

Driscoll didn't say anything.

"Would you describe yourself as a jealous man, Vincent?"

"No," Driscoll answered immediately, but without a trace of hostility. "And, like, believe me, I've had plenty of opportunities to find out."

"Did Rumour ever introduce you to her friends," Valkyrie asked, "the ones who came over every few weeks?"

"No – but it wasn't because she didn't want to. She was... See, they were all into horror. And they'd meet up to watch a film or go to the movies and have a drink after and talk about it and it seemed – it sounded – fun. And she asked, kept asking, if I wanted to hang out with them. Go to a movie with them or just knock on the door next time they were over... But I never did. I'm not good with new people. I'm not good with people full stop. She was always trying to get me to break out of my shell, but I think I like my shell too much."

He hesitated, and then gave a desperate shrug, and laughed.

"She gave me so many chances to be a part of her life. But I always said no because I was too scared. And too settled. And I always thought I'd have time to change my mind and maybe, one day, surprise her. I'd knock on the door and join in and I'd be funny and everyone would like me, and over time Rumour would start to see me in a different light, and I'd start to dress properly and I'd grow up... But I didn't do any of that."

He looked so incredibly sad. "And now she's gone and I never will."

19

The next morning, when Valkyrie stepped into the High Sanctuary, before she'd even had a chance to look for Cerise, Tanith Low strode over. As the Cleaver Commander, a post that brought with it a staggering amount of responsibility and gravitas, Tanith was supposed to wear a variation of the redesigned grey uniform as worn by those who obeyed her orders – minus the visored helmet, naturally. To hide those blonde tresses from the world would be a sin both unforgivable and unfathomable.

But while Tanith did wear the same armoured trousers as the Cleavers – tight-fitting but pliable – she had taken the similarly tight-fitting armoured jacket and managed, somehow, to cut the sleeves off. She wore it half-zipped, like her old waistcoats, and instead of a Cleaver's folded scythe strapped to her back, she usually had her sword.

She didn't have her sword this morning, however. Today was an office day – the kind of day that made Tanith extraordinarily grumpy.

"Do you know someone called Handsome Whitlock?" she asked, reading from a small tablet.

"Unfortunately, yes," said Valkyrie. "We interviewed him about the Ersatz killings. Why?"

"He's gone missing. A group calling themselves Team Handsome got in touch with the American Sanctuary, who got in touch with us because you guys were with him last..."

"They're his PR team. Team Handsome. He's an online guy."

"I'm not sure what that means, but OK," said Tanith. "The Sanctuary sent some operatives to look round the hotel room he was staying at. There were signs of a struggle."

"But no dead body?"

"Would you expect one?"

"Since we're dealing with Ersatz – yeah, probably."

"When you say he's an online guy... would he be famous?"

"I suppose he's famous to the people who know him."

"So, if he turns up dead, how much trouble could this be for us?"

"It would get a fair bit of attention, I'd say."

"Then it needs to be handled right. The Americans have got people looking for him. Hopefully, he'll turn up unharmed. Oh, hey, if you're headed up to see Ghastly, will you tell him I have to stay at the barracks tonight? I'd call, but he never answers, and I'd text, but he never looks at his phone, so..."

"I don't know if we'll see him," Valkyrie said. "We're here to talk to a psychiatrist."

Tanith clapped her on the shoulder. "About damn time." She walked off, two Cleavers falling into step on either side of her.

Valkyrie checked her phone, expecting to see a missed call from Skulduggery, explaining his tardiness. Instead, there was a sweet message from Militsa that Valkyrie returned, smiling.

"Detective Cain."

Valkyrie put away her phone. "Good morning, Cerise. Busy?"

"As ever."

"I don't know how you keep this place running, I really don't. The other Administrators weren't half as good as you."

"Yes," Cerise responded, "but they had the distinct disadvantage of being traitors. I would expect that'd be quite a distraction from their regular duties."

"I'd imagine so. Has Doctor Elysian arrived yet?"

"I'm afraid we have been unable to secure an interview for you."

Valkyrie hesitated. "So he's... unavailable?"

"Unavailable, yes."

"Huh. And when will he be available?"

"I'm sorry, I wouldn't know," Cerise said, standing there with her tablet, the very picture of efficiency.

"I'm a little confused," Valkyrie said, smiling again. "You've never failed to get someone here for an interview before. Any obstacles that are thrown in front of you, you find a way around. And Doctor Elysian works for the Sanctuary. He's probably in this very building right now."

"He's unavailable, I'm afraid."

"Cerise, I'm an Arbiter. There *is* no *unavailable* when it comes to Arbiters."

"He's unavailable, I'm afraid."

Valkyrie looked at her. "Right," she said. "Could you get us in to see Ghastly?"

"Grand Mage Bespoke is in meetings all morning, but I may be able to slot you in later this afternoon."

"Thank you, Cerise."

Cerise gave a nod, and then walked away. Valkyrie stayed where she was, stewing. She didn't even hear Skulduggery approach.

"You look angry," he said.

"Cerise has informed me that Cyrus Elysian is unavailable for interview."

"And what did she mean by that?"

"She means she's not going to be able to facilitate our request for a conversation."

"Is he not on the premises? Is he—"

"Skulduggery, she won't set up the interview. Ghastly's avoiding us as well."

His head tilted. "Then there has been a breakdown in communication. Let's go fix it."

They took the elevator to Ghastly's office, ignored the protests of his assistants and walked right in. Ghastly was pacing back and forth between the flickering images of some very important-looking people.

"Everyone take a short break," he said. "We'll continue in five minutes." He waved his hand and the images faded to nothing. "I can't let you talk to him."

Skulduggery gestured and the office doors closed behind them. "Cyrus Elysian is a person of interest in an Arbiter investigation."

"So I understand," said Ghastly. "But I can't let you talk to him."

"Why not?" asked Valkyrie.

"Elysian is part of a team working on a high-priority project. I can't afford to let you distract him."

"This is a murder investigation," Skulduggery said.

"I'm aware," Ghastly said, sitting behind his desk. He looked exhausted and it was only just gone ten in the morning.

Skulduggery took one of the other chairs, crossed his legs and placed his hat upon his knee. "You told us, when you took on the role of Grand Mage, that you would not stand in our way."

"I remember," said Ghastly.

"You told us that you knew what it was like when those in power used bureaucracy to obfuscate the situation to their own ends."

"I'm relatively sure I didn't use those words, but that was the gist, yes."

"You told us we would have your unconditional support."

"And you do, Skulduggery – just so long as it doesn't conflict with my unconditional support for other endeavours."

"Ersatz has killed three mortals that we know of," Valkyrie said. "Elysian may hold the key to putting a stop to it."

"I have every faith that you'll find this killer and stop him."

"And talking to Elysian is how we do that."

"If you don't stop Ersatz, more mortals could die," Ghastly said. "I recognise what's at stake. I do. But what Elysian is working on could ensure the safety of billions. It could save the world."

"Why are you protecting him?"

"I just told you."

Valkyrie shook her head. "I mean, why? Has he done something wrong in connection with the Ersatz killings? If he has, then *you* tell us. We don't even have to talk to him if you fill in the blanks."

"I don't know what Doctor Elysian has or has not done. I just can't take the risk that you'll find something to arrest him for."

"Then how about we agree not to arrest him? We'll talk to him, find out what he knows, and, no matter what he's done, we'll let him go back to work and deal with him when your top-secret project is finished."

Ghastly looked at them both. "Elysian had a partner, twenty-odd years ago. A brilliant man, but a psychopath who was a danger to innocent people. If that man were working here today, would you allow him to stay at his post, or would you throw him in prison? Can you see my position? If Elysian is helping Ersatz, for whatever reason, or if he's involved to such an extent that he's putting innocent lives at risk – would you still walk away until his work here is done?"

Valkyrie didn't answer.

"I wish I could help you," Ghastly said. "I wish I wasn't in a position where I have to choose between my duty and my friends. But here I am."

Skulduggery took his hat off his knee and stood. "This is disappointing," he said.

"I know."

"Also, I need new shoes."

"Your shoes are fine."

"These are old shoes. They take twice as long to polish."

"Then polish them at double the speed."

"You said you would have new shoes to go with my new suit. I don't have my new suit, either."

"I've been busy. You'll get your suit and you'll get your shoes when they're ready. Besides, you have rooms full of suits and shoes and they're all in pristine condition."

"This," Skulduggery said, putting on his hat, "is just very disappointing."

Ghastly sagged. "I know."

Skulduggery walked out.

"I'm making you some new clothes, too," Ghastly said to Valkyrie.

"Why?"

"Your necronaut suit doesn't offer the kind of protection you need."

"I like my necronaut suit."

"I'm making you new clothes, anyway. You don't have to wear them."

"Tanith said to tell you she'll be staying at the barracks tonight."

"Thank you."

"I'm mad at you, by the way."

"OK."

"We've just had a personal conversation because we're friends, but I don't want you to think that I'm not mad at you, because I am. I'm going to walk out now without saying goodbye. Goodbye. Damn it."

She walked out.

When they were in the elevator and heading down, Skulduggery splayed his fingers, trapping their words in a bubble.

"You think they're listening to us?" Valkyrie asked.

"It's a possibility," he replied, "but probably not. Ghastly doesn't need to eavesdrop to know exactly what we're saying right now, and to know exactly what we're going to do."

She raised an eyebrow. "So he knows we're going to find Elysian and make him talk? Good. Just as long as we're all on the same page."

20

Cyrus Elysian lived in one of the nicest parts of Roarhaven, where they had the biggest houses with the best security systems: a combination of cutting-edge technology and cutting-edge magic. The security system, it was roundly acknowledged, was *virtually impenetrable*. It had taken Skulduggery the better part of twenty minutes to dismantle this one, and Valkyrie had spent that time texting Militsa. She read the latest message and laughed.

"What's funny?" Skulduggery asked, cutting a wire in the hidden panel on the roof.

"Never you mind," Valkyrie told him.

The breeze was warm and glorious. She would have happily sunbathed out here. She wrote that in a text and sent it, and Militsa's reply made her laugh again.

"What's funny now?" Skulduggery asked.

"Would you please just focus on getting us into this bloody house?"

"But I'm bored."

"If you tell me how we're going to lure Elysian out of

the High Sanctuary without bringing a load of Cleavers with him, I'll tell you what I'm laughing at."

"But that will ruin the surprise."

"Then you'll just have to live without knowing."

He sighed – heavily – and went back to work.

Valkyrie took a selfie and grinned as she sent it. When Skulduggery stood and turned, she smiled at him innocently. "Can we break in now?"

"Let's find out," he said.

They kicked the back door in and Skulduggery entered, Valkyrie behind him. No alarms went off.

The house was just as Valkyrie had imagined: ultramodern, with lots of glass and corners and white walls. Skulduggery found the secret switch under the mantelpiece within four minutes, and a staircase opened in the marble floor.

"Now this is interesting," Valkyrie said.

They descended into a vast room of paintings and sculptures and exotic masks of exquisite beauty.

"Doctor Elysian has a passion for art," Skulduggery told her. "More precisely, he has a passion for stolen art. He doesn't steal it himself, but once it's stolen, and it appears on the black market, he likes to acquire it for his private collection."

Valkyrie smiled. "So he wouldn't want any Cleavers or Sanctuary personnel accompanying him into this room, would he?"

"He would not," Skulduggery said, clicking his fingers. He summoned a flame that he turned into a fireball, and he held the fireball in his hand until the heat sensors picked it up and the lights started flashing red.

"So this is how we lure him to us," he said. "Now, tell me what was so funny."

"You wouldn't get it."

"Of course I would."

"It's a girl thing, Skulduggery. You really wouldn't."

She led the way upstairs and while they waited in the living room he kept asking until she eventually relented and told him.

He tilted his head. "I don't get it."

Valkyrie shrugged. "Told you."

They heard the front door burst open, and a moment later a man came stumbling into the room before freezing.

"Doctor Elysian," Skulduggery said, "so good to finally meet you."

Valkyrie saw a flicker of surprise briefly pass over Cyrus Elysian's features. "You've broken into my house," he said. "I could have you arrested."

"We all know you won't do that, Doctor."

Elysian was a trim, narrow man with a trim, narrow face. He wore an expensive suit and expensive shoes. His haircut probably cost more than most phones, and even his closely cropped beard could have applied for a small bank loan based on its credit history alone. He glanced at the secret stairs. "My collection?"

"Unharmed."

He nodded. "You tricked me. Very well, Detectives, you may have your interview." He walked over and sat on the couch and crossed his legs. "Of course, you understand that I am not at liberty to discuss my Sanctuary work."

"We understand," Skulduggery said. "Rumour Mills was a patient of yours?"

"I do not discuss my Sanctuary work and I do not discuss my patients."

"But she *was* your patient."

"I do not discuss my patients."

"You know what an Arbiter is and you know the power we have."

"I'm aware, yes, as you are no doubt aware of the protection that Grand Mage Bespoke himself has afforded me. You can ask your questions, and any that I can answer, I will. Any I cannot answer, you will have to accept my apology and move on."

"What do you know of Ersatz?"

"I don't know what that's in reference to."

"Have you heard the names of Gavin Fahey, Sarah Boyle, or Colleen Griffin before?"

"I've heard of Colleen Griffin, yes."

"Where did you hear about her?"

"I'm sorry, that's confidential."

"Those three people I just mentioned are dead, killed by a sorcerer calling himself Ersatz. Rumour may have been his first victim."

Elysian said nothing.

"What work do you do for the Sanctuary, Doctor?"

"Much of it is confidential."

"And the parts that aren't?"

"I have helped them, in the past, with various matters requiring highly trained Sensitives. I've looked into the minds of suspects, been responsible for locking away some of them and clearing others of suspicion."

"Where do your interests lie?"

Elysian allowed himself a quick smile. "The human mind, Detective, in all of its complexities."

"You work as a therapist for the Sanctuary, but also take on private patients, yes?"

"That's correct."

"Do you treat many patients suffering from depression?"

"Depression is a somewhat common complaint, yes, though there's nothing common about it. Depression affects everyone differently. Each case is unique and each treatment needs to be tailored to the individual." He looked directly at Valkyrie. "As you well know."

"I do."

Elysian nodded. "And how do you feel you're coping?"

"Better than I was," Valkyrie said. "Sometimes it's a struggle."

"That's an interesting word to use."

"Is it?"

"People struggle with depression, don't they? They suffer from it and they struggle with it, like it's an enemy that has attacked them, but can be beaten into submission."

"I think you might be reading too much into an everyday phrase."

"But you used it for a reason. You used it because, to you, it felt right."

"Maybe – but you're not my therapist, Doctor."

"Of course. If I were your therapist, I would be charging for this interaction." Another quick smile, this time at his own wit.

Valkyrie smiled in return. "If you were, how would you treat my depression?"

"There are different ways for different people. We would talk. You'd discover things about yourself."

"Would you suggest medication?"

"Medication can be very effective, yes. It's not for everyone."

"Would you suggest any psychic interactions?"

"They can be helpful, too."

"What about magic?"

"There are some magical avenues to treat depression, yes."

"What avenue did you use for Rumour Mills?"

"I'm afraid that's confidential."

"I read up on you," Skulduggery said.

Elysian nodded. "And I on you."

"You're an advocate for a controversial treatment for mental-health issues."

"*Issues*," Elysian repeated, almost in a murmur. "Yes, Detective, I am. I seek out therapies to help my patients. At times, they can be controversial. Such is the nature of this particular beast."

"Do you have a problem with my use of the word *issues*, Doctor?"

"Not at all. You are free to use whichever words you please. But I have a question for you. Do you think, because you have moved beyond the need for a physical brain and all of its pesky chemicals, that you have also moved beyond having any mental-health *issues*, as you put it, yourself?"

"You think I'm beyond such things?"

"I think you may regard yourself as being beyond such things, yes."

"But wouldn't that make me a superior being?"

"It all depends on your metric. I would certainly like to

take a peek into your mind. We'd have to do it the old-fashioned way, obviously, as you are annoyingly impervious to my – and who is this?"

Valkyrie glanced over her shoulder and then whirled as Ersatz walked into the room.

Elysian got to his feet. "Is this man with you, Detectives?"

Valkyrie tapped the skull on her belt and her necronaut suit flowed over her clothes as she went right and Skulduggery went left, circling Ersatz slowly. Ersatz, for his part, kept his focus on Elysian.

"Why's he looking at me?" Elysian asked. "Oh, God, this is the killer, isn't it? He's here to kill *me*? Why does he want to kill *me*? I haven't done anything." He spoke louder. "I haven't done anything! I don't even know you! You've got no reason to kill me!"

"Don't worry, Doctor," Skulduggery said. "Ersatz likes to take his time with his victims. You'll be safe enough while we—"

A flick of the wand and Elysian didn't even have time to scream before he was torn apart. His remains splattered to the ground.

"I may have misjudged that," Skulduggery muttered.

Valkyrie released a torrent of white lightning at Ersatz, who wheeled and flicked the wand like a conductor at an orchestra. A gash ripped through the marble floor and would have sliced her in two were it not for her suit. As it was, she went tumbling head over heels.

Skulduggery pushed at the air, but Ersatz cut his way through. The wand moved and Skulduggery slammed into the wall, the wall itself wrapping around his wrists before solidifying again, trapping him there.

Ersatz spun without looking as Valkyrie went to blast him from behind. An invisible force flipped her, sent her sprawling. She sprang back to her feet. The wand twirled again and a charge – that was the word that sprang to mind – hit the skull on her hip and the skull cracked. The necronaut suit flowed away instantly and Ersatz whipped the wand in a zigzag and Valkyrie opened up from the top of her right leg, across her stomach, and diagonally up to her right shoulder.

Skulduggery roared and Valkyrie fell, her body already numb. She landed and didn't roll, didn't tumble, didn't somersault. She lay on her back, gasping.

Ersatz approached, watching her. At the far end of the room, Skulduggery went quiet and very, very still. His head dipped, his hat obscuring his skull. She watched, through wide eyes, as the parts of the wall holding him in place started to crack. His wrists slipped through. He was moving in slow motion. Everything was in slow motion, even Valkyrie's own heartbeat and the splashing of her blood.

The air shimmered and Skulduggery came through the air, collided with Ersatz. Ersatz whirled so, so slowly, and they fought, and Valkyrie was aware of Skulduggery's roar once again filling the room. She was aware of it, but couldn't hear it. It was odd. It was an odd sensation.

Ersatz kept trying to use the wand, but Skulduggery, despite moving so slowly, was somehow also moving too quickly. The walls and the floor and the ceiling exploded like white fireworks of dust and rubble, and all the while Skulduggery was hitting and parrying and hitting and dodging – and then he had the wand, snatched it right out of Ersatz's hand as he stumbled.

It was so cold in here. Valkyrie was only realising that now. It was so incredibly cold. She wondered if that had anything to do with the fact that she could see her insides, and decided that yes, it probably did. She gazed at her jeans and her top. They were ruined. That was sad.

The air swelled beneath her and lifted her off the floor and Skulduggery was running at her. When she was waist-high off the ground, he reached her, his arms snaking in under her. He was carrying her now. That was nice of him. If he only had any warmth to his body, he could have warmed her. But probably not. She'd forgotten about her injuries.

Valkyrie smiled. So silly.

Then they were off the ground and the door ahead of them burst apart in a magnificent display of splinters and out they flew and it was really, really lovely.

21

She didn't die, which was the good news.

The bad news was that the Sanctuary technicians were, in Skulduggery's words, "entirely pessimistic" about their chances to repair the black skull that housed the necronaut suit. For the first few hours since waking up, Valkyrie lay in bed with the machines beeping all around her and vacillated between clenching her jaw in annoyance and clenching her jaw in pain. Whenever a nurse came by to offer her relief from that pain, she declined.

Once her condition had stabilised, Reverie laid her glowing hands on the stitches crossing Valkyrie's abdomen. Heat flooded her body and she closed her eyes and focused on not moving. Reverie worked for close to half an hour and Valkyrie felt her insides rearranging, her flesh knitting back together, her organs healing.

"You're going to need to rest," Reverie said when she was done, a light sheen of sweat on her face. "Your body has been through some unimaginable trauma, so allow twenty-four hours before the next stupid thing you do, OK? What's your pain level right now?"

"Like... five?"

"Five? Really? I know when you're lying, Valkyrie. Just for future reference." Reverie sighed. "Just do me a favour and try not to die on one of my beds, there's a good girl."

Reverie left and Valkyrie dozed. When she woke, Skulduggery was sitting in the chair next to her.

"My hero," she said dreamily.

"Dear God," he responded, then tilted his head. "Oh. You're being funny again."

"I'm laughing in the face of adversity," she told him. "Ersatz?"

"I had to let him escape. You took priority."

"Did you tell Militsa what happened?"

"You had an eighteen per cent chance of survival so, per your standing instructions: no, I did not inform your girlfriend of the danger you were in."

"Good. You only tell her—"

"If your chances are fifteen per cent or below. I remember. I'm assuming you'll tell her eventually?"

"When I'm recovered, absolutely." She sat up a little, as much as she was able. "So, to business. Where are we in the investigation? If I'm stuck in bed, let's take the opportunity to think about what we've learned so far."

His head tilted. "Have you not been thinking about any of this until now?"

"No, I have."

"Because that's part of what being a detective means."

"I know that," she said crossly. "But we have a chance to really get into it."

"It sounds like you haven't been devoting any time to this at all."

"I'm the action hero," she said. "You're the thinking guy. Has Handsome turned up yet?"

"He has not."

"So it's looking like Ersatz got to him."

"Very likely." Skulduggery took his hat off. "So let's compare theories. What do you think is happening?"

"You want me to go first? I was thinking maybe you go first, you start with your theory, and then I'll jump in with mine, and if they overlap so be it."

"I'm tempted to insist that you go first," Skulduggery said, "but you're injured, so I'll relent. Rumour Mills, a sorcerer, was part of a social circle of mortals which included Gavin Fahey, Sarah Boyle, Colleen Griffin, and Niamh Cairns."

"A social circle," Valkyrie said. "Yes, that's exactly what I was going to say. They were friends."

"They were friends." Skulduggery nodded. "Brought together through a shared love of...?"

"Italian food. Welsh poetry. Horror movies."

"Horror movies, yes – they would meet up to watch a film and then discuss it. It is entirely possible that they did this every week, and simply changed the location on a rotating basis."

"I agree," said Valkyrie.

"I'm so relieved," said Skulduggery.

"Do we know how they all met in the first place?"

"As of yet, we do not. They seem to have no one or nothing else in common, as evidenced by the fact that they were unaware that the members of their group were being picked off."

"The media blackout probably didn't help matters,"

Valkyrie said. "Maybe if they'd seen a picture of their friends on the news they'd have realised someone was after them."

Skulduggery shrugged. "It's standard operating procedure for Sanctuary investigations. I don't blame Avant Garde for implementing the blackout – we would have done the same. It allows us to operate more freely."

"So Ersatz, after making a deal with the Hidden God, and using a wand, of all things, has been tracking down and murdering each member of this little horror club."

"In an increasingly sadistic fashion, yes."

"So why the long gap between murdering Rumour nine months ago and murdering Gavin two weeks ago?"

"He might not have had the opportunity," Skulduggery said. "He may have been elsewhere. He may have been occupied. He may have been in prison."

"We should check with the Sanctuary, get a list of mages who were jailed after Rumour's murder and released before Gavin's." Valkyrie chewed her lip. "Maybe check the mortal prisons as well."

"Good idea."

"So why go for Rumour first? Maybe she knew Ersatz? Maybe she introduced him to the horror club, and that's why the horror club is being eliminated? Because they can identify the killer? But then why did Ersatz kill Elysian?"

"Elysian knew something," said Skulduggery. "Something about Rumour. Something she told him or something he saw in her mind."

"But what? If it was something, like, immediately damning, then Ersatz would have killed him first, right? Instead, he waited until we'd figured out that Elysian was someone we needed to speak to and then swooped in to silence him."

"Well," Skulduggery said, "not necessarily. We may have played into the enemy's hands there."

Valkyrie groaned. "Oh, God, what did we do?"

"Elysian had been working hard on Ghastly's secret project for months. He'd barely left the High Sanctuary."

"So?"

"Well… we lured him out into the open, didn't we?"

She stared. "We delivered Elysian to Ersatz? How mad is Ghastly with us right now?"

"*Quite*, bordering on *very*."

"Should we feel guilty? Oh, man, I'm feeling guilty. Ooh, I have that guilty feeling. Oh, it's horrible. We thought we were so clever and cool and badass."

"I *am* clever and cool and badass."

"But we ended up doing what the killer had been unable to do."

"Take my advice, Valkyrie: stop the killings now, and feel guilty later."

She sighed. "So what about this wand?"

"The experts are examining it as we speak."

"And we don't know yet how the Hidden God factors in to all of this, or what deal Ersatz made with him. Have they broken into Reverend Fervor's mind yet?"

"His defences are too strong."

"Has he said *anything*?"

"He just smiles. We can jail him for assault, but… I doubt we'll be able to find anything else to charge him with. There have, however, been new developments in other areas. Dermot Cairns called me. He found his wife's phone. Ersatz didn't get an opportunity to wipe it, so Dermot sent us the group messages for the horror club. The messages themselves are of no use, but we do have two names to add to the list of friends – Sean Dowling and Eimear Shevlin. Both of whom have dropped off the map, by the way. They vanished the day Niamh Cairns was killed."

"You think Ersatz got to them?"

"Perhaps. Or maybe they heard what happened to their friends, figured out they were probably next, and so they've gone into hiding. Their respective partners and families have no idea where they are. I've asked the Sanctuary to search hotels and rental properties, and we're keeping an eye on their phones."

Valkyrie's own phone pinged and she went to reach for it before groaning in pain. Skulduggery picked it up instead and passed it over.

"Thank you," she said, as the pain subsided. She read the screen. "Reggie's waiting to talk to us. Let's go."

Skulduggery put a restraining hand on her shoulder. "You probably shouldn't move."

Wincing only a little, Valkyrie gave what she hoped would be a reassuring shrug. "The doctors said I was grand to walk around."

"I just spoke to Reverie – she said no such thing."

"It wasn't Reverie who said it. It was another doctor. He's got long, curly eyes and brown, fuzzy teeth. You probably don't know him. He's new. Today was his first day. Then he quit. He couldn't handle the pressure. It got to him. Happens to the best of us. His name was Edward. Edward Doctor. Doctor Edward Doctor. Doctor Doctor. I asked him if that was a joke and he ran away, crying."

"Do you ever get tired of hearing yourself speak?"

Valkyrie sagged. "God, yes. Sometimes I just want to shut up and, like, glare at people in silence, but then... I don't know. You've infected me, is what you've done. I've spent so much time with you – I've known you for twenty years – that I now have a reservoir of excess silliness I need to empty every few days. What have you done to me? Seriously?"

"Excess silliness?"

"You're a very silly person, Skulduggery."

"I am a very serious person in a very silly world."

"All I'm saying is, I was a lot happier when I was more miserable. Now help me up."

"That is not advisable."

"Since when has that stopped us from doing literally anything?"

With his aid, Valkyrie got up, and Skulduggery turned his back while she dressed. It took a while. When she was done, she hobbled out of the room beside him. They walked a few more steps and then Skulduggery abandoned her, striding towards a room up ahead.

"Hey," she said.

"You're moving very slowly," Skulduggery called back to her.

"Because I've just been horrifically injured."

"Yes, but you're really slow, so it's very boring. I'll be here when you catch up."

She scowled and followed him, reaching the door almost a minute later. Avant Garde lay on the bed inside, hooked up to machines that beeped and whirred. He was deathly pale, with close-cropped dark hair, grey at the temples. His clothes and belongings were neatly placed on a table beside the door. A pair of trousers – what looked like all that remained of those impeccable suits that detectives like him wore. A black leather belt. A watch. A gun, still in its holster. A single brown leather shoe.

"Any improvement?" Valkyrie asked.

Skulduggery looked at the chart beside the bed. "Not much," he responded, and walked back to her. He used the air to lift her off her feet. Grinning, and making little "*wheee*" noises, she glided after him into the elevator, and they went up to the Research and Development Department.

They found Professor Reginald Regatta in his laboratory, and Skulduggery set Valkyrie's feet gently on the ground.

"Detective Cain," Regatta said, frowning at her, "are you all right? You're very pale."

"Don't worry about me, Reggie," she said, laughing. "I'm fit as a fiddle, right as rain, in fine fettle, and hunky-dory."

"Excuse me?"

Valkyrie's laugh died, and she frowned. "Sorry. The pain might be making me delirious. But hey, I've managed to get up here without my guts spilling out all over the floor, so why not make it worth my while? What've you got for us?"

Regatta led them to where the wand floated in the air, suspended between three carved metal sticks that stood upright on a desk. He waited for Valkyrie to hobble over before speaking.

"This is a truly fascinating artefact," he said. "It is, as you suspected, a human rib – the seventh. It's been shortened, with one end whittled down to a fine point. We've had no luck trying to trace the DNA – though we have noticed some irregularities on that front that we're investigating." He paused, gazing at the wand for a moment.

186

"The really interesting thing about the artefact, though, is that it's both magic and not magic."

"OK," said Valkyrie, nodding. "What?"

"As an object, it is exactly what it is: a whittled human rib. It has no magic of its own that we can detect. But, once a sorcerer holds it, that changes. It goes from an inert human rib –" Regatta plucked it from between the metal sticks – "to a massively powerful conduit through which my magic is pulled, absorbed, converted, magnified, and then expelled, all at the speed of instinct: a *wand*, as distasteful as that word may be to mages."

"When you say converted...?" Skulduggery said.

"The discipline I've trained in means nothing. My magic becomes nothing more than a power source. As for what it can do... I hesitate to use hyperbole, but it is entirely possible that this wand may be capable of doing anything."

Valkyrie frowned. "Literally anything? Like, if I wanted to switch off the sun..."

"It would take a much larger power source to draw from, but yes – the potential is there. We theorise that this wand is only limited by the wielder's imagination and experience, and the more they use it, the more it can do."

"How long would it take, do you think, to go from novice to expert?" Skulduggery asked. "How long, for example, before you could burn someone alive underwater?"

"Not much time at all, I shouldn't think," Regatta said. "Give something like this to a talented sorcerer and it would only be a few weeks before they could do something like that."

"Then it's a good thing we took it from Ersatz while we still could. Do you have any idea where it came from?"

"None yet."

Valkyrie looked at Skulduggery. "What are you thinking?"

"I'm thinking," he said, "that we may be in an inordinate amount of trouble."

"We usually are," she murmured, the room swaying for a moment.

Skulduggery used the air to scoop her up gently. "Professor," he said, "would you please keep us informed as to any further tests you run? I really have to get Valkyrie back to her hospital bed before she dies."

22

With each passing hour spent in the hospital bed, Valkyrie could feel herself getting stronger. She was incredibly bored, however, so much so that when Quiddling appeared at her door she was almost non-annoyed to see him.

"Detective Cain," he said, "I'd like a word, if I may?"

Valkyrie gestured to the chair. "I'm not going anywhere."

Quiddling walked in, put a small wooden box on the bedside locker, then sat. "I was pleased to hear that you survived your ordeal."

"Me too. What can I do for you?"

"I have," he said, "a dilemma."

"Never a good thing to have."

"Indeed. Detective, you think the advisory board that I am proposing is the thin end of the wedge."

"You say it's an advisory board, we say it's an oversight committee dictating which cases the Arbiter Corps can investigate."

"And, while that is the furthest thing from our minds, I appreciate it's the conclusion to which you would jump."

"If you think you're going to convince me as I'm lying

here in a weakened state, I'm afraid you'll be disappointed. Even if I were so delirious that I'd agree, Skulduggery never would, so what's the point?"

"We wouldn't need him to agree," Quiddling said. "All we need is for you to accept our proposal, and that decision would be binding."

From his jacket pocket, he took a thin yellow arkheia crystal, a far more rudimentary version of an Echo Stone, and placed it beside the wooden box. "You don't mind me recording this conversation, do you?"

"You expect me to change my mind in the next few minutes? That's optimistic."

"Which brings us to the dilemma I mentioned." Quiddling shifted in his seat. "Detective, I have been approached by someone I believe you are trying to find: a man called Ersatz."

Valkyrie's small smile dropped away. "You've talked to him?"

"I have. While I'm here, I have various matters to attend to and various people to talk to. I was in Dublin yesterday and, before my scheduled appointment turned up, I was confronted by an individual in a black mask, who identified himself as Ersatz and told me, briefly, of the people he had killed."

With some discomfort, Valkyrie sat up straighter. "Where was this?"

Quiddling took a notepad from his other pocket and handed it over. "All the information is contained in these pages. The location, time, and the exact words spoken. I will be happy to answer any other questions once we conclude our business."

"And what is our business, Mr Quiddling? Why did Ersatz go to you?"

"He is somehow aware of the proposal I have brought to you. To help facilitate a successful outcome for everyone, he has written his true identity on a slip of paper and deposited it in this box, which apparently will incinerate its contents if tampered with or if it has not been opened by twelve noon." He checked his watch. "In just under five minutes."

"Did you talk to Tanith Low? She might have someone on her staff who could deactivate that measure."

"I haven't told anyone about this. I even had to sneak the box into the building to ensure no one tried to interfere."

Valkyrie raised an eyebrow. "So you took a box from a known killer, without checking that it didn't contain a bomb, and you smuggled it through security, into the High Sanctuary, to give to one of the detectives trying to stop him? And you thought this was a good idea?"

Quiddling went very, very pale.

"How do I open the box without incinerating what's inside?" Valkyrie asked.

"Maybe we should call in the Cleavers," he responded.

"Mr Quiddling, pay attention."

"You, ah, you have to agree to our proposal."

"Seriously?"

"The box is keyed to the arkheia crystal. Once the crystal documents your acceptance, the box will open on its own."

"So all I have to do is say yes, and I have Ersatz's identity?"

Quiddling nodded, perspiration on his upper lip.

"That seems way too easy for something like this."

"Those are the terms. Your acceptance of the proposal

is binding, and will immediately facilitate an advisory board to assist with all Arbiter investigations."

"Whatever," Valkyrie said, taking the box. Then she frowned. "How binding is it?"

"I'm not sure I understand. Binding is binding."

"But I can say *yes*, the box opens, I read what's inside, and then I can go, *oh, on second thoughts, no.* Right?"

He shook his head. "Your acceptance will set in motion a process that cannot be reversed."

"But we can agree that my answer isn't serious. You and me, we can shake on that here and now because lives are at stake and a killer is on the loose and what's inside this box can stop it all."

"I'm sorry, Detective, that's not how it works."

"People are dying, Mr Quiddling. Mortals are being murdered."

"I am aware of the situation in which you currently find yourself."

"You work for the English Sanctuary. You represent an international group of Sanctuaries. The whole purpose of the Sanctuary system is to protect mortals. That's your primary concern."

"Yes, it is. And I want Ersatz stopped as much as the next person. And this is a way to do exactly that."

"What you're talking about right now is extortion."

"Detective, I have to disagree with you. None of this has anything to do with me. These are the terms set by Ersatz."

"You're forcing me to choose between letting your bosses dictate what we can investigate, and letting a killer continue killing."

"I'm not forcing you to do anything," Quiddling said.

"And, furthermore, I reject your phrasing. The Sanctuaries I represent only wish to aid you in your duties as Arbiters, and in no way want to dictate—"

"Once we let them in, there'll be no getting rid of them."

"I sincerely don't know why you would want to. This is an opportunity for synergy, Detective. You're already using the Irish Sanctuary in your investigations, aren't you? Their experts are at your beck and call. Their operatives do the legwork that you don't have time to do. Their Sensitives interview witnesses and suspects. You're already co-operating with this institution, and every other Sanctuary you request aid from gives it freely and without complaint. The advisory board would ensure this continues."

"They co-operate because they have to," said Valkyrie. "Because we're Arbiters. Our authority supersedes their own. You're not doing us a favour when you work with us, Mr Quiddling, you're doing what you're told. Those are the rules."

"Rules that were put in place when the Sanctuaries were just coming into being, before they'd settled into what they are today. These were wartime rules, for God's sake."

"Just because they're old doesn't mean they're obsolete."

Quiddling sighed. "I've done my best," he said. "I've presented the proposal to you as clearly as I am able. I didn't expect to be coming to you today with a deadline, let alone with this *kind* of a deadline, but so be it. It is almost noon, Detective, so make your choice. What is more important – the idea of having someone to answer to, or stopping a serial killer from murdering more innocent people?"

Valkyrie lunged and Quiddling jerked back so suddenly he tipped his chair over. It crashed to the floor and he sprawled, but Valkyrie was in too much pain to enjoy it. Holding the box in one hand and her belly with the other, she got out of bed and said through gritted teeth, "You'd better find a way to rephrase that question before I lose my temper."

"If you assault me, you're going to prison," Quiddling said, getting to his hands and knees. "Your Arbiter status doesn't put you above the law, Detective Cain." He glanced at his watch. "You have one minute."

Energy crackled round Valkyrie's eyes and she did her best to dampen it, to draw it back in.

Quiddling got to his feet, regarding her warily. "However," he said, "I do apologise, and I will rephrase. What is more important to you: accepting the advisory board and all that entails, or learning Ersatz's true identity?"

"How do we know the box contains his true identity?"

"I'm afraid I can't answer that."

"For all we know, the piece of paper is blank."

"Yes. You have forty seconds."

She chewed her lip. "I think his name is in there. This is a test, and the test only means something if it's honest."

"What do you mean, a test?"

"Ersatz has some idea in his head about who I am, and so long as I pass the test I'm, I don't know, worthy to continue the investigation. The last detective assigned to this case failed, and Ersatz nearly killed him."

"But you have recovered Ersatz's weapon, haven't you? Or are my sources incorrect?"

"We have the wand, yeah, but we're still being tested."

"Fifteen seconds."

"I either accept your proposal and put the practical matter

194

of stopping a killer before the integrity of the Arbiter Corps, or I reject it and put my principles before an easy solution to a difficult problem."

"Detective, seven seconds."

Valkyrie stared at the box.

"Three, two, one—"

Valkyrie sent a charge through the box that blasted it apart, but the paper inside was already turning to ash.

Quiddling breathed out. "So do you think you passed?"

"I have no idea," she answered, lying back. "I suppose it depends on what Ersatz thinks the right choice was for me to make."

"For what it's worth, Detective, I really wish I hadn't had to come to you with such an ultimatum. This was not part of my strategy."

"I believe you. You gonna leave us alone now?"

"I'll report back to the Elders, they'll talk to the other Councils, and I'll get my orders, whatever they may be."

"Fair enough, Mr Quiddling. On your way out, could you do me a favour? Could you send a nurse in? I think I've ripped open some stitches."

23

As he walked, Mr Herringbone sorted through the pile of books he was holding. One of them slipped from his grip and, when he went to grab it, the rest of the pile tumbled from his hands. His bag slid off his shoulder, landing heavily.

"Let me help you, sir," Mia called, running forward.

Winter watched her load the books back into Mr Herringbone's arms, chatting amiably as she did so. This was not the plan. The plan was to leave school grounds without anyone noticing.

"Thank you, Mia," Mr Herringbone said, resting his chin on the uppermost book. "How are the exams going?"

"Brilliantly, sir," Mia responded. "Absolutely brilliantly. They're going so brilliantly that I wish we could have more of them. I just don't want them to end."

Herringbone raised an eyebrow. "I think you're overdoing it ever so slightly, Mia. What about you, Winter? Are the exams going as brilliantly for you?"

Winter shrugged. "They're going OK, yeah."

Mia picked Herringbone's bag off the floor, grunting

slightly with the exertion. "Wow. What do you have in here, sir? Bricks?"

Herringbone manoeuvred his shoulder into the strap. "Just more books."

"Knowledge is heavy, sir."

"It is, indeed. Where are you two going? You have another exam this afternoon, don't you? I would have thought you'd need to spend the next hour revising."

Mia nodded. "That's what we're doing, sir. We're going to find a quiet spot in the sun, away from everyone else, and get in some last-minute swotting."

"I see," said Herringbone. "And where are your books, may I ask?"

Mia blinked. "Our books, sir?"

"For your swotting."

"Oh! Our books! Yes." Mia turned to Winter and Winter had the sinking feeling that Mia expected her to trade banter. "Winter, I thought you were bringing our books."

Winter did her best not to glare. "No," she said.

"You mean you thought *I* was bringing them? So we both thought the other person was bringing the books? That is hilarious! It really is! And it's so *us*, wouldn't you say?"

"Yes."

Mia laughed. "Hilarious! We're always doing stuff like this!"

Mr Herringbone looked at them both, and then sighed. "Good luck in the exam, ladies," he said, and walked on towards the gates.

"What a nice man," said Mia.

"You didn't have to run over to him, you know," Winter said.

"Meh," Mia said, shrugging one shoulder. "OK, stay here. I have to pee." She ran off, passing Tier on his way over.

"She has to pee," Winter explained.

"Thanks for the information," he responded.

They stood together. Cars passed beyond the gates and a tram glided by. The silence between them was awkward.

"Is it just us three, then?" Tier asked. "I thought Aphotic was coming."

"He'll probably meet us there," said Winter. "He's been preoccupied with exams."

"I don't want to be mean to your friend, but he's a strange guy."

"Oh, Aphotic isn't our friend. He got obsessed with Brazen and that's as much as we really know about him. He changed his name because of her."

"Seriously?"

She nodded. "Brazen likes a certain kind of guy and Aphotic has been trying his best to be that."

"What about you?"

"What about me what?"

He looked at her. "Do you like a certain kind of guy?"

Winter blushed. Oh, God, she blushed, right here, right in front of him. "I don't know," she said, trying to be casual, but there was no salvaging it. "I just like who I like. They don't have to be a particular type."

"Yeah, me too," said Tier. "Having a type is a little restrictive, y'know? My sister, she's older than me, she has a list of qualities that whatever guy she's seeing must possess – height, look, job, whatever. She hasn't been able to find a guy who ticks all those boxes so now she's expanding her options by including girls. But it's not going to be any different. She just can't seem to accept that everyone brings something different."

"I didn't know you had a sister," said Winter. "If I ask you something, will you not get offended?"

Tier laughed. "I can't promise that."

"OK, no, but if I ask you something and it's so completely wrong, or even if it's right, then can you accept that I don't mean it in a bad way? It's just a question?"

"Sure," said Tier. "Ask away."

She hesitated. "Are your parents Eliza Scorn and Baron Vengeous?"

"Is that what people are saying about me? Didn't Baron Vengeous die, like, twenty years ago?"

"Nineteen, I think."

Tier smiled at her. "Baron Vengeous is not my dad."

"OK, cool. And your mum?"

"If Eliza Scorn was my mother, she'd probably have told me never to tell anyone, one way or the other, because she has so many enemies in the world. But what I will tell you is that my mother loves me and she's a good person."

Winter nodded. "Cool."

"What about you? Anyone evil in your immediate family?"

"Not any more."

"Cool."

He smiled at her, and she smiled back.

"I can't believe it's taken us this long to talk," he said.

"In my defence, you don't come across as the friendliest of people."

"And you do?"

"I'm super friendly."

"You scowl at everyone."

"No, I don't."

"You're scowling now."

"Only because you said I scowl at everyone."

"People are terrified of you," said Tier.

"What are you talking about? People barely even know I exist."

"Winter, listen to me: you're one of the most intimidating people in school, and that includes the teachers. The only person more intimidating than you is Principal Sorrows."

"So, what, the only reason we haven't become friends up till now is because you were too intimidated by me?"

"Honestly?" said Tier. "Yeah. I really wanted to, like, get friendly with you, but you were always—"

She laughed. *"Get friendly with me?"*

He grinned. "How else would you say it? I've fancied you for years."

Winter's laugh died and her mouth dried. "I'm sorry, what?"

His grin turned to a smirk. "Was I not supposed to say that?"

"You fancy me?"

"Hugely."

"Like, still? Like right now?"

"Like right now, yeah." He moved closer.

"Golly," she said.

"Could I kiss you?" he asked.

"Sure," she whispered.

He leaned in and her lips parted.

"This is the worst possible time, isn't it?" said Mia from right beside them.

They immediately drew away from each other and looked at her.

Mia put her hands to her face. "I am so incredibly sorry. Oh my God. I was halfway over and I was thinking they're having a nice chat, they seem to be really getting on well, and then I got nearer and you went to kiss and it was way too late for me to turn round and I couldn't just stop because then I'd be standing there, watching, and wouldn't that ruin your first kiss, whenever you thought back on it? At least this way you still have it to look forward to." She gave an apologetic shrug. "But I peed, so... So *that's* good news."

"That's great news," said Winter.

"And no sign of Aphotic yet?"

"He'll probably meet us at the demonstration."

"Yes. He probably will. So shall we go? We can see if Brazen's about, and then get back in time for the exam and we'll just, all three of us, try to pretend this awkwardness doesn't exist. That cool with you two?"

"Let's go," said Tier, and led the way to the gates.

Mia made a face at Winter. "I'm so sorry," she whispered.

Winter rolled her eyes at her friend, and then frowned. "Hey," she said, "am I intimidating?"

"Yep."

"To everyone?"

"Pretty much."

"So how come you're my friend?"

Mia shrugged. "I took pity on you on account of how ugly you are."

"Oh. Cheers."

They got on the tram when it passed, and Winter sat beside Mia, and Tier sat opposite, and they didn't say anything the whole way there. Winter wasn't especially familiar with the Humdrums. This part of the city had been the worst hit during Devastation Day, when Darquesse had torn through town. Even though it had been rebuilt, as good as new, it retained the after-effects of a massive psychic discharge that still affected sorcerers today, thirteen years later.

So it had been handed to the mortals from Dimension X, the Leibniz Universe, the parallel Earth once ruled by Mevolent where the sorcerers had taken over and the mortals had been slaves. Unable to assimilate into the regular mortal population outside Roarhaven, these Leibniz mortals had begun to flourish, setting up their own businesses and establishing their own culture, despite being surrounded, at all times, by the kind of people they feared most.

The tram came to a stop and the three of them got off and started walking. There was a small crowd of mages ahead, watching a woman make a speech. Nervous mortals peered out through shop windows, but there were half a dozen Cleavers standing around to handle any trouble if it broke out. A few observers, probably from the mayor's office, stood at a distance and talked among themselves.

It was a fairly low-key affair, in all honesty, and not what Winter had been expecting. This was no riot. This was no march. This was a clumsy, angry speech that sought to echo what Icious Staid had been saying at the underground bar.

Tier nudged Winter. She frowned, trying to find what he was looking at, and then she took off, tearing through the crowd until she was yanking on the arm of Brazen Yarrow.

"Hey," she said, because now that she'd found her she didn't know what to say.

A look passed over Brazen's face, a look that told Winter

she'd been expecting them. Winter led her out of the crowd, away from the speech, Mia and Tier following.

When they were far enough away, Brazen pulled free of Winter's hand and raised both eyebrows expectantly.

"We've been looking for you," said Winter. "You haven't been in school in a week. Sorrows called us into her office."

"We're worried about you," Mia said.

"Since when?" Brazen responded. "And what business is this of yours?"

"You're missing the exams."

Brazen laughed. "I really don't care. You were looking for me, you found me, so now you can run back to Principal Sorrows like good little children. In case you haven't noticed, we stopped being friends a while ago."

Brazen went to return to the crowd, but Winter stepped into her path, and there was a moment when she thought Brazen was going to hit her. Winter was ready for it.

"And these are your new friends, are they?" Mia asked. "These people? Mortal-haters and the Order of the Ancients?"

Brazen fixed Mia with a glare. "By *these people*, do you mean people who actually pay attention to what's going on in the world? People who actually care about making a difference? Because if so, then yeah, these people are my friends."

"So you're friends with a bunch of bigots."

Anger flashed and Brazen stepped up to Mia, and Winter shoved her away. Immediately, Brazen came back, shoulders squared, hands clenching to fists, but Winter shot out a hand to keep her at a distance.

"Don't," Winter said.

"You push me?" said Brazen. "You push me? I'll tear you apart, you spoiled little brat."

Tier stepped between them, his own hands up. "You gonna start a fight in the middle of the street?"

"She's the one starting it," Brazen snarled. "And what are *you* doing, taking their side? I thought you were one of us. I thought you saw things clearly."

"If you think Imperator Dominax is someone who sees things clearly, you need some serious adjustment, Brazen."

Brazen made a visible effort to calm down, switching her attention more fully to Tier. "Oh, that's right," she said. "You *were* on our side, you *did* see things clearly, and then this bimbo started laughing at all your jokes, didn't she?"

"Not *all* of them," said Mia, feigning offence. "Just the jokes I understood."

"I'm not talking about you," Brazen snapped, but she was too late, because Winter was already laughing despite herself. Robbed of the angry response she'd been aiming for, Brazen sneered. "Go back to school, kiddies. The rest of us are trying to do some good in the world."

She barged through them, hitting her shoulder off Winter's, and they watched her go.

"Oh, for God's sake," Mia muttered, and Winter saw Aphotic standing in the crowd with the rest of Brazen's new friends. He met Winter's eyes and then turned away.

"Come on, kiddies," Winter said. "Let's get back to school."

24

Valkyrie got up to use the bathroom. As she sat on the toilet, she gazed out of the window. It was a blue-sky morning, looking like it'd be a blue-sky day.

She hobbled back to bed, climbed slowly beneath the covers, and Militsa snuggled up to her.

"How you doing?" her girlfriend mumbled, eyes still closed.

"Feeling better," Valkyrie replied. "And there was no blood in my pee."

"Oh, well done, you."

Valkyrie moved some of Militsa's hair away from her nose, where it tickled, and lay there, looking at the ceiling. She traced her fingers along the scar that zigged and zagged up her torso. Reverie had assured her it would heal completely so long as she used her ointments. Valkyrie wasn't too worried about how it looked – it'd certainly have made bikini season interesting – but she wasn't keen on the idea of having the wound reopen at some stage in the future. She didn't like carrying weakness with her.

Militsa was handling it well, all things considered. In the

past, she'd freaked out whenever Valkyrie sustained any kind of significant injury, and concern would generally give way to random, aimless anger. Their primary source of arguments, in the old days, tended to be Valkyrie's job and the risks she took. Militsa understood what was required as an Arbiter, and she'd entered into this relationship fully aware that Valkyrie's life was fraught with danger – but there was a difference between understanding something intellectually and understanding it *actually*.

Once Militsa understood the risks *actually*, they found themselves on shaky territory where Valkyrie couldn't predict which way things would go. She hoped Militsa's love for her would overwhelm the fear of losing Valkyrie to any of the enemies or monsters or entities she tended to face on a semi-regular basis – but she couldn't be sure.

And yet here they were, sharing a home and an increasingly elderly dog, lying in bed on a Sunday morning with the sun streaming through the window, the birds singing outside, and Valkyrie recovering from a disembowelment.

If that wasn't true love, Valkyrie didn't know what was.

She dozed for a bit, and when she woke next Militsa was scrolling through her phone. Valkyrie reached for her own phone – slowly, stifling a groan of pain so as not to worry her girlfriend – and they lay like that for close to an hour, scrolling, showing each other videos, chatting and laughing about whatever there was to chat and laugh about. Then Militsa helped Valkyrie out of bed – with Valkyrie exaggerating her discomfort ever so slightly so as to garner some extra nuggets of sympathy in her time of need – and Valkyrie took a shower while Militsa headed downstairs to take Xena outside. When Valkyrie was dressed, she went down and Xena grabbed a toy in her mouth and trotted over to show her.

"Who's that you've got there?" Valkyrie said, nuzzling the dog. "You've got Mister Moo, have you? You've got Mister Moo?"

Xena had, indeed, got Mister Moo, and she happily showed off the floppy little cow toy.

By mid-afternoon, Valkyrie was feeling a lot stronger. She could walk without hobbling and bend over without groaning. Taking the dog for a run was still beyond her, however, so Militsa dropped her off outside her parents' house and continued on to the beach, Xena's tail wagging madly.

Valkyrie let herself in the front door. "Hello?" she called.

"In here!" her mother answered from the living room.

Melissa Edgley, clad in workout gear, lay sprawled, face down, on the yoga mat she'd placed in the middle of the floor. Valkyrie walked over.

"Mother," she said, "are you all right?"

Without turning her head, Melissa reached out, searched around for a moment, and then weakly tapped Valkyrie's foot. "I'm good, sweetie. I'm just doing my Pilates. I'm engaging my core."

"Are you, though? Because it looks like you've collapsed."

"Am I not moving?"

"Not even a little."

"Damn."

Melissa heaved herself up on to her elbows and turned her sweaty head towards her daughter as Valkyrie sat on the couch. "Pilates is hard," she said.

"But amusing," Valkyrie responded.

"I'm usually a lot more active than this, you know. You've caught me at the end of my session. You should have seen me at the beginning. I was a dynamo."

"I can believe it. Do you... do you want help getting up?"

"Am I not getting up right now?"

"You are not."

"Damn. I think I'll stay down here for a few minutes more – just until I get my second wind. And how are you, sweetheart?"

"I'm good," Valkyrie said. "I'm taking a day off, so I thought I'd stop by the old homestead, see how the family is. Where's Dad?"

"Playing golf with Fergus."

"Dad doesn't play golf."

"Neither does Fergus, but they've both decided that, as men of a certain age, they should start to do what men of a certain age do. Apparently, that means giving golf another try. They've been golfing every Sunday for the past month."

"Do they like it?"

"No," said her mother. "They hate it. They're miserable. But they're miserable together, so I encourage it. Men spend so little time with other men that if you don't push them to be sociable they'll end up completely alone if their wives ever decide to leave them."

"Are you planning on leaving Dad?"

"Not planning on it, no. But if he doesn't stop complaining about golf, Steph, I swear to God..."

Valkyrie grinned. "I suppose it's nice that he gets to see his brother every week."

"Fergus has started to mellow, actually," said Melissa, finally sitting up. "Ever since I've known him, he's been this stick-in-the-mud —" she searched for the right word — "curmudgeon, but in the last few years... I don't know. Maybe it's all to do with getting older. When you realise you only have so long left on this Earth, you start to appreciate the things that have always been in front of you. Not that you'll ever have to deal with stuff like that."

"You think I don't have a healthy sense of my own mortality?"

"Oh, I know you do," said Melissa, narrowing her eyes. "You've almost died a few times, have you not? Despite my pleading with you to be safe? But no — what I'm referring to here is the value you place on things and people when you age. But you don't have to experience that. You look like you're barely past twenty and how long are you going to stay like this? The next five hundred years?" Melissa sighed happily. "That lightens my heart, it really does."

She started getting up and Valkyrie eased herself off the sofa to help her stand.

"Are you hurt?" her mother asked, frowning.

"Pulled a muscle in my back this morning," Valkyrie lied. "Even sorcerers pull muscles."

"Well, yes," Melissa said, leading the way to the kitchen, "but you were probably lifting weights at the time, were you? You see, everything about you is strong and vibrant and healthy and wonderfully, eternally young."

"Not eternally."

"Eternally young," Melissa insisted. "You will be young and beautiful and healthy and happy for the next thousand years. I just know it."

Valkyrie had to smile. "OK, fine. I'll be eternally young

for a thousand years, but then I'm going to slow down, all right?"

"Deal. Would you like a coffee, sweetheart?"

"That would be lovely."

Melissa busied herself at the coffee machine beside the kettle. "I was talking to Hannah Foley's mother at the carpet shop. I'm going to get a rug for the landing so I've been looking for— Anyway, she was asking how you were, what you've been up to, and I did my usual spiel, you know, whenever anyone asks about you. I said Steph is handling her uncle's estate, dealing with lawyers, dealing with publishers, with movie studios. I said she's still living in Grimwood House with her beautiful girlfriend. I said there *might* be wedding bells, there might *not*—"

"Mum."

"—and doing all the requisite bragging that any mother would do when talking about her first-born. Without, obviously, getting to brag about all the *other* stuff you do, like saving the world, restarting the universe, and becoming God."

"I didn't restart the universe and I'm not God."

"Yes, but you *practically* did and you *practically* are, so I think I should be applauded for my restraint whenever you come up in conversation."

Valkyrie clapped once, and very lightly.

"Thank you," said Melissa. "And then I asked about Hannah. You know she has five kids now?"

"I heard that, yeah."

Her mum put Valkyrie's coffee in front of her and went back to pour a cup for herself. "I always liked Hannah. She was a bit of a handful, a bit too... nice, but generally a fine girl."

Valkyrie took a sip. "We were best friends in primary school."

Melissa turned, resting her hip against the worktop, coffee in her hand. "Her mother didn't give details but, just from the way she was talking, I got the impression that Hannah and her husband are going through something. The way she presents herself to the world – this constantly happy, bright family where everything is perfect and positive – that's not her life. That's the life she pretends to have."

"I'm not surprised," said Valkyrie. "Everyone wears a mask, don't they?"

"I suppose." Melissa drank some coffee and looked distracted for a moment. "But I used to see Hannah and her marriage and her kids and I used to worry that this was something you were going to miss out on. You and Alice. Yes, you both have magic and Alice is in wizard school and you're off saving everyone and, like we agreed, you're going to be eternally young and happy until you're at least a thousand years old and so is your sister... but the fact that you might never get to experience the smaller joys in life – that worried me."

"Not everyone needs marriage and kids, Mum."

"Absolutely," said Melissa. "And you're still young, and you're going to stay like this for centuries, so you've got time to experience it all, I suppose. You don't have to rush into marriage and you don't have to start a family until some far-flung stardate in the future. And that's great."

"But...?"

Melissa smiled. "But then I realised that the thing that was making me sad wasn't what you or Alice were going to miss out on, but what *I* was going to miss out on. So my worries, actually, weren't even about you – they were about me. Hannah's mother, no matter what else was going on, she had her daughter and she had her grandchildren. And I could just see the love. It radiated from her."

"You want grandchildren," said Valkyrie.

"It's selfish, but a part of me does, yes. And, OK, your father and I realised early on that you might be far too busy to provide any, but at least we'll have Alice, you know? Alice can get married, Alice can start a family, your dad can be a grandfather and I can be the cool nana who bakes apple tarts and is always there with little bits of advice for everyone while the granddad potters about behind her like some kind of delusional idiot."

"That *is* my father."

"But now, with Alice being magic and her life opening up in the ways that yours did... It's great for her, and it's great for you. It's not so great for your dad and me."

"I can see how that would be the case."

"I don't want you to change your plans. I'm not asking for it and I'm not expecting it. I want you and Alice to follow your own course. So I'm not saying any of this to persuade you one way or the other. I think I'm just saying it because your dad and I are getting old."

"You're not old."

"I said *getting* old," Melissa responded. "And getting old is a strange sensation. I still think of myself as someone in their late thirties – maybe early forties, depending on how long I spend recovering after Pilates. Basically, you're forever in my head as a teenager, and I'm forever the mother of a teenager. I never expected to get old. I knew it was coming, technically, but it's something that happens to other people, and maybe your father, while I remain young and laugh at him."

"But you're still the mother of a teenager," said Valkyrie. "Fair enough, it's not me, but even so..."

"I suppose," Melissa said, coming forward to sit opposite. "And I'm still making all kinds of new mistakes that, in theory, should keep me feeling young." She took another sip of coffee. "Alice is not like you."

Valkyrie grinned. "I'm aware."

"And I mean she's *really* not like you. You were a model child. You had your moments, don't get me wrong, but you never really caused us any great worry. Granted, if we'd known you were out risking your life every day, that might have affected our opinion, but you weren't stroppy, you weren't argumentative, you didn't storm through the house, slamming doors..."

"I saved all my arguments for Skulduggery."

Melissa smiled. "Then he was welcome to them. But Alice..."

"Should we be talking about this where she can overhear us?"

Melissa waved a hand. "She's up in her room. Whenever she's home from wizard school, she's up in her room. She ventures down for food and then she's right back up there. Whatever we managed to do with you, we're completely failing with her. Do you have any advice? Do you remember something I ever said or did that got you firmly on my side, or snapped you out of a bad mood, or impacted you in any positive way whatsoever?"

"Nothing that springs to mind."

Her mother sighed.

"I mean..." Valkyrie said.

"Yes? What? Any advice, Steph, would be hugely appreciated."

"Maybe she'd be in a better mood if you called her by her taken name."

Melissa folded her arms. "Her name is Alice."

Valkyrie winced. "Not any more, though."

"I understand the name thing, and I understand how important it is, but her name is still Alice in this house. You don't mind that we call you Stephanie. You never did. You were never offended by that. But she's choosing to be offended by this." A moment passed, and Melissa frowned. "You are OK with us calling you Stephanie, aren't you?"

"I mean, yeah," said Valkyrie. "Sure."

Melissa stared. "Oh, God. You're not OK with it."

"It's just that Stephanie isn't my name," Valkyrie said, shrugging, "and it hasn't been since I was twelve."

"But we named you Stephanie! I love the name Stephanie! I also love the name Valkyrie, of course I do, but it's..." Melissa paused, and exhaled. "I'm in the wrong, aren't I?"

"This isn't about being in the wrong."

"Des said that I've got to start respecting Alice's decisions. It's just... it's so hard. Calling her by another name confirms that she's not my little girl any more. I don't want her to grow up. You grew up way too fast."

"Mum, she's fifteen."

"She's still my little girl. So are you, for that matter. One day, when you do have kids of your own, you'll understand."

Valkyrie smiled. "You respected me when I was her age. She deserves that much, at least."

"I know." Melissa nodded. "OK. I'll make a concerted effort to try it out. That's the best I can do right now."

"I think that'd improve things between you," Valkyrie said. "She's in her room now?"

"Go on up. Say hi. Put in a good word for me."

Valkyrie smiled, finished her coffee, and kissed the top of her mother's head. She went upstairs and knocked on the door to her old bedroom.

"Hey," she said. "Can I come in?"

There was a pause. "Sure."

Valkyrie opened the door and stepped in. "Hey, Winter."

25

"Hey," Winter responded.

Valkyrie, wearing jeans and a top that showed exactly how much time she spent in the gym, closed the door behind her. Winter had been trying lately to not let those things get to her, but it wasn't easy. No matter how tall she got, Valkyrie was taller. No matter how strong she got, Valkyrie was stronger. No matter how good she got, Valkyrie was better.

She watched as her sister looked around, probably noticing every little change. This used to be her room. The desk used to be her desk. The bed used to be her bed. When Valkyrie sat on the end of it, there was probably a teeny-tiny thought in the back of her mind, like, *This is the bed I slept in after I saved the world that time.*

Winter had never saved the world. Winter had never wanted to.

"How are the exams going?"

Winter shrugged. "I'll know when I get the results."

"Feeling confident?"

Winter shrugged again.

Valkyrie nodded. She glanced at the wardrobe, the only piece of furniture that hadn't once been hers. "How's your reflection working out?" she asked. "Making things easier?"

"Not really," said Winter. "We're not allowed to get them to do homework and we still have to take the exams ourselves. The only thing it does is go to all these extra classes so at the end of the day I actually have more work to do, not less."

"Ah," said Valkyrie. "Have you talked to China about it?"

"Principal Sorrows is your friend. Not mine."

A text came in from Mia, and Winter answered. As her fingers danced over the screen, she glanced up. "I can text and talk at the same time, you know."

"Of course," said Valkyrie. "So what's been going on? Anything much? I thought you Corrival students were always getting into adventures, but I haven't heard one peep from you on that front."

"No adventures to report, sorry."

"Maybe next year, right?"

Winter gave another shrug. "Maybe. Or maybe adventures are more your thing."

She put the phone away, enjoying the look of awkwardness on her big sister's face.

"Yeah," Valkyrie said. "I suppose. Hey, you want to get back to some sparring? I could pick you up next week when the exams are over and—"

"No, it's OK," said Winter. "Combat class keeps me well practised."

"But you'll need to keep your skills up over the summer."

"I'll be grand."

Valkyrie nodded. "Right. How's everyone? How's Mia and Brazen?"

"Mia's good, but I haven't been friends with Brazen for a while."

"Oh. Sorry, I should have known that. So, like, term ends in a few days, right? You gonna meet up with Mia over the summer?"

"Probably not."

Valkyrie pulled her leg in, curled it under herself like they were gal pals settling down for a heart-to-heart. "Winter, is everything OK? I get that you might not want to talk to me about it. I was the same. I didn't see the point in talking about my feelings or what I was going through. I figured I could deal with it. And I could. I know that you can, too, but I had Skulduggery in my corner, and that meant the world to me. I knew that no matter what happened, what I went through, what I did... I knew there was someone there who would understand, who wouldn't judge me. I could be your Skulduggery, if you need me to."

Winter looked deep into her sister's eyes. "No, I'm grand, thanks."

It was funny, the expression on Valkyrie's face, the disappointment mixed with annoyance. Winter had to fight not to break out into a grin.

"Cool," said Valkyrie, and she got up off the bed that used to be hers. "If you want to come take Xena for a walk over the next few days, just let me know, OK?"

Winter would have loved to take Xena for a walk. "I'll probably be busy," she said, eyes back on her phone.

She was aware of Valkyrie nodding and then leaving the room, heading back to whatever adventure she was in the middle of. Back to Skulduggery, the dark and dangerous partner. Back to Militsa, the gorgeous and awesomely cool girlfriend. Back to her life as a hero with the perfect amount of dark edge to make her interesting – the dark edge that should have been Winter's.

Once upon a time, Alice Edgley had been on track to become the Child of the Faceless Ones, to call herself Malice, to embark on an adventure of her own. But instead of allowing her to experience this, to fight her own battles, to find her own way out of the darkness and back into the light, Valkyrie had decided, without consultation, to take on that burden. To take on that responsibility. It wasn't enough that she'd already had her adventure. It wasn't enough that her true name had gained sentience. It wasn't enough for Darquesse to go from being the universe's greatest threat to its greatest hero. That wasn't enough for Valkyrie Cain, oh no. She just had to snatch Winter's journey away from her before Winter had even taken her first step.

And what did that leave Winter with?

A life where all the difficult decisions had been made for her. A life that may have had meaning once, but was now so anodyne, so sterile, so safe that it was impossible to view it as anything but a cotton-wool, mollycoddled existence. Winter had gone bowling once, when she was a kid, and her life was like a bowling alley with those plastic bumpers in the gutters – a life without risk. A life without the possibility of failure.

Valkyrie had robbed so much from her – had robbed her of the person she would have otherwise become – that there were now parts of Winter's life that she refused to share, even though she knew that sharing might help. Because despite Valkyrie's best efforts, despite the things she had done through love and devotion, there had been traumas inflicted upon Winter that Valkyrie knew nothing about. Traumas that reverberated, that ricocheted against the corners of her mind. In seeking to protect her little sister from the pain and horror she could see coming, Valkyrie had allowed in *new* pain and *new* horrors that she hadn't anticipated. That she wasn't even aware of.

Winter loved her sister. There had been a time when her sister had been her absolute hero, when she had been everything Winter wanted to be when she grew up.

Now there was a piece of Winter who ever so slightly hated her.

26

Valkyrie started Monday with a jog. Xena accompanied her halfway, then lay down in the shade to rest and waited for her to complete her usual circuit. When Valkyrie returned, she stood up, tail wagging, then trotted beside her back inside.

Valkyrie showered and had breakfast. She was feeling good. Feeling strong. Reggie called and told her he had some new test results from the wand. She took one of the bikes – the BMW R nineT – to the High Sanctuary and parked next to the Bentley where Skulduggery was waiting for her.

"You're pleased with yourself," she said, hanging her helmet from the handlebars.

"I haven't said one word," he replied.

"You've got that look on your face."

"My façade isn't up."

"I'm not talking about your façade." She swung her leg off the bike. "I'm talking about your face."

"The one I don't have?"

"That's the one. What's happened?"

"Something happened to Rumour Mills six years ago," he said. "Something traumatic enough to trigger a life-changing depression."

"The Faceless Ones appeared and the world went to hell."

"Yes. It struck me that when digging into Rumour's life there are two pasts requiring investigation. Just because the world has moved beyond the Deletion doesn't mean all the people have. I went over the accounts of what happened back then, and it seems that the Faceless One over Dublin—"

"Khrthauk."

"—had, in its intangible state, been standing with one of its feet – or paws, or claws – on or near the road outside Rumour's apartment building. If the horror group kept to its regular schedule, according to the messages on Niamh Cairns' phone, then this would have happened on an evening when they were due to meet up."

"So that's where they'd have been when Khrthauk became corporeal."

"Indeed. They would have been faced with a monster appearing right outside the front door, obliterating everything within the space it occupied. At which point, of course, the entire world fell apart."

"And you think this has something to do with why Ersatz is killing them?"

"It may not – but we have to keep in mind that we should be looking for possible motivation in two different timestreams."

Valkyrie stared at him. "Why would you want to make this any more complicated than it already is?"

"The world got complicated all by itself without any help from me."

"That's not exactly true, though, is it?"

"Well… fair enough, no. It was my idea to send someone back in time to recruit Darquesse so I suppose you could argue that these unnecessary complications are *all* my fault, but then you'd have to admit that my idea saved all of existence and I know you hate doing that, so let's move on."

"Let's. OK, so the horror group were together when this happened. Now that we know this, we can speculate on what happened next. And you have that look on your face again."

"The face I don't have."

"What new piece of information are you going to astound me with?"

"The Faceless Ones announced their presence and the mortals' initial response was to attack," Skulduggery said. "When their first attempts didn't work, there was a slight pause as the world reassessed how to deal with the problem – and in that pause the Shalgoth emerged. Mortals were being slaughtered in the streets by the Faceless Ones' little pets."

"Little?"

"Relatively little."

"Monsters the size of trucks."

"The Shalgoth first appeared in Dublin, and then they were everywhere, in every city around the world, in every town, wherever there were people. But one of the first locations they were reported was at Khrthauk's clawed foot – on Rumour's street."

"So if the horror group was still there, if they were too

scared to leave, or if their building was damaged and they were stuck, the Shalgoth would have gone straight for them."

Skulduggery nodded. "And what would Rumour have done?"

"She'd have fought back. In front of her friends. Her mortal friends who had, until recently, no idea that magic existed, and *absolutely* no idea that Rumour was a sorcerer."

"The question now becomes," Skulduggery said, "what happened then?"

The tiles brought them to the foyer and they took the elevator to the Research and Development Department. The doors pinged open and a man went to step in before he noticed them. He froze, staring first at Skulduggery and then at Valkyrie.

"Hey," Valkyrie said, giving him a nod. He didn't respond, just continued to stare in that starstruck way. This kind of thing tended to happen a lot in Roarhaven, even in the High Sanctuary.

Skulduggery stepped out first, and then Valkyrie squeezed by. The man watched them go. They found Professor Regatta in his office.

"Come in, come in," he said, barely looking up from the papers spread over his desk. "Detective Cain, I hope you're feeling better. These are the readings we've just taken from the wand. We had to completely recalibrate our instruments – we even had to build a new scanner from scratch, just to take into account what we're dealing with. Do you see? Do you?"

There were stacks of graphs and mathematical equations. Valkyrie stared at them, eyes moving from one to the other, and she gasped out, "I'm so bored."

Skulduggery picked up two of the sheets, held them beside each other, and tilted his head. "These are accurate, I assume?"

"Yes," Regatta said excitedly.

"When you told Valkyrie the wand was capable of doing anything... you weren't exaggerating."

"The wand generates a sort of..."

"A warp in physics," Skulduggery said.

"Yes. Exactly. We're calling it an Unreality Field. Fuelled by the wielder's magic and directed by sheer intent, the wand rewrites the rules as it goes. It is, judged purely on the basis of everything we know about both physics and magic, an impossible device and yet, obviously, it exists."

"Do we know where it came from?"

"We do not."

"Do we know whose rib it's made from?"

"We do not."

"Professor, would I be right in saying that this wand is possibly one of the most powerful weapons on the planet?"

"You absolutely would, Detective."

Skulduggery nodded. "Then we'll be taking it with us."

Regatta's delighted smile dropped off completely. "What? But our tests—"

"You'll be able to continue with your tests," Skulduggery said, "but only when Valkyrie or I are in attendance. We trust you, we absolutely do, and we trust Grand Mage Bespoke, but we do not trust the Sanctuary system. We cannot risk a weapon such as this falling into the hands of those who would use it for their own gain."

"Detective Pleasant, this is a far too—"

"Professor – this wand could change everything. If we'd

had this when Mevolent attacked, one flick of the wrist and the threat would have ended. If we'd had this when the Faceless Ones attacked, we could have wiped them away in an instant, yes?"

"Assuming you had some experience using it... yes."

"It could ensure this world's safety and survival for centuries to come, if not longer."

"All the more reason to carefully study and catalogue its qualities."

"All the more reason to keep it away from self-serving leaders and the people they prioritise."

Regatta rubbed his face with his hands. "And you think you should be the ones entrusted with it?"

"Arbiters answer to no one, Professor."

"Surely you're not so naive as to believe that, Detective. You are Irish, based here in Ireland. You have close ties with the Irish Sanctuary. If it came down to it, you would prioritise us, you would prioritise your home, over any other people or territory that was under threat."

"You're quite right," Skulduggery said. "Not even we are truly impartial. But, right now, we're the closest thing to incorruptible that this world has got. Plus... we brought the wand in. It's ours to do with as we choose."

"And you'll still be able to study it," Valkyrie said, "but be honest, Reggie – do you trust the people in charge to act in the best interests of everyone, or do you think they'd use the wand to secure their own position *before* lending aid to whoever else needed it?"

"I don't trust anyone to do anything," Regatta answered. "That's why I chose science. Science doesn't take sides. But if you two are holding yourselves up as paragons of virtue,

I'm afraid I'd have to object. Everyone who knows about you, everyone who's ever heard about the things you've done, would all agree on one thing: you value each other more than anyone else. What is that thing you say? What was it I read in that transcript from years ago? Oh, yes. *Until the end.* It's Skulduggery Pleasant and Valkyrie Cain, together against the world. You're not any more or less incorruptible than the rest of us. All it takes is the right sort of leverage."

Skulduggery tilted his head. "We'll be taking the wand now, Professor."

Regatta sighed, and got up, and they followed him out of the office and down the corridor, towards the laboratories. He got them through the security doors and past the scanners and into the Restricted Area. But when they got to the lab where the three metal sticks kept the wand hovering between them, the sticks were there, but the wand was gone.

27

"Professor?" Skulduggery said quietly.

Regatta practically lunged to the other side of the desk, as if the wand might have just fallen out of sight. He turned, spinning in place, eyes scanning the floor and then the pristine, ordered tables around him.

"This isn't..." he said. "This shouldn't..."

He slapped a button on the desk and, after a chime, a voice answered. "Hello, Reginald. What can I—?"

"The wand," Regatta interrupted. "Do you have it?"

"Do I—? No, I don't have it. You have it. It's in your lab."

"It's not here. It's gone."

"It can't be gone," said the scientist on the other end. "The wand can't just—"

Regatta slapped the button again, ending the conversation, and looked up at Skulduggery and Valkyrie. "It was here twenty minutes ago. We'd just finished the latest tests and I was retrieving the results and I put it back. I put it back here."

"Is there a log?" Skulduggery asked. "A log of who entered this lab?"

Regatta ran to a monitor, waved his hand in front of the screen to activate it, and tapped on the hard-light keyboard that materialised on the table before him. Seconds dragged by.

"Shrill," he said at last. "Tomoltach Shrill. Sanctuary operative. I don't know him. Look."

He turned the monitor to them. Footage played from the camera in the ceiling, showing a man hurrying over to the wand. The man they'd passed as they got out of the elevator.

"Access the rest of the cameras," Skulduggery said to Regatta as Valkyrie bolted to the doors. "Find where he's gone."

She sprinted through the Restricted Area, scattering scientists in her path.

"I'll go down," Skulduggery called from behind her. "You go out."

She veered towards the first window she came to, blasted it apart, and leaped through. The wind whipped at her hair and her clothes and her magic ignited, tripling the speed of her descent to street level. She pulled up, her energy singeing the uppermost leaves on one of the trees planted along the pavement. Shrill wasn't on the steps of the High Sanctuary and he wasn't hurrying away, not that she could see. How long since he'd taken that elevator down? Six minutes? Eight? He could be anywhere by now. If he had access to a Teleporter – or if he knew how to use the wand to teleport himself – he could literally be anywhere.

Her phone buzzed and she landed in a run, accidentally barging into a group of people and then apologising as she took the phone out.

"He left the High Sanctuary four minutes ago, through

the main doors," said Regatta. "I don't have access to the cameras outside the building."

"Call Tanith," Valkyrie instructed. "Tell her to locate him, then call Skulduggery and fill him in."

She put the phone away and blasted off again. A four-minute head start. He could have crossed the square or hopped into a car or taken a tram or stayed on foot. Keeping low, skimming over the roofs of moving vehicles, Valkyrie flew up one street and down the next. She was never going to find him like this.

She pulled up, flying now for Shudder's Gate. By the time she got there, the Cleavers were already stopping people from leaving. She landed on a rooftop, slapping at her smouldering jeans. Her T-shirt was already scorched beyond repair. She called Skulduggery.

"Tanith found him and then lost him," he told her. "He'd already sabotaged the surveillance cameras, but she tracked him heading for the gate."

"I'm there now," Valkyrie responded. "No one's getting past those Cleavers."

"Hold on," Skulduggery said, his voice becoming slightly fainter as he moved his phone away. "I'm reading his file. He's an Elemental – described as an adequate flier."

Valkyrie scanned the wall that encircled the city and saw movement. "Got him," she said. "To the west of the gate."

Phone stuffed back in her pocket, she ran and jumped off the edge of the rooftop, piling on the speed. Ever since Skulduggery had unlocked the secret to flight, Elementals around the world had been struggling to master the ability like he had. None of them had managed to even approach his level, yet the increasing number of serious injuries, not to mention fatalities, had not deterred them from trying.

Tomoltach Shrill may have been listed as adequate, but as she watched him hover unsteadily over the top of the wall, Valkyrie realised that the standard must be pretty damn low.

"Hey there," she said, snatching the back of his jacket and yanking him off course.

Shrill screamed and flailed, grabbing on to her wrists so tightly he was going to leave bruises, and Valkyrie did not bruise easily.

"Please let me down!" he shrieked. "Please!"

She angled them towards the ground on the other side of the wall. Although her grip was strong, he was still about to slip from her hands, and she reflected that her decision to carry him had been the wrong one.

The long grass of a meadow zoomed towards them and Valkyrie did her best to slow before they hit, but that just made Shrill drop from her grip. He cried out in pain as he landed and she tried to pull up, but went tumbling through the grass instead. Such a landing was no big deal in her necronaut suit. Doing it in jeans and a T-shirt was something else entirely.

She came to a stop and groaned, looking up at the blue sky. While Shrill continued to yell, Skulduggery came into view, drifting gently down to land beside her.

"That was very impressive," he said.

"Shut up."

She got up. Her elbow was bleeding and the knees were torn out of her jeans, which were smoking slightly due to her energy expenditure, but that seemed to be the extent of the damage. Her wound hadn't reopened and her insides were good.

Shrill got to his feet, too, then stumbled. His face was ashen and his leg looked broken. He reached into his jacket.

Skulduggery pulled out his gun and thumbed back the hammer in the same instant that Valkyrie raised her hand, which crackled with energy.

"Do not move," Skulduggery warned.

Shrill froze. "Please don't shoot me."

"Take your hand out of your pocket and I won't have to."

A nod, and Shrill complied.

"Why'd you do it?" Valkyrie asked.

"You don't understand," said Shrill. "Ersatz has my wife and children. I had to take the wand or... or my family..."

"You could have come to us," Skulduggery told him.

"I was warned what would happen if I did. I wanted to. Of course I wanted to. I didn't want anything to do with that psychopath, but my family..."

"What do you know about Ersatz?"

"Nothing," said Shrill. "Nothing I haven't seen reported on the Network or heard around the High Sanctuary. If you're looking for a name or a description or a location, I'm sorry. I don't know anything. My wife and children went missing and I got a phone call and a picture and... I had to steal the wand."

Shrill's phone rang in his pocket – the same pocket he'd been reaching for. He licked his lips nervously. "I have to answer that."

Skulduggery tilted his head. "Is that Ersatz?"

"I don't know. I have to answer it."

"Loudspeaker."

Shrill pulled out his phone and jabbed the screen.

A woman's voice – relief bordering on hysteria. "We're safe. Sweetie? We're here. We're safe."

"Oh, thank God," Shrill said, and sobbed. "Oh, thank God."

Skulduggery stepped closer to the phone. "This is Skulduggery Pleasant. Who took you?"

"Oh," the woman said. "Um, a man. A man in a mask."

"Where is he now?"

"Gone. We were in a van. He left us alone a few minutes ago and we just got free."

"Where are you?" Valkyrie asked. "Did he say anything?"

"He didn't say one word. He grabbed us and tied us up and put us in the van. Then he drove us here and parked and he waited for a bit, and then he left."

"Drove you where? Where are you?"

"Roarhaven. We're at the corner of Languid Street, right where it meets the Circle Zone. Where's Tomoltach? I want to speak to Tomoltach."

"I'm here," said Shrill. "You're sure you're OK? You're sure the kids are OK?"

"They were so brave, sweetie. I was so proud of them. They're OK. They're not hurt. What happens now?"

"Your husband will call you back in a few minutes," said Valkyrie, and nodded to Shrill. He said goodbye to his wife and hung up. She held out her hand. "Wand."

Shrill hesitated. "I don't have it."

"You stashed it?"

"I was told to leave it at the base of the clock monument in the Circle."

Valkyrie glanced at Skulduggery and he swept both hands

233

up and a wave of air lifted her. The wind propelled her halfway up the wall, at which point her own magic kicked in and she cleared the top of it and then, like a missile, aimed herself directly at the Circle Zone, passing over Languid Street at the van that was parked there.

She landed in a run, snagged the monument to stop from overshooting, and checked around it. Nothing. No wand. There were a few people sitting by the fountain across the way and she ran over.

"Did you see anyone by the clock?" she asked. "Anyone stop to pick something up? Anyone in the last few minutes?"

"Hey," said one of the men, "you're Valkyrie Cain."

"Did you see anyone by the clock?" she said, louder now.

They blinked, and shook their heads. They hadn't noticed. Of course they hadn't noticed. No one had. She turned, looking around. She doubted the CCTV cameras had picked up anything, either. Ersatz was careful about things like that.

Skulduggery landed beside her, letting Tomoltach Shrill limp over to the fountain to sit.

"He has it," she said. "Ersatz has the wand back." She glared at Shrill. "You were told to lead us away, weren't you?"

"I'm sorry," he muttered, then looked up, lurched to his feet and hobbled over to his wife and kids, as they ran up, tears in their eyes.

Valkyrie wiped the blood from her knee. "I am so sick of this. How does he know? How is he always one step ahead?"

"One step ahead, or several," Skulduggery said, "sooner or later Ersatz will stumble. And then we'll have him."

28

Xena used to tear round Haggard beach, chasing after sticks and diving into the crashing waves. When Winter took her for walks, it was a full-time job trying to keep her under control. Xena obeyed every command Valkyrie uttered, but for everyone else she'd been a demon of energy and unpredictability.

Those days, it seemed, were gone.

Winter had last taken her for a walk months ago, just after Christmas, and she'd been her usual self. Time, however, had caught up with her, and today she walked at Winter's side happily, no longer interested in the things that used to distract her. They met a mortal and a small dog coming the other way and the small dog yapped and jumped against his lead and Xena practically rolled her eyes as they passed.

Winter sat on a rock, looking out to sea, and Xena lay down beside her, tongue hanging out. It was a gorgeous evening.

"Cute doggy."

Winter looked round, then quickly stood.

Alter Veers approached. He was slender and clean-shaven, his lip, nose, ears, and eyebrow pierced, in black jeans and a tattered hoody. Tattoos curled up his neck and peeked out at his wrists. He pulled down his hood. His hair was blue.

Xena sat up, wary.

"Easy, girl," said Winter.

"You know who I am?" asked Alter.

"How did you find me?"

"I can find anyone."

"Not me," said Winter.

"You *were* more difficult than most," Alter said, smiling. "Do any of your friends know who you are? Who your sister is? No? Not even Mia? That's interesting. I hope I don't upset you too much, turning up like this. I know how much you value your privacy."

"You don't know anything about me," Winter said.

Alter smiled. "I know a little. When you started at Corrival, I didn't have a clue who you were. I never even noticed you. You were just like all the other First Years, wandering around, confused and frightened and hilarious. But then a friend of mine, whose parents worked in the High Sanctuary, pointed you out one day and said, 'See her, that blonde girl? That's Valkyrie Cain's sister.'"

"I mean, I was shocked. I was. Because this friend, she'd already told me everything that she'd learned about you from her parents. How you were supposed to be the Child of the Faceless Ones. How you were supposed to grow up to be Malice, this uber-powerful sorcerer, and how you came back from the future as sentient energy. *Sentient energy*, man! How cool is that? And not only was there a version of you that was sentient energy, and not only did it travel back in

236

time, but it travelled back from a future that no longer exists! *What?* My mind, Winter! Mind blown!"

Winter watched him, said nothing.

"My friend told me that this version of you, this Malice, is still around. Is that right? She's kept in a Soul Catcher in the High Sanctuary or Coldheart Prison or somewhere. Doesn't that freak you out? There is an older version of you, of who you are, of who you were meant to be, and she's sitting in a Soul Catcher. I don't know. That would seriously mess with my head."

Alter thought about it some more, and gave a little laugh. "Anyway, when my friend pointed you out, I thought no way. No way can that little girl be the great and powerful Malice. No way is she Valkyrie Cain's sister."

"Sorry to disappoint you," Winter said.

"But that's exactly it," said Alter. "You don't disappoint me, Winter – not at all – though I can understand why you'd think that. Those thoughts must be in your head constantly, am I right? You're the sister of a living legend. Valkyrie Cain isn't just the detective or the badass or the hero, she's... I hope you don't mind me saying this, but she's *everything*. She's so freakin' *hot*. She's beautiful and tall and strong and confident and she's mean and tough and she doesn't care what anyone thinks. Not everyone loves her – loads of people hate her – but she doesn't care about that, either. She's just so goddamn *cool*, Winter. Your sister is *cool*."

"She's pretty cool, all right."

"And don't get me wrong. You're cool, too. From what I've heard, you're also smart as hell – the kind of smart that you try to hide. Would I be right? Do we have a budding genius on our hands? My point is, you've got everything

237

you need to be a legend – but you're never going to get the chance, are you?" Alter shook his head sadly. "You're trapped in your sister's shadow. And that's where you're gonna stay – unless you can find a way out. Unless you can forge your own identity."

"And that's why you're here, is it?" Winter asked. "To help me forge my own identity?"

"If anyone knows about forging their own identity, you're looking at him. What, you think this was easy to come by? This person you see before you? Nuh-uh. I had to fight to be who I am. I had to fight *myself*. I was born in the wrong body, for one thing. I came into the world in the body of a girl and I didn't realise until it was too late to say, 'Uh, hello, excuse me? Someone has obviously made a dreadful mistake...' It took me years to figure myself out, years to reconcile how I viewed myself compared to how everyone else saw me. And it's not over yet. Although –" he leaned forward – "have you heard? There's a new procedure. A group of doctors – sorcerers, obviously – in Seattle have come up with a way to flip your gender."

Winter raised an eyebrow. "Seriously?"

"Flip it," said Alter. "Like a switch. Well, maybe not like a switch. I don't know too much about it, but wouldn't that be amazing? It'd change the world – especially for people like me. Born a girl? Flip the switch, and your own body is now the opposite gender. Even cisgendered people would want to give that a go! Wouldn't you like to live as a male version of yourself for twenty-four hours? I'm not sure which side I come down on – this enterprise is riddled with ethical quandaries – but it would appear that gender-flipping might very well be the way of the future."

"And what does any of this have to do with me?"

Alter smiled. "I look at you and I see someone who needs to forge their own identity, just like I did."

"You want to recruit me."

"I do, yeah. I think the Order of the Ancients would be lucky to have you. Hell, give it a few years and you'll be running the show."

"Your current leader might not be overly thrilled about that."

"Imperator Dominax is way too limited. You're not. You're a freakin' *leader*, Winter. You've got power and you've got brains. You're what we need."

"But I'm not a bigot."

"Me neither. I just don't like mortals."

"You realise how risky this is, don't you? Trying to recruit the sister of Valkyrie Cain? One word from me and she'd swoop in and crush the Order under her boot. You think you have anyone who could stand against her? And if she brings Skulduggery along, forget it."

Alter shrugged. "Yeah, it's a risk – but it's a risk with or without Valkyrie in the mix. I talked to Brazen about recruiting you, around the time we were recruiting her, and she said no way. I asked her again before coming to see you today. Know what she said? She said if Winter says yes, if she agrees to join, she'll be lying. She'll take the opportunity to look around, gather names and information, and then she'll use it against us. Brazen doesn't even know who your sister is, and she still can only see you as the hero in this equation."

"Which would make you the villain."

"Or it would make Brazen kinda biased," Alter said,

grinning. "You're sick of living in Valkyrie's shadow? Well, Brazen's sick of living in yours."

"That's why she joined your lot?" asked Winter. "Because she wants her moment in the spotlight?"

"That's a part of it, yeah."

Winter considered this. "That's a little pathetic."

"See, that's what I was thinking."

"What about Aphotic? Did you ask him?"

Alter sighed. "That boy just repeats what Brazen says. He doesn't give a damn about the cause or the mission – he's just besotted with Brazen. I mean, whatever. It's not like we're ever going to use him for anything. He's just there to make up the numbers at speeches."

"Brazen has a point, though. If I do join you, how could you trust me?"

"I wouldn't," Alter said. "Not initially. But if you give us a chance I think I could persuade you that what we're doing is necessary, and right. We can't live with the mortals – you know that. Everyone knows that."

"Why aren't you advocating peaceful isolation? Why are Imperator Dominax and all his lackeys preaching violence?"

"Because violence will get the job done faster," Alter replied. "If we strike against the mortals, if we leave bodies in our wake, we risk magic being exposed. We don't *want* it exposed, God, no. We've all seen what would happen in that scenario. But we're willing to run the risk if it means the Sanctuaries will pull out of the mortal sphere sooner rather than later."

"So you want more cities like Roarhaven?"

"Roarhaven is a beginning, but it's not the end point.

Tell me why. Tell me why Roarhaven isn't our idea of paradise."

Winter watched him. "Because it's surrounded by mortals."

Alter smiled. "Exactly."

"So what do you want? You want mages to have our own country?"

"Essentially, yes."

"And you don't care how many mortals you have to kill to get it?"

"*Au contraire, mon amie.* We absolutely *do* care how many mortals we kill. The higher the body count, the louder the message."

"I don't want to kill anyone."

"So help us find another way. You don't want us to take lives? Then point us at another target. I'll happily destroy some property, blow up some pipelines, disrupt some systems... But it's got to be effective. It's got to get the conversation started."

"You realise you're inviting me into a terrorist organisation in order to change the fundamental nature of that organisation?"

Alter shrugged. "I'm just shaking things up, Winter. So, what's it gonna be? You interested in joining us, or what?"

"If I say yes, it'd just be to spy."

"Then are you interested in spying on us, or what?"

"Sure," she said. "I'll spy on you."

29

Valkyrie couldn't sleep.

She got up a little after dawn and drove to Roarhaven and worked out in the gym. She showered and had breakfast. By the time she got to the High Sanctuary, it was approaching seven. Skulduggery was late, and she didn't fancy hanging around the foyer in case she bumped into Cerise, who was still annoyed at them for luring Cyrus Elysian out into the open and getting him killed.

Valkyrie went up to the security floor, to the office that had been allocated to the Arbiters – the office they rarely used, with the window looking out over Roarhaven. The city was waking, stirring to life. The morning sun cast a deep shadow along the wall, but glowed golden upon the streets and avenues. All those sorcerers, and all those mortals from another dimension. Her life sometimes seemed like it had come straight from one of her uncle's books. She liked that.

She turned from the window and picked up a large brown envelope from Skulduggery's desk. She flipped it over to the sticker on the other side, where a typewritten message read:

```
Fo. the attention of ?iste.
Skuldugge.y Pleasant and ?iss Valky.ie
Xain
```

Valkyrie slid her fingernail under the flap, tearing it open smoothly. From it, she drew out a single page with a photograph paper-clipped to it.

Oh, hell.

She placed the envelope, the page, and the photograph on the desk and took out her phone. Skulduggery answered.

"He sent us another letter," she said, "and a picture. A photo. Handsome Whitlock tied to a chair."

"I've just got into the building," he replied. "I'll be right there."

Valkyrie put the phone away, then took a pair of latex gloves from the desk drawer and put them on. She picked up the envelope. In the top right-hand corner was a stylised skull in a circle, complete with date, that the Sanctuary stamped on whatever piece of mail came in. The package had been delivered two days ago – the day after Handsome went missing. Since then, it had been sitting on the desk in this office they barely used.

She put the envelope down, ignoring the photograph for the moment, ignoring the dried blood on Handsome's face and the look of terror in his eyes, and focused on the letter.

It was three paragraphs of utter gibberish.

```
O dv srftt yd kye ulof foiysyg. S
fytpfk htkjyt fymgtmj npgyf bydffhtg yu
ijt hruyvutbtg ttylf yg hpn myovk
jdh. O dv mui jdmovk goc. Ekfy p hp
```

pg mui guu ni yev ktdiohtvdiouc noi tdijtu o dv sv tmfitovrvi ph fifioby. Njypg vifi nt gojhrg. Duvrutntg o ulovg o kfbt xrtc nuum hyt ulof. Ijdi o kfbt crnyt myrv libfm. Ulsu t jdmr dhedod myrv f etfouc. Uup fu cpu pmgytfisvh ijdi bo bpnypvd dur dhttysgo hrdh.

Jdcffynt tjpikunl pg sjurdhu gysg xiu tjtljtu jt td uy nt ktdcyth s uyniytduu yyoytrny gyotcff ym iyi. P hpoxy ulof td d irfi uup ephh ifdf. T fupnu opo ftt nsifnjy. Uupt utnt td umry.

Opo ftt f fyfhuc nyyijly gyev xu furdus. D hoyy euhg hykjyf mo s ftmjhr dutut. S flsyg fyyevtmj tm d uou yg uf. Uupt ifdftmj ephk vyy my nuytvyf, ffbt urylsig ni ijt gojymu hrdh, jtffpch mfvh ip rft. Htkjtmj td dhk iyi kfbt ybtu ntym jypg jpy. Ty pg s uuspi et gjdur. Ry yky dkfnth. Yky ttkttiydxkt jrr. Xruiry ip rfkh tmuy yky npgyf fmg urlymv yiy fmbyduytf tm ulr uijtueuukg. T ephk fymg opo ip byru ijtv duym.

Valkyrie was still trying to decipher it when Skulduggery strode in. His hat flew to the hatstand in the corner and he stood beside her.

"I see," he said.

"It's been here two days," she told him. "We might be too late. Handsome could already be dead."

"Let's operate on the assumption that he is not," said Skulduggery.

"Yeah. OK, cool. That's a lot cheerier than what I was thinking. Do you recognise the code? It's different from the last one. Maybe if we turn it the other way round." She tilted her head. "No, now it's just upside down. Do we have a mirror? Maybe it's backwards."

"I appreciate your enthusiasm for the oblique, Valkyrie, but it would appear, with the use of punctuation and paragraphs, to be a straightforward substitution code. Nothing overly complicated."

"So how do we crack it?"

"The first thing you do is look for single-letter words – these are going to be either *a* or *I*. Once you have them, you can look for double letters. The English language only has a certain amount of letters that double up in a word. From that point on, you can start playing hangman with what you know, and the rest should fall into place."

"OK," said Valkyrie. "So what's it say?"

"I have no idea. It's not obeying the rules. Ersatz, it seems, has decided to be awkward." He picked up the envelope. "But this is interesting."

"A question mark instead of the letter *M*," Valkyrie said, "a full stop instead of *R*, and an *X* instead of a *C*. Is he being sloppy, or is this part of the code?"

"This is making me think of things," Skulduggery murmured. "What is it making me think of?"

"Can we trace the typewriter? I don't know anything about typewriters. Can they be traced? Am I being dumb?"

"Christopher Lathan Sholes sold the QWERTY keyboard to Remington in 1873," Skulduggery said, straightening. "Remington released the typewriters to great success after making a few alterations – like putting the *R* key where the full-stop key was, putting the *M* where the question mark was, and switching the *X* and *C*."

"How do you even *know* things like this?"

"I was there when it happened."

"Were you really, though?"

"No," he said. "But I read about it, and I remember things I read."

"What's it like being you?"

"Never less than amazing."

"So OK, we've solved the mystery of the envelope. Now what about the message?"

"The envelope gives us the clue to solving the message," Skulduggery said. "We just have to find out what it is. Ersatz is using a keyboard substitution, but it's not a simple one. It has a pattern, but it's... it's as if the pattern has a rhythm."

A gesture, and the chair slid over and he sat at his monitor. The screen came alive, the keyboard lighting up. He put the letter before him. "OK, the first three words. *O dv srftt.* If we assume he's starting with the first-person singular pronoun *I*, which would seem logical in a letter, then, in his code, he's moving one key to the right, and substituting O for I. So to solve it, we move one key to the left, which leaves us with..."

He typed out: *I sc aedrr.*

Valkyrie leaned in. "This is a good start."

"Hush," he said. "So that's wrong. What's a typical two-letter word that would follow the word I in a sentence?"

"Am?"

"Which means *D* is actually *A* and *V* is actually *M*. *D* is two keys away from *A*. *V* is three keys away from *M*, but going to the left instead of the right, because the right doesn't have enough letters on that line." His head tilted. "All right then, maybe if there isn't space to go left to right, we just flip it, and go right to left. Fairly simple."

"What?"

"The code so far is one, two, and three keys away from the letters Ersatz wrote. If this continues, then the next letter – *S* – will actually be the fourth key along, and so on, which would make *srftt* into... Huh. No. We'd quickly run out of space."

"I'm barely hanging on here," said Valkyrie, "but, since Ersatz is such a fan of the rule of three, maybe it just repeats. One, two, three, one, two, three, and on like that."

"Which would mean, once all that is flipped round to *undo* the code, *srftt* is actually... A W A R E."

Valkyrie grinned. "Now I get it."

"We immediately get into difficulty as, according to our code-breaking, the first line translates as *I az aware of hew this aiyears* – but I think we can take into account how he got there, using his own rules, and compensate accordingly."

"What?"

Skulduggery's fingers flew over the keys as he translated the code.

```
I am aware of how this appears. A
serial killer sending coded messages
to the detectives reeks of fun being
had. I am not having fun. What I do
```

is not for my own gratification but rather I am an instrument of justice. Blood must be spilled. Sometimes I think I have been born for this. That I have never been human. That I have always been a weapon. You do not understand that my victims are already dead.

Handsome Whitlock is already dead but whether he is to be granted a temporary reprieve depends on you. I doubt this is a test you will pass. I doubt you are capable. Your time is over.

You are a dragon brought down by spears. A dire wolf felled by a single arrow. A shark drowning in a pit of tar. Your passing will not be mourned, save perhaps by the silent dead, heading back to war. Killing is all you have ever been good for. It is a trait we share. We the shamed. The regrettable few. Better to walk into the mists and rejoin our ancestors in the otherworld. I will send you to meet them soon.

"The third paragraph," Skulduggery said once he'd finished typing.

Valkyrie got to the last word and then looked at him. "What?"

"Three, as they say, is the magic number. The first

paragraph is his rationale. The second is the challenge. The third is the clue. A dragon, a wolf, a shark. The rule of three means we focus on the shark in the pit of tar. Do you know what tar is?"

"Of course I know what tar is," Valkyrie said.

"But do you *actually* know what it is?"

"Yes," she insisted. "It's a thick, goopy... goop." She took out her phone, searched, and after a moment looked up. "Produced from coal, wood, petroleum, or peat through destructive distillation."

Skulduggery went silent for a bit, tapping his chin. Then the tapping stopped. "Ah," he said.

"*Ah* what?"

"Do you know what was also used as tar? A substance called bitumen."

Her fingertips glanced over her phone. "Of course," she said. "Everyone knows that. Because bitumen, you see, bitumen is... Yes. Bitumen was used as an adhesive and waterproofing as far back as 5,000 BC. Did *you* know *that*? It was also used, like you say, as tar, and these days it's the major component of asphalt."

Skulduggery got up and looked out of the window. "It was also thought, wrongly, that it was used to embalm the dead in ancient Egypt. Some bright spark reckoned that bitumen's medicinal qualities would have transferred to the mummies themselves, which meant that a lot of them were dug up in the Middle Ages and consumed to cure various illnesses."

Valkyrie made a face. "People ate mummies?"

"Bits of them, yes. The practice only died out relatively recently. When I was around two hundred or so, I remember that certain apothecaries in Paris and London still sold mummia as a remedy for various afflictions like gout, migraines... even the plague."

"Does this have anything to do with when doctors used to prescribe, like, ground-up bones to people?"

"It all comes from the same pseudoscientific theory, yes. European society had a definite thing for cannibalism back then."

"People are messed-up," said Valkyrie, "and they always have been. But what does this have to do with the riddle?"

Skulduggery turned to her. "Dragon, dire wolf, mummia, and shark. Does this not ring a bell? *Scale of dragon, tooth of wolf, / Witches' mummy, maw and gulf / Of the ravin'd salt-sea shark, / Root of hemlock digg'd i' the dark.*"

"Sorry?"

"The three witches in *Macbeth*."

"Oh, those guys," she said, tapping her phone. "Deffo."

"And the *silent dead, heading back to war* probably refers to the *Pair Dadeni*."

"I was about to say that, actually. Yeah. How are we spelling that?"

"In English, it's the Cauldron of Rebirth, destroyed by Efnysien in a battle with the Irish king Matholwch. The dead would be placed in the cauldron and return to life to fight on, though without the power of speech."

"Efnysien and Matholwch," Valkyrie repeated, thumbs hovering over her screen. "Is there anyone in that story named Dave or Ray or...?"

"*Killing is all you have ever been good for,*" Skulduggery read off the monitor. "*It is a trait we share. We the shamed. The regrettable few.* Maybe there's a riddle in there, but I doubt it. It sounds like he's just being dramatic. Then, *Better to walk into the mists and rejoin our ancestors in the otherworld.*"

"The Otherworld!" Valkyrie shouted. "Otherwise known as *Tír na nÓg*, the Land of the Young!"

"And why did you shout that, may I ask?"

"Because it's the one thing I actually know. Yes, everyone in Ireland also knows what that is so it's hardly impressive, but you've got to let me feel good about this because with everything else I'm just caught up in a whirlwind as you're figuring stuff out. Honestly, if that is genuinely how quick your mind works, why do you waste time talking to people like me?"

"People like you?"

"Non-geniuses."

"Oh. There are a myriad of reasons why I talk to you, Valkyrie. If you'd like me to—"

She held up a hand. "It's OK. You don't have to list them. Just tell me what I need to know."

"The Otherworld is supposedly occupied by the Tuatha Dé Danann, who some scholars believe were the Ancients by another name. The Tuath Dé received their instruction in magic in four great cities, on four islands in the far north, off Ireland. From the city of Murias, the Tuath Dé brought the Dagda's Cauldron, which could feed an army because it never ran dry."

Valkyrie put away her phone. "The Dagda's Cauldron, the Cauldron of Rebirth, and the three witches from... Ah. *Double, double toil and trouble; / Fire burn and cauldron bubble.* So that's cauldron, cauldron, and cauldron." She pounded her fist into her open palm. "Holy bar names, Skulduggery! The Cauldron bar in LA!"

His hat flew into his hand. "That's a *Batman* reference, isn't it?"

"You're supposed to say, 'Good work, old chum,' or something like that, but whatever." She pointed at the door. "Quick! To the Teleporter!"

30

Fletcher wasn't available, so one of his protégées teleported them to the Cauldron bar. It was nearing midnight and there was a queue of people waiting outside. The door staff were polite but firm, refusing to allow a small group of people access. Valkyrie switched to her aura-vision, which identified the group as mortals. They were highly indignant, their frustration mounting because no one would tell them quite why they weren't being let in.

Faint strands of anxiety twisted through Valkyrie's mind. Her aura-vision, for which she had never managed to come up with a cooler name, used to be so much more vibrant, the colours almost breathtaking in their stark beauty. Now she could barely see them.

She shook her head, dislodging the anxiety before it had time to settle.

She hadn't donned a different outfit, hadn't bothered with make-up, but Skulduggery had spent the last few minutes cycling through façades until he was happy with the face he was wearing.

They skipped the queue. The door staff recognised

Valkyrie immediately and unhooked the velvet rope, allowing them through. They entered the bar to howls of protest from the mortals behind them, and Skulduggery's façade dropped.

Valkyrie led the way, Skulduggery at her shoulder, waving his hand gently, using the air to form a path through the crowd. The mages that were nudged to the side turned to glare angrily before realising there were Arbiters in their midst, at which point they averted their eyes and did their very best to look innocent.

A woman with a fantastic Afro glided towards them, beaming a megastar smile that almost hid the panic on her face. "Skulduggery Pleasant and Valkyrie Cain," she said, speaking over the perfectly modulated music, "it is an honour to welcome you to the Cauldron! Is this your first time?"

"Yes, it is," Valkyrie said, responding with a smile of her own. "We've heard so much about it that we just had to visit."

"I am flattered," said the woman, her hand fluttering to her chest. "I'm Glorious – Glorious Gautreaux – proprietor and manager. There's a private area in the back if you get tired of the crowd, and all the drinks are on the house. I will not entertain arguments on this matter: it's the least we can do for bona fide heroes who've saved the world."

"That's very nice of you," said Valkyrie. "We're wondering if a friend of ours is here – Handsome Whitlock?"

Glorious looked surprised. "He never mentioned that he knew you two – which is an achievement, as he can't help but name-drop. I'm kidding, I'm kidding! We love Handsome here! I don't think he's in tonight, though.

But take a look around. He might have decided to come incognito."

"It was very good to meet you," Valkyrie said, going to shake her hand and then being pulled into an embrace and a triple cheek-kiss.

"Oh, likewise," said Glorious, giving her an extra squeeze before sashaying back into the crowd.

"I'll check the basement," Skulduggery said into Valkyrie's ear. "You try upstairs." And then he was gone, the people parting like snow before a snowplough.

Valkyrie looked around. There were a lot of tall people here – or, at the very least, a lot of people wearing high heels – so she couldn't immediately see the best path to take. There was a door marked PRIVATE to the left of the bar and she made her way over, arrived at a bottleneck between the bar and a booth and there was a girl with blonde hair standing with her back to her, swaying to the song that was playing.

"Excuse me," Valkyrie said, tapping her shoulder ever so slightly as she went to move by.

The girl turned and Valkyrie's eyes widened at the smile that greeted her, at the smile she never should have seen again.

"Hello, Valkyrie," said Melancholia St Clair.

The music faded to nothing and everyone else went away as the world tilted.

"I saw you walking in," Melancholia said. "I hadn't intended to announce my presence quite yet, but it appears that fate has thrown us together."

She still looked the same as when Valkyrie last saw her, battling Darquesse fourteen years earlier. No – not the same.

The sigils that had been carved into her skin, transforming her into the Death Bringer, were gone. Her skin was unmarked.

Valkyrie grabbed her, hugged her, felt her laughing as the music rushed back in and the bar filled up with people.

"Darquesse brought you back," Valkyrie said into her ear.

"Kind of," Melancholia responded. "Dear me, Valkyrie – where did all this muscle come from?"

Valkyrie moved back a little, just enough to take another look at her friend. "Why didn't you come see me?"

Melancholia screwed up her face a little. "There's a lot going on."

"You've been back for six years!"

"And I've been busy."

"Doing what?"

"Sorry?"

"What have you been doing for six years?" Valkyrie said, louder this time.

Melancholia laughed. "You're not the only one with a mission, Miss Cain. What are you doing here, anyway?"

"I'm looking for someone. Handsome Whitlock. You know him?"

"I know *of* him."

"He's in danger. We think he's here somewhere."

"Let's go look for him," Melancholia said, grinning as she took Valkyrie's hand and led her to the door marked PRIVATE. They passed through and the door shut, muting the bar behind them.

"This is so weird," Valkyrie said, following her through the narrow, brightly lit corridor. "And so amazing. I mean... Jesus. I just can't believe you're back."

"With a few alterations," Melancholia said, glancing behind her. "It isn't St Clair any more. It's Wreath."

"Melancholia Wreath," Valkyrie said. "I like it. Solomon would have liked it, too, I'd say."

"Oh, he does."

Valkyrie snagged Melancholia's shoulder, turned her. "Solomon's alive?"

"Solomon and a few others. He led us back."

"What do you mean?" A member of staff saw them and walked quickly over, but Valkyrie flashed her Arbiter badge and he left them alone. "Solomon's alive, and he hasn't come to tell me, either?"

"He knew you'd be mad."

Valkyrie needed time to process all this. She took the lead, heading up a set of stairs.

"Everyone knows that Darquesse brought people back from death," Melancholia said. "Some of them she brought back deliberately and some, well, it kind of looked accidental."

"There do seem to be a number of those," Valkyrie agreed.

"But for me and a few other Necromancers it was different. We were adrift – maybe because of our training – but when Darquesse remade the universe we saw our chance. Solomon led us out and we... emerged."

"I'm going to need a few more details than *we emerged*."

"I'm afraid that's all I can give you right now," said Melancholia. "We were alive again, and that was pretty traumatic, and Solomon had a plan so we took his name. It just seemed right, you know? To reinvent ourselves."

They walked out into a corridor, broader than the one below, with open doors.

"So there are a bunch of Wreaths now, wandering around town?" Valkyrie asked.

"Some of us have been assigned to LA, yes."

"Is Solomon here?"

"I'm afraid I can't tell you that."

"What's your assignment? What's Solomon's plan? What is... why are... *what is going on*?"

"Sorry, Valkyrie. You've got your secrets and I've got mine. Though I *have* been keeping tabs on you. You're bisexual now, huh?" Melancholia gave her a slow smile. "Cool."

Valkyrie looked away before she started blushing.

They passed a storeroom and a tech room and an office and a bathroom, and right at the end of the corridor, tucked to the side, were six narrow steps leading up to a closed door.

"So what's Handsome Whitlock got himself mixed up in?" Melancholia asked, keeping her voice down.

"A man named Ersatz is killing mortals," Valkyrie answered, climbing the steps. "If the bad guy's up here, you run, you hear me? Ersatz has a weapon you can't defend against."

"Duly noted," said Melancholia, joining her. "I'll run right after you do."

Valkyrie turned the handle, pushed open the door, and climbed a few more steps.

The attic was big and cluttered and dark. There was a single window, a crescent on its side, that let in the streetlights, but all it managed to do was lighten the gloom a little. Whatever this place was before it became a bar, all that junk was stacked up here. Tables, chairs, boxes, lamps, old cash registers – all layered with dust.

Valkyrie pushed a whisper of magic into her hand and her fist lit up, crackling, throwing shadows against the walls and the ceiling and the wooden floor that creaked under every footstep. From somewhere, a skittering.

"Does this place have rats?" Melancholia asked softly. "I love rats."

Up ahead, someone sitting in a chair, their head down, silhouetted by the window.

"Handsome?" Valkyrie said.

The head raised and then the darkness lifted from the chair as Ersatz got to his feet. Valkyrie unleashed a lightning strike that flipped the chair, but Ersatz twisted sideways and she glimpsed the wand. The floorboards bent inwards and Valkyrie yelped as she dropped through the floor, fell into the corridor beneath. She scrambled up to the sound of smashing furniture, went to fly back up, but the ceiling repaired itself. Cursing, she got to the stairs just as the door slammed shut.

She twisted the handle, rammed it with her shoulder. It shuddered but stayed closed. She blasted a hole into it and charged through, saw Melancholia stumbling and Ersatz advancing. Ersatz raised the wand, but Melancholia vanished into the darkness, reappearing behind him, the shadows curling around her fingers like talons. She sent them out, raked them across Ersatz's back and he hissed in pain and whirled, knocking her away.

The crescent window exploded and Skulduggery landed in a crouch, firing his revolver. Valkyrie caught Ersatz in the side with her lightning, sent him spinning into a stack of boxes. Skulduggery darted in, ready to fire again – but Ersatz was gone.

Skulduggery looked at Valkyrie as she hurried over. "Are you all right?"

"I'm good," she said. "Melancholia?"

"Unhurt," Melancholia answered.

Skulduggery tilted his head at Melancholia. "This is surprising."

"Not for me."

He shrugged and turned, then waved his hand, and a pile of junk moved sideways, revealing Handsome Whitlock, tied to a chair with a gag over his mouth. Handsome gave a muffled greeting.

"Oh, good," Skulduggery said without enthusiasm. "You're alive."

While he went to release Handsome, Valkyrie turned to Melancholia. "Thank you," she said.

"What are friends for? Hey, now that you know I'm alive, we can hang out or something, right?"

"I'd like that."

Melancholia smiled. "Excellent. Oh, on a related note, are you still seeing Militsa Gnosis?"

"I am. Do you know her?"

"Not very well, but I was just thinking, like, if you ever break up and you're in the market for another hot Necromancer..."

"I'm sorry?"

"Until that happens, though, you and me? We're just friends."

Valkyrie blinked. "I... what?"

"Do you think you can manage that, Valkyrie? Do you think you can control yourself around me?"

"What?"

"Ah, monosyllabic but still pretty." She patted Valkyrie's cheek. "You're a good girl."

"What?"

"See you around, Skulduggery," Melancholia called as she walked for the door.

Valkyrie stared after her. "What?"

31

They went downstairs, into the VIP section of the club, where Skulduggery made some calls and arranged for a private security team to join them. Handsome perched on the edge of his chair like he was getting ready to bolt. He smelled *really* bad. He said something, but the music drowned it out.

"Would he have killed me?" he asked when Valkyrie told him to repeat it. "Ersatz said he'd kill me if you didn't come, but... would he have? Was that true?"

"We told you Ersatz has been murdering people," Skulduggery said. The pulsing lights glinted off his skull as the mages around them tried not to stare.

"*People*, yeah," Handsome responded, "but not *me*. You never said he'd want to murder *me*. What have I ever done to him, or to anyone?" He shook his head. "I'm just living my life the best way I can live it. I'm just doing my thing. I haven't hurt anyone, I haven't upset anyone – I haven't done anything wrong *ever*."

"You've cheated on a few girlfriends," said Valkyrie.

He blinked. "So?"

"Some people take that stuff seriously."

Handsome made a face. "Seriously enough to, what, send someone to kill me?" He sagged back in his chair. "I don't believe it. This is what I get for sharing myself? This is what I get for loving someone?"

"As a point of interest," said Valkyrie, "how many girlfriends have you cheated on?"

"I guess it depends on how you define *cheated*. If you're talking about overlapping relationships, then I guess I've cheated on most of my girlfriends. I haven't had any boyfriends yet. It's not that I'm not open to the possibility, it's just at this time in my life I find myself focused primarily on women. The female form, I think, is most pleasing to me at this present juncture. I also like their faces more. You've got a pretty face. Would you be interested in...?"

"No," said Valkyrie.

"Maybe after I've showered, with clean clothes?"

"No."

His grin returned. "Never hurts to enquire, am I right?"

"Let's get back to the serial killer," said Skulduggery.

The grin vanished. "I just don't understand why anyone would want to hurt me."

"Apart from all the aforementioned girlfriends you cheated on," Skulduggery said. "Yes, we remember. What can you tell us about your interactions with Ersatz? How did he grab you?"

"I was out," said Handsome. "Me and my crew, we were here, at the Cauldron. The plan was, we start here, then we go on to the Firehand. We were getting ready to leave and I excused myself to use the facilities, and when I'm done... I just remember reaching for the door handle and

263

then it all went dark. I woke up tied to the chair. I knew I was still on the premises because I could hear the music. My magic was bound and I had a gag in my mouth, and the chair wasn't budging. Then the bar closed and I was still there and I spent the whole night sitting in that attic."

"Ersatz didn't appear to you that first night?" Skulduggery asked.

Handsome shook his head. "I woke up and it was morning and I was hungry and I needed to pee and the gag was drying out my mouth and I sat there, waiting for someone to find me. I figured, hey, I was in the attic of a popular bar, you know? A janitor or someone would find me sooner or later."

Valkyrie frowned. "Did you not notice the mess?"

"I noticed the mess, yeah."

"Did you not notice the dust?"

"I noticed the dust, too."

"So why would you think a janitor would be visiting the attic anytime soon?"

"I guess – I guess I didn't consider that."

"When did Ersatz appear?" Skulduggery asked.

"Later that morning," Handsome answered. "I think. I don't know. It was impossible to keep track of time up there."

"You were beside the window," Valkyrie pointed out.

"Yeah, but there was no clock or anything outside. LA doesn't have that big clock tower thing that you guys have."

"Yeah, but the sun. You can tell what time it is by the position of the... Wait. Do you mean Big Ben? That's in London."

"Cool."

"We're from Ireland."

"All right."

"London is not in Ireland."

"Yeah," said Handsome, "but Ireland's in... Wait, Ireland isn't in London, is it?"

"London's in England. Ireland is a whole different country."

"I know that!" Handsome said with a laugh. "But it's all part of the same group of little islands, right?"

Valkyrie wanted to crack her knuckles. "You're thinking of Britain, aren't you? Ireland isn't part of Britain."

"Is it part of France?"

"It's not part of anything except Ireland. The Republic of Ireland."

"OK, but that's not what I'm thinking of. What am I thinking of? Where's the place with the big clock? Is that not Ireland? Where's Ireland?"

"We're straying off-topic again," Skulduggery said.

"How can you not know where Ireland is?" Valkyrie asked. "It's one of the Cradles of Magic, for God's sake. Do you know where Australia is? Africa?"

Handsome nodded. "Vaguely."

"You should know where the Cradles of Magic are, Handsome."

He shrugged. "I didn't go to Corrival Academy. I went to a mortal school where they don't teach you useful stuff like how to forge documents or set up fake identities or where Ireland is on a map."

"*Ersatz*," said Skulduggery, clicking his fingers to draw Handsome's attention.

"Right, yeah," Handsome said. "So, he walks in with that

mask on and just, like, stands there, watching me, for, I mean, it might have been thirty seconds, might have been ten minutes. Like I said, it's pretty hard to keep track of time up there on account of us not having a Big Ben like you guys have in Ireland."

Valkyrie kept her mouth shut.

"And I'm sitting there, and I'm not saying anything either because of the gag, and I know what he's thinking. He's thinking, *He's peed himself.* And it's true, I had. I had to pee, and so I peed, and that's what happens when you've been to a bar and then you get tied to a chair all night. Then he says, 'You have failed.' He says that. To me. He says, 'You have failed.' He tells me I've failed humanity. I don't know whether that was because I'd peed myself or what, but if it was, that's a hell of a burden to put on someone who didn't have access to a toilet. Then he says, like, unless—"

"Don't paraphrase," Skulduggery said. "Repeat what Ersatz said, as precisely as you are able."

Handsome sighed, thought about it for a moment, and nodded. "All right. He said, 'You have failed. You have failed humanity. In three days – unless Skulduggery Pleasant finds you – you're going to die. But I'm not going to use magic to kill you. I'm going to use a knife.'" Handsome shuddered. "Who says that? Seriously, what kind of person says something like that?"

"A serial killer," Valkyrie responded.

"Yeah, fair point," Handsome murmured. "Then he left and I stayed like that, sitting in that chair, not eating, not drinking, peeing myself, sleeping, getting weaker and weaker, until you found me. How *did* you find me?"

"Ersatz sent us a riddle."

"Like in *Batman*?"

"Yes," Skulduggery growled.

"And it took you two days to solve it? I thought you were supposed to be smart."

"It got lost in the mail for a little bit," Valkyrie said before Skulduggery could respond. "Is there anything else you can tell us? Anything you saw, you heard? Anything you smelled?"

"I heard music at night and traffic during the day. I saw the inside of the attic. And I smelled pee. But I got used to that pretty quick, and then I didn't smell it any more."

"Tell me, Handsome," Skulduggery said, "do you remember much about the Deletion?"

Handsome shrugged. "As much as anyone, I guess, but I don't dwell on it. I think it's healthier to just focus on the new timeline. Keeps you sane."

"Were you going out with Rumour Mills at the time?"

"I was, yeah. That was coming to the end of round one of our relationship."

"What happened to her apartment?" Valkyrie asked. "Was it damaged?"

"During the Deletion? No, but her car was trashed. There was a Faceless One standing directly over her building. I mean, it's a Faceless One, so it's huge, and standing over a lot of buildings, but it's got a foot – was it a foot? A paw? A claw, maybe? – on her street. When it moved off, when it went walking, I got a Teleporter buddy to take me over there immediately. I hadn't heard from Rumour in days. There was no cell reception, nobody had Wi-Fi – it was hell. It was literal hell. So I got over there and Rumour's in tears and then there was one of those smaller things, you know the ones? The smaller monsters?"

"Shalgoth," said Valkyrie.

"Yeah, there was one of them outside, and my buddy, the Teleporter, he's not due to pick me up for another few hours and I'm just like... *ohhhh, this is a mistake.* I went directly into the warzone to see the woman I loved, I was risking life and limb, and when I get to her apartment there are monsters outside and her face is all blotchy from crying."

"Must have been hard for you," Valkyrie said.

"It was," said Handsome, looking at Valkyrie like she was the only one to understand his pain. "All she wanted to talk about was the state of the world and how everything was awful and her stupid dead neighbour."

"I'm sorry?"

"Her neighbour," said Handsome. "The guy living opposite. Don't remember his name, but a typical mortal. And I don't mean that in a bad way. They just have a certain look. Kind of like... you know... *Duhhh.*" He mimicked a plodding movement.

"Right," said Valkyrie slowly.

"Anyway, he was dead?" said Handsome, making it sound like a question. "He was going out to find her some food, because they were starving by that stage, and the Shalgoth got him when he was halfway across the road. Rumour saw it happen, saw him being torn apart." Another shrug. "So that bummed her out."

"What about her friends?" Skulduggery asked. "The other mortals?"

"Oh, them," said Handsome, making a face. "Yeah, they were not cool. And I'm saying this as someone who likes mortals. You think sorcerers make up the bulk of my social-media followers? Nuh-uh. Ninety-nine point nine per cent of them are cast-iron mortal, and they have no idea that I'm a sorcerer. They just like me for me, which is kinda life-affirming, you know what I mean? So I am good with the non-magical, ordinary, mundane people of the world." He took a breath. "But Rumour's friends were jerks."

"In what way?"

"They were with her, watching their scary movies, when the Faceless One went solid. That's how Rumour used up all her food – because they were too terrified to leave for the first few days. Then the Shalgoth were everywhere and hundreds of thousands of people were dying around the world."

"Did the Shalgoth, the one who killed her neighbour, did it try to get into the building?" Valkyrie asked.

"It did, and Rumour fought it off. Now, you'd expect the mortals to be cheering her on, but they were all, like, *Naw*. They were freaked out basically. The moment they could, they hightailed it outta there, left her alone to cry and to look out at her dead neighbour's remains spread across the road."

"And then you arrived," said Skulduggery.

"Handsome to the rescue. Yes, indeed."

"And did you rescue her?"

"Well, like, I stayed for a few hours, but I had to get home."

"You didn't take her with you?"

"You think I should have?"

"Yes," Skulduggery said. "I think that would have been the nice thing to do."

"Well, maybe. Hindsight being twenty-twenty and everything. But she had her own stuff to deal with. Like, when I was there, Simone came round."

"Simone Ruddy who doesn't like you for some reason," Valkyrie said.

"Yeah, that's her. But during the Deletion she didn't like Rumour, either, and I sincerely don't know why. She turned up screaming, calling Rumour all kinds of horrible names. She said something about watching her parents being killed."

"And *had* her parents been killed?"

"By the Shalgoth, yep."

"So Simone's parents get killed by magical monsters," said Valkyrie, "and she goes to the only magical person she knows – her best friend – to lash out, and you *sincerely don't know* why she might have blamed Rumour?"

"It's not like Rumour killed her parents."

"But her parents were just butchered," said Valkyrie. "Simone was obviously not thinking clearly."

"I still reckon it was unfair." Another shrug. "She stood on the doorstep and screamed and cried and then ran off. Not that it matters, though. After Darquesse reset the universe, all that stuff got wiped from the minds of every mortal in the Deletion, right? And Simone's folks never even got killed in the first place."

Valkyrie looked at Skulduggery. "But Rumour would have remembered it. And she'd have remembered how the horror club reacted."

Skulduggery stood as someone approached, someone huge, and Valkyrie turned and jumped up, grinning, as Ragner, son of Quietus, grabbed her in a hug.

"Greetings, my friends! Greetings and salutations! Valkyrie, you look beautiful and lovely, and Skulduggery, you also look beautiful, and also lovely! Two beautiful people! And what is this? A third beautiful person?"

"Ragner," Skulduggery said, "this is Handsome Whitlock. He'll be needing the services of you and your team."

"By all means!" Ragner said, leaning forward to grasp Handsome's hand in his meaty fist. "It is very nice to be making your acquaintance, Mr Whitlock. For the last three years I have been the proud owner of a private security firm, and I look forward to working together! May I suggest, however, that the first place we escort you, in absolute safety, of course, would be a shower? You may not know this, because persons in polite society are loath to give beautiful people distressing news, but there is somewhat of a maliferous quality to your aroma! A most unhelpful miasma! A fetor, if you will!"

"I don't know about any of that," said Handsome miserably, "but I stink."

"You stink!" Ragner roared. "Yes, you do! But come now! To the showers!"

32

Lunchtime in Dublin on a sunny day and all the mortals were sitting outside the cafés and sharing benches and generally acting like they weren't all a load of murderous bigots who'd turn on those different from themselves the moment the cracks started to appear in their safe little lives. Winter walked among them, their inane chatter biting at her patience. She may just have been in a bad mood – the only city centre she actually liked was Roarhaven's – but they did seem especially aggravating today. Maybe it was the gorgeous weather. Maybe she didn't like being reminded of the ugliness the mortals were capable of when the world itself was so pretty.

Not that mages could make any great claims to beauty of purpose, she conceded. The King of the Darklands, Mevolent, Serpine, Abyssinia, not to mention Darquesse herself... The list of evil, destructive sorcerers who'd brought this civilisation to the edge of oblivion was somewhat exhaustive.

Mortals and mages, Winter figured, were just as bad as each other.

Alter was waiting for her amid the crowds on Grafton Street. Beside him, Brazen and Aphotic stood.

"What's *she* doing here?" Brazen asked, the moment Winter came into view.

"Winter's one of us now," said Alter.

"What? Since when?"

"Since yesterday."

Brazen shook her head in disbelief. "Are you actually stupid? Are you? I told you about her. I told you she only joined up to spy on us."

"Winter," said Alter, "why did you join up?"

"To spy on you," said Winter.

Alter nodded, pleased. "So now that we're all agreed, let's move on."

Winter shot a withering look at Aphotic, who averted his eyes, and continued to ignore Brazen as she addressed Alter. "So what's up? What's the emergency? If I'd known I'd be getting Avengers Assemble texts in the middle of the morning on my summer holidays, I wouldn't have given you my number."

"But this is, as you say, an emergency," Alter replied. "Everyone's been mobilised, kiddies. We're on a search-and-destroy mission – or, at the very least, a search-and-shout-about-it mission. Phones out."

Alter tapped his phone, and the headshot of a bearded man appeared on their screens.

"Who's this?" Brazen asked.

"His name is Sage Highbrow. A pretentious name, I know, but the man is, admittedly, a genius. Imperator Dominax recruited him personally to a team of scientists he had working on a top-secret project."

"What was the project?" Aphotic asked.

Alter frowned at him. "Winter here has already acknowledged that she's spying on us, and I've known you for a week. What makes you think I'd trust you with top-secret information?"

Aphotic was too busy blushing to respond.

Alter continued. "Doctor Highbrow has had a change of heart, and he has absconded with an item belonging to Dominax. Belonging to us. He is on the run somewhere in the city. Our fearless leader has teams searching for him. We think – we only *think*, mind you – that we have him cornered. Our orders are to comb this street forward and back, for the rest of the day if we have to, and if we see him we call in the big guns. We do not engage ourselves, do you understand?"

Brazen sneered. "He doesn't look dangerous."

"I appreciate the toughness, Brazen, I really do. But you're fifteen years old, and Sage Highbrow – while a self-confessed nerd – is over two hundred, is a grown goddamn man, and is scared and desperate. Scared and desperate makes him dangerous. He's more than you can handle. Are we all clear?"

Winter nodded along with the rest of them.

"Look at his face. Memorise it. Keep your phone handy. We're going to be walking up and down this street in a line, looking at every single dude of average height that we pass. Highbrow is slightly heavy, but nothing that'd stand out. Any questions?"

"Do I have to do this?" asked Winter.

"This is your chance to prove yourself useful," said Alter. "If you want to go back home, go right ahead. You won't get to spy on us, and I won't get my opportunity to show you why we're in the right, and why you should come over to our side. But hey – there's the door." He pointed behind her. "Metaphorically speaking."

Winter hesitated, then sighed. "Fine. I'll walk up and down for hours like the rest of you idiots."

Alter grinned. "That's what I like to hear."

They spread out across Grafton Street, with Brazen on the left and Aphotic on the right, and between them Alter and Winter. They walked up the street. They walked down. They walked up again. They walked down again.

Everywhere Winter turned, she was met with a deluge of faces. She skipped over the women, her eyes flickering from man to man. She got quite a few smiles when they'd catch her eye, but she ignored that and walked on, even when the younger men stopped to initiate conversation. *Not interested!* she wanted to shout.

Her annoyance grew with each pass until she realised she was walking with a scowl. True, it worked to deter most of the younger men from wanting to chat, but now it invited older men to wink and tell her to smile. Winter didn't know which irritated her more.

As she walked, she'd see Brazen and Aphotic and even Alter glance at their phones to remind themselves what their quarry looked like. She didn't need to. Faces and names, facts and figures, things said and done, they all stayed in her head. In many ways, she was a lot like her reflection – she tended to remember stuff other people forgot.

Sage Highbrow, for example. His sandy-coloured hair was receding. His eyes were hazel and his eyebrows were surprisingly fine. He had extra weight in his cheeks, and his nose was long and slightly crooked. His beard was full and flecked with grey. In the photo, he was smiling. His teeth were straight, and a little yellowed. No Hollywood smile for Doctor Highbrow. He was too busy conducting top-secret work and then absconding with it.

If Imperator Dominax had mobilised everyone in the Order of the Ancients – including newbies like Aphotic and sceptics like Winter – then Highbrow's work must have been very valuable to the leadership. Winter wondered what qualified as *valuable* to a terrorist organisation. Was it money that defined a project's value? Or was it the threat level?

Had Highbrow stolen weapon plans?

In his photo, he'd been wearing a thin silver chain around his neck. On it was a cheap love heart, the kind made by pouring glue into a mould and then painting it. Something only a kid would do, and something only a loving parent would wear.

The picture, presumably, was recent, and the paint on the love heart hadn't yet started to fleck, so presumably the kid was still a kid. So Highbrow was a dad, and his kid was young, and if he had been working on a weapon, might his devotion to the cause have wavered slightly? Might a few doubts have started to creep in? Had he decided that he couldn't let someone like Imperator Dominax get his hands on such a device? Is that why he ran? Is that why Winter was searching for him – to return the plans to the terrorists so that they could destroy and maim and murder?

And suddenly there he was, walking towards her in the crowd.

He was wearing a baseball cap and he'd shaved his beard, but now the lower half of his face was slightly paler than the rest and Winter recognised him immediately and – stupidly – she froze. Her arrested motion in a sea of movement caught his attention and their eyes locked.

He turned abruptly, tried to blend in among a fresh wave of mortals. Winter plunged in after him. She lost him almost immediately, turned in a circle, glimpsed Brazen running and followed, just in time to see Highbrow darting into Johnson's Court, a much narrower street no less packed with people. Aphotic was on his heels, and then Brazen.

Winter raced to catch up, barging through protesting mortals.

Highbrow had collided with a pram. He stumbled, nearly fell, allowing Aphotic to close the distance. The mortals around them cried out in alarm and concern. Highbrow was running again and Aphotic reached for him, barely missed. Now they were running side by side, and Aphotic glanced behind him, searching for backup, terrified because now he didn't know what to do. The decision was taken away from him when Highbrow put his hand against Aphotic's head and shoved him into the wall. Aphotic hit it with his face and bounced off, his black coat flapping as he fell like a stunned pigeon who'd just flown into a window.

Brazen leaped over his dramatic sprawl. The mortals ahead saw the commotion and stood aside, allowing them an unimpeded path. Highbrow suddenly stopped and Brazen crashed into him and he threw her over his hip. It wasn't a particularly skilful throw, but he was bigger and stronger and he slammed her into the ground. A mortal man jumped in to intercede and Highbrow swung at him. His hand didn't connect, but Winter saw the ripple of air and the do-gooder was hurled off his feet and Highbrow ran on.

Alter was somewhere behind Winter. It was up to her.

She piled on the speed, passing both Aphotic and Brazen. Highbrow was a fast mover, both for a heavier guy and a scientist. He burst out on to Clarendon and a car nearly hit him, had to brake sharply. Winter got a hand to the bonnet and vaulted, sliding across it without slowing down. Highbrow banged his hip against a bollard and crashed into a middle-aged woman and sent her to the pavement. Winter jumped over her.

Highbrow tried suddenly stopping again, like he'd done with Brazen, reaching out to grab her. But Winter jumped, her knee slamming into his chest. They went down, Highbrow making a *"whoof"* sound. All credit to him, he was instantly up, snapping his palm towards her. They were so close that the startled onlookers probably thought he hit her, but it was the air that launched Winter backwards. She cracked a shop window and rebounded, fell to one knee.

He ran down Coppinger Row and Winter went after him, leaving the crowd in her wake. She lost sight of him behind a parked delivery truck that was taking up half the road. As she reached the rear of the truck, the thought occurred that this was the perfect ambush point, and then he jumped at her, grabbed her, smashed her into the wall.

"Leave me alone!" he gasped, the exertion making him sweat. He smashed her into the wall two more times and then went to throw her, but she had grabbed him by now and she got her foot behind his and they both fell.

They rolled behind the delivery truck and then he was on top and so, so heavy. He hit her in the face. He was a big guy, but she'd been hit harder when sparring and so she absorbed the blow without caring about it. She grabbed his wrist and he pulled away and she took the opportunity to hook her right leg over his shoulder. He pressed against her, tried to rise, but she yanked his arm across her torso, curled her left knee round her right instep. The triangle choke wasn't perfect, but she adapted and when she brought her knees together and pulled down on his head his eyes bulged and he made a noise down deep in his throat, the same noise she'd made a thousand times whenever Valkyrie caught her with this exact same move.

He struggled and struggled and then stopped struggling, his eyes rolling back in his head, his body going limp.

"Pretty sure I told you not to engage," Alter said, strolling up.

"He was going to get away," said Winter, releasing the choke.

"I'd already called it in," Alter said, hunkering down and searching Highbrow's pockets. "There was no way he was escaping us." He pulled out a vial of green liquid.

"That's what he stole?" Winter asked.

Alter smiled, and didn't answer, just helped her to her feet. Brazen and Aphotic came round the delivery truck. The side of Aphotic's face was cut and swelling. Brazen was pale, and held her shoulder like it was broken. She glared at Highbrow and then at Winter, and then back at Highbrow.

A woman joined them, her hair in tight cornrows, her outfit the height of fashion. "He wants to see you," she said. "All of you. Please step on the unconscious man."

Alter placed his foot on Highbrow's leg, and Aphotic and Winter did the same. Brazen delivered a swift kick before grinding her heel on to the side of his neck. The woman lightly touched Alter's shoulder.

"Hold on to your lunch," she said, and teleported them to the middle of an empty office. There were twelve or thirteen desks and a phone ringing on one of them. The windows looked out over a car park.

Aphotic dived for the nearest bin and puked into it, and the woman disappeared without saying anything more.

Winter frowned. "Is this the... Is this your...?"

Alter grinned. "Say it."

"Is this your lair?"

He laughed. "You were expecting a castle? A dungeon? Do you have any idea how expensive those places are to run? And forget about Wi-Fi access. Any secret, underground magical-terrorist organisation worth their salt is located in a business park like this – and if they're not, they should be."

"So where is everybody?"

"Out looking for Doctor Highbrow here. You've done us a big favour."

The Teleporter appeared back with half a dozen sorcerers. Most of them went straight to their desks, but two came over and dragged Sage Highbrow away.

"Come on," said Alter. "The boss wants to say hello."

He led them to a door and knocked, and a voice said, "Enter."

They walked in. The office was a good size, and had a large window looking out on to some trees. The middle-aged man standing behind the desk wore gloves and he had thin chains criss-crossing his chest under a leather coat, its shoulders studded with spikes. He looked like somebody's uncle had wandered into a post-apocalyptic society and decided to set up a mid-sized accountancy firm.

"I am Imperator Dominax," he announced. "Welcome to the inner sanctum of the Order of the Ancients."

"Cool," said Winter.

"Imperator," said Alter, "this is Brazen Yarrow, Aphotic Atramentous, and Winter Grieving."

"I have heard great things about you all," said Dominax, sitting. "Well, maybe less about the boy, but Brazen, you definitely show promise."

Brazen bowed. "Thank you, Mr Dominax."

"Call me Imperator. And Winter... Alter believes that you have the potential to become our most valuable member."

"Winter single-handedly apprehended Sage Highbrow," Alter said, passing over the vial of green liquid.

"Is that so?" Imperator said, much to Brazen's obvious annoyance. He examined the vial, then opened his drawer and placed it inside. "In that case, it would appear that Alter was certainly right to sing your praises. Maybe in a few days, once we've demonstrated to the Sanctuaries how committed we are to isolation, you'll be persuaded to join our ranks."

Winter couldn't help it. She had to ask. "What happens in a few days?"

"What happens indeed?" Imperator Dominax said, steepling his fingers and laughing. "What happens indeed?"

It was deeply, truly lame.

33

Teleporting from LA at night to Roarhaven at mid-morning was a shock to the system, no matter how many similar trips Valkyrie had taken in the past. Just when she was settling into one groove, she was wrenched into another. For Teleporters, that readjustment was one of the first things they were taught to deal with. In a weird way, however, she quite liked those brief periods of mild stupefaction: they stopped her from taking all this for granted.

When they arrived back in the High Sanctuary, they got a message from Cerise, and dutifully reported to the Administrator's office. Valkyrie had only been here once before, but that had been a friendly visit. Now, like errant schoolchildren, they stood before her.

"You requested surveillance on the phones of the friends and families of Sean Dowling and Eimear Shevlin," Cerise said, sliding a report towards them while she typed one-handed. "Dowling called his wife fifteen minutes ago. The call originated from these coordinates."

Skulduggery glanced at the paper. "Thank you," he said.

"Are you annoyed with us?" Valkyrie asked.

"Very," Cerise answered.

"Oh."

"We'd better go," Skulduggery said quietly.

Valkyrie nodded, went to follow him out, then turned. "We're annoyed with you, too, by the way. We've always been on the same side and I get that you had to protect Cyrus Elysian because of the work he was doing, but we're trying to save lives."

"You didn't save *his* life."

"OK, fine, fair point."

"So it was a mistake? To lure him out of the High Sanctuary?"

"It... Yes."

"All right then," said Cerise.

Valkyrie went to argue some more in the hope that she'd arrive at a defensible position as she talked, but Skulduggery spoke again.

"We have to go."

More annoyed than ever, Valkyrie spun on her heel and followed him out. Instead of heading for the elevators, they walked towards the balcony.

"We're not driving?" she asked.

"The coordinates are in Crone Wood, about fifty kilometres from here. We'll be faster flying."

Valkyrie sagged. She'd really liked this T-shirt.

They got out on to the balcony and took off, Valkyrie doing her best to keep the crackling energy from singeing her top. As they left Roarhaven behind, they flew high enough to be practically invisible from the ground, and in the bright sunshine her trail of lightning was a lot less noticeable. Within minutes, they were over trees.

They found the cabin tucked away in Crone Wood, where the forest thinned ever so slightly, and landed behind it. Valkyrie was pleased to discover that her top was relatively undamaged. They approached quietly. Skulduggery picked the lock on the back door. The hinges squeaked a little as they moved in. The kitchen worktop was filled with takeaway boxes and bags of rubbish: the signs of someone hiding out.

Voices from the other room, two people in quiet conversation.

"Don't scare them," Valkyrie whispered.

"I'm not going to," Skulduggery assured her.

"They're obviously freaked out enough as it is. They've been living in fear for days. Just let me handle the initial conversation, all right?"

"Absolutely." His façade flowed up. "You go in first and ease them into it."

She nodded. "All right then."

Squaring her shoulders, Valkyrie took a breath, exhaled, and walked slowly into the small living room. "Hello," she said.

Sean Dowling and Eimear Shevlin had their backs to her and at the sound of her voice they screamed and whirled and Skulduggery ran in, his façade dropping and his gun in his hand, searching for the non-existent threat, and they saw him and screamed louder, backing away and falling over furniture.

"It's OK!" Valkyrie shouted over their screams. "We're not here to hurt you! We're not going to kill you!"

"You're here to kill us?" Sean screamed.

"No!" Valkyrie shouted. "We're *not* going to kill you!"

"You have nothing to be scared of," insisted the living skeleton with the gun.

"Oh my God!" screeched Eimear.

Skulduggery looked at Valkyrie. "This is not going well."

Sean grabbed Eimear's wrist and they bolted for the door, but Valkyrie got in their way, energy crackling around her hand. They saw it, their eyes widened, and they backed off.

Once she was sure they weren't going to jump out of the window, Valkyrie let the energy fade.

"We're not here to hurt you," she told them in a much calmer voice. "Sean, Eimear, you're safe with us. I'm sorry we scared you, but we're here to help. My name is Valkyrie Cain. This is Skulduggery Pleasant."

"Neither of those are names," Sean said in a hushed voice.

"Well, they're *our* names," Valkyrie responded, giving a small smile. "We're detectives. We're the good guys, OK? Even Skulduggery."

"People tend to equate me with Death, or the Grim Reaper, or evil personified," said Skulduggery. "*Jason and the Argonauts* did me no favours, either. Have either of you seen that movie? No? Valkyrie, what about you?"

She frowned at him. "What?"

"*Jason and the Argonauts*," he said. "From 1963? There's a famous sword fight between the Argonauts and seven of Ray Harryhausen's stop-motion skeletons. No?"

"I mean... I've seen the stop-motion skeletons in *Army of Darkness*, but... OK, now isn't really the time for this. Sean, Eimear, we know you're scared. We know what happened to your friends. We're here to stop that from happening to you."

Sean did not appear reassured. "How do we know you're not the ones who killed them?"

"That is a very good point," Skulduggery said. "You do not know that. But seeing as how I have a gun, and I could kill you both very easily from where I'm standing, the fact that you're alive right now is testament to our good intentions." To reinforce his point, he put his gun away.

"We're here to help you," Valkyrie said. "But in order to do that you have to help us. How much do you know about Rumour Mills?"

"I know she's dead," Sean replied. "That's what I know about her."

"Eimear, what about you?"

"Just tell us why all this has been happening," said Eimear, her voice quiet.

"A man, who calls himself Ersatz, murdered Rumour and is making his way through her group of friends," said Skulduggery. "I'm sure you know by now that you two are the only ones left."

"But why? Why are we being targeted? What did we do?"

"That's what we're trying to uncover. Did Rumour ever introduce you to anyone? A friend of hers, an acquaintance, a colleague? Specifically, anyone right before she died?"

Eimear shook her head.

"I don't think so," said Sean, still looking freaked out. "I don't remember her introducing us to anyone. Apart from her neighbour."

Eimear nodded. "Her neighbour, yes. Vincent."

"Vincent Driscoll," said Valkyrie. "We've talked to him. He seems nice."

"Very nice," Eimear said. "From what we saw of him, anyway."

"He was kind of awkward around us," said Sean. "Shy,

you know? That's the only person I remember her introducing us to."

"How did you all meet?" Skulduggery asked.

"Can I sit down?" Eimear asked.

"Please," said Valkyrie.

Eimear went to an armchair and sat, hugging herself, keeping her knees pressed together. "A movie marathon," she said. "Ten, twelve years ago, maybe, at Halloween, in the Irish Film Institute. You know the cinema there? They had this movie marathon thing that went on for the whole weekend."

Sean must have realised how weak his own knees were, because he gratefully sank into the couch. "It was a good marathon. It was great, actually. The best they'd put on in years."

"And that's where you met?"

He nodded. "We all went with friends, with our own groups. But halfway through all of our friends faded. Like, they couldn't handle it. They were too tired, they were too overloaded, they just weren't into the whole... experience, you know?"

"The crowd was whittled down," Eimear said, "and by the last night there were only a few dozen people left. And we'd all been talking to each other over the weekend, and we kind of... we congregated. And that's how we became friends."

"And you met up every week after that?" Valkyrie asked.

"Pretty much. We'd get together in different people's houses and watch obscure horror movies or we'd head to the cinema if there was a theatrical release or..."

"When was the last time you met up?" Skulduggery asked.

"Six or seven years ago, maybe?" said Sean.

"Six," said Eimear.

"Six," said Sean. "Fair enough. I can't remember why we stopped. I think there was some friction in the group? Eimear?"

"I can't remember."

Sean shrugged. "People fall out. Friends drift apart. It happens. There was no big bust-up, if that's what you think. No major argument or whatever. We drifted apart; we all got on with our lives. To be honest, I hadn't thought about the old group until Eimear got in touch to tell me about the others."

Valkyrie looked at Eimear. "You figured out the group was being targeted?"

"I just heard from a friend of a friend," Eimear said. "Niamh's cousin was going out with my friend's housemate. It's a small world, you know? And then I called Colleen, but she wasn't answering, so I tried to find her online and I saw... I saw her family had put up a death notice. And then I looked for the others and saw that Sean was the only one alive."

"The obituaries all said they died from natural causes or accidents or whatever," said Sean, "but we knew something was happening. We'd been through the *Final Destination* franchise. We knew a pattern when we saw one."

"So we came here," said Eimear. "To a cabin in the woods. No one knows where we are and... and no one we love would be hurt if someone came for us."

Skulduggery moved past Sean, who shrank back, and sat in the armchair opposite Eimear. He crossed his legs and took off his hat. "Eimear," he said, "what's your favourite scary movie?"

34

Eimear laughed, then frowned, flustered. "Sorry. I wasn't expecting you to quote *Scream* to me."

"I am full of surprises," Skulduggery said. "We talked to Vincent Driscoll and he wears the horror T-shirts and he has the figurines, and Rumour had all those posters in her apartment... but you don't strike me as the horror type."

"I don't know what to tell you," Eimear said. "I got into horror as a kid and I just love it. The first real horror movie I remember seeing was probably *A Nightmare on Elm Street*. The original, obviously. It was showing one night and I caught the start of it, the bit where Freddy's walking down the alley and his arms are stretching out either side, and his claws are raking against the wall? I must have been eleven or twelve, so way too young to watch something like that, but I couldn't turn it off. It had me. I had nightmares for weeks, but I think that's probably my favourite horror movie."

Sean sat forward. "My favourite is an obscure Korean movie called—"

"Just one moment there, Sean," Skulduggery said, not

looking away from Eimear. "And your favourite horror novelist, Eimear?"

"It, uh, it's sounds so obvious, but I just love Stephen King."

"I thought you might," Skulduggery said. "I met him, actually, back in the 1980s. Gordon Edgley introduced us."

Eimear's eyes widened. "You know Stephen King?"

"You know Gordon Edgley?" Sean said, eyes equally as wide.

"I met Stephen King," Skulduggery said, "but I knew Gordon, yes. He introduced me to a lot of the contemporary horror novelists."

"Gone too soon," Sean said, shaking his head.

"Damn right," said Valkyrie.

"Eimear," Skulduggery said, "what's your favourite Stephen King book?"

"Oh, God, there's so many," said Eimear. "*The Shining, Carrie, The Dead Zone*. I read *Firestarter* when I was a kid and it just... It resonated."

"That's interesting."

She smiled. "Is it? Why? Because I don't seem the type?"

"No," Skulduggery said, "because you were lying earlier."

Eimear's smile slipped. "I'm sorry?"

"When Sean asked you why the group broke up six years ago. You claim not to remember, but you're lying."

"No, I'm not."

"Why did the group break up, Eimear?"

"Listen, I don't know what you—"

"Why did *Firestarter* resonate with you as a child?"

"I don't know. It just did."

Skulduggery glanced at Valkyrie. "Have you read Stephen King?"

"Of course," she said. "Gordon had me reading all the classics."

"Is there a common theme in Eimear's favourite novels?"

"*Firestarter* is about a little girl who's a pyrokinetic. Little Danny Torrance in *The Shining* is a psychic, as is Johnny Smith in *The Dead Zone*, and, of course, Carrie White is a telekinetic."

"All psychics," said Skulduggery. "All what we could label *Sensitives*. Why did these stories resonate with you as a child, Eimear?"

"I don't know," Eimear said, her voice thick.

Skulduggery tilted his head. "What were you like as a child?"

Eimear stood up. "I don't appreciate these questions. I don't appreciate being accused of lying. I've done nothing wrong. Why are you interrogating me when there's a serial killer out there who wants to kill us?"

"We're trying to stop him, Eimear," Skulduggery said. "We're trying to stop him before he gets to you – but the only way we can do that, the only way we can save your life and Sean's, is if we know why this is happening. Tell me what you were like as a child."

"I was normal!" Eimear said, upset. "I was just a normal kid!"

"You're lying again."

"What do you expect me to say?" she responded, her voice rising. "How do you expect me to answer that?"

"Truthfully. Eimear, I know what you are. I know what you were. You've hidden all your life, but you don't have to hide from us. Look at me. I'm a living skeleton. Why would you think you have to keep anything from us?"

"What's he talking about?" Sean asked.

Eimear swallowed, and sat down slowly.

"I *was* a normal kid," she said softly. "I was a normal little girl. And then when I was eleven I started hearing voices. Other people's voices, the voices in their heads. I told my parents and eventually they took me to a bunch of doctors and everyone asked questions and started looking at me differently and I didn't like it. My parents had to take me out of school. They so worried about me. They told me it was all going to be OK, but I could hear their thoughts. I knew they were lying. Then I read the Stephen King book and I read about the government agency coming after the little girl with the special talent and so I stopped telling people that I could hear their thoughts."

"These abilities," said Valkyrie, "they sometimes manifest during puberty."

Eimear nodded. "But I kept pushing it down. When I couldn't push it down, I ignored it, or I did my best to." She gave a grim, humourless smile. "That wasn't easy. Not when you're a teenage girl. Not when you're in your twenties. Not when you're in your thirties. Not when you're out in a bar or when you're at work or when you're on a bus or when..." She shuddered. "It's never easy to ignore people's thoughts about you."

"Rumour was magic," Skulduggery said. "You knew that, didn't you?"

"Not when I first met her," Eimear said. "I mean, I knew there was something different about her because I couldn't hear what she was thinking. I'd met a few people over the years whose thoughts were quiet, but she was the first friend I'd had who... who didn't hit me with a barrage of thoughts."

Valkyrie looked over at Sean. He was staring at the floor. "You doing OK there, Sean?"

"Not really," he said, his voice quiet. He looked up. "Rumour was magic? Eimear, you... you can read my mind?"

She nodded.

He paled. "And you've been able to do that since we met?"

She nodded again.

"But... but some of my thoughts..."

"It's OK," Eimear said. "Everyone has them."

"But—"

"Sean, seriously, everyone has them. Everyone has normal thoughts and weird thoughts and lovely thoughts and nasty thoughts, and they can happen one after another or all at the same time. You're not a bad person because you have a bad thought. I judge you solely on what you do and what you say. You make a decision at every moment about which thoughts to let rise to the surface, and I judge you on those. You're my friend and you're a good guy. We're cool, OK?"

Sean sat back, too shocked to respond.

Eimear looked at Valkyrie. "I can't hear your thoughts. There's a wall between us." She looked at Skulduggery. "But you... it's just empty. I don't know how you even think."

"I am an enigma," he said. "What happened six years ago, Eimear?"

She didn't move, but she seemed to immediately get smaller. "Nothing happened," she said.

"You remember," Valkyrie said, watching her. "You remember the Deletion."

Eimear didn't look up. "I don't know what that is."

"Six years ago, the world ended, and then it restarted. When it restarted, there were suddenly two timelines. There was the timeline that ended the world, with monsters and death and darkness, and there was the timeline where the world never ended, and everyday life continued as normal. Mortals – or non-magical people like Sean – can only remember the timeline without the death and the monsters. People like us can remember both."

Eimear exhaled shakily. "I thought I was going mad."

"It must have been terrifying for you."

A fluttering hand raised to her mouth. "I honestly thought I was going mad. Oh my God. Oh my God, now I see what... Oh my God."

"I don't understand any of this," said Sean.

"So it all happened?" Eimear asked, looking up. "The creatures? Those giant monsters? The missiles and the tanks and the bombs and all those news reports?"

"It all happened. That's how the world ended."

"Oh my God."

"You were in Rumour's apartment when it started, weren't you?" Skulduggery asked. "When the giant monster appeared over Dublin, it trapped you in the apartment?"

Eimear nodded. "We were too scared to leave. The whole world went... Everything was crazy. Rumour told us not to panic. She said everything would be all right. She kept us together." She glanced at Sean. "You were great," she said. "You were really brave."

"That's nice of you to say," he responded, "but I sincerely don't know what you're all talking about."

"Eimear, what happened then?" Valkyrie said as gently as she could.

"The creatures – not the giant monster, but the smaller monsters – they attacked. We saw them kill people, people driving past. These creatures would just flip the cars and... and rip the people out. Then they noticed us. They saw us through the window and they came for us, but Rumour stopped them."

"She fought them off," said Valkyrie.

"She saved us."

"How did the group react to this?" asked Skulduggery.

He didn't get an answer.

"Eimear?" Sean said. "How did we react?"

"Oh, Sean," Eimear said, starting to cry. "Oh, Sean, we didn't... we didn't react how we should have."

"What do you mean? What does that mean?"

"Rumour saved us. She used magic and we saw, we all saw what she could do, and... The group was scared. We were all terrified, but we were also hungry, and the water had shut off, and the power, and days had gone by, and then Rumour... We saw what she could do and what she was and all of that misery and anger and fear became paranoia. And hostility. We said horrible, horrible things to her."

Sean looked away for a moment. "Who said these things? Was it me?"

"It was all of us."

"Even you?" Valkyrie asked.

Eimear shook her head. "But that just makes me worse than any of them, doesn't it? They didn't know what was going on, they didn't know there was magic in the world, but I did. I could read people's minds! So when they turned against Rumour I should have defended her. I should have stood with her..."

"But you were too scared," Sean said quietly. "Because we'd turned against Rumour so quickly, you thought we'd turn against you, too."

Eimear wiped at her eyes, and nodded.

"Tell us what happened," Skulduggery said.

"We left," Eimear said, after a big, shaky breath. "We wouldn't stay with Rumour. There was some... Some of us wanted to throw her out of her own apartment, but we were too scared of her, of what she could do." A sudden, violent sob, and then Eimear pulled it back in. "She even volunteered to leave. She said we could stay in the apartment and she'd go, but no one wanted to do that, so we all left. We got out of there. We left her alone. Just her and her neighbour. He wasn't afraid of her like the rest of us. I think he was too much in love with her.

"We got two streets over, but there were more of those creatures so we ran into a hotel. You know the hotel there? It was empty, and we barricaded off a part of it and stayed there for days. The power came back on for a few hours at a time. We watched the news reports and whenever we could get internet access we'd read these, you know, theories about what was happening. People were blaming all kinds of groups. Every religion was blaming every other religion, and all of them were blaming atheists, and conservatives were blaming liberals and liberals were blaming conservatives, racists were blaming different ethnicities, bigots were blaming gay people... It was horrible. All those thoughts that everyone had been keeping private, the thoughts that I heard over and over growing up... they were now out in the open. People were voicing them. Acting on them. Hatred was, literally, everywhere.

"And, of course, there were loads of theories about all these people with amazing powers who were showing up. The fact that they were fighting the monsters and saving our lives didn't seem to get through to anyone that maybe they were on our side? So the theories started that the people with magic were battling the monsters for control. That this was a... what do you call it? When two gangs fight?"

"A turf war," said Valkyrie.

"A turf war, that's it. So we were reading about how the true enemy are these people with the magic powers and, for some reason, we got it into our heads that it had all started with... with Rumour."

"Oh, God," said Sean.

"We decided that she was the one responsible. We thought she was controlling everything, all the monsters, all the people with the powers... She was behind it. And if we... if we stopped her, we'd stop everything that was happening. We'd save everyone."

Eimear took another shaking, trembling breath. "So we waited for night and then we... we sneaked back to Rumour's apartment. And, while she was sleeping, we..."

Her voice cracked and her jaw clenched.

"What did we do?" Sean asked dully.

"We grabbed her. We... we hit her."

"What did we do, Eimear?"

"We dragged her outside and we... we burned her."

Sean's hands went to his open mouth. "No. Please."

"I'm so sorry, Sean," Eimear said, tears rolling down her cheeks. "I didn't want to tell you."

"Was she alive? Was she alive when we...?"

Eimear nodded.

Sean stared at her. "And I did it? I did it, too?"

"I'm so sorry."

"Who lit the fire, Eimear?" Skulduggery asked.

"I don't... I don't remember. I think it was Colleen. But we were all... It was all of us."

"It wasn't you," Valkyrie said.

"It was me, too," Eimear told her, her face buried in her hands. "I was too scared to say anything. I went along with it. I helped carry her. I helped tie her. I helped... oh, God, I helped burn her because I was too scared not to."

"Jesus."

"We murdered her," said Eimear. "All of us. We murdered our friend. And then a day later, two days later, all that went away, and life was normal and the monsters had never appeared. But no one could remember it the way that I did! I had two sets of memories. I was alone with the knowledge of what we'd done. I couldn't face the others. I couldn't even talk to them."

"And Rumour," Valkyrie said, "she would have remembered everything, too."

"I never even apologised," said Eimear. "I didn't know she remembered, but even so I... I just didn't want to see any of them again."

"So you pulled out of the group," Skulduggery said, "and I assume Rumour wouldn't have been overly eager to associate with the people who had burned her alive in another timeline, so she pulled out too, and the group disintegrated."

Eimear nodded.

Sean stood. "I can't be here," he said, and walked towards the door.

"Keeping close to us is your best chance of staying alive," said Skulduggery.

Sean turned. "Maybe I don't deserve to stay alive. If that's the kind of person I am, then maybe this Ersatz guy *should* kill me."

"That wasn't you," said Valkyrie. "It's hard to understand, and it's harder to truly accept, but the version of you in that timeline is not the man standing in front of us. That version of you went through a horrific ordeal, he was terrified, his whole world was crumbling, and he got swept up in one terrible idea. But that's not you. That stopped being you the moment that timeline was deleted."

"I don't just watch slashers and monster movies, you know," Sean said. "I watch science fiction, too. I'm aware of the concepts at work here. And thank you for trying to make me feel better, but attacking an innocent person, burning her alive... that is something that I am capable of doing. You push me the wrong way, you take away certain particular things, and this is what I will do."

"Sean, please don't go," Eimear said.

"I can't be around... this," he replied. "I can barely be around *me*."

He opened the door and came apart, his flesh dividing, his organs splitting, his blood becoming a fine red mist that hung in the air and then parted, allowing Ersatz to walk through.

A wave of the wand, and Sean's shredded remains collected neatly on the floor.

35

Skulduggery's gun had cleared its holster and he was already firing by the time Valkyrie unleashed twin handfuls of lightning.

The bullets hit Ersatz in the torso and head and the lightning struck him in the chest, dead centre, and all Ersatz did was take a couple of steps back.

Valkyrie grabbed Eimear and they ran for the rear of the cabin as Skulduggery sent a wall of air slamming into the killer.

Eimear was panicking. Valkyrie's feet got tangled with hers and they tripped over each other, but managed to remain upright and stumbled to the back door. A turn of the handle and it was open and they were outside, and Valkyrie bent her knees to launch them both into the sky.

But something snagged her foot and Valkyrie fell, cursing, leaving Eimear to run on a few steps before turning back. The grass was lengthening, wrapping around Valkyrie's ankles.

"Go!" she shouted. "Keep running!"

Ersatz walked through the back door and Eimear sprinted for the trees.

Valkyrie sent a jolt of power through her legs, frying anything that touched them, but immediately more grass reached up, wrapped around her. Ersatz passed within touching distance and she lunged, but weeds burst from the scorched earth, clutching at her wrists, flattening her to the ground. She tried tearing her arms free, but the grasses were twisting, snaking around her midsection, her throat.

Skulduggery came striding out of the cabin, reloading his pistol. He clicked the cylinder back into place and started firing, six bullets ricocheting off the black mask as Ersatz turned. Skulduggery opened his hand and the gun shot from his grip, striking Ersatz in the forehead, and a heartbeat later he crashed into him.

Valkyrie scrambled up as Ersatz flicked the wand. Skulduggery staggered, roaring in pain as bone shards cut through his suit from within. Lengthening and curling like antlers, the tines found each other, interlocking and bending him backwards like some bizarre, obscene sculpture.

A wave of the wand and Ersatz disappeared, and Valkyrie came to a sliding halt beside Skulduggery.

"Help her," he gasped.

There was a moment when a wall descended in her mind, when her feet wouldn't move, when the only thing that mattered was getting Skulduggery to the Infirmary in the High Sanctuary. But she smashed through it, forcing her legs to work, and sprinted into the trees, into the sudden gloom. Ducking branches, she caught sight of Eimear ahead.

Eimear heard her coming and glanced round, saw who it was, stopped to wait and then a branch swung into Valkyrie's chest, knocking her on to her back.

Struggling for breath, she leaned on one elbow, looked blearily to see who had hit her, and the branch bent, much like the grasses and weeds had, and came for her.

Eimear reached her, hauled her to her feet, and Valkyrie blasted the branch, but succeeded only in scorching the bark. The trees around them twisted and Valkyrie blasted again, but the branches and the twigs had her right wrist, and there were vines curling around her left knee. The woodland was alive with the groaning of old trees and the rustling of leaves, and those branches were everywhere, and they were forcing Valkyrie and Eimear apart.

Valkyrie tried to shout, to tell Eimear to keep running, but there were leaves in her mouth, thin vines wrapping around her head, gagging her. The branches lifted her off the ground, cutting into her ankles and wrists, drawing blood. They were in her hair, tugging her head painfully back. They were scratching her skin, squeezing her throat. They were strangling her.

Through shifting leaves that threatened to obscure her vision, Valkyrie saw Eimear whirling to face Ersatz. She stood there, crying, talking, saying something, her back to Valkyrie, and Ersatz raised the wand.

Valkyrie focused, drawing on the other magic that coursed through her system, the magic she'd absorbed from the katahedral crystal the day the Sceptre of the Ancients exploded in her hand. She crackled with black energy and she sent it through her body, and the branches and the twigs and the vines turned to dust and she dropped, landing in a crouch, feeling the power inside her, her entire being filled with an unstoppable destructive force.

She felt her eyes turn black and start to leak black vapour.

Ersatz watched her and she raised one hand and the killer disappeared.

Valkyrie dropped to her knees, looking at her hand, looking at all those tendrils of black energy dancing over her skin. Her lungs were burning and she breathed out, distorting the air around her. Her hair moved like she was caught in an updraught. She fought to contain the magic, to rein it in, to keep it under control.

The woodland floor blackened beneath her. The trees around her turned to solid ash with a chorus of weakening cracks.

"Valkyrie."

"Stay away," she whispered.

He didn't stay away. Skulduggery never stayed away. He came forward, stepped round her, knelt. His hat was gone. His suit was in ribbons, but the antlers, the spurs and the tines had retracted. He was his old self again.

"Hello, Valkyrie," he said softly. "Look at me, please."

Slowly, she raised her head.

"You can control this," he told her. "You've done it before. You'll do it again. You can do it now."

"I can't."

"This power is not your master."

"Keep back."

He brought his hand up. Even his gloves were torn, she saw, as he moved his fingers closer to her face.

"Please don't," she said.

"I trust you."

"Please."

"I trust you," he said again.

An instant before Skulduggery touched her cheek, she drank that energy back into her body, and felt her eyes return to normal.

"One of these days," she said, "that's not going to work."

He pulled her to her feet. Holding on to him for support, Valkyrie hobbled out of the blackened circle towards Eimear, who was still standing there, trembling.

Valkyrie said her name, and when Eimear neither responded nor turned, she gathered her strength and moved round.

Eimear stood, her hands by her sides and her eyes open, quite dead. Her face was bruising, turning a deep, dark purple. Her head bowed to one side and she collapsed. The way she fell, the way she crumpled, Valkyrie knew that Ersatz had sliced her into pieces, just like he'd done to Niamh Cairns. But he hadn't gone through the skin. It was her insides that he'd cut up. All those diced cubes of meat and bones and organs jostled and tumbled, contained within the unmarked skin, within the layers of clothing, before finally, eventually, mercifully settling in a pile on the ground without anything tearing. Without anything spilling.

Valkyrie dropped to her knees, her stomach roiling, bile rising, vomit spewing.

Skulduggery didn't say anything.

36

It was nice to be back in Roarhaven, even after a few days of living in the mortal world. There were no real crowds, there was no pollution, no litter in the streets, and people walked with real purpose. They weren't just clocking in at work to keep the mortal machine churning – everything these mages did made a difference to somebody else in the city. Magical communities worked for the betterment of every sorcerer. Mortal communities were barely communities.

Winter met up with Mia and they walked through Corrival's gates. It was odd seeing the students in their everyday clothes. When they joined their classmates in their form room, Tier saw them, came over.

"Nervous?" he asked.

"Do I look nervous?" Mia responded.

"Yes, actually."

"Oh, yeah, well – it's not my results I'm nervous about. It's what we're doing after."

He frowned. "What are you doing after?"

But before she could answer Mr Herringbone came in, carrying a thick briefcase. He held up a finger and the chatter died down. A moment later, Principal Sorrows' image faded up beside Herringbone's desk.

"Welcome back, students of Corrival Academy," she said. "Before you receive your exam results, I would like to offer my congratulations to those of you who did the best, given your limitations. The rest of you, the staff and I expect better. That doesn't necessarily mean we expect higher marks: just that we expect *better*. School is training. We are training you to work. You will, upon graduating, apply that skill to whatever you decide to do with your lives. Work is essential, because nothing good ever comes easily – and if it does, it's seldom worth it. You would do well to remember that. Your form teachers will now distribute your results, and we will see you all in September." Then she added sternly, "Until then, stay alive."

Mr Herringbone opened his briefcase. One by one, the students went up, collected their envelope, and either hurried or sauntered out into the corridor to rip it open in private. When Winter and Mia left the room they exchanged envelopes, opened them, and read the results.

"You did well," said Mia. "Not brilliantly, but you did well."

"You did really good," Winter said. "High marks in everything except maths and forgery."

"Did I pass them?"

"You did."

They swapped the results back, and read their own.

Winter shrugged. "I'm OK with this, actually."

"Me too," said Mia. "Though Dad's not gonna be happy with the forgery mark. He always says a sorcerer's greatest power is using the mortal system against the mortals. I've

306

always said that a sorcerer's greatest power is magic, but what the hell do I know?"

Tier came over. "I'm assuming you both did fine, but I honestly don't care enough to ask. The only important question is what are you doing now? It's something dangerous, isn't it?"

"Actually, it isn't," Mia replied. "It's something *potentially* dangerous, which means it might be barely dangerous, not dangerous at all, or incredibly dangerous."

"I'm in, either way."

"You're not," said Winter.

"Yes, I am. Unless you think you can't trust me?"

"It's not about whether or not I trust you," she said, keeping her voice down. "It's about whether or not you should be trusted."

"I'm on your side."

"You don't even know what side that is."

"So? I don't care enough about any of this for that to make a difference. If you're into mortal-hating, then fair enough: I can find reasons to hate them. If you're working against the mortal-haters, I can find good reasons for that, too."

"So why do you want to help?" asked Mia.

"Because I fancy your friend and I'm looking for an excuse to spend time with her," he answered.

Mia blinked. "Well, OK then. Winter?"

Winter hesitated. "I mean... I suppose that's fine."

He nodded. "Cool. So what are we doing?"

"The Order of the Ancients has a scientist that I helped capture. He had a little bottle, a vial of something green, when we caught him. We're gonna break him out of their headquarters, and steal the vial, whatever it is."

Tier chewed his lip, then nodded. "Nice."

All the other students had left and Mr Herringbone stepped into the corridor, briefcase in hand.

"Well done, the three of you," he said. "You did some good work this year. Some mediocre work, too, let's be honest, but by and large good. Are you off now to celebrate? To paint the town red?"

"A quiet afternoon in, actually, sir," said Mia. "What about you? You've got three months off work – how are you going to spend your time?"

"Suffice it to say, Miss Pizazz, that a teacher's work is never done."

"Because of poor time management? I get that, sir, I really do. Fare thee well." She curtsied, then twirled and walked away.

"What the hell was that?" Winter asked when she and Tier had caught up with her.

"I'm not sure, but then I have no idea why I do half the things I do. It's what makes me so fun to be around."

They tracked down Genial Waylay, the only student in their class good enough to teleport them into Dublin. When she dropped them off, they flagged the first empty taxi that passed. Tier used the mortal driver's given name to wrangle a free ride out of the city and into the suburbs, where the Order of the Ancients had their headquarters.

"It's on the third floor of that building," Winter said once they were out of the car. She passed the sign listing all the businesses in the park and stepped on to the grass.

"The villain's evil lair is in *here*?" Tier asked.

"It's something to do with the Wi-Fi," Winter responded. She picked a heavy stone from the flowerbed and they went round the side of the building. "The point is, the offices on the first and second floors are mortal workplaces, so bear that in mind. I'm assuming they're keeping Doctor Highbrow on the third floor – unless this place has a basement, which I doubt."

"Question," said Tier. "Are we going in guns blazing? Because if we are, we're probably gonna get killed."

"There will be no blazing guns."

"Shouldn't we call someone?" Mia asked. "I don't want to be the one to say *let's call the cops*, but honestly... let's call the cops. Let Tanith Low break down the door and get her Cleavers to storm the place. If this is going to be properly dangerous, why the hell are *we* doing it?"

"Mia does have a point," said Tier.

"We're doing it because we can," Winter said. "We're doing it because we're capable of doing it. This is the Order of the Ancients we're talking about. Not the Soldiers of Magic. Not anyone we have to take seriously."

Mia looked uncertain. "I think we might have to take them at least a little bit seriously. They might be all talk, but if they're about to use whatever weapon they've been developing, it means they're ready to take the next step. What are you always telling me about fighting, Winter? You should never underestimate your opponent."

"I'm not underestimating anyone," Winter said, "and that includes the two of you." She nodded upwards. "That's the window to Imperator Dominax's office. Dominax is a weak little man who has to wear a stupid costume because of his fragile sense of self-worth. He will not be able to endure anyone undermining his authority."

Tier frowned at her. "And how does this help us?"

"We're going to break his window, then you two are going to cause a fuss, get him good and angry so that he charges out of his office, at which point you'll run the hell away."

"I don't like this," said Mia. "What are you going to be doing while we're running away?"

"I'm going to retrieve the vial that Highbrow stole, and then rescue Highbrow himself. Are we ready?"

"No," said Mia.

Winter grinned happily. "Good luck!" she said, and the air rippled around her hand and the stone smashed through the window.

37

Winter dodged into the bushes, leaving Mia and Tier standing there, dumbstruck. Imperator Dominax appeared at the window, gesticulating madly and shouting obscenities.

"Oh, for God's sake," muttered Tier, and clicked his fingers. He yelled an insult back and hurled a fireball, and Mia pushed at the air and the window flexed, the cracks spreading across what remained of the glass.

"You wait right there!" Dominax shrieked, and ran out of sight.

Tier and Mia sprinted away, and Winter focused on the window. She forced herself to breathe evenly, letting the space she was looking at fill her mind. She willed herself there. She was an average Teleporter, but she could do this. She knew she could. It was just like moving from one side of the hall to the other. Sure, in school, there were all these safety precautions and everything was quiet and calm and there was nothing to distract her, and she could take the time she needed, but she was certain she could do this. She was fairly certain she could do this. She was almost fairly certain –

– and then she was inside Dominax's office, but she was in mid-air, halfway over his desk, and she fell and her left foot caught on the desk and her leg curled beneath her and she collapsed in a graceless heap on the thinly carpeted floor.

"Ow," she whispered.

The door to the office was closed and nobody came barging through to investigate the noise – probably because they were too busy listening to Dominax scream about the kids outside. Winter searched the desk but it was empty. No vial. Grimacing with displeasure, she went to the door, squared her shoulders, and walked out.

No one saw her.

Dominax was at the far window with two others, issuing directions to the people below them in the car park. "Check the sign!" he shouted. "The sign! Check the big sign behind you! They might be hiding there! The sign!"

Winter hurried to the exit, slipped through and then closed the door silently. There was a lift and a stairwell opposite, and another door a bit further up. It was locked when she tried it, but she turned the handle with one hand and pushed at the air with the other, and it burst open.

There were two doors for the bathrooms and a third marked STAFF ONLY. It was locked, too. She knocked. Knocked again. When nobody answered, she broke it open.

Sage Highbrow sat on the floor in the corner of the small room, gagged, with his hands shackled behind him, and a short chain securing him to the radiator. He blinked at Winter as she came over.

"Doctor Highbrow," she said. "Or Sage. Can I call you Sage? Sage, I know that the first time we met I choked you unconscious, but now I'm here to rescue you." She pulled down his gag. "Are you cool with that?"

He tried to answer, but could manage only a dry croak, so he nodded instead. She pulled him to his feet and while he worked to get the stiffness out of his legs, she examined the chain.

"OK," she said, "I wasn't expecting this. To be honest, I don't have anything to cut it with. I thought you'd be tied up, you know? With rope? The chain's a bit much. A bit dramatic, you know what I mean?"

"Key," he managed to say.

"The key! Yes, of course! Do you know where it is?"

Sage cleared his throat. "The guy who takes me to the toilet – he has it in his pocket."

"Who is he? What does he look like?"

"He's a big guy, lots of muscles. His name's Slam. Slam Debacle."

"Well, at least he doesn't have a dumb name. Get the circulation back into your legs. I'll either return with the key or I'll run off and leave you here. Sorry, but I'm not gonna get killed trying to rescue you, no offence."

"No, no," he said. "That's fair."

She hurried out, strode to the next door just as it opened and a huge man who could only be Slam Debacle stepped through.

"Who the hell are you?" he growled, or at least Winter assumed that's what he was about to say before she hit him in the windpipe. He staggered against the wall and she darted forward, shutting the door behind him, and then stepped back to kick at his leg. His knee barely buckled so she kicked again, remembering everything her Muay Thai coach had taught her, sweeping his legs from under him and sending him crashing to the floor. She pulled a small key from his pocket as he rolled around, clutching at his throat.

"Hope you don't die," she told him, then back into the small room she went.

"That was quick," said Sage, in the middle of doing lunges.

"I am very efficient," Winter murmured, releasing him from the chain. He still had the shackles, though, so he'd be pretty much useless in a fight. "Stay behind me," she told him.

They crept by Debacle and took the stairs down. Through the windows, they watched the Order of the Ancients office workers heading back inside, empty-handed. They hid behind a corner and listened to them grumbling about being sent after a couple of stupid kids when they should have been putting the finishing touches to the demonstration. When the last of them had passed, Winter led Sage out of the building. Keeping low and tight to the walls, they moved to the other side of the business park and climbed the slight hill, slipping through the trees.

They came down the other side and Winter called Mia's phone. They met up at the nearest bus stop and caught a bus within sixty seconds. They climbed to the top deck and went to the back, where they'd be alone.

"Doctor Sage Highbrow," said Winter, "this is Mia and Tier."

"Thank you," said Sage. "Thank you, all of you. I owe you... I probably owe you my life. But listen: you have to call the Sanctuary. Imperator Dominax has a weapon, a bomb. I tried to get away with a piece of it, but he has that now, too."

"The vial?" Winter asked. "With the green stuff inside?"

"The liquid is achtolycerin helphate. We use its individual components in various things like cloaking spheres and protective garments, but when mixed together it becomes an explosive. In small quantities, like the vial, it's quite safe. In larger quantities, it becomes volatile. Once it's fitted into the bomb, it goes live. Once the bomb is activated, you've got ten seconds to get clear of the area. Only a Teleporter could manage it, and they have a Teleporter."

"What kind of bomb?" asked Mia.

"It's called a Desolation Engine," he said. "As far as I know, there were only three ever made, by a man called Kenspeckle Grouse. Somehow Dominax got hold of the early designs, the prototypes. I was part of a team assigned to figure out how to build one of our own. So that's what we did. Only... only I had a change of heart."

"Because of your child," Winter said.

Sage frowned. "Yes. How did you know?"

"Tell us about the bomb. What does it do?"

"It obliterates. Turns whatever is in its blast radius to ash. There really is no limit to its yield. If you build the bomb big enough, if you have enough achtolycerin helphate, it could take out an entire continent."

Mia paled. "Is that what Dominax wants to do?"

Sage shook his head. "He'll start off small. If that's enough to force every sorcerer to adopt Isolation, then that's all he'll use it for. If not, he'll go bigger."

Tier frowned. "What's the target, Sage-the-Mage? He'll start off small? How small? It's the Humdrums, isn't it? He's going to kill all the mortals in Roarhaven."

"No," said Sage. "He's going small, but not that small. It's Dublin. The whole county, not just the city. If the bomb goes off, then by this time tomorrow every person, every building, every blade of grass in Dublin will be nothing but ash."

They stared at him.

"Damn," said Tier.

They got into Dublin and Mia called Genial Waylay because Mia was by far the nicest, and people didn't seem to mind doing favours for her. Genial teleported in, frowned suspiciously at Sage and his shackles, but delivered them into the grounds of Corrival without asking any questions.

"Take Sage to Stagger Aimes," said Winter, once Genial had left. "He lives on Bushwack Avenue – you know it? He's probably the best at picking locks so he'll have those shackles off in minutes. If he's not home—"

"We'll find him, don't worry," said Tier. "What are you gonna do?"

"I need to report what Dominax is planning. If the Cleavers raid the place in the next hour, they might still catch them."

"You want help? Getting in to see Tanith Low will not be easy."

"It'll be easy for me," said Winter. "She's a family friend."

Mia frowned. "Since when?"

"Since before I was born. Go on now. I'll meet up with you when I'm done."

Tier and Mia escorted Sage on to the tram, and Winter took the tram heading in the opposite direction. If they were lucky, this would all be over by dinnertime.

Her foot tapping impatiently, she focused on the streets that passed as the tram slowly emptied. When there was one more stop left, a man stood in front of her. She frowned, looked up to tell him to keep moving, and he hit her and the world plummeted into darkness.

38

When Ghastly died, the shop where he'd made and repaired all those exquisite suits and immaculate dresses was sold and converted into a coffee shop. Valkyrie had visited once, just to see what it was like. The tables were solid wood and the décor was rural-chic, designed to look like everything had been gutted from an actual barn. The coffee wasn't bad. The music was inoffensive. The windows let in a lot of light. The whole thing was awful.

Valkyrie had sat there, listening to the inoffensive music, drinking her not-bad coffee, looking out of the big windows. The entire street was different. It used to be run-down. Dirty. Squalid. All the better to deter the casual mortal from stopping for too long. But behind each front door was a sorcerer's house. It was a small community, consisting of one single street in the middle of Dublin, but it didn't need to be anything else. This was a street that attracted little drama, and that's how the residents liked it.

Now they were all living in Roarhaven, most likely, having sold up to mortal developers. The road had been redone and the houses were apartments and everything looked clean and new.

Valkyrie had preferred it the old way.

When Ghastly had come back, he'd reopened in Roarhaven, having sought out the narrowest building in a dead-end street in a quiet area where even the air seemed to slow down. His work at the Sanctuary kept him busy – kept him *more* than busy – but Bespoke Tailors was his refuge. It was where he came to relax.

Valkyrie walked in. 'Come Away With Me' by Norah Jones played and two mannequins – one in an astonishing gown and the other dressed only in a basted suit jacket – waltzed across the open floor while four other mannequins, in various articles of clothing, looked on and applauded in silence, their sculpted hands never quite touching. The door clicked as it closed behind Valkyrie and all six mannequins stopped what they were doing and snapped their heads towards her.

There were an awkward few moments where nothing and nobody moved.

And then Ghastly came through from the back room, humming along to the song, his eyes on the fabric he was carrying. Upon his arrival, the mannequins immediately separated and froze in various poses, but something caught Ghastly's attention because he looked up sharply.

"Valkyrie," he said, glaring at the mannequins.

"Ghastly," she said in return.

"Valkyrie, when you came in, were these mannequins moving?"

"These mannequins?" she asked as he walked up to the one in the gown and peered at it suspiciously.

"These ones," he said. "They've been misbehaving of late and I told them what would happen if I caught them moving without permission. In particular, were they dancing? They used to dance, back in the old place, and I was fine with it until one of them split the crotch of its trousers."

One of the mannequins behind Ghastly quickly shook its head.

"No," said Valkyrie. "They were just standing there. No dancing."

Ghastly grunted, folded the fabric and placed it in a nook within a section of the wall that was full of them. "What can I do for you?" he asked.

"I can't just call round for a chat?"

"This is just a friendly conversation, is it? You haven't approached me here because you thought I might be more amenable? I'm going to have to disappoint you, I'm afraid. I try to leave Sanctuary business for the Sanctuary, but after the fiasco yesterday..."

"Fiasco?"

"Two mortals died, Valkyrie."

"And we tried to stop that from happening."

"And you failed."

"So we try again tomorrow."

"You should have called in backup."

"That's not how we generally work."

"And that generally works out for you," Ghastly said. "I know that better than almost anyone. But it didn't this time, did it? This time, you went up against an opponent you still don't understand, wielding a weapon you haven't yet learned to counter."

"A weapon that was stolen from *your* building by one of *your* people."

"And because of that I've now got reports being compiled on how to ensure that never happens again," Ghastly said, "because I like to learn from my mistakes."

"Are you saying we don't?"

"That's exactly what I'm saying. You and Skulduggery, you're just going to keep throwing yourself at this problem until you throw yourself hard enough that something breaks. You never alter your approach, no matter how many mistakes you make."

"We're Arbiters," said Valkyrie. "We deal with our own problems."

"No matter what?" Ghastly replied. "Even if there's a better way, an easier way, a safer way? I could have given you an army of Cleavers if that's what you needed. An army of sorcerers. Instead, you went in alone."

"We didn't know Ersatz would turn up."

"He's been a step ahead all along. What made you think he wouldn't turn up when you least expected him to? Where's Skulduggery?"

"He's meeting me here."

"Then I'll wait," said Ghastly. "I want him to hear this, too."

She folded her arms. "Fine."

They looked at each other.

"Would you like a cup of tea?" he asked.

"Sure."

She followed him into the kitchen, but didn't unfold her arms. He put the kettle on.

"How's Militsa?" he asked.

"She's fine."

"Your parents?"

"Fine."

"How's your sister?"

"She's OK."

"Dog?"

"Getting old."

"Aren't we all?"

"No."

He shrugged. "I suppose not. Do you want a biscuit?"

"I'm grand, thanks."

He took two mugs from the cupboard, put a teabag in each, and turned to her while he waited for the kettle to boil.

She sighed. "How's Tanith?"

"You know how Tanith is. You talk to her almost every day."

"Yes, but I'm enquiring because it's polite."

"In that case, Tanith is fine, thank you for asking. She's great, in fact."

"You've been together for a few years. Do I hear wedding bells in your future?"

A smile. A small smile. "I don't think Tanith's the marrying kind, do you?"

"Maybe not. Probably not. Another thing we have in common. She's working with the church, I see."

"Just arranging security, crowd control, things like that. Right now, she's meeting with a delegation from the Dark Cathedral about whatever that big event is that's coming up." He frowned. "What is it, actually?"

"Why would I know?"

"Darquesse is a part of you."

"She *was* a part of me. Then she went off and became God."

"So you have no idea what big religious event the Dark Cathedral is about to hold?"

"None at all," Valkyrie responded. "They tried to involve me in the early days, but I think they got the message that I have no interest in participating. I didn't pray to the old God and I'm not praying to the new one."

"Fair enough," Ghastly said as the kettle boiled. He poured the water in, prodded the teabags to within an inch of their little teabag lives, then scooped them out and into the food bin. He passed a mug to Valkyrie and she blew on it, took a sip.

"He's scary sometimes," she said.

Ghastly watched her. "Skulduggery?"

"Like, in a different way than you'd expect. We all know he's scary when he gets angry. We all know there are things about his past that make him scary. But the way he thinks, how smart he is..."

"Ah, yes. It's a different kind of scary."

"Isn't it? I don't know how he can slow down enough to talk to the rest of us. Isn't that hell for him? It must be like dealing with toddlers. We're stumbling around behind him and he has to wait until we comprehend something before he can continue on."

"This surprises you?"

"No," she said. "I've seen it before. We've been solving mysteries together for almost twenty years. But every so often I step back and it's like I'm seeing it for the first time. There's something that goes along with that, too..."

"Yes," said Ghastly. "Guilt."

Valkyrie didn't respond.

"You feel a special kind of guilt when you're around him," Ghastly continued. "You're ashamed that you're so pedestrian. You're worried you're slowing him down, dragging him back, not letting him sprint the way you think he was born to."

"Yeah," she murmured.

"And then you wonder why he's wasting his time on you," Ghastly said. "Have you ever asked him?"

"Sure."

"Have you ever asked him seriously? And has he ever answered seriously?"

"I don't think so."

"Maybe you should." Ghastly sipped. "It's not like him to be late, though."

"He's been late a lot in the last few weeks," she replied. "He's got something going on that he won't tell me about."

"Does that bother you?"

"No. I've got things going on that he doesn't know about, too. I don't mind secrets. It'd be a boring world if we didn't have secrets."

Ghastly watched her as he drank his tea.

She rolled her eyes. "And now you're wondering if these secrets are a threat to, what, national security?"

"*International* security, actually."

"You can keep wondering."

"I trust you, Valkyrie. I do. Just like I trust Skulduggery. If I were a tailor full time, then I'd trust you over the Sanctuary any day. But being Grand Mage means I have to think on a different scale. The things I'd risk as an individual just can't be... tolerated, I suppose, when viewed in a larger context."

"You think we should accept this oversight committee," Skulduggery said from the doorway.

Valkyrie glanced over at him as he came into the kitchen. Grey suit and hat today.

"I'm starting to wonder," Ghastly said with a single nod. "You messed up against Ersatz."

"We'll try again tomorrow."

"That's what Valkyrie said."

"It's how we work."

"And how many targets does Ersatz have left? Is there anyone on his list that he hasn't been able to kill? There's very little point in resolving to try again tomorrow if the bad guy finishes his work today."

Skulduggery didn't have an answer for that.

"If you'd been working within the Sanctuary," said Ghastly, "if this oversight committee, or some version of it, had been keeping an eye on things, we could have teleported an army right to your side. Those mortals didn't have to die. They died because you went in alone, because you thought you could handle whatever was thrown at you. Yes, in the past, that's how it has tended to happen and every time you save the day. But you didn't save the day yesterday, did you?"

"We did not."

Ghastly put his mug on the worktop. "I'd support your independence if I wasn't Grand Mage," he said. "I'd support it because we've all seen what happens when the Sanctuaries try to rein you in. Their rules become interference. Their vast reach becomes a liability. The more moving parts a machine has, the more things there are to break down along the way."

Skulduggery tilted his head. "And that's what you would say if you weren't Grand Mage."

"But, since I am Grand Mage, I can protect you from that. The oversight committee – or advisory board, or whatever they call it – wants to steer you towards only the important cases. That's ridiculous, and open to unconscious manipulation at best and sheer corruption at worst."

"So you wouldn't be in favour of the oversight committee as proposed by Quiddling."

"No, I wouldn't. You're Arbiters. You have to maintain your independence. The Sanctuaries, the Councils of Elders, the Grand Mages themselves... sometimes they're the ones who need to be investigated. There need to be people they can't control. There need to be people they're scared of. That's you."

"Prove it," Skulduggery said.

"I'm sorry?"

"If this is what you truly believe, then prove it to us and we'll think about it."

"Tell us about Elysian," said Valkyrie.

Ghastly soured. "That's... I can't."

Skulduggery shook his head. "You're not filling us with confidence here, Ghastly."

"He's dead," said Valkyrie. "Surely you can tell us something about him."

"I can tell you lots about him," Ghastly responded. "I can give you his life story. But I can't tell you what he was working on."

"Because you don't trust us?"

"Because every Sanctuary has its secrets. It'd be a boring world without them, right?"

"You can talk about his work with Rumour Mills, though," said Skulduggery. "Surely there's no confidentiality clause that survives the death of both doctor and patient."

"Unless his work with Rumour is linked to his work with the Sanctuary," Valkyrie said.

"I can't discuss any aspect of Doctor Elysian's work," Ghastly said.

"You've got to give us something, otherwise Ersatz is going to get away with what he's done. Will you be able to live with that, knowing a killer is still out there? A killer with a weapon we know nothing about?"

Ghastly was silent for a few seconds. "That's not entirely the case," he said.

"What isn't?"

"We do know something about the wand."

"Professor Regatta said their scans—"

"Professor Regatta didn't have enough time," Ghastly said. "If he'd had a year, or three, his examination would have been a lot more thorough. Or if he'd been part of the original team I'd assigned."

Skulduggery pulled out a chair and sat. Ghastly took a breath, exhaled, and did the same. Valkyrie stayed standing and confused.

"What?" she said.

"A sorcerer named Reliance Bask arrived in our reality three years ago," Ghastly said. "He was badly injured and he was on the run. That's all we were able to ascertain. Someone was after him, chasing him through dimensions, and he was terrified. He died soon after he got here."

"And he brought the wand with him," said Skulduggery.

"He did. I assigned a team to it, kept it all top secret. A weapon like that, it shouldn't even function. Four of our top scientists worked in absolute secrecy with every resource at their disposal and they could barely crack the surface of what this thing could do."

"Professor Regatta said the wand is inert until a sorcerer holds it."

Ghastly nodded. "At which point, the sorcerer's magic is pulled in and converted. Our team had theories about how something like that might be possible given what they'd discovered about the wand, but it hasn't been easy. We had the strictest measures in place, which meant that none of the team were ever alone with the wand, or ever had any kind of unsupervised access."

"You didn't trust them."

"A weapon like that is too powerful. Too tempting."

"Did you ever try it?" Valkyrie asked.

Ghastly nodded. "You don't really understand it until you use it. The moment I understood it, I put it down."

"So how did Ersatz get his hands on it?"

"I have my suspicions, but I don't know. Work on the wand had slowed. The lack of progress was frustrating and, frankly, the sense of urgency dissipated the longer Reliance Bask's pursuers failed to materialise. The original team had taken on new assignments and the wand was locked away. Honestly, we don't know when it was taken. The last time it had been examined was almost a year ago. It was locked away and that's where I thought it stayed until you brought it in for Regatta to examine."

"Tell us about your suspicions," Skulduggery said. "Who do you think took it?"

Ghastly sighed. "Cyrus Elysian."

Skulduggery tilted his head. "Elysian was part of the team?"

"Not originally," said Ghastly. "He was brought on in an attempt to find out how the wand interacted with the wielder – whether there was a psychic connection to the mind, or if it was something else."

"Did he find anything?"

"Nothing conclusive."

"Why would Elysian have given the wand to Ersatz?"

"I don't know that he did. I just know that he was one of a very small group of people who had access – and I trust the others more."

"And why didn't you tell us any of this when we first went up against Ersatz?"

"Because you're not part of the Sanctuary," said Ghastly, putting a little more iron in his tone. "Because we have secrets that we need to keep, and the people who know those secrets have to follow our rules and understand our priorities."

"Our only priority is stopping the bad guy at the earliest opportunity," Valkyrie said.

"Exactly," Ghastly responded. "But, as awful as it sounds and as awful as it is to say aloud, sometimes stopping the bad guy at the earliest opportunity is not in the best interests of the Sanctuary."

He looked at her and sat back, and then looked away.

"Is that the case here?" Skulduggery asked, his voice quiet.

Ghastly sounded so incredibly tired. "In this instance? No. There's no strategic advantage to having a psychopath kill a group of innocent mortals."

"That's nice to know. Elysian's home – has the security system been repaired since he died?"

"Not that I'm aware of. Why?"

"We're going to break into it again. I trust you won't have a problem with that."

"So long as you turn over any Sanctuary-related documents you might find, no, I have no problem with that at all. There could still be a police presence, of course – it is, technically, an active crime scene."

"I'll let the mayor's office know we're coming," Skulduggery said. "It's always good to have friends in high places."

They left Ghastly in his shop.

39

Skulduggery made a call to the mayor and, by the time they pulled up outside the late Cyrus Elysian's house, the Roarhaven Police had been told to expect them. The two cops still guarding the place nodded in greeting and stood aside.

A search of the top floors found nothing pertaining to the case. They found nothing pertaining to much of anything, really. Elysian had little in the way of personal effects, and had mostly surrounded himself with works of art displayed in cases or on plinths.

They went downstairs, into the private museum. Most of the pieces here had tags on them denoting the actual owners, and some had already been shipped back. Skulduggery didn't seem interested in the artwork, however. Most of his attention was on the walls and floor.

Valkyrie's phone rang and she answered.

"That was Reverie," she said when she hung up. "Avant Garde is awake."

"Is he talking?" Skulduggery asked, running his hands over the wall.

"He's conscious and communicating. I told Reverie we'd

call by as soon as we're done here. He might know something useful."

"Yes, he might," Skulduggery murmured, and clicked a hidden panel. A door slid open. As much as she disliked Elysian, Valkyrie did appreciate a good secret room.

They stepped into a mid-sized, windowless office. One wall was lined with filing cabinets; the opposite wall was lined with monitors. The remaining walls held various boards covered in small, neat handwriting. In the middle of the room was a desk and a chair. Beside the desk, Cyrus Elysian stood.

"Detective Cain," he said, glowing ever so faintly. "Detective Pleasant. What an unwelcome surprise."

"Huh," said Valkyrie, walking over to the desk and taking the Echo Stone from its cradle. It was pretty much identical to the one that had once housed her uncle's personality. She put it back. "The real Elysian copied you on to the Stone so he could finally have an intelligent conversation, is that it?"

Elysian smiled. "You sound like you've heard that joke before."

"My uncle used it a few times."

"Ah, yes, Gordon Edgley. I must admit, I have never read his work. I prefer my novels to be better written."

"Risky talk for an easily deactivated hologram."

"I would not stay deactivated for long, I'm afraid. My expertise is too widely sought-after."

Skulduggery opened the first filing cabinet.

"Those are confidential," Elysian said, irritation in his voice, but Skulduggery ignored him and proceeded to rifle through the files.

"So the real Elysian used you as a sounding board, right?" Valkyrie asked, sitting herself in the chair. "He bounced ideas off you?"

"The ideas bounced back and forth," Elysian said. "I *am* capable of having an original thought every now and then."

"Did he tell you about Rumour Mills?"

"I don't discuss my clients."

"When was the last time you talked to him?" Skulduggery asked.

"The morning before he died."

"You're aware that he's dead. How?"

"I am thoroughly capable of contacting the outside world. The cradle is designed to activate the Echo Stone each morning at the same time. While Doctor Elysian travelled to the High Sanctuary to work, I stayed here. Everything in this office is voice-activated. Occasionally, I will take part in conference calls and I'm always ready to answer questions from members of whichever team I happen to be assigned to that week. The fact that Doctor Elysian is dead has not altered my daily routine one bit."

"How did you react when you discovered that the real you had been killed?" Valkyrie asked.

"I *am* the real me," said Elysian. "When the *other* me died, I lamented the loss of a beautiful mind and a unique talent, and then I got back to work. Which I am keen to do now, as a matter of fact."

"How much do you know about his killer?" Skulduggery asked.

"This Ersatz person? Just what I read in the reports."

"He used a wand, the killer. A wand that the other Elysian had access to."

"I'm sure I wouldn't know anything about that."

"We spoke to Elysian before he died," Skulduggery said. "I didn't like him."

"Few do."

"He started telling us about his work with the Sanctuary, and how it linked to his treatment of Rumour Mills. He was murdered before he could tell us what we needed to know. Perhaps you can fill in the blanks."

Elysian smiled. "I don't discuss my clients – not even my dead ones."

"But she wasn't your client, was she? She was the *other* Elysian's client. You're free to tell us whatever we want to know."

"Do you think I am less intelligent than the original, Detective Pleasant? Do you think I am more gullible? I am not the same man as the Elysian you spoke with, of course – we stopped being the same man the moment I was recorded on to this Echo Stone. But I am not inferior, either. Come to think of it, due to his current status – which is to say deceased – I can now claim, without worry of contradiction, to be, in fact, the superior version." His smile broadened. "How delightful."

Skulduggery closed the filing cabinet and came over, taking the Echo Stone from the cradle. "You are obviously a valued asset to the Sanctuary," he said. "Your knowledge, experience, and expertise undoubtedly combine to make you invaluable."

"Quite."

"So threatening to deactivate the Stone is not something you'll take seriously. You are, as you say, too much in demand."

"I'm glad we agree."

Skulduggery tossed the Echo Stone to Valkyrie. "So we'll threaten to destroy it instead."

The smile faded from Elysian's face. "You wouldn't dare."

"I don't know how much energy it would require to fry an Echo Stone – to literally burn you out of it – but I'm sure Valkyrie could manage it without too much effort. Valkyrie, what do you think?"

Valkyrie put her feet up on the desk and shrugged. "I'd say it'd take more energy than I use to heat up a cold cup of coffee, but less than I'd need to blast a hole through a wall."

"You're bluffing," Elysian said. "The Sanctuary would never allow—"

"We don't work for the Sanctuary," Skulduggery said. "We're Arbiters, remember? We answer to no one but ourselves."

Valkyrie flipped the Stone in her hand and Elysian stepped forward.

"Be careful," he said tightly. "I am too valuable to the realm of science to risk damaging."

She shrugged. "Then if I damage you by accident, I'll apologise to the realm of science. But if I damage you, I promise it'll be on purpose."

"You won't get away with—"

"We'll get away with whatever we want," Skulduggery said. "You're a recording, Doctor. You're an imprint."

"I am a sentient being! If anyone understands that, it is Valkyrie Cain! Your reflection evolved into a real person, did it not? Your own uncle was in the very same state as me and you treated him—"

"I treated him with love and respect because I loved and respected him," Valkyrie interrupted. "I don't have either of those feelings about you." She held the Stone out towards him, and white energy crackled around her hand.

"OK!" Elysian yelled, his image flickering. "OK, do not harm the Stone! What do you want to know? I'll tell you! Do you want to know about Rumour Mills? Do you want to know how I treated her? Do you want to know what I was working on for the Sanctuary?"

Skulduggery straightened his tie a fraction. "That's exactly what we want to know."

"Mind control," said Elysian. They looked at him and he continued. "The project I'm working on in the Sanctuary is called Veritas. It's a technique – well, a device, really – that reaches into the soul in order to extract the true name."

Valkyrie took her feet off the desk.

"I see that I have your attention," Elysian said. "Good. It really is as impressive as it sounds. This is something I've been obsessed with for decades, following the ground-breaking work pioneered by Doctor Nye during the—"

"You worked with Nye?" Skulduggery said.

"There were times when I worked by its side, yes, but mostly I took its research, I examined its experiments, I tried to replicate its results... With all due humility, I am a genius and a leader in my field, but Doctor Nye is something far more. Or it was, anyway, before *Professor* Nye replaced it. I have not yet had the pleasure of meeting the professor, but I hope to rectify that within a reasonable—"

Energy crackled around Valkyrie's fist and Elysian's image flickered violently.

"Please!" he shouted. "Please!"

She eased off, and his image faded up once more.

He continued, with obvious nervousness. "Using, ah, using Doctor Nye's research and adding it to our own, we—"

"Who is *we?*" asked Skulduggery.

"My old partner and I. Decades ago, I had come up with the idea for Veritas with Clutter Gaines, a brilliant scientist who is sadly no longer with us. Nye's research opened up so many possibilities that, working with the team at the Sanctuary, I was able to transform our theoretical machine into a physical device that could reach into the soul. Please understand that the terms I'm using, clumsy and misleading as they may be, are for your benefit. The, ah, the so-called soul, the life force, is where the true name resides. The device, essentially, reads the true name, translates it, and presents it to us. Again, I'm using radically simplified terms to describe an incredibly complex procedure."

"So you wanted power?" Valkyrie asked. "You wanted to become the next Darquesse, is that it?"

"Far be it. In fact, the Veritas device is designed to prohibit an individual from using it on themselves."

"Then what's the point of finding out someone's true name?"

Elysian frowned. "Like I said, it's mind control. The purpose is to control people's minds."

"And Ghastly Bespoke is allowing this to continue?"

"'Allowing'? Detective, Grand Mage Bespoke initiated the revival of the project in the first place."

Valkyrie stood. "You're lying."

"I assure you, I am not."

"So Ghastly told you to construct this device, did he?"

"Well... yes. I told him about my work, I told him that

337

Veritas was the next inevitable breakthrough, and either he gets ahead of it, or he falls victim to it. He decided on the wisest course of action."

"Who have you used it on?" Skulduggery asked.

"It is still in its testing phase."

"Who have you used it on?"

"No one!" Elysian said. "Practically no one!"

Valkyrie tightened her grip on the Stone and Elysian's eyes widened.

"Volunteers!" he said quickly. "Twelve volunteers, as part of a test group. There was a twenty-five per cent success rate."

"So you discovered the true names of three people," Skulduggery said.

Elysian nodded. "And once those names were used on those volunteers, once we confirmed that they were accurate, we destroyed that information, paid the volunteers, and said goodbye to them. No harm was done. Obviously, there were risks. If a volunteer discovered their true name before we could use it, we could have been facing another Darquesse or Argeddion situation. Rest assured, Grand Mage Bespoke insisted on strict protocols regarding the volunteers and these protocols were adhered to rigidly."

"Was Rumour Mills part of this group?" Valkyrie asked.

"No. Not officially."

"You'd better keep talking."

"Rumour came to me in my capacity as a therapist," said Elysian. "I knew her father through Clutter Gaines, and he told me she had experienced something during the Deletion that she was having trouble dealing with."

"She was burned alive."

"Quite. Her experience, naturally, traumatised her. She was plagued by nightmares, she was developing agoraphobic symptoms, she was highly distrustful of strangers, and, quite honestly, deeply resentful of mortals."

"Understandable."

"Rumour was not a stupid person, and she recognised these burgeoning traits and did not welcome them. She was a *people person*. She saw where her trauma was taking her and she wanted no part of it. She wanted help."

"Did you help her?"

"I did what I could," said Elysian. "My work as a therapist utilises my skills as a Sensitive, but despite popular opinion I do not simply barge into my patients' minds and clear away their bad thoughts. It is not *my* work that cures them. It must be their own."

"So how did Rumour respond to the therapy?"

"She made good progress at first. Then she deteriorated. I happened to mention my work at the Sanctuary—"

"You happened to mention your top-secret, highly confidential, hugely problematic work at the Sanctuary?" Valkyrie said. "What, it slipped out mid-conversation?"

"Or were you looking for a new volunteer?" Skulduggery asked.

Elysian's jaw clenched. "I happened to mention it and Rumour saw a chance to rid herself of her pain."

"She wanted you to use the Veritas device and find out her true name," said Skulduggery. "She didn't want power, though. She had no interest in becoming a god. She wanted to be instructed to forget what had happened to her."

"Not forget, no," said Elysian, "but to forgive. Her trauma was a boulder obstructing her future. She wanted to move beyond it, to pass it by, and to forgive the mortals who had put it there. She wasn't capable of doing that by herself, but if ordered to do so, she wouldn't have had to think twice."

"And what happened?" Valkyrie asked.

"I don't know."

"I'm sorry?"

"All I know is that the other Doctor Elysian, the flesh-and-blood Doctor Elysian, was planning to use Veritas on her. When I asked him about it later, he wouldn't discuss it."

"Why not?"

"I have no idea."

"But you're him," said Valkyrie. "Even if something went wrong, why wouldn't he discuss it with himself?"

"Because he wouldn't have been discussing it with himself," Skulduggery said. "He'd have been discussing it with an arrogant, cruel, egomaniacal alternate *version* of himself."

Elysian shrugged. "I can be quite cutting, it's true."

"So he didn't talk to you about it," Valkyrie said, "because you're too mean? And he never told you how it went? He never mentioned Rumour again?"

"Not until he told me she was dead."

40

They parked beneath the High Sanctuary and took the tiles up to the foyer. They passed behind Cerise and stepped into the elevator without her noticing. Valkyrie was glad.

"What do we do about Ghastly?" she asked when the elevator doors closed.

"We get over our disappointment as quickly as possible," Skulduggery answered.

"It's a little more than disappointment, though, isn't it? He's got people working on a way to control everyone on the planet. That's not good-guy behaviour, Skulduggery."

"I'm aware."

"If it were anyone else doing that—"

"We'd burn it all to the ground," Skulduggery said.

"So what do we do?"

"We get over our disappointment, we calm down, we talk to Avant Garde and then, on our way out, we talk to Ghastly. We hear his reasons. We present our argument. We reach an understanding. And *then* we burn it all to the ground."

Valkyrie nodded. "Cool."

Cadence Clearwater was already in the Infirmary when they arrived. "They won't let me see him," she said.

"You can see him once we've finished asking him questions," Skulduggery said.

"I'm afraid I won't be much good to you."

They turned as Avant Garde walked slowly out of his room. He was pale, with bags under his eyes, but his dark suit was impeccable. He did up both buttons on his jacket as he made his way over, squaring his shoulders as he neared.

Skulduggery shook his hand. "Avant, very good to meet you."

"Same here," Avant said. "I'd like to say Cogent talked about you, but Cogent didn't talk about anyone. Detective Cain, pleasure to meet you, too."

They shook hands. Cadence just stood there like she didn't know what to do.

"You're awake," she finally said.

"Yeah," Avant replied, "but I'm going to need some time before I can give anyone any answers. My head's a mess. Everything's foggy."

Reverie hurried over. "Detective Garde, did I or did I not give you strict instructions not to exert yourself?"

He frowned. "Did you?"

"If you can't remember, then you definitely shouldn't be—"

"Oh, wait, it's coming back to me now. You said I shouldn't get out of bed." He looked down at himself. "Aw, hell. Doc, I got out of bed."

"You are not as charming as you think you are, Detective."

"But I do make the effort."

She turned to Skulduggery and Valkyrie. "He has

responded very well to our treatments, but there are still unanswered questions about his injuries and I'm sorry, we need to conduct more tests before I can allow you to talk to him."

Valkyrie's phone buzzed and she took it out, read the message, then glanced at Skulduggery. "Ersatz has sent us another letter," she said. "Avant, give us a call when you can talk, OK?"

"What will I do?" Cadence asked.

Skulduggery responded. "If you want to be useful, Detective Clearwater, you'll stay here. Ersatz tried to kill Avant once; he might return to finish the job. Keep an eye on your phone and we'll call you if we need you."

Cadence nodded. "I will, sir. Yes, sir."

They took the elevator to the security floor, heading straight to their office. The envelope sat on Valkyrie's desk, addressed simply to The Arbiters.

Skulduggery opened it, took out the page, and they read it.

```
I have just one more puzzle for you,
Detective Pleasant. You have impressed
me, so far, with your deductive
reasoning, with your intellectual
prowess, with your sheer intelligence,
which — I happily admit — far exceeds
my own. I have tried, in my way, to
test you, to challenge you, to
provoke you, and while you have
solved the first riddles with what I
can only imagine to be consummate
```

ease, you have also failed to catch
me. Or even identify me.

   My work is almost done, so I will
give you one more riddle. This is a
riddle, in fact, that Valkyrie may
well ask of you, Detective Pleasant,
if she puts on her detective's cap:
what is it that separates you from me?

Valkyrie frowned. "That's it? A single riddle?"

"Interesting," Skulduggery murmured.

"What happened to the rule of three? He's got a last
chance to mess with us and this is what he does? So the
answer to the riddle is something that separates us?"

Skulduggery looked at her. "List them."

"List the things that separate us?"

"You have fifteen seconds to list as many as you can."

"I'm female, you're male. I'm alive, you're dead. I'm tall,
you're taller. I'm funny, you're not. I'm young, you're old.
I'm cool, you're annoying. Um... this isn't as easy as it—
OK, I'm flesh and blood, you're a skeleton. I'm—"

"Time's up."

"How did I do? Did I solve it?"

"I have no idea. Without some kind of framework, it will
be virtually impossible to pin down where we should be
focusing."

"Do you think he ran out of time, and that's why there's
only one riddle? Or maybe he ran out of riddles. It can't
be easy thinking them up."

Skulduggery's head tilted. "Or maybe there isn't only one."

"No, there is. See?" She pointed. "One."

"But the solution could be anything, agreed? He has asked one single question, but the amount of potential answers is almost endless."

"You think he's looking for three answers from one riddle?"

"And, when they're combined, they'll lead us to him."

Valkyrie sighed. "I still don't see how that helps. The solution might be in the differences between us in music, fashion, and favourite movies – but even in those categories alone there are literally thousands of options. Hundreds of thousands. Millions."

"But he didn't ask for the difference between us, did he? He's asking what *separates* us. He calls me *Detective Pleasant* but he calls you *Valkyrie*, and refers to *her* detective's cap, which might serve to put an emphasis on the fake names we use when posing as Guards. The question is *what is it that separates you from me?* If the *you* in this question refers to your Garda alias, then what he's actually asking is what separates *Her* from *Me*."

Valkyrie closed her eyes. "I'm so confused, but OK. What separates us, in that case, is the fact that I'm a Detective Sergeant and you're a Detective Inspector." She frowned. "But would Ersatz even know about our fake names?"

"Let's assume that he's done his homework. Let's leave that train of thought aside for the moment. What else separates you from me?"

"I don't know," she said. "*You from me*. The letter *r*? Ersatz likes letters so much, you got, what, nine letters in *you from me*. Four on each side, separated by the one in the middle: *r*. Does *r* mean anything? Is that a clue?"

"*R* is the eighteenth letter, and the fourteenth consonant, in the English alphabet," Skulduggery said. "From the Greek *rho*. It's the *littera canina*."

"The what?"

"The canine letter. It sounds like a growling dog when you say it. Shakespeare referred to it as *the dog's name*. *R* is used as the written abbreviation for *rex* and *regina*, or king and queen."

"How do you know all these things?"

"I read a lot."

"But how can you just know, like, random facts about random letters?"

"They're not random facts. They're just facts."

"Do you know one of the most irritating things about you?"

"That there is *nothing* irritating about me?"

"Oh, there are plenty of irritating things about you, believe me. But one of the *most* irritating is that I can point to literally anything in this room and I bet you'd be able to tell me something incredibly, randomly stupid about it."

"I don't think that's accurate at all, actually." Valkyrie pointed at the door handle, but he shook his head. "Pick something else. I was around when metalworking advanced to such a degree that locks could use a twisting motion to open, which, as you can imagine, led to a boom in decorative door handles. Basically, I know a lot about them, but that's just because you happened to pick a topic I found very interesting once upon a time."

Valkyrie pointed to the bulletin board mounted on the wall.

"I only know what *everyone* knows about the humble corkboard," Skulduggery said, "in that it was initially a

German invention, primarily used as insulation, until an American gentleman patented it, in 1924, as a bulletin board you could stick drawing pins into. His patent lasted until 1941 because back then, in America, as you know, the lifespan of a patent was only seventeen years."

"No, Skulduggery, I did not know that the lifespan of a patent was only seventeen years in America in 1924," Valkyrie said. "Neither did I know that corkboard was a German invention."

"Then what on earth did you learn about in school?"

"Nothing like this," Valkyrie said. "But whatever, y'know? It's fine. Your head is full of random yet useful information and mine is full of half-remembered song lyrics. We each bring something to the table." She sighed. "So what were you saying? The letter *R* is Shakespeare's dog, or something?"

"Shakespeare called it *the dog's name*, yes."

"Did Shakespeare even have a dog?"

"I don't know, actually. I never asked him. I'd imagine he would have had – or his family would have had one, at least, maybe on his Stratford estate. He could also have had some hunting dogs."

"And we don't know any of their names? So that's probably not a clue."

Skulduggery hesitated.

"Oh, God," she said. "You've got another random piece of information, haven't you?"

"Just that *Shakespeare's Dog* is a novel by Leon Rooke, published in 1983, an amusingly bawdy novel told from the point of view of Shakespeare's pet, a dog named Hooker."

"Hooker," Valkyrie repeated.

"A hooker is—"

"I know what a hooker is."

"—one of the eight forwards in a rugby team."

"Oh," Valkyrie said. "Yeah. So you think the clue has something to do with rugby?"

Skulduggery tapped his chin. "Maybe. But there is a Rook Hill in Galway, and another one just outside Dublin, though neither Rook is spelled with an e at the end, like the writer…"

"Wait," Valkyrie said. "I know where you're getting Rook from, obviously, but you plucked Hill out of nowhere."

"Not really. It came back to what you were saying about our Garda aliases."

"Explain that one to me."

"What separates a Detective Inspector from a Detective Sergeant? The answer is rank. Rank is slang for stench. Another way of saying something has a stench is saying it reeks."

"Ersatz is in the mountains!" Valkyrie said, snapping her fingers. "He's at MacGillycuddy's Reeks! Where the Remnant Receptacle was!"

"Maybe."

She soured. "You mean no."

"Reek means a *rick* or *stack* in Irish, and yes, it is sometimes used to name hills."

"So Rooke and Rank equals Rook Hill," Valkyrie said. "That is quite a stretch."

"Yes."

"Like, quite a ridiculous stretch."

"True."

"I'm not saying all of it doesn't add up. I'm just saying there are probably an infinite number of other possibilities.

The chances of these leaps of yours, from one fact to another, adding up to the riddle's solution is..."

"Highly unlikely," Skulduggery said, taking out his phone. "I agree with you wholeheartedly."

"So what are you doing?"

He started tapping and swiping the screen. "I'm looking at a map of the closest Rook Hill to us, just to see if anything else fits."

Valkyrie watched him. "If this turns out to be the answer to the riddle, I'll... I'll... I don't know what I'll do."

"I will share in your astonishment if that is the case."

More swiping. Some zooming in and then zooming out.

"You can't just solve problems like that," she told him. "You can't just head down one avenue of thought and find tenuous links to other things that you then knock into shape. That's not how life works."

"You're correct," said Skulduggery. "Although that wasn't what I was doing."

"Then what were you doing?"

"I was heading down multiple avenues of thought at the same time, bouncing between each of them, searching for links. For instance, something that separates you from me is age, so the question *what is it that separates you from me?* could be rephrased as *what is age?* And what *is* age? Well, the word itself is from the Latin *aevum*. As a noun, it can either mean the length of time that a thing has existed or a distinct period of history. But that's too broad. Let's narrow it down to you, because it's a question he wanted *you* to ask. So what is your age, Valkyrie? You're thirty-one. Does that number hold any relevance to you?"

"I don't—"

"Since we're dealing with the killer of a group of horror fans, *31* is a 2016 horror movie directed by Rob Zombie. Not one of his better films, admittedly, but who am I to judge? Thirty-one is also the date in October of Halloween, and the title of a 1978 John Carpenter movie, the remake of which Mr Zombie directed and released in 2007. What separates, in years, the original from the remake is twenty-nine. The answer to what separates twenty-nine from thirty-one could, arguably, be either three, one, or thirty."

"Wait, what? How did you get—?"

"Add them up and you have thirty-four. Thirty-four is the atomic number of selenium, from the Greek *selene* meaning *moon*. It is the number of the house where your girlfriend Militsa lives in Roarhaven. There can be up to thirty-four vertebrae in the spinal column. Thirty-four is a semiprime number, and the smallest number to be surrounded by numbers with the same amount of devisors as it has. Thirty-four is also the age at which I proposed to my future wife. We were married a year later. Does any of that hold any relevance to this case?"

Valkyrie stared at him. "No?"

"Exactly."

"So you headed down all these different avenues of thought and you only told me about the most promising one?"

Skulduggery looked up at her for a moment. "See?" he said. "You *do* understand me. Could you look up Quality Fresh Farms, in Rook Hill?"

Valkyrie took out her phone while he continued to search the map, and found what she was looking for. "OK," she said, "it's been closed down for over twenty-five years."

"What was it?"

"Farm and butcher, apparently."

"They had their own abattoir?" Skulduggery asked. "On-site?"

"How did you know?"

He tapped a message on his phone before putting it away. "What separates you and me, Valkyrie? What was one of the first things you said? I'm a skeleton, and you're flesh and blood. So, meat. Meat separates us."

"Meat," she said. "Slaughterhouse. I mean, it's a little unsubtle, but I suppose it kinda fits."

"*Kinda fits* is good enough for me," Skulduggery said. "Let's roll, Robin."

"I am not Robin in this equation."

"You can't be Batman. I'm Batman."

"We can both be Batman."

Skulduggery considered this. "Fine," he said. "You can be Batman, too. Does Batman need to pee?"

"I'm sorry?"

"It's a bit of a drive, and we'll probably be plunged into a life-or-death battle at the end of it. If you have to use the facilities, now would be the best time."

Valkyrie sighed, and led the way out. "Yes, Batman needs to pee."

41

Valkyrie peed, then went straight down to the Bentley. She ended up waiting there for ten minutes before Skulduggery joined her. He didn't explain why he was late. She was getting used to that.

They drove for almost an hour without saying much. This part was pretty typical. Knowing she was about to enter into a violent situation tended to either make Valkyrie talk a whole lot of nonsense or clam up. She distracted herself with other thoughts. The other thoughts led to a question.

"What's it like to be you?"

"It's wonderful," Skulduggery replied, taking the Bentley round a slow-moving tractor and speeding on, fields and meadows whipping by on either side. "Why do you ask?"

"The way your mind works," Valkyrie said, "it must seem like you're wading through quicksand when you're talking to the rest of us. How annoying is it to be partnered with someone like me? Oh, I know I'm smart – don't worry about that. I've got no inferiority complex there. But compared to you I'm as dumb as a bag of hammers."

"There are other qualities you have that keep me interested."

"Well, they must be spectacular, because if I were you I'd just be going around with a scowl and a headache all day."

"Then it's a good thing I don't scowl or get headaches. We're here, by the way."

They slowed, turning on to a disused driveway. They drove up as far as they could, stopping before a padlocked iron gate. Huge sheds sat in the concrete yard beyond. Between the sheds, more iron gates and railings – lots of railings, the kind sturdy enough to corral livestock. The place was empty and quiet, and looked like it had been that way for years.

Skulduggery used the air to lift them both over the gate, and they walked towards the largest shed: a squat, ugly building of concrete and small, frosted windows darkened by decades of grime.

The heavy door, the one used by the cattle, was open slightly. Skulduggery took out his gun and led the way in.

It was dark inside. Years ago, Valkyrie would have sent a ball of crackling white energy into the air so that it could hover overhead, illuminating their surroundings. But she'd lost the knack of that, so Skulduggery conjured a fireball and held it in his left hand as they advanced up a ramp wide enough to fit two cars.

The ramp continued round a corner. Ahead, thick plastic curtains – clouded and dirty – hung from the ceiling. There were lights on the other side. Skulduggery let the flames in his hand go out.

They reached the plastic curtains, nodded to each other, and pushed through.

The killing floor was wide. Pipes and cables and railings crossed the ceiling. The walls were tiled. A machine stood quietly in the far corner. There were hoses everywhere, and sluice gates, and hooks, and the place was lit by floodlights.

There were three large objects covered in sheets and behind them, raised up on a wooden platform, stood Ersatz, the wand in his hand.

The whole thing reeked of performance, of drama, of spectacle. Skulduggery's final test had been the riddle to get them here. Valkyrie had a feeling that she was looking at her final test right now.

"Congratulations," Ersatz said. "You have followed the clues as I have laid them out. Welcome to the end."

"I'm not terribly *au fait* with horror movies," Skulduggery responded, taking off his hat like he was getting ready for a fight, "but is this the moment when the killer unmasks?"

"Traditionally? Yes. But the unmasking only happens if you earn it, Detective."

"The middle one," Valkyrie called out.

Ersatz turned his head a fraction to focus on her.

"The middle one," she repeated. "You're going to make me choose, aren't you? That's why these things are covered in sheets. You're going to pull the sheets off and force me to make a moral choice. Well, screw it. I pick the middle one. Boom. Game over."

Ersatz's tone was playful. "How presumptuous of you. How daring. You don't even know what the stakes are."

"Oh, I'm sure they're something predictably awful. So I'm going to take whatever impossible decision you're going to try to get me to make, and skip to the end. No matter what my options are, I pick sheet number two."

"I see. I'm afraid that's not how it works. That's not how the game is played."

"That's how it's gonna work today."

"Why don't I give you the options, anyway?" said Ersatz. "Then you can make up your mind. There are three lives at stake, Detective Cain."

"Don't care."

"Before you stands—"

"Blah blah blah."

Ersatz flicked the wand and Skulduggery hurtled back, his hat falling from his hand. Another flick and a wall of red energy descended, cutting the room in two and sealing Skulduggery off from Valkyrie.

Before she could formulate a plan of action, Ersatz swished the wand and the first sheet flew off, revealing an upright casket, an iron maiden, its open door festooned with spikes. Within the casket, bound by ropes and shackles, her mouth gagged, stood Militsa.

42

Energy surged through Valkyrie's body before she was even aware that she had bolted towards her girlfriend.

"No, no, no," said Ersatz.

Valkyrie froze. Militsa watched her with eyes brimming with tears.

"If you attempt to interfere with the iron maiden," said Ersatz, "the door will spring shut. I built these maidens myself. The hinge mechanisms are inordinately powerful, and the spikes ridiculously sharp."

"Let her go or I'll kill you," Valkyrie said quietly.

"*You* can save her, if you want," Ersatz replied. "There's a release catch halfway down that will open the shackles and retract the spikes. But saving one occupant will trigger the remaining two maidens, killing the occupants instantly."

"I choose Militsa."

"Are you sure? You don't want to see who else is in danger? You might change your mind..."

Valkyrie glanced at Skulduggery, who was standing helplessly on the other side of that energy wall. She turned again to Ersatz, but didn't say anything. He took her silence as permission, and flicked the wand.

The sheet on the third iron maiden dropped to the floor. Simone Ruddy, Rumour Mills' best friend in all the world, stood in the casket. She immediately started screaming behind her gag.

"Can you still choose your girlfriend over this mortal?" Ersatz asked. "Do you still value the life of the woman you love over this poor, defenceless civilian? Can you decide to be selfish and think only of yourself, only of what *you* want, what *you* need, or can you rescue, instead, someone you barely know?"

Valkyrie forced herself to be calm. She drank in all the excess energy that was scorching her clothes and let it settle. "You don't have to do this," she said.

"I won't be doing anything, Detective Cain. Or can I call you Valkyrie? Valkyrie, you're going to be the one making the choice, not me."

"But why?" Valkyrie asked. "You've killed them all. You've killed everyone who hurt Rumour Mills."

"Yes. All of them. All except for Handsome Whitlock."

"But you let him live."

"And yet it wasn't mercy that stayed my hand, Valkyrie. It was you and your partner. And you have a chance to do so again – to save another life."

"And if I refuse to make the choice?"

"If you fail to choose before the clock reaches zero? Then the iron maidens will close. All three of them."

On the wall at the far end of the room was a digital readout, a countdown. Valkyrie had just under sixteen minutes. Plenty of time – though the seconds were moving fast.

"Or," she said loudly, "we could solve the mystery. We could figure out who you are."

"That's not your test, Valkyrie. That's not your challenge. Your test—"

"I don't care!" she roared. "These tests are stupid! They suck! Why do you have me making these moral decisions? Why are my tests all about goddamn ethics and Skulduggery's are about solving riddles?"

"Skulduggery's tests are to gauge whether or not he is a smarter person than me. Your tests are to gauge whether or not you're a *better* person than me. Different tests for different people."

"Oh, I'm pretty sure that I'm a better person than you. I think I've answered that question, you *dribbling psychopath*. But you want to test me? You want to actually challenge me? If I can figure out who you are, you let Militsa and Simone and whoever's in the last iron maiden go. Agreed?"

Ersatz paused. "I accept your challenge. And to help you, you can confer with Skulduggery. My only condition is that he may not assist in your deductions."

"That's fine with me," said Valkyrie. "I don't even need him to solve this. You think you're so clever, don't you? Skulduggery, have you worked out who he is yet?"

"I have," Skulduggery replied.

"And do I have everything I need to figure it out myself?"

"You do."

Valkyrie nodded, not taking her eyes off Ersatz. To look at Simone right now would be a distraction. To look at Militsa would be heartbreak.

"OK," she said, pacing. "OK, first thing is the *why*. Once I know why you did it, the *who* will follow. Why did you kill all those people? Why did you kill the mortals, and why did you kill Rumour Mills and Cyrus Elysian and why did you try to kill Handsome Whitlock? Six mortals and three mages. Why?"

Ersatz didn't react. Ninety seconds had passed on the clock already.

"It was personal," Valkyrie said. "Those mortals, especially. How you killed them was... cruel. Sadistic. You hated them. You wanted them to suffer."

"And how they did suffer," said Ersatz. "How they did scream. How they did beg."

"Yeah, whatever. We thought they might have been able to identify you. We thought Rumour knew you, had introduced you to them, and then maybe they saw you do something and so you needed to eliminate the witnesses. But that's not it. This is about Rumour. This is all about Rumour.

"The mortals were her friends. Handsome was her boyfriend. Elysian was her doctor. We know about what happened during the Deletion. We know they burned her alive. We know Handsome broke up with her because he couldn't handle how her trauma was affecting her and we know Elysian was going to let her try his Veritas device to eradicate all the bad feelings.

"You killed the mortals in revenge for what they'd done. You killed Elysian because he'd failed her as a doctor. You went after Handsome because he let her down when she needed him the most. You're very big on failure, aren't you? That's why you picked the name Ersatz. You see yourself as an inferior substitute, don't you? An imitation of who you're meant to be. Why? Because you failed Rumour as well?"

Ersatz didn't respond.

"That's it, isn't it?" said Valkyrie. "You failed her. You blame yourself. You reckon you're just as guilty as the people you've killed."

"Your time is running out, Valkyrie. Who are your suspects?"

"Well," she said, "Rumour's father is the obvious one, right? Salter Such. He'd have all the motivation in the world as far as revenge goes. He's definitely suspect number one. Suspect number two is Handsome."

Ersatz inclined his head. "Handsome Whitlock? That's an interesting addition. Especially seeing as how you saw me in the same room as him."

"No, we didn't. We saw you, and then we saw him, *after* you'd teleported out. He told us you wanted to kill him, but why delay it? He was sitting in that attic for days before we even realised you'd sent us a letter. Why didn't you kill him when we failed to turn up after twenty-four hours? Maybe because Handsome is not that big of a creep, after all. Maybe he'd actually seen the error of his ways and so, tormented by the part he played in Rumour's death, he put on that mask and picked up that wand and embarked on a crazy revenge scheme."

"What an intriguing theory. You might be right, of course. Or you might be giving Handsome far too much credit."

"Yeah, maybe – though establishing himself as just another victim did throw us off his scent."

"So that's Salter Such and Handsome Whitlock," Ersatz said. "Suspects one and two. Do you have a Suspect Number Three?

"Vincent Driscoll," said Valkyrie. "The lovestruck

neighbour. The horror fan too shy to ever ask Rumour out. Mortal – as far as we know. But even the faintest trace of magic would be enough to power that wand of yours – and if he *did* have magic he'd be able to remember what happened during the Deletion, just like Eimear Shevlin did. That would have been enough to fuel his rage. There are other suspects, of course. You could be Catherine Dennehy, Rumour's mother. You're always in the same outfit, after all. What's so special about it? Skulduggery wears clothes that fill out – no reason you couldn't, too, changing a female form to male. And that mask disguises your voice."

Ersatz glanced at the clock. Eleven and a half minutes left.

"But one thing still doesn't fit," Valkyrie continued. "Why did you kill Rumour? If this is about revenge, like I think it is, then why start by killing somebody you loved? Unless that's the guilt driving you. Unless you killed Rumour in a rage, during an argument, and once you'd realised what you'd done you turned the hatred that you felt for yourself outwards so you wouldn't have to admit what you'd done. Is that it? It is, isn't it? I know who you are! You're Handsome Whitlock! I've won!"

"You're wrong," said Ersatz. "And because you are wrong, you'll have to choose who lives and who dies. And to make it easier..." He flicked the wand. The final sheet flew off and all the strength left Valkyrie's legs.

"No," she whispered.

Winter struggled against her bonds, a gag in her mouth, her eyes narrowed in fury.

"You have just under eleven minutes to decide who to save," Ersatz said. "Who will it be? Your girlfriend, a mortal, or your sister?"

"Please," Valkyrie said, "don't do this."

"Make your choice," said Ersatz. "Save who you're going to save. Say goodbye to the others."

Valkyrie stepped towards the casket on the right. "I'm sorry," she said to Simone. "I'm so very sorry."

Simone stared at her, then did her best to shake her head, her protests muffled by the gag.

On stiff legs, Valkyrie took three steps to her left. To Militsa.

"I'm sorry, baby," she said, tears starting to roll down her cheeks. "I'm so sorry. I'm sorry I got you involved in this. I'm sorry I haven't already stopped him. I'm sorry that you're... I love you. Militsa, you've got to understand that. I love you, baby. But I have to save my sister. There's no choice here. There's no decision. Letting a mortal die... It'll torture me and I'll hate myself forever, but I can live with it. But if I save you and not Winter, you'll never be able to forgive yourself."

Militsa gave her a gentle nod, and smiled behind the gag.

"I love you," Valkyrie said. "With all my heart."

The clock on the wall showed ten minutes remaining.

Valkyrie ran over to Winter's iron maiden. Her sister watched as she reached out, frowning slightly when Valkyrie's finger hovered over the release catch.

Winter mumbled something. A question. Valkyrie looked at her and then at Simone.

The seconds ticked down.

"Let Simone go," Valkyrie said to Ersatz. "She's innocent."

"Oh, but Simone started all this," Ersatz replied. "During the Deletion, she went to see Rumour. She blamed her for the Shalgoth killing her parents."

"How did that start anything? She was traumatised! She was—"

"After she'd screamed at Rumour, she ran, and took refuge in a hotel where she met Rumour's so-called *friends*, who had also chosen that building in which to cower. She told them this was all Rumour's fault. Simone planted the idea in their heads."

"But that wasn't her!" Valkyrie shouted. "That was another version of her! And she didn't even know what she was saying. She'd just lost her parents. She was angry; she was lashing out. She didn't mean any of it!"

"And because of this I have shown mercy. I have given you a chance to save her. I have given her a chance to live."

"If I may interject," Skulduggery said.

"This isn't about you, skeleton," Ersatz warned. "Your tests are over. Your part in this is done."

"But my tests were to gauge which one of us is smarter. Solving the riddles doesn't prove anything. If you truly are smarter than me, I won't have correctly worked out who you are, will I? Indulge me. We've indulged you, have we not? These games, these riddles, these challenges. We've played along quite dutifully. The least you can do is hear my deductions."

"Very well, Detective. I admit I am curious. But the seconds slip by."

"Then I'll speak quickly," Skulduggery replied. "Everything Valkyrie said has been accurate. Her conclusions are sound. This has all been about a young woman tormented by the memories of something that no longer happened. A young woman so besieged by trauma that she was willing to undergo a process to find out her true name:

363

not to use that power to exact revenge on those who wronged her, but to be instructed to forgive them. Rumour Mills was an extraordinary person, an extraordinarily good person, a person of such compassion, such love, that she may well have gone on to change the world.

"But we'll never know, because, in her efforts to forgive the people who turned against her, she took Cyrus Elysian's Veritas device when it was offered. But she couldn't let him operate it. Who would entrust their true name to someone like that? No, she needed someone she loved. Someone who loved her. Someone who would never betray her, never use her true name against her. She needed her father.

"But something went wrong. She learned her true name before you did. The power exploded through her. She couldn't control it. She attacked you and you defended yourself, didn't you? You killed her. Salter Such, you killed your own daughter."

43

Ersatz reached up, undid the latches on the black mask, and took it off, freeing his long grey hair. His face was flushed and coated with perspiration.

"None of us are innocent," Salter said. "We all deserve to be punished. We all deserve what's coming to us."

"You didn't know what you were doing," Skulduggery responded. "You used the Veritas device, didn't you? But something went wrong. Did it malfunction?"

"No, it worked, it found her true name," said Salter. "But I couldn't pronounce it right. It's a word that didn't exist until that moment so I kept trying, kept repeating it in different ways, but Rumour realised how it was meant to sound before I did."

"And, by realising it, she was the one to discover it."

"And suddenly she had all this new power," said Salter. "It would have overwhelmed even the strongest mind for a time, but Rumour was fragile. Her trauma had left her vulnerable."

"What happened?"

"It tore her mind apart. It broke her. She didn't stand a chance."

"So you hid her away," said Skulduggery, "somewhere you thought she'd be safe, and you went to see Elysian. You demanded that he help."

Salter's lip curled. "It was his fault. He'd told Rumour about that damn Veritas thing. I thought he'd be able to reach into her mind, calm her down."

"What did he do?"

"He said if the Sanctuary got involved they'd lock Rumour up. In order to save the rest of us from what she was becoming, a god they wouldn't be able to control, they'd decide to kill her. So he took back the Veritas device and he gave me this wand. He said it would do whatever I willed it to – that it would be powerful enough to contain her. In the early stages, at least."

"Before she figured out that she had no limits," Valkyrie said.

"I went back to Rumour and I tried. But there's a learning curve with the wand, and it takes a while to figure it out."

"And Rumour was getting worse," Skulduggery said quietly.

"She was terrified of what she might do. Can you imagine that? Her biggest fear was going after her *friends*, the very people who'd killed her."

"An extraordinary person," Skulduggery said quietly.

"She collapsed. She was unconscious, or she was in a coma, or something. She was sleeping, and I was exhausted, and I hadn't eaten."

"You went home," said Valkyrie. "You needed to eat and rest. But she called you, didn't she? She called you and you drove back to her."

"She didn't want to risk hurting anyone so she went to

the park. It was night, but she was all lit up with a... a golden energy. I ran to her, but all she could do was beg me to kill her."

"And then she lost control," Skulduggery said.

"I tried to use the wand to calm her down, but when I saw her power, her sheer destructive *power*, there was a moment of fear and she came at me. I remember wanting to keep her away, just to get some space so I could think of something. I used the wand and..."

"And you killed her," said Valkyrie.

Salter squared his shoulders like he was shifting into another gear.

"You were always a prime suspect," Skulduggery said. "How could you not be? But Rumour's death threw me off your trail, almost eliminating you from my list of possibilities. Almost but not quite. I don't like to ever discount a possibility if I can help it. It wasn't until your final riddle that it all fell into place. This was your family's farm, wasn't it? This is where you were brought up."

"My family have been butchers since the 1600s," said Salter. "Not all of us had magic in our veins, but we had this place – until it wasn't viable any more. How did you know?"

"You've got meat cleavers on display in your home, some of them stamped with a butcher's guild logo that hasn't been used in over three hundred years. You don't strike me as the overly sentimental type, but it's your wife who keeps the Mother's and Father's Day cards, so I'd assume the interior design was down to Catherine. The knives were in storage, I'd imagine, maybe in a crate somewhere until she found them and decided to put them on display. This would have been, what, ten years ago? Maybe a little less? It strikes me as a rather sudden need to acknowledge heritage, to show where both sides of the family come from."

"Those plates she put up are from her side," Salter said. "She thinks they're antique, but they're not. They're cheap, mass-produced things."

"I'm interested in where you got that mask."

"I'd say you are. I made a deal to get this mask. I sold my soul."

"Was it even yours to sell?"

"A rhetorical question signals the end of intelligent conversation," Salter said. "And now the time has come for the choice to be made. Valkyrie, you have just under three minutes left."

Valkyrie glanced back at Skulduggery. "Please tell me you have a plan."

"Plans are for other people," he told her. "I merely have a meticulous schedule of non-spontaneous improvisations. One of the items on that schedule was placing a phone call before we left the High Sanctuary."

The plastic curtain behind him parted, and Catherine Dennehy stepped on to the killing floor.

"Salter?" she said, grief and confusion etched into her face.

"This is your last attempt at getting through to me, is it?" Salter said, anger biting at his laugh. "To use my wife against me? Do you seriously think that's going to work?"

"I heard you," Catherine continued. "Just now, I heard you. You were trying to help her. I know that. It wasn't your fault. You should never have been put in that position. Salter, please, let these people go. I love you. We lost our daughter, but I still love you."

"And you think that I still love you, is that it?" Salter asked. "Cathy, sweetheart, you must listen to me and understand. I hate you."

Catherine's face crumpled. "You don't mean that."

"I hate your entire species," said Salter. "I hate your weakness. I hate how small you are."

"Salter, please..."

"A sorcerer gets older, their mind expands, and they want to try new things, take on new experiences, experiment with new perspectives. For a sorcerer, the years are merely opportunities to grow. But... the older a mortal gets, the narrower their mind becomes."

"Rumour wouldn't want—"

"Do you know why?" Salter asked, interrupting. "Because you mortals are nasty little creatures whose culture is built on a bed of superstition and fear. The older you get, the more resistant you are to change." His face twitched. For a moment, it looked like he couldn't get the words out, but then they spilled from his lips. "Change terrifies you. Ageing terrifies you. So all that superstition and fear rises up from the depths of your very souls and it infects you. It gets into your blood, it gets into your thoughts. Some of you, you're born closer to that darkness than others.

"You, my dear, have gone a long time – relatively speaking – without succumbing, but I can see it starting to happen. Starting to change you. Little things you say, ordinary little things that hint at something worse. But Rumour's friends... they were never very far from that darkness to begin with. They succumbed immediately. They lashed out; they blamed her; they murdered her. Her first death is on their hands, and her second is shared between us. I should die for what

I did, and, when my work is over, I'll welcome it. But not just yet."

Catherine stared at her husband, aghast, and Skulduggery tilted his head.

"This is not going the way I hoped it would," he said. "I thought arranging for Catherine to come here would be enough to stop you."

"There is no stopping me," said Salter. "And I'm sorry, Valkyrie – it looks like your time is just about up."

"No," Valkyrie said.

"You failed to make a choice," said Salter. "You failed your final test. Now all three will die."

"No!" Valkyrie screamed.

"If I may interject a second time," Skulduggery said.

Salter shook his head. "I'm afraid not, Detective Pleasant."

"Save your sister, Valkyrie," Skulduggery said from the other side of that wall of red energy, his right hand going to his left wrist.

The countdown reached zero.

Skulduggery teleported in beside her, stepping over his hat with both hands splayed, the air around Militsa's casket shimmering as the door tried to slam shut but couldn't. Valkyrie was aware of this, but her focus was on the iron maiden containing her sister, twin streams of katahedral energy bursting from her black eyes, turning the door of that iron maiden to dust. And something had caught the door to her right, keeping those nails from Simone Ruddy, and she watched as the door was wrenched from the casket and went hurtling into the far wall. A moment later, Cadence Clearwater leaked into visibility.

Skulduggery twisted his hands and the mechanism on Militsa's casket cracked and the door swung wide.

"Fine," Salter growled, raising the wand, "then I'll do it myself."

In an eyeblink, he was surrounded. Valkyrie didn't have time to count the Sanctuary mages or the sheer number of Cleavers. She barely had time to register Tanith, leaping at Salter, her sword swinging for his head, before Salter flicked the wand and vanished.

"Fletcher!" Skulduggery roared.

Valkyrie felt Fletcher's hand on her shoulder and then they were on a hillside under the warm grey sky, beside an old tree, a grave in front of them and Salter, whirling, the wand rising.

Valkyrie dived to one side and avoided the wave that threw Skulduggery and Fletcher off their feet. She lunged, batting the wand away from her, feeling a rush of energy sizzle past her ear as she rammed the heel of her palm into Salter's chin. He stumbled and she pressed into him, wrapped his right arm with her left, hit him again, then grabbed his shoulder and pulled him into a headbutt. He wrenched himself away, staggering, hands at his face, the wand falling to the grass.

Valkyrie kicked him, driving her full weight into his midsection. He went backwards but didn't fall. Just growled.

She sent lightning into his chest, blasting him backwards, and he hit the tree with a grunt. She tried for his head, the one part of him that wasn't protected, but she was too close. She missed and he was on her, lifting her into the air.

Oh, he was strong.

He slammed her to the ground, emptying the wind from

her lungs. She drove a knee into his side, tried to get up, but he scrambled round, gripping her wrist as he went, and he broke her arm and she screamed. He hit her, his massive fist knocking the scream right out of her. He jumped up, went to stomp on her, but she turned over, got her legs around his and twisted, buckling his knee. He went down, face first, and Valkyrie rolled over him, their legs still intertwined, and she broke something of his that made him cry out.

She came out of that roll on her feet and she stumbled, clutching her arm, taking her eyes off him for a split second as she regained her balance, and when she looked back he was pointing the wand at her.

Crap.

"My work isn't done," Salter said, snarling. "Handsome Whitlock and Simone Ruddy deserve to die."

"No, they don't," Valkyrie replied.

Salter got up slowly, favouring his right leg. "They betrayed Rumour."

Valkyrie shrugged and pain shot through her. That was dumb. "They're human," she said, gritting her teeth. "They're not responsible for what happened to your daughter. Listen to me. What those people did to her was unforgivable. But they weren't the people you killed."

"You're arguing semantics," Salter said. "Just because they didn't have all the same memories doesn't mean they're not the same people."

"That's exactly what it means."

"You won't change my mind, Valkyrie. I won't change yours."

"Put the wand down, Mr Such. There's been enough blood spilled for your daughter already."

"Has there?" he asked, smiling. He had blood on his teeth. "See, I don't think there has. I was going to stop once they were all dead. I thought that crossing out each name on my list would bring me closer to a sense of... completion. Closure. And then I'd be able to die, knowing that my death would close that circle. But I'm no closer. Not even with all those names crossed out."

"Put down the wand," Skulduggery said, walking up beside Valkyrie.

"I don't think I will. It isn't over yet. Not by a long way."

"Whitlock and Simone will be under Sanctuary guard," Skulduggery said. "You'll never even find them, let alone get close enough to kill them."

"It isn't about those two any more. I don't think it ever was. Not really. It's about... *them*." Salter waved his free hand in the air. "The mortals. I was too narrow before. My focus was too limited. I've been doing my research. There are places on the internet where mages document the crimes committed against them during the Deletion. Did you know that? It's where all these anti-mortal groups are finding their voice. I'm making a new list. I'm like Santa Claus, except my list is just the names of all the naughty children, the naughty little mortals. I'm going to visit them, every single one. They're going to pay for what they did to us. For what they did to my daughter."

"We'll stop you," Valkyrie said.

"No, you won't."

He went to flick the wand and Fletcher was beside him, swinging one of Salter's antique cleavers down through his wrist.

It may have been centuries old, but the blade was still

sharp and Salter's hand fell to his daughter's graveside. Salter stared at it, eyes wide, mouth open, then jammed his wrist under his armpit.

"Thank you, Fletcher," Skulduggery said.

"I cut the dude's hand off," Fletcher said dully.

"So you did. Maybe now you could take him back to the High Sanctuary."

Fletcher nodded. "High Sanctuary."

"Maybe the Medical Wing?"

"For his hand."

"For his hand, yes."

"And then jail."

"Then he'll be going to jail, that's right."

Fletcher nodded, and teleported away.

A moment later, he was back.

"I should take the bad guy with me," he said.

"Good idea," said Skulduggery.

Fletcher disappeared with Salter, who still hadn't even screamed, and Valkyrie looked at Skulduggery.

"You think he'll remember to teleport back for us?" she asked.

"Probably not. How's your arm?"

Now that the adrenaline was fading, the full force of the pain was hitting her in waves.

"It's great," Valkyrie responded, grimacing. "It's wonderful. Let's go bowling. How do you think it is? It's broken."

"You get really sarcastic when you're in pain."

"Oh, gee, do I?"

Skulduggery picked up Salter's hand and prised the wand from its fingers. "I bet I could use this to teleport us straight to the Infirmary, first try."

"Don't you dare. You have no idea how to use that."

"Oh, Valkyrie, you worry too much. Nine-tenths of magic is confidence."

"I thought nine-tenths of magic was practice."

"We can argue about this all day, but is your arm getting any better?"

"Do not try to teleport us anywhere, Skulduggery."

He sighed and she moaned as a fresh wave of pain hit.

"What do we do with it?" she asked. She was sweating now. "We can't let the Sanctuary keep a weapon like that. We can't let *anyone* keep a weapon like that. It's far too dangerous."

Skulduggery nodded. "We should destroy it."

"I agree."

He put it in his pocket. "Or I could keep it."

"What? No."

He took out his phone. "Hush now. I'm calling Fletcher to come back for us."

"Skulduggery, you can't—"

"Fletcher!" he said loudly, the phone pressed to the side of his skull. "How are you? Have you deposited the bad man in the Infirmary? Is he surrounded by Cleavers? Oh, good! Would you mind coming back for us? Valkyrie needs to visit the doctor, too. That's right. Because of her arm, yes. Thank you ever so much!" He hung up. "Straight to voicemail," he said. "Let's try flying there. What do you say?"

44

Once Salter Such's arm was treated and bandaged, Tanith and two Cleavers escorted him to the cells. He didn't pose much of a danger – not with a fresh injury, his weapon taken away, and his magic bound – but he was a big man, and obviously intelligent. He didn't make any trouble, though. Tanith had seen this before, had seen dangerous people crumble the moment their plans were scuppered. For some of them, it took a while before they reorientated. For others, that never happened. It was too soon to tell which way Salter Such would go.

She went back upstairs. Cerise had a delegation waiting to discuss religious matters with Ghastly. They'd already been in to see the mayor, but the Sanctuary was just as big a part of the upcoming events as Roarhaven's government. As usual, Ghastly had found a reason to push back the meeting, thereby jamming it up against his remaining appointments for the day so that, when it did finally go ahead, he would have to get through it as speedily as possible.

Tanith smiled politely at the delegates – two women, one man – then nodded to Cerise, and let herself into Ghastly's office. Ghastly himself was behind his desk, writing, while Cadence Clearwater and Avant Garde stood beside the two empty chairs. Tanith nodded to them as she walked over and kissed Ghastly's cheek. Unprofessional it may have been, but hey, her boyfriend was the boss.

"How long have the delegates been outside?" she asked.

"Not long enough," Ghastly responded, finishing up the notes he was making in the margins of a report. A few more seconds and he put his pen down, looked up. "Detective Garde, sorry for keeping you. How are you feeling?"

"Much better," Avant said. He was looking positively healthy. He had colour back in his cheeks and he stood straight and easy. His suit, expensive and well tailored as it was, may not have been as fine as something Ghastly would make, but it was close. Beside him, Cadence looked nervous.

"And Detective Clearwater," Ghastly said.

"Yes, Grand Mage."

"You can relax, Detective. You're not in trouble. You played a big part in today's success. Well done."

She positively beamed.

Ghastly glanced at Tanith. "Any sign of Skulduggery and Valkyrie?"

Like they'd been waiting for their cue, the doors opened and the Arbiters strode in, brash as hell – which is how Tanith liked them.

"The conquering heroes have returned," Skulduggery said. His suit was dirty and his hat was missing. Valkyrie's clothes were tattered and burnt and her arm was in a sling. They sat in the chairs like they owned the place.

"Where's the wand?" asked Ghastly.

"Destroyed," Skulduggery said. "It crumbled away to

nothing, actually, the moment Fletcher teleported away with Mr Such."

Ghastly nodded slowly, the way he did when he didn't believe something. "That's very unfortunate. We really could have used that wand. We tend to encounter impossible threats every now and then and it'd be useful to have a weapon like that to face them down. Any idea why it crumbled away to nothing?"

"Maybe it forms a bond with its wielder. Maybe it can't be separated by too great a distance. They're just my theories. We might never know the truth."

"Uh-huh." Ghastly looked at Valkyrie. "And you didn't have anything to do with it crumbling away to nothing, no?"

"I can honestly say that I've got nothing to do with what happened to that wand," she replied. "But I have questions."

"Well," Ghastly replied, "I'm afraid while we're in this office, I'll be the one doing the—"

"Question number one," Valkyrie said, "is for Tanith. How the hell did you arrive when you did?"

"We were listening in," Tanith replied. "Cadence had a livestream going so we were seeing and hearing everything you were. Fletcher teleported in and out to get his bearings, and we stood ready."

"And how did Cadence know what was happening?"

"I messaged her," Skulduggery said. "Before we left, I spoke to a few people."

"And you didn't bother to tell me?"

"You're the one who wanted to solve this yourself. Besides, I needed Salter to believe your bewilderment."

"I was hardly bewildered."

"You looked bewildered."

Valkyrie rolled her eyes. "It's called acting. I was in on it the whole time."

"Of course you were. Somehow Ersatz knew where we were going and what we were doing at every stage, so I began to suspect that he'd used the wand to keep a watch on us. I couldn't take the risk of discussing any of this with you, since we would have been his primary focus. Unfortunately, keeping you out of that particular loop meant that I had to make a decision alone that affects us both."

"What kind of decision?"

"We were walking into an unknown situation against an enemy with a weapon we couldn't defend ourselves against. We needed help."

Valkyrie frowned. "OK. So the Sanctuary helped us. That's what the Sanctuary does."

"We needed more than that," Skulduggery said. "I didn't know what we were going to find when we got to the abattoir – all I could predict was that Salter Such would present you with an impossible choice for your final test. A choice that would leave you with no option to emerge unscathed." He hesitated. "So I contacted Mr Quiddling and accepted his proposal."

Tanith watched the colour drain from her friend's face.

Valkyrie stared at Skulduggery. "You agreed to the oversight committee?"

"Within reason," Ghastly interjected. "You will remain free to choose your own investigations. You will continue to make your own calls and your authority will not be lessened in the slightest."

Valkyrie didn't take her eyes off Skulduggery. "I can't

believe you agreed to that. We could have found a way to beat Salter on our own. We *would* have found a way."

"But we would have lost Militsa and Simone Ruddy," Skulduggery said. "Would it have been worth it?"

She didn't answer, so Skulduggery continued.

"I knew Ersatz would already have dismissed Cadence from his considerations, so I was confident that he wasn't watching her."

"And, after Skulduggery messaged her, she contacted me," said Tanith, "so I had my teams standing by. We didn't know where we were going or what the plan was because, for all Skulduggery knew, Ersatz had been watching *us* as well. We were kept in the dark until Cadence called."

"Working more closely with the Sanctuaries *does* give us access to emerging technologies," Skulduggery said. "Quiddling agreed to loan us some of his gadgets – including the cloaking skin that Cadence used. Then I sent her the coordinates and she met us there – invisible, of course."

"And the teleportation butterfly thing," Valkyrie said in that voice she used when things were slotting into place. "The Gadda-Da. You hid it in your hatband."

"And which Mr Quiddling now has safely back in his possession," said Ghastly, taking Skulduggery's hat from one of his desk drawers and handing it over.

"Thank you," Skulduggery said. He flicked a piece of dust from the brim and placed it on his knee. "This arrangement might even work out for the best."

"But Arbiters are not supposed to have bosses," Valkyrie said quietly.

"And you don't," Ghastly responded. "You're fully independent. You have my word." He sat forward. "You stopped a killer today. From what Fletcher has already told me, he would have gone on to murder countless more innocent people. You saved their lives. That's precisely why the Sanctuaries still exist: to protect the mortal world from magical threats. Well done."

Skulduggery gave him a nod, put on his hat, and stood. He walked towards the door and Valkyrie groaned with the effort of following. Before he got there, however, he stopped, and slowly spun on his heel. "There is just one more thing..."

Ghastly sighed. "I really can't keep the delegates waiting any longer."

Skulduggery wandered back. "I'll be quick, I promise. Cadence?"

Cadence straightened. "Yes, sir."

"You don't have to call me sir. It's nice that you do and I wish Valkyrie would, but you don't have to. You can call me Skulduggery, if you like. Cadence, you're the youngest here so I'm going to ask you: what is the key to overcoming psychic domination?"

"I'm, uh, sorry?"

"A Sensitive is trying to read your thoughts, Cadence. What is the first step in keeping them out?"

"Repetition."

"Repetition, exactly. As anyone who's ever had to establish a psychic defence knows, repetition is essential in building those first blocks."

Tanith watched Valkyrie frown.

"The rule of three," she murmured.

"Yes, Valkyrie," said Skulduggery. "Establish a pattern. Repeat the pattern. Focus on the pattern. It can be images, memories, sounds, colours, words... or in this case a number.

You see, Salter Such had been fighting a battle no one else was even aware of. This technique has spilled over into every other aspect of his life, as it tends to do. It permeated the letters he sent to us, all those tests and taunts. It even infiltrated his speech patterns. Until a certain point in the abattoir, when he finally lost his battle, Salter had been talking either in three-sentence bursts or in three-word sentences."

"I don't understand," Cadence said.

"He was being controlled," said Valkyrie.

Tanith felt the need to sit down, so she perched on the edge of Ghastly's desk. "So he was forced to kill those people?"

"He was forced to kill them and forced to taunt us," Skulduggery said. "He was trying to build a psychic defence against this control and, under normal circumstances, he may have succeeded. But these were not normal circumstances."

"So who was controlling him?"

"That's a question I asked myself," Skulduggery said. "Who would go to all this trouble? Who would care enough about Rumour to do this?"

They all looked at Skulduggery expectantly.

"Her father," he said at last.

"I have such a headache," Valkyrie muttered.

"But Salter *is* her father," Cadence pointed out.

"Apologies, I meant her *biological* father."

"Explain," said Valkyrie.

"It was the Father's Day cards. What did you notice about them?"

"Like... they were cute? All of them were home-made except for two."

"Sent when Rumour was eleven and twelve, yes. I imagine Rumour was eleven when her parents finally told her that Salter was not her biological father. She spent close to two years processing this, probably deciding how she felt about this apparent betrayal, about her parents lying to her, before realising that she loved her dad no matter what."

"So who is Rumour's biological father?" asked Ghastly.

Skulduggery tilted his head at Valkyrie. "You wanted to solve this one, didn't you? Go ahead."

Valkyrie glared. "Don't do this to me. Not in front of people."

"I have absolute faith that you'll be able to answer correctly."

"Fine. OK." She stood in silence for a bit. "All right then – Rumour's mum, Catherine, had a boyfriend before Salter. He was a mage, and not a nice guy. He was a friend of – no, an *acquaintance* of – Salter's." She frowned. "He may also have been an acquaintance of Cyrus Elysian. Oh, wow." She looked up. "Is it Clutter Gaines? Is it? Have I just worked it out?"

"The scientist?" Ghastly said.

"Oh, *scientist* is but one aspect of who he is," Skulduggery responded. "You also have recluse, psychopath, narcissist, and co-inventor of the Veritas device. Gaines embarked on a relationship with Catherine Dennehy and she became pregnant. That relationship ended and Gaines did not take it well. You have access to his files, Ghastly. What happened?"

"I'd have to look it up to remind myself of all the details, but from what I can remember he tried to kill his girlfriend. Sanctuary operatives went after him and he fled the country, disappeared."

Valkyrie raised an eyebrow. "And he's stayed disappeared for all this time?"

"There weren't many photographs of him – one of the advantages of being a recluse – but he destroyed what there was. Hell, I'd say Doctor Elysian was the last person alive who'd have been able to visually identify him. We didn't have much to send to the other Sanctuaries so he was able to sink beneath the radar. And remember, he was – or *is* – a highly intelligent individual."

"And once Gaines was out of her life," Skulduggery said, "Catherine married Salter Such. She gave birth to a little girl and they raised the child together. The years passed and Clutter Gaines watched her grow up from afar. We can only imagine his rising levels of bitterness and resentment. Rumour, after all, was his one chance of that absolute, unquestioning love that a narcissist like him would have always wanted."

"And then Rumour died," said Valkyrie.

"And Gaines forged a new identity and returned to Ireland. He found out that it was Salter who'd killed Rumour but, like Salter, he felt that the blame almost rested with the others. So he used the Veritas device to find Salter's true name and from that point on he dominated his will entirely. Salter was a weapon Gaines wielded to not only get his revenge on the people who wronged Rumour, but also to leave enough clues that would take us straight to Salter once it was all done."

"But why didn't he just take the wand and do all this himself?" Valkyrie asked.

"*That* I do not know."

"So who is he?" Avant asked. "Who is Clutter Gaines?"

"He's you," said Skulduggery.

With a startled yelp, Cadence leaped away from Avant's side.

"Excuse the hell out of me?" said Avant.

"You're not one of Cogent Badinage's detectives," Skulduggery said. "You know a lot about him, this is true, so you've talked to someone who did know him. But Cogent produced detectives just like him. That was a requirement. It was one of his adorable quirks. If they couldn't match his sense of style, for example, how could he trust them to match his dedication?"

"You're accusing me of being Clutter Gaines because of my suit? What the hell's wrong with it?"

"This one? Nothing. It's perfect. But when you were attacked, when you arranged for Ersatz to injure you severely but not fatally, you were wearing brown leather shoes and a black leather belt."

Ghastly suddenly stood, a gun in his hand pointed right at Avant. Avant froze.

"I thought, OK, everyone's entitled to one bad day," Skulduggery continued. "But then you confirmed that you weren't who you claimed to be. You're standing before us now with your jacket open, but earlier, at the Infirmary, both buttons were fastened."

"I'm a little lost," Valkyrie said quietly.

The gun in Ghastly's hand didn't waver. "You don't use the bottom button of a jacket or blazer. Ever. It pulls on the fabric and disrupts the silhouette."

"That's an Italian suit you're wearing," Skulduggery said. "Italian suits are all about the silhouette."

"This is ridiculous," Avant said.

"Isn't it?" Tanith said as she stepped over to him. "Making these assumptions because of errors in fashion sense? It's preposterous, is what it is." She shackled his hands behind his back, then removed his gun from its holster. "Clutter Gaines, I'm placing you under arrest for conspiracy to commit murder, coercion to commit murder, the framing of an innocent man—"

"Salter Such is not an innocent man," Avant snarled as the two Cleavers by the door came over and shackled his wrists behind him. "He stole my family."

"You controlled his will," said Skulduggery. "You twisted his mind. You made him want what you wanted."

"He hated those mortals almost as much as I did."

"Oh, I'd say he hated them more, because he actually loved Rumour. You poured your corruption into him. You made a deal with Arava Kahann to get him that mask and then you gave him the wand and orchestrated every step he took from that moment on."

Clutter sneered. "You think you're smarter than me, don't you? You think you have it all figured out? Then answer me this, skeleton: why didn't I use the wand myself? You see, you think you understand my motivations, and yet you haven't even *begun* to grasp at the—"

"No, no," said Skulduggery, "I've worked all that out, as well. But your part in this is done, so you can leave. Please enjoy your stay in prison."

"What? Wait, what?"

Tanith nodded and the Cleavers escorted Clutter Gaines out.

Cerise passed them without even acknowledging the fact

that Gaines was in cuffs. "Grand Mage," she said, "you really must talk to the delegation."

Ghastly sighed. "Can't you do it?"

"It has to be you, I'm afraid."

"What if I make you Grand Mage for the day?"

"Not for all the money in the world," Cerise answered.

"Come on," said Valkyrie, nudging Cadence. "We'll buy you a coffee to celebrate."

"I don't drink coffee," said Cadence.

"Then today is a good day to start."

They left, and when Cerise went to fetch the delegation Tanith stole another kiss from Ghastly. "I'll see you at home?"

"At some stage," he said wearily.

Tanith laughed. "I could invent some emergency, you know. Pretend there's about to be an attempt on your life?"

He smiled back at her. "Ah, the old *assassination attempt to get out of a meeting* routine. Thank you, my sweet, but if we keep doing that then no one will believe it when somebody *does* want to assassinate me. I'll soldier on."

"My hero," Tanith said, pretending to swoon as she walked to the doors.

Cerise stepped in with the delegates. "Grand Mage Bespoke," she announced, "may I introduce Bennet Troth, from the Darquesse Society, Languid Crokebane, representing the Dark Cathedral, and, speaking on behalf of the Masked Sisters, Rapture Scathe."

Tanith smiled as she passed them, and closed the doors on her way out.

45

She knocked on his door and turned as she waited.

A man and a woman emerged from the funeral home on the right side of Cemetery Road, the funeral director accompanying them to their car. When they drove off, he gave a single, respectful wave, and stood with his hands clasped until they had gone. Then he turned to the funeral home across the road and thrust his middle finger into the air. Valkyrie watched the owner of the second funeral home lean out of an open window and do the same back.

Skulduggery opened his front door and Valkyrie turned. His façade was of a young man, an eyebrow arched in mild surprise.

"Are you early?" he said.

"No. I'm exactly on time. Two o'clock."

"It's two o'clock already?"

"It's funny how that happens, isn't it? I swear it was one o'clock just an hour ago. Everything OK, Skulduggery? I don't think I've ever seen you looking so casual."

He was in shirtsleeves and his tie was loose. "I was reading," he replied. "I didn't expect you to be early, that's all."

"I'm not early. I'm on time."

"Then I don't expect you to be on time." He held his hand behind him and his jacket and hat floated into his grip. He stepped out of the door and put them on. "Fletcher will be here in a moment."

"Where are we going?"

"Tying up loose ends."

"Yeah, OK. Speaking of which, we still haven't talked about what you've done and what it's going to mean for us."

"Agreeing to Quiddling's proposal was the only way I could get my hands on those gadgets and secure the Sanctuary's aid."

"You couldn't think of anything else?"

"There were options," he conceded, "but I had no time to implement them. I didn't know what we'd be going up against, but I did know that Ghastly and Tanith would be able to adapt and improvise once they had a live feed. Which is exactly what they did."

"They would have helped us, anyway."

"Are you so sure?"

Valkyrie frowned. "You think Ghastly would have hesitated?"

"He's running an organisation that needs to be in control," Skulduggery said. "If we'd stayed on the outside, we would have seen our support being slowly whittled down over the next few years."

"But he's our friend."

"He has a responsibility now to something more than friendship."

"And Tanith?"

"Tanith's not quite so rigid in her thinking. She'd have come down on our side in an emergency, but it would have damaged her position. We need her to stay where she is, and we need her record unblemished."

"You sound like you're expecting trouble."

"I'm always expecting trouble."

"Trouble from Ghastly?"

"Not from him, no. Not specifically. But from the other Sanctuaries, yes."

"So we play along, is that it? Now that we're back in the Sanctuary system, we follow the Sanctuary rules?"

A shrug. "We follow our own rules, just like we've been doing. But we don't trust them, Valkyrie. People in charge can never be trusted. They like to think they've got their eyes on the bigger picture, but if there are three layers to any image, they're focused solely on the middle ground. We've got to take care of everything else."

"And we still have to deal with the fact that Ghastly authorised the work to continue on the Veritas device," Valkyrie said. "Mind telling me why we haven't raised that subject quite yet?"

"Sometimes it's better to only play your cards when you need to."

She rubbed her face and sighed. "Why can't things be easy?"

"Where's the fun in easy?"

Fletcher appeared beside them. "Sorry I'm late," he said, glancing at the notepad in his hand. "Let's see... you're going to Coldheart Prison. I've already cleared it with the warden so we'll be able to teleport straight in. You'll need a return trip?"

"We will," Skulduggery said.

"Then I'll take you to the staff canteen and grab some lunch while I wait. Link up, please."

They both put their hands on his arm and an instant later they were in Coldheart. Fletcher wandered off to get some food and Valkyrie followed Skulduggery down the corridor.

"Mind telling me why we're here?"

"Because sometimes, Valkyrie, there are riddles within riddles."

"Aw, man. Am I going to have to use my brain again?"

"It's quite likely, yes."

The Cleavers ahead parted and the security doors opened, then clunked shut behind them.

"When I was running through the possible solutions to the third riddle," Skulduggery said, "you may remember I mentioned the number thirty-four, which was, as I said, the age at which I proposed to my wife."

"I remember that, yes. My brain is working so far."

"You do look genuinely relieved. The proposal changed me. I realised that I'd found someone to love, someone I wanted to spend the rest of my life with."

"That's sweet."

"In the first riddle, reference was made to the tenth ancile."

Valkyrie nodded. "The sacred Roman shield thing."

"According to legend, the first of these divine shields fell from heaven during the reign of Numa Pompilius."

"That's a made-up name."

"He was the second king of Rome."

"Well, I've never heard of him."

They took the stone stairs, heading down. "You've heard of the first king of Rome, though, haven't you? Romulus?"

"I've heard of the *planet* Romulus."

"Not a real planet. Where Romulus had been a king of war, Pompilius had been a king of peace, celebrated for his wisdom and piety."

"What has he ever done for us, though?"

"A lot, actually. He's widely credited to have been the one to add January and February to the calendar."

"He did what?"

"The old calendar started in March, but he added two new months and everything else shifted up. That's why October, from the Latin and Greek *ôctõ*, meaning eight, became the tenth month."

Valkyrie gasped. "*That's* why it became the tenth month?"

"Your mocking tone notwithstanding, Numa Pompilius paved the way for the modern age."

"And what a cool guy he was, too. But what does Numpty Consillious have to do with what we're talking about?"

"That's not at all how his name is pronounced – but the changes he made to the calendar, plus the reference to the number ten, makes me wonder if we're not meant to focus on October here."

"All right. So?"

More Cleavers standing guard below them. More security doors sliding open and then clunking closed once they'd passed through.

"October is the month I died."

Valkyrie took a moment. "OK. So the age in which you proposed to your wife, and the month in which you died.

Is there something in the second riddle that references another big, life-changing event?"

"Very possibly, and it's something you should recognise. Do you remember the first paragraph of that riddle?"

"You know I don't, Skulduggery."

"*What I do is not for my own gratification but rather I am an instrument of justice. Blood must be spilled. Sometimes I think I have been born for this. That I have never been human. That I have always been a weapon.*"

"OK."

"What do you think of, from your own life, when I say the words *instrument of justice*?"

"From my own life? I... I don't know. Honestly, the first thing that comes to mind would be one of Gordon's crime novels."

"The Vargas and Webb trilogy, of which *A Cold, Clean Instrument of Justice* was the first. How about the words *Blood must be spilled*?"

Valkyrie narrowed her eyes. "The second book – *Spilled Blood on a Linoleum Floor*."

"And what about *That I have never been human. That I have always been a weapon*?"

"Book Three – *Human Weapon, Human Target*. So, what, Gordon Edgley is the answer?"

"My friendship with Gordon led me to you, another significant, life-changing event."

Valkyrie nodded. "Possibly the most significant of all."

"I wouldn't say that."

"Definitely the most important thing that has ever happened to you. So the hidden riddles are all about... you?"

"But Salter Such would not have known I viewed these things in that way. Neither would Clutter Gaines."

"Hold on, wait a second. Clutter Gaines was behind Salter Such, but you're saying there's someone else behind Clutter Gaines?"

"If that is the case," Skulduggery said, "then they would have had to have known that Gaines was Rumour's biological father. They may have been the one to facilitate Gaines's re-emergence as Avant Garde, feeding him the information he needed. And, obviously, they would have had to have known those things about me."

They stepped out into a vast, enclosed space where cold air howled up from the chasm in the rock floor. Hovering over the chasm, in his cell of glass and metal, a skeleton in an orange jumpsuit tilted his head at them.

46

"I knew you'd solve it," Cadaver Cain said. "I knew you'd visit. It's a good thing, too. We don't have an awful lot of time."

"You're behind all of this?" Valkyrie said, approaching the edge of the chasm. "Why? Please tell me that you have an actual reason and you didn't do it all just because you were bored."

"Valkyrie," Cadaver replied, "you've barely come to see me in the six years I've been here and, when you do, you come hurling sharpened words. I do have feelings, you know."

"Cadaver, I swear to Jesus."

He made a sound that could have been a chuckle, and shifted his head slightly. "Hello, Skulduggery. You're looking devilishly handsome as usual. How's the head?"

"No complaints," Skulduggery responded.

Cadaver ran the tips of his distal phalanges over the metal staples holding his own fractured skull together. "I do miss it," he murmured. "I don't suppose you'd agree to an occasional swap, would you? I have it every second weekend and Bank Holidays, maybe?"

"I don't see that happening," Skulduggery said. "How did you know about Rumour Mills?"

"About her sad demise? I keep abreast of security reports from the Sanctuaries."

"You're not supposed to have that type of access."

"Would *you* let that stop you?"

"And what about her connection to Clutter Gaines?"

Cadaver shrugged. "In my timeline, those of us who opposed Damocles Creed found ourselves making the unlikeliest of allies. Cyrus Elysian was on Creed's side, and we had Clutter Gaines on ours. In order to keep him placated, we had to – very gently – abduct Rumour. I learned about her true parentage when Salter Such went to rescue her. The rescue turned incredibly violent and astonishingly bloody, of course, but that's to be expected when you're dealing with volatile people whose minds are full of murder."

Valkyrie folded her arms. "So what happened? You read about Rumour's death and decided to play a ridiculously elaborate game?"

"My game-playing days are over," Cadaver said. "My time in this cell has allowed me to reflect on who I have become, and who I want to be. I'm not meant to sit in prison. I should be out there, fighting the good fight. Saving people."

"By helping Salter Such murder innocent mortals?"

"The murders had nothing to do with me," said Cadaver, "but I understand your suspicions. It's why I arranged for you to visit me today – so we could talk. I knew Rumour's death would drive Clutter Gaines out of hiding and on to a path of destruction. He had the potential to stir the Isolationists to overt acts of terrorism that would plunge us all into a fate we could not escape. In an effort to mitigate this destruction, I made contact."

"How?" Valkyrie asked.

"I am a model prisoner, and as such I have access to certain devices that I have adapted to my communication needs. Sadly, by the time contact was made, Clutter's plan was already underway."

"So you knew what he was doing? You knew he was responsible for the murders Salter Such committed? You knew this and yet you didn't tell anyone? Why the hell not?"

"Because you locked me away in prison, Valkyrie. Because I am still human enough to need some retribution for that." Cadaver's head tilted. "A petty excuse, I freely admit, and one that is possibly unworthy of my lofty goals. But while I had no intention of informing on Clutter Gaines or his manipulations, I did some manipulating of my own. I convinced him to prove his intellectual superiority to my younger self by outwitting Skulduggery with codes and messages and hidden clues – all those elements that make crime-solving so fun."

"So you're taking credit for allowing us the chance to stop Salter Such?" asked Skulduggery.

"Indeed. That wand is far too dangerous for someone like Salter Such or, more pertinently, Clutter Gaines to possess. It could do a lot more good in the hands of someone like you, for example."

"OK, so you made sure there were certain elements to Ersatz's riddles that would draw us here," Skulduggery said, "and now, here we are. What do you want to tell us, Cadaver? What has all this been about?"

Cadaver took a moment. "There was a time, thanks to the training of the Viddu De, when I could see every possible path that lay before me, and choose whichever one I deemed most beneficial. That is no longer the case. And I like that. It makes life interesting. But while I cannot see the future, I can anticipate it, and I've arrived at the conclusion that we're all in grave danger."

"Continue," said Skulduggery.

"The Isolationist movement poses a far greater threat than anyone yet appreciates," Cadaver responded. "If I'm right – and I usually am – it will cause a rift between the mortal and the magical worlds that will never get the chance to heal. Once this rift occurs, once there is a schism between us, we will be vulnerable."

"Vulnerable to whom?" Skulduggery asked.

"There are too many potential threats at this current juncture to narrow it down, but the consequences range from the merely dystopian to the downright catastrophic. The apocalypse is on the horizon and every moment it draws closer."

"But just so we're clear," said Valkyrie, "this is what you *think* might happen, right? It's not actually real."

"If I've imagined it," said Cadaver, "then it's possible. And if it's possible then it's likely. And if it's likely, then it's real. Our only hope is that I haven't imagined this too late."

"And what do you want?" Skulduggery asked.

"I want to get out of here," said Cadaver. "I'm being wasted, languishing in a cell like this. The Sanctuaries need me. The world, in all its diverse splendour, needs me. I daresay you need me, though you don't yet realise it. I want you to talk to Ghastly for me. Tell him we need to have another chat."

They didn't talk much as they walked back to meet Fletcher. He recognised the silence and didn't try to puncture it. He just took them back to Cemetery Road, said his goodbyes, and left.

"You're taking this seriously," Valkyrie said. She stood by her car. Skulduggery stood by his front door.

"I am," he said. The façade he wore had day-old stubble and blue eyes.

"But Cadaver's staying in prison, right? We can't let him out. He's far too dangerous."

"He is far too dangerous," Skulduggery conceded. "But the question is who is he a bigger danger *to* – us, or whichever threat is first over the horizon?"

"We can't trust him. He's too ruthless."

Skulduggery paused before speaking. "Cadaver likes to think he sees the bigger picture. He's in that cell and he's got nothing else to do but figure out the threats we're going to face before we face them. But he doesn't see everything. There are possibilities open to us that just aren't open to him, because he doesn't have you to force him to come up with a better way."

"I'm relying on you to find that better way."

"I'm relying on you for the same thing."

Valkyrie turned to her car, then turned back. "You've been hiding something from me."

He frowned at her.

"You've been late and you're never late," she said. "You've been cagey and you're never cagey."

"I'm always cagey."

"You're never cagey with me – not unless you've got a secret. When I got here earlier, you weren't wearing your jacket."

"I don't always have to be wearing a—"

"Were you afraid you'd get something on it?"

His eyes widened slightly.

"And why haven't you invited me in to talk about this?" she asked. "Why am I standing here, and why are you standing there? Standing on your front step means you need to keep your façade activated. You know the disadvantage of that? You still haven't figured out how to control it."

"I have more control over my façade these days than I've ever had in the past. It's thought-activated."

"I mean you haven't learned how to control your expressions. When it's you, the real you, the glorious skeleton that I know and love, you don't need to even think about that. You don't have a face to betray you. But the face you're wearing right now? It's showing guilt, Skulduggery."

"Then the face is faulty," he said. He opened his front door and stepped to one side. "But if you honestly don't believe me, if you cannot trust that I am telling the truth, then feel free to search my house, Valkyrie. If I'm hiding something, I'm sure you'll—"

"Thanks," Valkyrie said, walking in.

Skulduggery followed quickly, his façade flowing off his skull. "I didn't think you'd actually come in."

"I know," she said, heading straight for the living room.

"You realise this is a betrayal of our entire relationship?"

"No, it isn't."

"You are doubting my integrity."

"You've had very fine hairs on your jacket sleeves and your trouser cuffs for the last few weeks. The hairs on your trousers stop halfway to your knees, suggesting something small has been rubbing itself between your feet."

She stepped into the living room and two little kittens bounded over to meet her. "I knew it!" she squealed.

"I don't know where they came from," Skulduggery said immediately.

Valkyrie dropped to her knees and scratched their little heads. "How could you hide these from me?"

"They must have broken in while we were out."

She scooped one of them up. "These are the most adorable little things ever in the world."

"Valkyrie, I swear to you, I have never seen these animals before this very moment."

The other kitten, the one she hadn't scooped up, launched itself at Skulduggery's leg and quickly claw-climbed its way to his shoulder.

"Help," Skulduggery said while the kitten nuzzled into his jawbone. "They're attacking."

"You're just a big softy, aren't you? Just a big giant softy."

"I resent that," he said, taking the kitten away from her. Her put them both down on the floor and stepped back. "Watch this," he said as the kittens launched themselves at each other and went tumbling.

Valkyrie made noises she only made for puppies, kittens, and very small babies as they watched the impossibly cute wrestling.

"You asked what it's like for me," Skulduggery said,

keeping his attention on the cats, "to be so smart and surrounded by people who don't think as fast as I do. It can, at times, be difficult – but it's only ever aggravating when I have to deal with an incurious mind. You do not have an incurious mind, Valkyrie. Because of that you are unpredictable, incisive, and challenging. In his timeline, Cadaver was alone for so long. He didn't have you. He didn't have anyone. He forgot the value that other people bring. He is intellect and will. He has no warmth or compassion. He does not view outside perspectives as being worthy of his consideration. These are the things you allow me to have. That, and strength. One of these days, I'll have to face Cadaver and it will be him, or it will be me. He thinks he'll win because my connections, my attachments, make me weak. But he has forgotten how strong you make me." He turned his head to her. "That's why I keep you around."

Valkyrie looked up at him from the floor, feeling the knot of emotion rise through her throat. When she was sure that her voice wasn't going to crack, she smiled, and said, "Lame."

He laughed.

47

There was a small farm a few kilometres to the east of Dublin Airport. The couple who owned it were dead, murdered as they ate breakfast that morning. The farm employed two full-time workers. They were dead, too.

The farm had a large concrete shed where some of the tractors and machinery were stored. There was also a workbench, fitted tight against one breeze-block wall, on which stood the Desolation Engine, a stone hourglass about six inches long with only one glass bulb. That bulb was filled with achtolycerin helphate. The other bulb of green liquid was in the hand of Imperator Dominax as he made his grand speech to Brazen and Aphotic and seven other members of the Order of the Ancients.

There were two doors into the shed. The first was small and near the corner. The second was a large sliding door of corrugated iron, and it stood half open.

Winter Grieving walked through the second one, interrupting Imperator's flow. The nine terrorists – plus their idiot leader – glared at her as she approached. She couldn't see Alter among their number, but the look on Slam Debacle's face was especially hostile.

"I'm here to give you a chance to surrender," Winter said. "Imperator Dominax, you'll be arrested and you'll go to prison, but the rest of you have a chance at making a deal."

"Traitor!" Brazen shouted.

"In order to betray you, I'd have had to be with you," said Winter. "And I was never with you. Surrender, come quietly, and no one needs to get hurt."

"Surrender to whom?" Dominax asked, the green liquid sloshing in the bulb. "I see no army of Cleavers descending upon us. Did you even alert the Sanctuary? You didn't, did you? You wanted to be the hero. You wanted to stop us single-handedly and claim all the glory for yourself. You stupid little girl."

"I don't care about the glory," Winter responded. "I don't want to be a hero. I came in here to give the rest of you a chance because hey, we all do stupid things every now and then. Any of you going to take me up on it?"

Some of them looked unsure, but no one said anything and no one surrendered.

Dominax smiled. "We won't kill you," he told her. "We'll tie you up, absolutely, but we won't hurt you – not if we can help it. Then I'll fit this vial into this bomb and we'll teleport away. Within ten seconds of our departure, you'll be dead. You'll be incinerated. The explosion will cover a twenty-five-kilometre radius at a rate of 4,572 metres per second. Do you know how long it will take to kill everyone in the entire county of Dublin?"

"No," said Winter. "Do you?"

"Approximately five and a half seconds. The same as a nuclear blast, but with none of the structural damage or pesky radiation."

"Radiation *is* pesky."

"You should have called in the Cleavers, little girl."

"I didn't need to."

He chuckled. "Oh, didn't you?"

"Nope," she said. "Not when I could just call my sister."

Valkyrie walked in behind her, dressed in the black clothes that Ghastly Bespoke had made for her, her jacket zipped halfway up and her eyes crackling with white energy.

Dominax yelled an unintelligible order and Valkyrie raised her hands, catching two wannabe terrorists with bolts of lightning. They flipped over, unconscious before they hit the ground, and Winter watched her sister leap on to the front tyre of an old tractor, then to the bonnet, then to the rear mudguard, dodging panicked streams of energy as she went. Valkyrie dropped on to the man standing on the other side, her knee smashing into his face. They went down. She tumbled back to her feet. He didn't.

Winter looked round as someone ran at her and Brazen punched her, knocked her back. With Brazen yanking her hair with one hand and scratching at her face with the other, they fell against a piece of farm machinery. Winter ignored all that, clasped her hands to the back of Brazen's neck, and drove a knee into her stomach. Brazen gasped and Winter sent a knee into her hip, then her thigh, then her chest, attacking with precision.

Behind Brazen, she saw Valkyrie break somebody's arm and throw them, screaming, to the floor. Another of Dominax's followers grabbed her and Valkyrie flipped him and then Winter was focusing on Brazen again, shoving her away.

"What's wrong with you?" Brazen screeched. "Why couldn't you just let me have this?"

Winter didn't know what the hell she was talking about, but, when Brazen dived at her, Winter punched, sending her toppling over a pile of tools that had been dumped off the workbench with the Desolation Engine on it. Brazen snatched up a hammer, but then Aphotic grabbed her from behind, trying to pin her arms to her sides.

"What are you doing?" Brazen shouted. "Let me go!"

They started grappling and Winter turned in time to see Slam Debacle barrelling towards her.

This, she figured, was going to hurt.

He lifted her off her feet and then, true to his name, slammed her to the ground. It hurt way more than she expected, but she'd kept her chin tucked in and her head protected so she was still conscious and still alert. She dug her thumb into his left eye. He snarled, batted her hand away, but a gap opened up while he did it and she brought her legs in, hooked her feet under his groin and lifted, elevating his hips. Jesus, he was heavy – this was much easier on people her own size – but for a few moments she was negating his superior strength.

"Winter!" Aphotic yelled, and she turned her head as he slid the hammer towards her. It was a weak effort and it stopped halfway between them so she pulled at the air and it slid the rest of the way into her hand.

She whacked it into Slam's head and he fell sideways, dazed. Winter went to hit him again, but his huge hand closed around her wrist. Bellowing, he stood, swinging her easily. She collided with the side of a tractor and fell, gasping, to her hands and knees. He came for her again and she flattened, rolled beneath the tractor, coming up to her feet on the other side in time to see Valkyrie punching the crap out of Imperator Dominax. Her fist connected with the hinge of his jaw and he collapsed like his bones had turned to rubber.

Slam came round the tractor. Winter tried pushing at the air, but the pain in her ribs made it impossible to concentrate her magic. She backed up. Stumbled.

Then Valkyrie tackled him, her arms wrapping around his waist, knocking him against the tractor. He went to break her hold, but she got her feet under her and, incredibly, lifted. She roared and arched her back, slamming Slam into the floor behind her. Winter heard his shoulder break.

Howling, Slam rolled away, got to his knees, twisting towards Valkyrie. She caught him with twin blasts of energy that burst from her eyes and when Winter's vision cleared he was lying there, unmoving, smoke rising from his shirt.

Valkyrie came over, her eyes back to normal. "You hurt?" she asked.

"Ribs," Winter said. "Might be broken." The sudden silence seemed, for some reason, artificial. "Did we do it? Did we win?"

Valkyrie showed her the bulb of achtolycerin helphate. "We stopped them from arming the Desolation Engine. That's a definite win."

Aphotic limped into view. His lip was bleeding. "Brazen got away," he said, and then extended his wrists like he expected to be cuffed. "I surrender."

"You're OK," Winter said. "We'll tell the Cleavers you were led astray by love."

He nodded and looked grateful, and then anxious. "Do you think Brazen will ever forgive me?"

"Not a chance," said Winter.

He nodded again, and looked like he might cry.

Valkyrie called Tanith and she arrived within five minutes with a load of Cleavers. A medic gave Winter a leaf to chew on to dull the pain, but Winter asked for a moment before they teleported her to the High Sanctuary to get her ribs sorted. While everyone else was focused on carting off the bruised and battered members of the Order of the Ancients and making sure the bomb was made safe, Winter wandered over to the farmhouse and made herself a cup of tea.

She sat at the kitchen table. The bodies of the owners were slumped on the floor, waiting for the professionals to come in and disguise the crime, perpetrated by sorcerers, as a more mundane crime perpetrated by mortals.

Winter sipped her tea, and gazed at the corpses. The door behind her opened.

Alter came in slowly, and peered down at the bodies. "They really are mayflies, aren't they?"

"Are they?" said Winter.

"They live for such a short length of time, but they lead such good lives. Such varied, worthy lives. It's a beautiful thing, when you think about it."

"That's funny," Winter said. "I *was* thinking about it. I was just thinking how pointless their lives are. Take these two. They meet, get married, and run this farm. They grow crops. Harvest the crops. Sell the crops. They have kids.

The kids grow up and move away. They've achieved nothing except to propagate their own species."

"Yeah," said Alter. "Like I said – it's a beautiful thing."

Winter raised her eyes to him. "Imperator Dominax is in shackles."

"Which is where he deserves to be quite honestly. Hey, fair do's to him: he had his little idea and he made the absolute most out of being a very limited person. But he was never worthy of being followed. He was never worthy of being obeyed."

"That's why you betrayed him? Because he was a bad leader?"

"Dominax didn't deserve to succeed. Whoever strikes the first real blow for the Isolationist cause, they're going to need to inspire people. He was never going to do that. He's not capable. He was too focused on twirling his diabolical moustache and making his diabolical speeches. We're not looking for a villain here. We're looking for a hero. We're looking for you."

"Now you are being funny," said Winter. "I'm not a hero."

"But you're a leader," Alter said. "You might not be ready to lead us now, but, when you are, you'll have people like me waiting to join you."

"You realise I'm only fifteen, right?"

"Your sister was fifteen and she'd already saved the world. You can do more than that."

"Oh, yeah?" Winter said as he went to leave the way he'd come in. "What can I do? Tell me. My sister saved the world, so what can I do to top that?"

Alter paused before leaving. "You can rule it."